THE
EPISTLE TO THE EPHESIANS

BY THE REV. PROFESSOR
G. G. FINDLAY

THE INTRODUCTION.

CHAPTER i. 1, 2.

G.G Findlay

The Epistle To the Ephesians

G.G Findlay

The Epistle To the Ephesians

1st Edition | ISBN: 978-3-75233-154-7

Place of Publication: Frankfurt am Main, Germany

Year of Publication: 2020

Outlook Verlag GmbH, Germany.

Reproduction of the original.

CHAPTER I.

THE WRITER AND READERS.

"Paul, an apostle of Christ Jesus through the will of God, to the saints, who are indeed faithful in Christ Jesus: Grace to you and peace from God our Father and the Lord Jesus Christ."[1]—EPH. i. 1, 2.

In passing from the Galatian to the Ephesian epistle we are conscious of entering a different atmosphere. We leave the region of controversy for that of meditation. From the battle-field we step into the hush and stillness of the temple. Verses 3–14 of this chapter constitute the most sustained and perfect act of praise that is found in the apostle's letters. It is as though a door were suddenly opened in heaven; it shuts behind us, and earthly tumult dies away. The contrast between these two writings, following each other in the established order of the epistles, is singular and in some ways extreme. They are, respectively, the most combative and peaceful, the most impassioned and unimpassioned, the most concrete and abstract, the most human and divine amongst the great apostle's writings.

Yet there is a fundamental resemblance and identity of character. The two letters are not the expression of different minds, but of different phases of the same mind. In the Paul of Galatians the Paul of Ephesians is latent; the contemplative thinker, the devout mystic behind the ardent missionary and the masterly debater. Those critics who recognize the genuine apostle only in the four previous epistles and reject whatever does not conform strictly to their type, do not perceive how much is needed to make up a man like the apostle Paul. Without the inwardness, the brooding faculty, the power of abstract and metaphysical thinking displayed in the epistles of this group, he could never have wrought out the system of doctrine contained in those earlier writings, nor grasped the principles which he there applies with such vigour and effect. That so many serious and able scholars doubt, or even deny, St Paul's authorship of this epistle on internal grounds and because of the contrast to which we have referred, is one of those phenomena which in future histories of religious thought will be quoted as the curiosities of a hypercritical age.[2]

Let us observe some of the Pauline qualities that are stamped upon the face of this document. There is, in the first place, the apostle's intellectual note, what has been well called his *passion for the absolute*. St Paul's was one of those minds, so discomposing to superficial and merely practical thinkers, which cannot be content with half-way conclusions. For every principle he seeks its ultimate basis; every line of thought he pushes to its furthest limits. His gospel, if he is to rest in it, must supply a principle of unity that will bind together all the elements of his mental world.

Hence, in contesting the Jewish claim to religious superiority on the ground of circumcision and the Abrahamic covenant, St Paul developed in the epistle to the Galatians a religious philosophy of history; he arrived at a view of the function of the law in the education of mankind which disposed not only of the question at issue, but of all such questions. He established for ever the principle of salvation by faith and of spiritual sonship to God. What that former argument effects for the history of revelation, is done here for the gospel in its relations to society and universal life. The principle of Christ's headship is carried to its largest results. The centre of the Church becomes the centre of the universe. God's plan of the ages is disclosed, ranging through eternity and embracing every form of being, and "gathering into one all things in the Christ." In Galatians and Romans the thought of salvation by Christ breaks through Jewish limits and spreads itself over the field of history; in Colossians and Ephesians the idea of life in Christ overleaps the barriers of time and human existence, and brings "things in heaven and things in earth and things beneath the earth" under its sway.

The second, historical note of original Paulinism we recognize in the writer's *attitude towards Judaism*. We should be prepared to stake the genuineness of the epistle on this consideration alone. The position and point of view of the Jewish apostle to the Gentiles are unique in history. It is difficult to conceive how any one but Paul himself, at any other juncture, could have represented the relation of Jew and Gentile to each other as it is put before us here. The writer is a Jew, a man nourished on the hope of Israel (i. 12), who had looked at his fellow-men across "the middle wall of partition" (ii. 14). In his view, the covenant and the Christ belong, in the first instance and as by birthright, to the men of Israel. They are "the near," who live hard by the city and house of God. The blessedness of the Gentile readers consists in the revelation that they are "fellow-heirs and of the same body and joint-partakers with us of the promise in Christ Jesus" (iii. 6). What is this but to say, as the apostle had done before, that the branches "of the naturally wild olive tree" were "against nature grafted into the good olive tree" and allowed to "partake of its root and fatness," along with "the natural branches," the children of the stock of Abraham who claimed it for "their own"; that "the men of faith are sons of Abraham" and "Abraham's blessing has come on the Gentiles through faith"?
[3]

For our author this revelation has lost none of its novelty and surprise. He is in the midst of the excitement it has produced, and is himself its chief agent and mouthpiece (iii. 1–9). This disclosure of God's secret plans for the world overwhelms him by its magnitude, by the splendour with which it invests the

Divine character, and the sense of his personal unworthiness to be entrusted with it. We utterly disbelieve that any later Christian writer could or would have personated the apostle and mimicked his tone and sentiments in regard to his vocation, in the way that the "critical" hypothesis assumes. The criterion of Erasmus is decisive: *Nemo potest Paulinum pectus effingere.*

St Paul's doctrine of *the cross* is admittedly his specific theological note. In the shameful sacrificial death of Jesus Christ he saw the instrument of man's release from the curse of the broken law;[4] and through this knowledge the cross which was the "scandal" of Saul the Pharisee, had become Paul's glory and its proclamation the business of his life. It is this doctrine, in its original strength and fulness, which lies behind such sentences as those of chapter i. 7, ii. 13, and v. 2: "We have redemption through His blood, the forgiveness of our trespasses—brought nigh in the blood of Christ—an offering and sacrifice to God for an odour of sweet smell."

Another mark of the apostle's hand, his specific spiritual note, we find in the *mysticism* that pervades the epistle and forms, in fact, its substance. "I live no longer: Christ lives in me." "He that is joined to the Lord is one spirit."[5] In these sentences of the earlier letters we discover the spring of St Paul's theology, lying in his own experience—*the sense of personal union through the Spirit with Christ Jesus.* This was the deepest fact of Paul's consciousness. Here it meets us at every turn. More than twenty times the phrase "in Christ" or its equivalents recur, applied to Christian acts or states. It is enough to refer to chapter iii. 17, "that the Christ may make His dwelling in your hearts through faith," to show how profoundly this mysterious relationship is realized in this letter. No other New Testament writer conceived the idea in Paul's way, nor has any subsequent writer of whom we know made the like constant and original use of it. It was the habit of the apostle's mind, the index of his innermost life. Kindred to this, and hardly less conspicuous, is his conception of "God in Christ" (2 Cor. v. 19) saving and operating upon men, who, as we read here, "chose us in Christ before the world's foundation—forgave us in Him—made us in Him to sit together in the heavenly places—formed us in Christ Jesus for good works."

The ethical note of the true Paulinism is the conception of the *new man* in Christ Jesus, whose sins were slain by His death, and who shares His risen life unto God (Rom. vi.). From this idea, as from a fountainhead, the apostle in the parallel Colossian epistle (ch. iii.) deduces the new Christian morality. The temper and disposition of the believer, his conduct in all social duties and practical affairs are the expression of a "life hid with Christ in God." It is the identical "new man" of Romans and Colossians who presents himself as our ideal here, raised with Christ from the dead and "sitting with Him in the heavenly places." The newness of life in which he walks, receives its impulse and direction from this exalted fellowship.

The characteristics of St Paul's teaching which we have described—his logical thoroughness and finality, his peculiar historical, theological, spiritual, and ethical standpoint and manner of thought—are combined in the conception which is the specific note of this epistle, viz., its idea of *the Church* as the body of Christ,—or in other words, of *the new humanity* created in Him. This forms the centre of the circle of thought in which the writer's mind moves;[6] it is the meeting-point of the various lines of thought that we have already traced. The doctrine of personal salvation wrought out in the great evangelical epistles terminates in that of social and collective salvation. A new and precious title is conferred on Christ: He is "Saviour of *the body*" (v. 23), *i.e.*, of the corporate Christian community. "The Son of God who loved *me* and gave up Himself for *me*" becomes "the Christ" who "loved *the Church* and gave up Himself for *her*."[7] "The new man" is no longer the individual, a mere transformed *ego*; he is the type and beginning of a new mankind. A perfect society of men, all sons of God in Christ, is being constituted around the cross, in which the old antagonisms are reconciled, the ideal of creation is restored, and a body is provided to contain the fulness of Christ, a holy temple which God inhabits in the Spirit. Of this edifice, with the cross for its centre and Christ Jesus for its corner-stone, Jew and Gentile form the material—"the Jew first," lying nearest to the site.[8]

The apostle Paul necessarily conceived the reconstruction of humanity under the form of a reconciliation of Israel and the Gentiles. The Catholicism we have here is Paul's Catholicism of *Gentile engrafting*—not Clement's, of *churchly order and uniformity*; nor Ignatius', of *monepiscopal rule*. It is profoundly characteristic of this apostle, that in "the law" which had been to his own experience the barrier and ground of quarrel between the soul and God, "the strength of sin," he should come to see likewise the barrier between men and men, and the strength of the sinful enmity which distracted the Churches of his foundation (ii. 14–16).

The representation of the Church contained in this epistle is, therefore, by no means new in its elements. Such texts as 1 Corinthians iii. 16, 17 ("Ye are God's temple," etc.) and xii. 12–27 (concerning the *one body and many members*) bring us near to its actual expression. But the figures of the *body* and *temple* in these passages, had they stood alone, might be read as mere passing illustrations of the nature of Christian fellowship. Now they become proper designations of the Church, and receive their full significance. While in 1 Corinthians, moreover, these phrases do not look beyond the particular community addressed, in Ephesians they embrace the entire Christian society.

6

This epistle signalizes a great step forwards in the development of the apostle's theology—perhaps we might say, the last step. The Pastoral epistles serve to put the final apostolic seal upon the theological edifice that is now complete. Their care is with the guarding and furnishing of the "great house"[9] which our epistle is engaged in building.

The idea of the Church is not, however, independently developed. Ephesians and Colossians are companion letters,—the complement and explanation of each other. Both "speak with regard to Christ and the Church"; both reveal the Divine "glory in the Church and in Christ Jesus."[10] The emphasis of Ephesians falls on the former, of Colossians on the latter of these objects. The doctrine of the Person of Christ and that of the nature of the Church proceed with equal step. The two epistles form one process of thought.

Criticism has attempted to derive first one and then the other of the two from its fellow,—thus, in effect, stultifying itself. Finally Dr. Holtzmann, in his *Kritik der Epheser-und Kolosserbriefe*,[11] undertook to show that each epistle was in turn dependent on the other. There is, Holtzmann says, a Pauline nucleus hidden in Colossians, which he has himself extracted. By its aid some ecclesiastic of genius in the second century composed the Ephesian epistle. He then returned to the brief Colossian writing of St Paul, and worked it up, with his own Ephesian composition lying before him, into our existing epistle to the Colossians. This complicated and too ingenious hypothesis has not satisfied any one except its author, and need not detain us here. But Holtzmann has at any rate made good, against his predecessors on the negative side, the unity of origin of the two canonical epistles, the fact that they proceed from one mint and coinage. They are *twin* epistles, the offspring of a single birth in the apostle's mind. Much of their subject-matter, especially in the ethical section, is common to both. The glory of the Christ and the greatness of the Church are truths inseparable in the nature of things, wedded to each other. To the confession, "Thou art the Christ, the Son of the living God," His response ever is, "*I will build my Church*."[12] The same correspondence exists between these two epistles in the dialectic movement of the apostle's thought.

At the same time, there is a considerable difference between the two writings in point of style. M. Renan, who accepts Colossians from Paul's hand, and who admits that "among all the epistles bearing the name of Paul the epistle to the Ephesians is perhaps that which has been most anciently cited as a composition of the apostle of the Gentiles," yet speaks of this epistle as a "verbose amplification" of the other, "a commonplace letter, diffuse and pointless, loaded with useless words and repetitions, entangled and overgrown with irrelevancies, full of pleonasms and obscurities."[13]

In this instance, Renan's literary sense has deserted him. While Colossians is quick in movement, terse and pointed, in some places so sparing of words as to be almost hopelessly obscure,[14] Ephesians from beginning to end is measured and deliberate, exuberant in language, and obscure, where it is so, not from the brevity, but from the length and involution of its periods. It is occupied with a few great ideas, which the author strives to set forth in all their amplitude and significance. Colossians is a letter of discussion; Ephesians of reflection. The whole difference of style lies in this. In the reflective passages of Colossians, as indeed in the earlier epistles,[15] we find the stateliness of movement and rhythmical fulness of expression which in this epistle are sustained throughout. Both epistles are marked by those unfinished sentences and *anacolutha*, the grammatical inconsequence associated with close continuity of thought, which is a main characteristic of St Paul's style.[16] The epistle to the Colossians is like a mountain stream forcing its way through some rugged defile; that to the Ephesians is the smooth lake below, in which its chafed waters restfully expand. These sister epistles represent the moods of conflict and repose which alternated in St Paul's mobile nature.

In general, the writings of this group, belonging to the time of the apostle's imprisonment and advancing age,[17] display less passion and energy, but a more tranquil spirit than those of the Jewish controversy. They are prison letters, the fruit of a time when the author's mind had been much thrown in upon itself. They have been well styled "the afternoon epistles," being marked by the subdued and reflective temper natural to this period of life. Ephesians is, in truth, the typical representative of the third group of Paul's epistles, as Galatians is of the second. There is abundant reason to be satisfied that this letter came, as it purports to do, from *Paul, an apostle of Christ Jesus through God's will*.

But that it was addressed to "the saints which are *in Ephesus*" is more difficult to believe. The apostle has "heard of the faith which prevails amongst" his readers; he presumes that they "have heard of the Christ, and were taught in Him according as truth is in Jesus."[18] He hopes that by "reading" this epistle they will "perceive his understanding in the mystery of Christ" (iii. 2–4). He writes somewhat thus to the Colossians and Romans, whom he had never seen;[19] but can we imagine Paul addressing in this distant and uncertain fashion his children in the faith? In Ephesus he had laboured "for the space of three whole years" (Acts xx. 31), longer than in any other city of the Gentile mission, except Antioch. His speech to the Ephesian elders at Miletus, delivered four years ago, was surcharged with personal feeling, full of pathetic reminiscence and the signs of interested acquaintance with the individual membership of the Ephesian Church. In the epistle such signs are altogether wanting. The absence of greetings and messages we could understand; these Tychicus might convey by word of mouth. But how the man who wrote the epistles to the Philippians and Corinthians could have composed this long and careful letter to his own Ephesian people without a single word of endearment or familiarity,[20] and without the least allusion to his past intercourse with them, we cannot understand. It is in the destination that the only serious difficulty lies touching the authorship. Nowhere do we see more of *the apostle* and less of *the man* in St Paul; nowhere more of *the* Church, and less of *this or that* particular church.

It agrees with these internal indications that the local designation is wanting in the oldest Greek copies of the letter that are extant. The two great manuscripts of the fourth century, the Vatican and Sinaitic codices, omit the words "in Ephesus." Basil in the fourth century did not accept them, and says that "the old copies" were without them. Origen, in the beginning of the third century, seems to have known nothing of them. And Tertullian, at the end of the second century, while he condemns the heretic Marcion (who lived about fifty years earlier) for entitling the epistle "To the Laodiceans," quotes only the *title* against him, and not the text of the address, which he would presumably have done, had he read it in the form familiar to us. We are compelled to suppose, with Westcott and Hort and the textual critics generally, that these words form no part of the original address.

Here the *circular hypothesis* of Beza and Ussher comes to our aid. It is supposed that the letter was destined for a number of Churches in Asia Minor, which Tychicus was directed to visit in the course of the journey which took him to Colossæ.[21] Along with the letters for the Colossians and Philemon, he was entrusted with this more general epistle, intended for the Gentile Christian communities of the neighbouring region at large. During St Paul's ministry at Ephesus, we are told that "all those that dwell in Asia heard the word of the Lord, both Jews and Greeks" (Acts xix. 10). In so large and populous an area, amongst the Churches founded at this time there were doubtless others beside those of the Lycus valley "which had not seen Paul's face in the flesh," some about which the apostle had less precise knowledge than he had of these through Epaphras and Onesimus, but for whom he was no less desirous that their "hearts should be comforted, and brought into all the wealth of the full assurance of the understanding in the knowledge of the mystery of God" (Col. ii. 1, 2).

To which or how many of the Asian Churches Tychicus would be able to communicate the letter was, presumably, uncertain when it was written at

Rome; and the designation was left open. Its conveyance by Tychicus (vi. 21, 22) supplied the only limit to its distribution. Proconsular Asia was the richest and most peaceful province of the Empire, so populous that it was called "the province of five hundred cities." Ephesus was only the largest of many flourishing commercial and manufacturing towns.

At the close of his epistle to the Colossians St Paul directs this Church to procure "from Laodicea," in exchange for their own, a letter which he is sending there (iv. 16). Is it possible that we have the lost Laodicean document in the epistle before us? So Ussher suggested; and though the assumption is not essential to his theory, it falls in with it very aptly. Marcion may, after all, have preserved a reminiscence of the fact that Laodicea, as well as Ephesus, shared in this letter. The conjecture is endorsed by Lightfoot, who says, writing on Colossians iv. 16: "There are good reasons for the belief that St Paul here alludes to the so-called epistle to the Ephesians, which was in fact a circular letter, addressed to the principal Churches of proconsular Asia. Tychicus was obliged to pass through Laodicea on his way to Colossæ, and would leave a copy there before the Colossian letter was delivered."[22] The two epistles admirably supplement each other. The Apocalyptic letter "to the seven churches which are in Asia," ranging from Ephesus to Laodicea (Rev. ii., iii.), shows how much the Christian communities of this region had in common and how natural it would be to address them collectively. For the same region, with a yet wider scope, the "first catholic epistle of Peter" was destined, a writing that has many points of contact with this. Ephesus being the metropolis of the Asian Churches, and claiming a special interest in St Paul, came to regard the epistle as specially her own. Through Ephesus, moreover, it was communicated to the Church in other provinces. Hence it came to pass that when Paul's epistles were gathered into a single volume and a title was needed for this along with the rest, "To the Ephesians" was written over it; and this reference standing in the title, in course of time found its way into the text of the address. We propose to read this letter as *the general epistle of Paul to the Churches of Asia*, or *to Ephesus and its daughter Churches*.

But how are we to read the address, with the local definition wanting? There are two constructions open to us:—(1) We might suppose that a space was left blank in the original to be filled in afterwards by Tychicus with the names of the particular Churches to which he distributed copies, or to be supplied by the voice of the reader. But if that were so, we should have expected to find some trace of this variety of designation in the ancient witnesses. As it is, the documents either give Ephesus in the address, or supply no local name at all.

Nor is there, so far as we are aware, any analogy in ancient usage for the proceeding suggested. Moreover, the order of the Greek words[23] is against this supposition.—(2) We prefer, therefore, to follow Origen[24] and Basil, with some modern exegetes, in reading the sentence straight on, as it stands in the Sinaitic and Vatican copies. It then becomes: *To the saints, who are indeed faithful in Christ Jesus.*

"The saints" is the apostle's designation for Christian believers generally,[25] as men consecrated to God in Christ (1 Cor. i. 2). The qualifying phrase "those who are indeed faithful in Christ Jesus," is admonitory. As Lightfoot says with reference to the parallel qualification in Colossians i. 2, "This unusual addition is full of meaning. Some members of the [Asian] Churches were shaken in their allegiance, even if they had not fallen from it. The apostle therefore wishes it to be understood that, when he speaks of the saints, he means those who are true and steadfast members of the brotherhood. In this way he obliquely hints at the defection." By this further definition "he does not directly exclude any, but he indirectly warns all." We are reminded that we are in the neighbourhood of the Colossian heresy. Beneath the calm tenor of this epistle, the ear catches an undertone of controversy. In chapter iv. 14 and vi. 10–20 this undertone becomes clearly audible. We shall find the epistle end with the note of warning with which it begins.

———————

The Salutation is according to St Paul's established form of greeting.

11

FOOTNOTES:

[1] The translation given in this volume is based upon the Revised Version, but deviates from it in some particulars. These deviations will be explained in the exposition.

[2] The case against authenticity is ably stated in Dr. S. Davidson's *Introduction to the N. T.*; see also Baur's *Paul*, Pfleiderer's *Paulinism*, Hilgenfeld's *Einleitung*, Hatch's article on "Paul" in the *Encyclopædia Britannica*. The case for the defence may be found in Weiss', Salmon's, Bleek's, or Dods' *N. T. Introduction*—the last brief, but to the point; in Reuss' *History of the N. T.*; Milligan's article on "Ephesians" in *Encycl. Brit.*; Gloag's *Introduction to the Pauline Epp.*; Meyer's, or Beet's, or Eadie's *Commentary*; Sabatier's *The Apostle Paul*.

[3] Rom. xi. 16–24; Acts xiii. 26; Gal. iii. 7, 14.

[4] Gal. iii. 10–13; 2 Cor. v. 20, 21, etc.

[5] Gal. ii. 20; 1 Cor. vi. 17.

[6] See ch. i. 9–13, ii. 11–22, iii. 5–11, iv. 1–16, v. 23–32.

[7] Gal ii. 20; Eph. v. 25.

[8] Rom. i. 16; Eph. ii. 17–20.

[9] 1 Tim. iii. 15, 16; 2 Tim. ii. 20, 21.

[10] Eph. iii. 21, v. 32.

[11] *Kritik d. Epheser-u. Kolosserbriefe auf Grund einer Analyse ihres Verwandtschaftsverhältnisses* (Leipzig, 1872). A work more subtle and scientific, more replete with learning, and yet more unconvincing than this of Holtzmann, we do not know.

Von Soden, the latest interpreter of this school and Holtzmann's collaborateur in the new *Hand-Commentar*, accepts Colossians in its integrity as the work of Paul, retracting previous doubts on the subject. Ephesians he believes to have been written by a Jewish disciple of Paul in his name, about the end of the first century.

[12] Matt. xvi. 15–18; John xvii. 10: *I am glorified in them.*

[13] See his *Saint Paul*, Introduction, pp. xii.–xxiii.

[14] See Col. ii. 15, 18, 20–23.

[15] *E.g.*, in Rom. i. 1–7, viii. 28–30, xi. 33–36, xvi. 25–27.

[16] See the Winer-Moulton *N. T. Grammar*, p. 709: "It is in writers of great mental vivacity—more taken up with the thought than with the mode of its expression—that we may expect to find anacolutha most frequently. Hence they are especially numerous in the epistolary style of the apostle Paul."

[17] Eph. iii. 1; Phil. i. 13; Philem. 9.

[18] Ch. i. 15, iv. 20, 21.

[19] Col. i. 4, ii. 1; Rom. xv. 15, 16.

[20] "My brethren" in ch. vi. 10 is an insertion of the copyists. Even the closing benediction, ch. vi. 23, 24, is in the *third person*—a thing unexampled in St Paul's epistles.

[21] Ch. vi. 21, 22; Col. iv. 7–9.

[22] Compare Maclaren on *Colossians and Philemon*, p. 406, in this series.

[23] Τοῖς ἁγίοις τοῖς οὖσιν ... καὶ πιστοῖς ἐν Χριστῷ Ἰησοῦ. The interposition of the heterogeneous attributive between ἁγίοις and πιστοῖς is harsh and improbable—not to say, with Hofmann, "quite incredible." The two latest German commentaries to hand, that of Beck and of von Soden (in the *Hand-Commentar*), interpreters of opposite schools, agree with Hofmann in rejecting the local adjunct and regarding πιστοῖς as the complement of τοῖς οὖσιν.

[24] Origen, in his fanciful way, makes of τοῖς οὖσιν a predicate by itself: "the saints *who are*," who possess real being like God Himself (Exod. iii. 14) —"called from non-existence into existence." He compares 1 Cor. i. 28.

[25] See, *e.g.*, ver. 18, ii. 19, iii. 18, iv. 12, v. 3.

PRAISE AND PRAYER.

Chapter i. 3–19.

Οὓς προέγνω, καὶ προώρισεν
συμμόρφους τῆς εἰκόνος τοῦ υἱοῦ αὐτοῦ,
εἰς τὸ εἶναι αὐτὸν πρωτότοκον ἐν πολλοῖς ἀδέλφοις;
οὓς δὲ προώρισεν, τούτους καὶ ἐκάλεσεν;
καὶ οὓς ἐκάλεσεν, τούτους καὶ ἐδικαίωσεν;
οὓς δὲ ἐδικαίωσεν, τούτους καὶ ἐδόξασεν.

Rom. viii. 29, 30.

CHAPTER II.

THE ETERNAL PURPOSE.

We enter this epistle through a magnificent gateway. The introductory Act of Praise, extending from verse 3 to 14, is one of the most sublime of inspired utterances, an overture worthy of the composition that it introduces. Its first sentence compels us to feel the insufficiency of our powers for its due rendering.

The apostle surveys in this thanksgiving the entire course of the revelation of grace. Standing with the men of his day, the new-born community of the sons of God in Christ, midway between the ages past and to come,[26] he looks backward to the source of man's salvation when it lay a silent thought in the mind of God, and forward to the hour when it shall have accomplished its promise and achieved our redemption. In this grand evolution of the Divine plan three stages are marked by the refrain, thrice repeated, *To the praise of His glory, of the glory of His grace* (vv. 6, 12, 14). St Paul's psalm is thus divided into three strophes, or stanzas: he sings the glory of redeeming love in its past designs, its present bestowments, and its future fruition. The paragraph, forming but one sentence and spun upon a single golden thread, is a piece of thought-music,—a sort of *fugue*, in which from eternity to eternity the counsel of love is pursued by Paul's bold and exulting thought.

Despite the grammatical involution of the style here carried to an extreme, and underneath the apparatus of Greek pronouns and participles, there is a fine Hebraistic lilt pervading the doxology. The refrain is in the manner of Psalms xlii.–xliii., and xcix., where in the former instance "health of countenance," and in the latter "holy is He" gives the key-note of the poet's melody and parts his song into three balanced stanzas. In such poetry the strophes may be unequal in length, each developing its own thought freely, and yet there is harmony in their combination. Here the central idea, that of God's actual bounty to believers, fills a space equal to that of the other two. But there is a pause within it, at verse 10, which in effect resumes the idea of the first strophe and works it in as a *motif* to the second, carrying on both in a full stream till they lose themselves in the third and culminating movement. Throughout the piece there runs in varying expression the phrase "in Christ—in the Beloved—in Him—in whom," weaving the verses into subtle continuity. The theme of the entire composition is given in verse 3, which does not enter into the threefold division we have described, but forms a prelude to it.

"Blessed be the God and Father of our Lord Jesus Christ: who hath blessed us,
In every blessing of the spirit, in the heavenly places, in Christ."

Blessed be God!—It is the song of the universe, in which heaven and earth take responsive parts. "When the morning stars sang together and all the sons of God shouted for joy," this concert began, and continues still through the travail of creation and the sorrow and sighing of men. The work praises the Master. All sinless creatures, by their order and harmony, by the variety of their powers and beauty of their forms and delight of their existence, declare their Creator's glory. That praise to the Most High God which the lower creatures act instrumentally, it is man's privilege to utter in discourse of reason and music of the heart. Man is Nature's high priest; and above other men, the poet. Time will be, as it has been, when it shall be accounted the poet's honour and the crown of his art, that he should take the high praises of God into his mouth, making hymns to the glory of the Supreme Maker and giving voice to the dumb praise of inanimate nature and to the noblest thoughts of his fellows concerning the Blessed God.

Blessed be God!—It is the perpetual strain of the Old Testament, from Melchizedek down to Daniel,—of David in his triumph, and Job in his misery. But not hitherto could men say, Blessed be *the God and Father of our Lord Jesus Christ*! He was "the Most High God, the God of heaven,"— "Jehovah, God of Israel, who only doeth wondrous things,"—"the Shepherd" and "the Rock" of His people,—"the true God, the living God, and an everlasting King"; and these are glorious titles, which have raised men's thoughts to moods of highest reverence and trust. But the name of *Father*, and *Father of our Lord Jesus Christ*, surpasses and outshines them all. With wondering love and joy unspeakable St Paul pronounced this *Benedictus*. God was not less to him the Almighty, the High and Holy One dwelling in eternity, than in the days of his youthful Jewish faith; but the Eternal and All-holy One was now his Father in Jesus Christ. Blessed be His name: and let the whole earth be filled with His glory!

The apostle's psalm is a psalm of thanksgiving to God *blessing and blessed*. The second clause rhythmically answers to the first. True, our blessing of Him is far different from His blessing of us: ours in thought and words; His in mighty deeds of salvation. Yet in the fruit of lips giving thanks to His name there is a revenue of blessing paid to God which He delights in, and requires. "O Thou that inhabitest the praises of Israel," grant us to bless Thee while we live and to lift up our hands in Thy name!

By three qualifying adjuncts the blessing which the Father of Christ bestowed upon us is defined: in respect of its *nature*, its *sphere*, and its *personal ground*.

16

The blessings that prompt the apostle's praise are not such as those conspicuous in the Old Covenant: "Blessed shalt thou be in the city, and in the field; in the fruit of thy body, and the fruit of thy ground, and the increase of thy kine; blessed shall be thy basket, and thy kneading-trough" (Deut. xxviii. 3–5). The gospel pronounces beatitudes of another style: "Blessed are the poor in spirit; blessed the meek, the merciful, the pure in heart, the persecuted." St Paul had small share indeed in the former class of blessings, —a childless, landless, homeless man. Yet what happiness and wealth are his! Out of his poverty he is making all the ages rich! From the gloom of his prison he sheds a light that will guide and cheer the steps of multitudes of earth's sad wayfarers. Not certainly in the earthly places where he finds himself is Paul the prisoner of Christ Jesus blessed; but "in spiritual blessing" and "in heavenly places" how abundantly! His own blessedness he claims for all who are in Christ.

Blessing *spiritual* in its nature is, in St Paul's conception of things, blessing in and of the Holy Spirit.[27] In His quickening our spirit lives; through His indwelling health, blessedness, eternal life are ours. In this verse justly the theologians recognize the Trinity of the Father, Christ, and the Holy Spirit.— Blessing *in the heavenly places* is not so much blessing coming from those places—from God the Father who sits there—as it is blessing which lifts us into that supernal region, giving to us a place and heritage in the world of God and of the angels. Two passages of the companion epistles interpret this phrase: "Your life is hid with Christ in God" (Col. iii. 3); and again, "Our citizenship is in heaven" (Phil. iii. 20).—The decisive note of St Paul's blessedness lies in the words "in Christ." For him all good is summed up there. Spiritual, heavenly, and Christian: these three are one. In Christ dying, risen, reigning, God the Father has raised believing men to a new heavenly life. From the first inception of the work of grace to its consummation, God thinks of men, speaks to them and deals with them *in Christ*. To Him, therefore, with the Father be eternal praise!

> "As He chose us in Him before the world's foundation,
> That we should be holy and unblemished before Him:
> When in love He foreordained us
> To filial adoption through Jesus Christ for Himself,
> According to the good pleasure of His will,—
> To the praise of the glory of His grace" (vv. 4–6a).

Here is St Paul's first chapter of Genesis. *In the beginning was the election of grace.* There is nothing unprepared, nothing unforeseen in God's dealings with mankind. His wisdom and knowledge are as deep as His grace is wide (Rom. xi. 33). Speaking of his own vocation, the apostle said: "It pleased God, who set me apart from my mother's womb, to reveal His Son in me" (Gal. i. 15, 16). He does but generalize this conception and carry it two steps further back—from the origin of the individual to the origin of the race, and from the beginning of the race to the beginning of the world—when he asserts that the community of redeemed men was chosen in Christ before the world's foundation.

"The world" is a work of time, the slow structure of innumerable yet finite ages. Science affirms on its own grounds that the visible universe had a beginning, as it has its changes and its certain end. Its structural plan, its unity of aim and movement, show it to be the creation of a vast Intelligence. Harmony and law, all that makes science possible is the product of thought. Reason extracts from nature what Reason has first put there. The longer, the more intricate and grand the process, the farther science pushes back the beginning in our thoughts, the more sublime and certain the primitive truth becomes: "In the beginning God created the heavens and the earth."

The world is a system; it has a method and a plan, therefore a foundation. But before the foundation, there was *the Founder*. And man was in His thoughts, and the redeemed Church of Christ. While yet the world was not and the immensity of space stretched lampless and unpeopled, *we* were in the mind of God; His thought rested with complacency upon His human sons, whose "name was written in the book of life from the foundation of the world." This amazing statement is only the logical consequence of St Paul's experience of Divine grace, joined to his conviction of the infinite wisdom and eternal being of God.

When he says that God "chose us in Christ *before the foundation of the world*"—or *before founding the world*—this is not a mere mark of time. It intimates that in laying His plans for the world the Creator had the purpose of redeeming grace in view. The kingdom which the "blessed children" of the Father of Christ "inherit," is the kingdom "*prepared* for them *from the foundation of the world*" (Matt. xxv. 34). Salvation lies as deep as creation. The provision for it is eternal. For the universe of being was conceived, fashioned, and built up "in Christ." The argument of Colossians i. 13–22 lies behind these words. The Son of God's love, in whom and for whom the worlds were made, always was potentially the Redeemer of men, as He was the image of God (Col. i. 14, 15). He looked forward to this mission from eternity, and was in spirit "the Lamb slain from the foundation of the world" (Rev. xiii. 8). Creation and redemption, Nature and the Church, are parts of one system; and in the reconciliation of the cross all orders of being are concerned, "whether the things upon the earth or the things in the heavens."

Evil existed before man appeared on the earth to be tempted and to fall. Through the geological record we hear the voice of creation groaning for long æons in its pain.

> "Dragons of the prime,
> That tare each other in their slime,"

grim prophets of man's brutal and murderous passions, bear witness to a war in nature that goes back far towards the foundation of the world. And this rent and discord in the frame of things it was His part to reconcile "in whom and for whom all things were created." This universal deliverance, it seems, is dependent upon ours. "The creation itself lifts up its head, and is looking out for the revelation of the sons of God" (Rom. viii. 19). In founding the world, foreseeing its bondage to corruption, God prepared through His elect sons in Christ a deliverance the glory of which will make its sufferings to seem but a light thing. "In thee," said God to Abraham, "shall all the kindreds of the earth be blessed": so in the final "adoption,—to wit, the redemption of our body" (Rom. viii. 23), all creatures shall exult; and our mother earth, still travailing in pain with us, will remember her anguish no more.

The Divine election of men in Christ is further defined in the words of verse 5: "Having in love predestined us," and "according to the good pleasure of His will." *Election* is selection; it is the antecedent in the mind of God in Christ of the preference which Christ showed when He said to His disciples, "I have chosen you out of the world." It is, moreover, a *fore-ordination in love*: an expression which indicates on the one hand the disposition in God that prompted and sustains His choice, and on the other the determination of the almighty Will whereby the all-wise Choice is put into operation and takes effect. In this pre-ordaining control of human history God "determined the fore-appointed seasons and the bounds of human habitation" (Acts xvii. 26). The Divine prescience—that "depth of the wisdom and knowledge of God"— as well as His absolute righteousness, forbids the treasonable thought of anything arbitrary or unfair cleaving to this pre-determination—anything that should override our free-will and make our responsibility an illusion. "Whom He did *foreknow*, He also did predestinate" (Rom. viii. 29). He foresees everything, and allows for everything.

The consistence of foreknowledge with free-will is an enigma which the apostle did not attempt to solve. His reply to all questions touching the justice of God's administration in the elections of grace—questions painfully felt and keenly agitated then as they are now, and that pressed upon himself in the case of his Jewish kindred with a cruel force (Rom. ix. 3)—his answer to his own heart, and to us, lies in the last words of verse 5: "according to the good pleasure of His will." It is what Jesus said concerning the strange preferences of Divine grace: "Even so, Father, for so it seemed good in Thy sight." What pleases Him can only be wise and right. What pleases Him, must content us. Impatience is unbelief. Let us wait to see the end of the Lord. In numberless instances—such as that of the choice between Jacob and Esau, and that of

Paul and the believing remnant of Israel as against their nation—God's ways have justified themselves to after times; so they will universally. Our little spark of intelligence glances upon one spot in a boundless ocean, on the surface of immeasurable depths.

The purpose of this loving fore-ordination of believing men in Christ is twofold; it concerns at once their *character* and their *state*: "He chose us out —that we should be holy and without blemish in His sight," and "unto adoption as sons through Jesus Christ for Himself." These two purposes are one. God's sons must be holy; and holy men are His sons. For this end "we" were elected of God in the beginning. Nay, with this end in view the world was founded and the human race came into being, to provide God with such sons[28] and that Christ might be "the firstborn among many brethren" (Rom. viii. 28–30).

"That we should be holy"—should be *saints*. This the readers are already: "To the saints" the apostle writes (ver. 1). They are men devoted to God by their own choice and will, meeting God's choice and will for them. Imperfect saints they may be, by no means as yet "without blemish"; but they are already, and abidingly, "sanctified in Christ Jesus" (1 Cor. i. 2) and "sealed" for God's possession "by the Holy Spirit" (vv. 13, 14). In this fact lies their hope of moral perfection and the impulse and power to attain it. Their task is to "perfect" their existing "holiness" (2 Cor. vii. 1), "cleansing themselves from all defilement of flesh and spirit." Let no Christian say, "I do not pretend to be a saint." This is to renounce your calling. You *are* a saint if you are a true believer in Christ; and you are to be an unblemished saint.

Thus the Church is at last to be presented, and every man in his own order, "faultless before the presence of His glory, with exceeding joy."[29] God could not invite us in His grace to anything inferior. A blemished saint—a smeared picture, a flawed marble—this is not like His work; it is not like Himself. Such saintship cannot approve itself "before Him." He must carry out His ideal, must fashion the new man as he was created in Christ after His own faultless image, and make human holiness a transcript of the Divine (1 Peter i. 16).

Now, this Divine character is native to the sons of God. The ideal which God had for men was always the same. The father of the race was made in His image. In the Old Testament Israel receives the command: "You shall be holy, for I, Jehovah your God, am holy." But it was in Jesus Christ that the breadth of this command was disclosed, and the possibility of our personal obedience to it. The law of Christian sonship, manifest only in shadow in the Levitical sanctity, is now pronounced by Jesus: "You shall be perfect, as your heavenly Father is perfect." Verses 4 and 5 are therefore strictly parallel: God elected us

20

in Christ to be perfect saints; for He predestined us through Jesus Christ to be His sons.

Sonship to Himself is the Christian status, the rank and standing which God confers on those who believe in His Son; it accrues to them by the fact that they are in Christ.[30] It is defined by the term *adoption*, which St Paul employs in this sense in Romans viii. 15, 23, as well as in Galatians iv. 5. Adoption was a peculiar institution of Roman law, familiar to Paul as a citizen of Rome; and it aptly describes to Gentile believers their relation to the family of God. "By adoption under the Roman law an entire stranger in blood became a member of the family into which he was adopted, exactly as if he had been born in it. He assumed the family name, partook in its system of sacrificial rites, and became, not on sufferance or at will, but to all intents and purposes a member of the house of his adopter.... This metaphor was St Paul's translation into the language of Gentile thought of Christ's great doctrine of the New Birth. He exchanges the physical metaphor of regeneration for the legal metaphor of adoption. The adopted becomes in the eye of the law a new creature. He was born again into a new family. By the aid of this figure the Gentile convert was enabled to realize in a vivid manner the fatherhood of God, the brotherhood of the faithful, the obliteration of past penalties, the right to the mystic inheritance. He was enabled to realize that upon this spiritual act 'Old things passed away and all things became new.'"[31]

This exalted status belonged to men in the purpose of God from eternity; but as a matter of fact it was instituted "through Jesus Christ," the historical Redeemer. Whether previously (Jewish) servants in God's house or (Gentile) aliens excluded from it (ii. 12), those who believed in Jesus as the Christ received a spirit of adoption and dared to call God *Father*! This unspeakable privilege had been preparing for them through the ages past in God's hidden wisdom. Throughout the wild course of human apostasy the Father looked forward to the time when He might again through Jesus Christ make men His sons; and His promises and preparations were directed to this one end. The predestination having such an end, how fitly it is said: "*in love* having foreordained us."

Four times, in these three verses, with exulting emphasis, the apostle claims this distinction for "us." *Who*, then, are the objects of the primordial election of grace? Does St Paul use the pronoun distributively, thinking of individuals —you and me and so many others, the personal recipients of saving grace? or does he mean the Church, as that is collectively the family of God and the object of His loving ordination? In this epistle, the latter is surely the thought in the apostle's mind.[32] As Hofmann says: "The body of Christians is the object of this choice, not as composed of a certain number of individuals—a sum of 'the elect' opposed to a sum of the non-elect—but as the Church taken out of and separated from the world."

On the other hand, we may not widen the pronoun further; we cannot allow that the sonship here signified is man's natural relation to God, that to which he was born by creation. This robs the word "adoption" of its distinctive force. The sonship in question, while grounded "in Christ" from eternity, is conferred "through" the incarnate and crucified "Jesus Christ"; it redounds "to the praise of the glory of His *grace*." Now, grace is God's redeeming love toward sinners. God's purpose of grace toward mankind, embedded, as one may say, in creation, is realized in the body of redeemed men. But this community, we rejoice to believe, is vastly larger than the visible aggregate of Churches; for how many who knew not His name, have yet walked in the true light which lighteth every man.

There lies in the words "in Christ" a principle of exclusion, as well as of wide inclusion. Men cannot be in Christ against their will, who persistently put Him, His gospel and His laws, away from them. When we close with Christ by faith, we begin to enter into the purpose of our being. We find the place prepared for us before the foundation of the world in the kingdom of Divine love. We live henceforth "to the praise of the glory of His grace!"

FOOTNOTES:

[26] Ch. ii. 7, iii. 5, 21; Col. i. 26.

[27] Vv. 13, 14; Rom. viii. 2–6, 16; 1 Cor. ii. 12; Gal v. 16, 22–25.

[28] εἰς αὐτόν, *for Him*; not αὐτῷ, *to Him.*

[29] Ch. v. 25–27; Col. i. 27–29; Jude 24.

[30] On *sonship*, see Chapters XV.–XVII. and XIX. in *The Epistle to the Galatians* (Expositor's Bible).

[31] From a valuable and suggestive paper by W. E. Ball, LL.D., on "St Paul and the Roman Law," in the *Contemporary Review*, August 1891.

[32] See vv. 12, 13, where Jews and Gentiles, collectively, are distinguished; and ch. ii. 11, 12, iii. 2–6, 21, iv. 4, 5, v. 25–27.

CHAPTER III.

THE BESTOWMENT OF GRACE.

"Which grace He bestowed on us, in the Beloved One:
In whom we have the redemption through His blood, the forgiveness of our trespasses,
According to the riches of His grace:
Which He made to abound toward us in all wisdom and prudence, making known to us the
mystery of His will,
According to His good pleasure:
Which He purposed in Him, for dispensation in the fulness of the times,
Purposing to gather into one body all things in the Christ—
The things belonging to the heavens, and the things upon the earth—yea, in Him,
In whom also we received our heritage, as we had been foreordained,
According to purpose of Him who worketh all things
According to the counsel of His will,—
That we might be to the praise of His glory."[33]

EPH. i. 6*b*–12*a*.

The blessedness of men in Christ is not matter of purpose only, but of reality
and experience. With the word *grace* in the middle of the sixth verse the
apostle's thought begins a new movement. We have seen Grace hidden in the
depths of eternity in the form of sovereign and fatherly election, lodging its
purpose in the foundation of the world. From those mysterious depths we turn
to the living world in our own breast. There, too, Grace dwells and reigns:
"which grace He imparted to us, in the Beloved,—in whom we have
redemption through His blood."

The leading word of this clause we can only paraphrase; it has no English
equivalent. St Paul perforce turns *grace* into a verb; this verb occurs in the
New Testament but once besides,—in Luke i. 28, the angel's salutation to
Mary: "Hail thou that art highly favoured (made-an-object-of-grace)."[34] If
we could employ our verb *to grace* in a sense corresponding to that of the
noun *grace* in the apostle's dialect and nearly the opposite of *to disgrace*, then
graced would signify what he means here, viz., *treated with grace*, made its
recipients.

God "showed us grace *in the Beloved*"—or, to render the phrase with full
emphasis, "in that Beloved One"—even as He "chose us in Him before the
world's foundation" and "in love predestined us for adoption." The grace is
conveyed upon the basis of our relationship to Christ: on that ground it was
conceived in the counsels of eternity. The Voice from heaven which said at
the baptism of Jesus and again at the transfiguration, "This is my Son, the
Beloved," uttered God's eternal thought regarding Christ. And that regard of
God toward the Son of His love is the fountain of His love and grace to men.

Christ is the Beloved not of the Father alone, but of the created universe. All that know the Lord Jesus must needs love and adore Him—unless their hearts are eaten out by sin. Not to love Him is to be anathema. "If any man love me," said Jesus, "my Father will love him." Nothing so much pleases God and brings us into fellowship with God so direct and joyous, as our love to Jesus Christ. About this at least heaven and earth may agree, that He is the altogether lovely and love-worthy. Agreement in this will bring about agreement in everything. The love of Christ will tune the jarring universe into harmony.

1. Of grace bestowed, the first manifestation, in the experience of Paul and his readers, was *the forgiveness of their trespasses* (comp. ii. 13–18). This is "the redemption" that "we *have*." And it comes "through His *blood*." The epistles to the Galatians and Romans[35] expound at length the apostle's doctrine touching the remission of sin and the relation of Christ's death to human transgression. To *redemption* we shall return in considering verse 14, where the word is used, as again in chapter iv. 30, in its further application.

In Romans iii. 22–26 "the redemption that is in Christ Jesus" is declared to be the means by which we are acquitted in the judgement of God from the guilt of past transgressions. And this redemption consists in the "propitiatory sacrifice" which Christ offered in shedding His blood—a sacrifice wherein we participate "through faith." The language of this verse contains by implication all that is affirmed there. In this connexion, and according to the full intent of the word, redemption is *release by ransom*. The life-blood of Jesus Christ was the *price* that He paid in order to secure our lawful release from the penalties entailed by our trespasses.[36] This Jesus Christ implied beforehand, when He spoke of "giving His life a ransom for many"; and when He said, in handing to His disciples the cup of the Last Supper: "This is my blood, the blood of the covenant, which is shed for many for the remission of sins." Using another synonymous term, St Paul tells us that "Christ *bought us out of* the curse of the law"; and he bases on this expression a strong practical appeal: "You are not your own, for you were bought with a price."[37] These sayings, and others like them, point unmistakably to the fact that our trespasses as men against God's inflexible law, apart from Christ's intervention, must have issued in our eternal ruin. By His death on the cross Christ has made such amends to the law, that the awful sentence is averted, and our complete release from the power of sin is rendered possible.

On rising from the dead our Saviour commissioned the apostles to "proclaim in His name repentance and remission of sins to all nations" (Luke xxiv. 47). It was thus He proposed to save the world. This proclamation is the "good news" of the gospel. The announcement meets the first need of the serious and awakened human spirit. It answers the question which arises in the breast of every man who thinks earnestly about his personal relations to God and to the laws of his being. We cannot wonder that St Paul sets the remission of sins first amongst the bestowments of God's grace, and makes it the foundation of all the rest.

Does it occupy the like position in modern Christian teaching? Do we realize the criminality of sin, the fearfulness of God's displeasure, the infinite worth of His forgiveness and the obligations under which it places us, as St Paul and his converts did? or even as our fathers did a few generations ago? "It is my impression," writes Dr. R. W. Dale,[38] "that both religious people and those who do not profess to be religious must be conscious that God's Forgiveness, if they ever think of it at all, does not create any deep and strong emotion.... The difference between the way in which we think of the Divine Forgiveness and the way in which it was thought of by David and Isaiah, by Christ Himself, by Peter, Paul, and John; by the saints of all Christian Churches in past times, both in the East and in the West; ... by the leaders of the Evangelical Revival in the last century—the difference, I say, between the way in which the Forgiveness of sins was thought of by them, and the way in which we think of it, is very startling. The difference is so great, it affects so seriously the whole system of the religious thought and life, that we may be said to have invented a new religion.... The difference between our religion and the religion of other times is this—that we do not believe that God has any strong resentment against sin or against those who are guilty of sin. And since His resentment has gone, His mercy has gone with it. We have not a God who is more merciful than the God of our fathers, but a God who is less righteous; and a God who is not righteous, a God who does not glow with fiery indignation against sin, is no God at all."

These are solemn words, to be deeply pondered. They come from one of the most sagacious observers and justly revered teachers of our time. We have made a real advance in breadth and human sympathy; and there has been throughout our Churches a genuine and much needed awakening of philanthropic activity. But if we are *departing from the living God*, what will this avail us? If "the redemption through Christ's blood, the forgiveness of our trespasses," is no longer to us the momentous and glorious fact that it was to the apostles, then it is time to ask whether our God is in truth the same as theirs, whether He is still the God and Father of our Lord Jesus Christ— whether we are not, haply, fabricating for ourselves another gospel. Without a piercing sense of the shame and ruin involved in human sin, we shall not put its remission where St Paul does, at the foundation of God's benefits to men. Without this sentiment, we can only wonder at the passionate gratitude with which he receives the atonement and measures by its completeness the riches of God's grace.

II. Along with this chief blessing of forgiveness, there came another to the apostolic Church. With the heart the mind, with the conscience the intellect was quickened and endowed: "which [grace] He shed abundantly upon us *in all wisdom and intelligence*."

This sequel to verse 7 is somewhat of a surprise. The reader is apt to slur over verse 8, half sensible of some jar and incongruity between it and the context. It scarcely occurs to us to associate wisdom and good sense with the pardon of sin, as kindred bestowments of the gospel. Minds of the evangelical order are often supposed, indeed, to be wanting in intellectual excellencies and indifferent to their value. Is it not true that "not many wise after the flesh were called"? Do we not glory above everything in preaching a "simple gospel"?

But there is another side to all this. "Christ was made of God unto us *wisdom*." This attribute the apostle even sets first when he writes to the wisdom-seeking Greeks, mocked by their worn-out and confused philosophies (1 Cor. i. 30). To a close observer of the primitive Christian societies few things must have been more noticeable than the powerful mental stimulus imparted by the new faith. These epistles are a witness to the fact. That such letters could be addressed to communities gathered mainly from the lower ranks of society—consisting of slaves, common artizans, poor women —shows that the moral regeneration effected in St Paul's converts was accompanied by an extraordinary excitement and activity of thought. In this the apostle recognised the work of the Holy Spirit, a mark of God's special favour and blessing. "I give thanks always for you," he writes to the Corinthians, "for the grace of God that was given you in Christ Jesus, that in everything you were enriched by Him, in all word and all knowledge." The leaders of the apostolic Church were the profoundest thinkers of their day; though at the time the world held them for babblers, because their dialect was not of its schools. They drew from stores of wisdom and knowledge hidden in Christ, which none of the princes of this world knew.

Of such wisdom our epistle is full, and God "has made it to abound" to the readers in these inspired pages. Paul's "understanding in the mystery of Christ" was always deepening. In his lonely prison musings the length and breadth of the Divine counsels are disclosed to him as never before. He sees the course of the ages and the universe of being illuminated by the light of the knowledge of Christ. And what he sees, all men are to see through him (iii. 9). Blessed be God who has given to His Church through His apostles, and through the great Christian teachers of every age, His precious gifts of wisdom and prudence, and made His grace richly to overflow from the heart into the mind and understanding of men!

26

This intellectual gift is twofold: *phronēsis* as well as *sophia*,—the bestowment not only of deep spiritual thought, but of moral sagacity, good sense and thoughtfulness. This is a choice *charism*—a mercy of the Lord. For want of it how sadly is the fruit of other graces spoilt and wasted. How brightly it shines in St Paul himself! What luminous and wholesome views of life, what a fund of practical sense there is in the teaching of this letter.

St Paul rejoices in these gifts of the understanding and claims them for the Church, having in his view the false knowledge, the "philosophy and vain deceit" that was making its appearance in the Asian Churches (Col. ii. 4, 8, etc.). Our safeguard against intellectual perils lies not in ignorance, but in deeper heart-knowledge. When the grace that bestows redemption through Christ's blood adds its concomitant blessing of enlightenment, when it elevates the mind as it cleanses the heart, and abounds to us in all wisdom and prudence, the winds of doctrine and the waves of speculation blow and beat in vain; they can but bring health to a Church thus established in its faith.

Verses 9 and 10 describe the object of this new knowledge. They state the doctrine which gave this powerful mental impulse to the apostolic Church, disclosing to it a vast field of view, and supplying the most fertile and vigorous principles of moral wisdom. This impulse lay in the revelation of God's purpose to reconstitute the universe in Christ. The declaration of "the mystery of His will" comes in at this point episodically, and by the way; and we reserve it for consideration to the end of the present Chapter.

But let us observe here that our wisdom and prudence lie in the knowledge of God's will. Truth is not to be found in any system of logical notions, in schemes and syntheses of the laws of nature or of thought. The human mind can never rest for long in abstractions. It will not accept for its basis of thought that which is less real and positive than itself. By its rational instincts it is compelled to seek a Reason and a Conscience at the centre of things,—a living God. It craves to know *the mystery of His will*.

III. Verse 11 fills up the measure of the bestowment of grace on sinful men. The present anticipates the future; faith and love are lifted to a glorious hope. "In whom also—*i.e.*, in Christ—*we received our heritage*, predestinated [to it], according to His purpose who works all things according to the counsel of His will."

Following Meyer and other great interpreters, we prefer in this passage the rendering of the English Authorized Version (*we obtained an inheritance*) to that of the Revised (*we were made a heritage*).[39] "Foreordained" carries us back to verse 5—to the phrase "foreordained to sonship." The believer cannot be predestinated to sonship without being predestinated to an inheritance.[40] "If children, then heirs" (Rom. viii. 17). But while in the parallel passage we are designated heirs *with* Christ, we appear in this place, according to the tenor of the context, as heirs *in* Him. Christ is Himself the believer's wealth, both in possession and hope: all his desire is to gain Christ (Phil. iii. 8). The apostle gives thanks here in the same strain as in Colossians i. 12–14, "to the Father who qualified us [by making us His sons] to partake of the inheritance of the saints in the light." In that thanksgiving we observe the same connexion as in this between our *forgiveness* (ver. 7) and our *enfeoffment*, or investment with the forfeited rights of sons of God (vv. 5, 11).[41]

The heritage of the saints in Christ is theirs already, by actual investiture. The liberty of sons of God, access to the Father, the treasures of Christ's wisdom and knowledge, the sanctifying Spirit and the moral strength and joy that He imparts, these form a rich estate of which ancient saints had but foretastes and promises. In the all-controlling "counsel of His will," God wrought throughout the course of history to convey this heritage to us. We are children of "the fulness of the times," heirs of all the past. For us God has been working from eternity. On us the ends of the world have come. Thus from the summit of our exaltation in Christ the apostle looks backward to the beginning of Divine history.

From the same point his gaze sweeps onward to the end. God's purpose embraces the ages to come with those that are past. His working will not cease till the whole counsel is fulfilled. What we have of our inheritance, though rich and real, holds in it the promise of infinitely more; and the Holy Spirit is the "earnest of our inheritance" (ver. 14). God intends "that we should be to the praise of His glory." As things are, His glory is but obscurely visible in His saints. "It doth not yet appear what we shall be,"—and it will not appear until the unveiling of the sons of God (Rom. viii. 18–25). One day God's glory in us will burst forth in its splendour. All beholders in heaven and earth will then sing *to the praise of His glory*, when it is seen in His redeemed and godlike sons.

Verses 9 and 10 (*which He purposed ... upon the earth*) are, as we have said, a parenthesis or episode in the passage just reviewed. Neither in structure nor in sense would the paragraph be defective, had this clause been wanting. With the "in Him" repeated at the end of verse 10, St Paul resumes the main current of his thanksgiving, arrested for a moment while he dwells on "the mystery of God's will."

This last expression (ver. 9), notwithstanding what he has said in verses 4 and 5, still needs elucidation. He will pause for an instant to set forth once more the eternal purpose, to the knowledge of which the Church is now admitted. The communication of this mystery is, he says, "according to God's good pleasure which He purposed in Christ [comp. ver. 4], for a dispensation of the fulness of the times, intending to gather up again all things in the Christ—the things in the heavens, and the things upon the earth."

God formed in Christ the purpose, by the dispensation of His grace, in due time to re-unite the universe under the headship of Christ. This mysterious design, hitherto kept secret, He has "made known unto us." Its manifestation imparts a wisdom that surpasses all the wisdom of former ages.[42] Such is the drift of this profound deliverance.

The first clause of verse 10 supplies a datum for its interpretation. The *fulness of the times*, in St Paul's dialect, can only be the time of Christ.[43] The dispensation which God designed of old is that in which the apostle himself is now engaged;[44] it is the dispensation, or administration (*economy*), of the grace and truth that came by Jesus Christ, whether God be conceived as Himself the Dispenser, or through the stewards of His mysteries. The Messianic end was to Paul's Jewish thought the dénouement of antecedent history. How long this age would continue, into what epochs it might unfold itself, he knew not; but for him the fulness of the times had arrived. The Son of God was come; the kingdom of God was amongst men. It was the beginning of the end. It is a mistake to relegate this text to the dim and distant future, to some far-off consummation. We are in the midst of the Christian reconstruction of things, and are taking part in it. The decisive epoch fell when "God sent forth His Son." All that has followed, and will follow, is the result of this mission. Christ is all things, and in all; and we are already complete in Him.

What, then, signifies this *gathering-into-one* or *summing-up* of all things in the Christ? Our *recapitulate* is the nearest equivalent of the Greek verb, in its etymological sense. In Romans xiii. 8, 9 the same word is used, where the several commands of the second table of the Decalogue are said to be "comprehended in this word, namely, Thou shalt love thy neighbour as thyself." This summing up is not a generalization or compendious statement of the commands of God; it signifies their reduction to a fundamental principle. They are unified by the discovery of a law that underlies them all. And while thus theoretically explained, they are made practically effective: "For love is the fulfilling of the law."

Similarly, St Paul finds in Christ the fundamental principle of the creation. For those who think with him, God has by the Christian revelation already brought all things to their unity. This summing up—the Christian inventory and recapitulation of the universe—the apostle has formally stated in Colossians i. 15–20: "Christ is God's image and creation's firstborn. In Him, through Him, for Him all things were made. He is before them all; and in Him they have their basis and uniting bond. He is equally the Head of the Church and the new creation, the firstborn out of the dead, that He might hold a universal presidence—charged with all the fulness, so that in Him is the ground of the reconciliation no less than of the creation of all things in heaven and earth." What can we desire more comprehensive than this? It is the theory and programme of the world revealed to God's holy apostles and prophets.

The "gathering into one" of this text includes the "reconciliation" of Colossians i. 20, and more. It signifies, beside the removal of the enmities which are the effect of sin (ii. 14–16), the subjection of all powers in heaven and earth to the rule of Christ (vv. 21, 22),[45] the enlightenment of the angelic magnates as to God's dealings with men (iii. 9, 10),—in fine, the rectification and adjustment of the several parts of the great whole of things, bringing them into full accord with each other and with their Creator's will. What St Paul looks forward to is, in a word, the organization of the universe upon a Christian basis. This reconstitution of things is provided for and is being effected "in the Christ." He is the rallying point of the forces of peace and blessing. The organic principle, the organizing Head, the creative nucleus of the new creation is there. The potent germ of life eternal has been introduced into the world's chaos; and its victory over the elements of disorder and death is assured.

Observe that the apostle says "in *the Christ.*"[46] He is not speaking of Christ in the abstract, considered in His own Person or as He dwells in heaven, but in His relations to men and to time. The Christ manifest in Jesus (iv. 20, 21), the Christ of prophets and apostles, the Messiah of the ages, the Husband of the Church (v. 23), is the author and finisher of this grand restoration.

Christ's work is essentially a work of *restoration*. We must insist, with Meyer, upon the significance of the Greek preposition in Paul's compound verb (*ana-*, equal to *re-* in *restore* or *resume*). The Christ is not simply the climax of the past—the Son of man and the recapitulation of humanity, as man is of the creatures below him, summing up human development and lifting it to a higher stage—though He is all that. Christ *rehabilitates* man and the world. He re-asserts the original ground of our being, as that exists in God. He carries us and the world forward out of sin and death, by carrying us back to God's ideal. The new world is the old world repaired, and in its reparation infinitely enhanced—rich in the memories of redemption, in the fruit of penitence and the discipline of suffering, in the lessons of the cross.

All things in heaven and earth it was God's good pleasure in the Christ to gather again into one. Is this a general assertion concerning the universe as a whole, or may we apply it with distributive exactness to each particular thing? Is there to be, as we fain would hope, no single exception to the "all things"—

no wanderer lost, no exile finally shut out from the Holy City and the tree of life? Are all evil men and demons, willing or against their will, to be embraced somehow and at last—at last—in the universal peace of God?

It is impossible that the first readers should have so construed Paul's words (comp. v. 5). He has not forgotten the "unquenchable fire," the "eternal punishment"; nor dare we. "If anything is certain about the teaching of Christ and His apostles, it is that they warned men not to reject the Divine mercy and so to incur irrevocable exile from God's presence and joy. They assumed that some men would be guilty of this supreme crime, and would be doomed to this supreme woe" (Dale). There is nothing in this text to warrant any man in presuming on the mercy or the sovereignty of God, nothing to justify us in supposing that, deliberately refusing to be reconciled to God in Christ, we shall yet be reconciled in the end, despite ourselves.

St Paul assures us that God and the world will be reunited, and that peace will reign through all realms and orders of existence. He does not, and he could not say that none will exclude themselves from the eternal kingdom. Making men free, God has made it possible for them to contradict Him, so long as they have any being. The apostle's words have their note of warning, along with their boundless promise. There is no place in the future order of things for aught that is out of Christ. There is no standing-ground anywhere for the unclean and the unjust, for the irreconcilable rebel against God. "The Son of man shall send forth His angels, and they shall gather out of His kingdom all things that offend and them that do iniquity."

FOOTNOTES:

[33] The arrangement above made of the lines of this intricate passage is designed to guide the eye to its elucidation. Our disposition of the verses has not been determined by any preconceived interpretation, but by the parallelism of expression and cadences of phrase. The rhythmical structure of the piece, it seems to us, supplies the key to its explanation, and reduces to order its long-drawn and heaped-up relative and prepositional clauses, which are grammatically so unmanageable.

[34] Χαῖρε, κεχαριτωμένη. It is impossible to reproduce in English the beautiful assonance—the *play* of sound and sense—in Gabriel's greeting, as St Luke renders it.

[35] See Rom. i. 16–18, iii. 19–v. 21, vi. 7, vii. 1–6, viii. 1–4, 31–34, x. 6–9; 1 Cor. xv. 3, 4, 17, 56, 57; 2 Cor. v. 18–21; Gal. ii. 14–iii. 14, vi. 12–14. The latter passages the writer has endeavoured to expound in Chapters X. to XII. and XXVIII. of his Commentary on *Galatians* in this series.

[36] It is an error to suppose, as one sometimes hears it said, that *trespasses* or *transgressions* are a light and comparatively trivial form of sin. Both words denote, in the language of Scripture, definite offences against known law, departures from known duty. Adam's sin was the typical "transgression" and "trespass" (Rom. v. 14, 15, etc.; comp. ii. 23; Gal. iii. 19).

[37] Gal. iii. 13; 1 Cor. vi. 19, 20.

[38] See *The Evangelical Revival, and other Sermons*, pp. 149–170, on "The Forgiveness of Sins."

[39] Bishop Ellicott, who advocates the latter rendering, objects to Meyer's interpretation that it is "doubtful in point of usage." *Pace tanti viri*, we must retort this objection upon the new translation. *To obtain by lot, to have (a thing) allotted to one*, is the meaning regularly given to κληροῦσθαι in the classical dictionaries; and in O.T. usage the *lot* (κλῆρος) becomes the *inheritance* (the thing *allotted*). The verb is repeatedly used by Philo with the meaning *to obtain*, or *receive an inheritance*; whereas there seems to be no real parallel to the other rendering. It is true that κληροῦσθαι in the sense of the A.V. requires an object; but that is virtually supplied by ἐν ᾧ: "we had our inheritance allotted *in Christ*." Comp. Col. i. 12, "the lot of the saints *in the light*," which signifies not the locality, but the nature and content of the saints' heritage.

[40] See Gal. iii. 22—iv. 7; and Chapters XV.—XVII. in the *Expositor's Bible* (Galatians), on Sonship and Inheritance in St Paul.

[41] Compare Acts xxvi. 18, which also speaks to this association of ideas in St Paul's mind, with vers. 4, 5, 7, and 11 in this chapter.

[42] Vv. 8, 9, ch. iii. 4, 5; comp. Col. ii. 2, 3; 1 Cor. ii. 6–9.

[43] "The fulness of the time," Gal. iv. 4; "in due season," Rom. v. 6; "in its own times," 1 Tim. ii. 6. These are all synonymous expressions for the Messianic era. Comp. Heb. i. 2, ix. 26; 1 Pet. i. 20.

[44] Ch. iii. 8, 9; Col. i. 25; 1 Cor. iv. 1; 1 Tim. i. 4, i. 7; 2 Tim. i. 9–11; and especially Rom. xvi. 25, 26.

[45] Comp. ch. v. 5; 1 Cor. xv. 24–28; Phil. ii. 9–12; Heb. ii. 8; Rev. i. 5, xi. 15, xvii. 14; Dan. vii. 13, 14.

[46] One wonders that our Revisers, so attentive to all points of Greek idiom, did not think it worth while to discriminate between *Christ* and *the Christ* in such passages as this. In Ephesians this distinction is especially conspicuous

and significant. See vv. 12, 20 iii. 17, iv. 20, v. 23; similarly in 1 Cor. xv. 22; Rom. xv. 3.

CHAPTER IV.

THE FINAL REDEMPTION.

"[That we might be to the praise of His glory:]
We who had before hoped in the Christ, in whom also ye *have hoped*,
Since ye heard the word of truth, the gospel of your salvation,—
In whom indeed, when ye believed, ye were sealed with the Holy Spirit of the promise,
Which is the earnest of our inheritance, till the redemption of *God's* possession,—
To the praise of His glory."

EPH. i. 12–14.

When the apostle reaches the "heritage" conferred upon us in Christ (ver. 11), he is on the boundary between the present and the future. Into that future he now presses forward, gathering from it his crowning tribute "to the praise of God's glory." We shall find, however, that this heritage assumes a twofold character, as did the conception of the inheritance of the Lord in the Old Testament. If the saints have their heritage in Christ, partly possessed and partly to be possessed, God has likewise, and antecedently, His inheritance in them, of which He too has still to take full possession.[47]

Opening upon this final prospect, St Paul touches on a subject of supreme interest to himself and that could not fail to find a place in his great Act of Praise—viz., *the admission of the Gentiles* to the spiritual property of Israel. The thought of the heirship of believers and of God's previous counsel respecting it (ver. 11), brought before his mind the distinction between Jew and Gentile and the part assigned to each in the Divine plan. Hence he varies the general refrain in verse 12 by saying significantly, "that *we* might be to the praise of His glory." This emphatic *we* is explained in the opening phrase of the last strophe: "that have beforehand fixed our hope on the Christ,"—the heirs of Israel's hope in "Him of whom Moses in the law and the prophets did write." With this "we" of Paul's Jewish consciousness the "ye also" of verse 13 is set in contrast by his vocation as Gentile apostle. This second pronoun, by one of Paul's abrupt turns of thought, is deprived of its predicating verb; but that is given already by the "hoped" of the last clause. "The Messianic hope, Israel's ancient heirloom, in its fulfilment is *yours* as much as ours."

This hope of Israel pointed Israelite and Gentile believer alike to the completion of the Messianic era, when the mystery of God should be finished and His universe redeemed from the bondage of corruption (vv. 10, 14). By the "one hope" of the Christian calling the Church is now made one. From this point of view the apostle in chapter ii. 12 describes the condition in which the gospel found his Gentile readers as that of men cut off from Christ, strangers to the covenants of promise,—in a word, "having no hope"; while he and his Jewish fellow-believers held the priority that belonged to those whose are the promises. The apostle stands precisely at the juncture where the wild shoot of nature is grafted into the good olive tree. A generation later no one would have thought of writing of "the Christ in whom *you* (Gentiles) *also* have found hope"; for then Christ was the established possession of the Gentile Church.

To these Christless heathen Christ and His hope came, when they "heard the word of truth, the gospel of their salvation." A great light had sprung up for them that sat in darkness; the good tidings of salvation came to the lost and despairing. "To the Gentiles," St Paul declared, addressing the obstinate Jews of Rome, "this salvation of God was sent: they indeed will hear it" (Acts xxviii. 28). Such was his experience in Ephesus and all the Gentile cities. There were hearing ears and open hearts, souls longing for the word of truth and the message of hope. The trespass of Israel had become the riches of the world. For this on his readers' behalf he gives joyful thanks,—that his message proved to be "the gospel of *your* salvation."

Salvation, as St Paul understands it, includes our uttermost deliverance, the end of death itself (1 Cor. xv. 26). He renders praise to God for that He has sealed Gentile equally with Jewish believers with the stamp of His Spirit, which makes them His property and gives assurance of absolute redemption.

There are three things to be considered in this statement: *the seal* itself, *the conditions* upon which, and *the purpose* for which it is affixed.

I. A seal is a token of proprietorship put by the owner upon his property;[48] or it is the authentication of some statement or engagement, the official stamp that gives it validity;[49] or it is the pledge of inviolability guarding a treasure from profane or injurious hands.[50] There is the protecting seal, the ratifying seal, and the proprietary seal. The same seal may serve each or all of these purposes. Here the thought of possession predominates (comp. ver. 4); but it can scarcely be separated from the other two. The witness of the Holy Spirit marks men out as God's *purchased right* in Christ (1 Cor. vi. 19, 20). In that very fact it guards them from evil and wrong (iv. 30), while it ratifies their Divine sonship (Gal. iv. 6) and guarantees their personal share in the promises of God (2 Cor. i. 20–22). It is a bond between God and men; a sign at once of what we are and shall be to God, and of what He is and will be to us. It secures, and it assures. It stamps us for God's possession, and His kingdom and glory as our possession.

This seal is constituted by *the Holy Spirit of the promise*,—in contrast with the material seal, "in the flesh, wrought by hand,"[51] which marked the children of the Old Covenant from Abraham downwards, previously to the fulfilment of the promise (Gal. iii. 14). We bear it in the inmost part of our nature, where we are nearest to God: "The Spirit witnesseth to our spirit." "The Israelites also were sealed, but by circumcision, like cattle and irrational animals. We were sealed by the Spirit, as sons" (Chrysostom). The stamp of God is on the consciousness of His children. "We know that Christ abides in us," writes St John, "from the Spirit which He gave us" (1 Ep. iii. 24). Under this seal is conveyed the sum of blessing comprised in our salvation. Jesus promised, "Your heavenly Father will give His Holy Spirit to them that ask" (Luke xi. 13), as if there were nothing else to ask. Giving us this, God gives everything, gives us Himself! In substance or anticipation, this one bestowment contains all good things of God.

The apostle writes "the Spirit of the promise, *the Holy* [Spirit]," with emphasis on the word of quality; for the testifying power of the seal lies in its character. "Beloved, believe not every spirit; but try the spirits, whether they are of God" (1 John iv. 1). There are false prophets, deceiving and deceived; there are promptings from "the spirit that works in the sons of disobedience," diabolical inspirations, so plausible and astonishing that they may deceive the very elect. It is a most perilous error to identify the supernatural with the Divine, to suppose mere miracles and communications from the invisible sphere a sign of the working of God. Antichrist can mimic Christ by his "lying wonders and deceit of unrighteousness" (2 Thess. ii. 8–12). Jesus never appealed to the power of His works in proof of His mission, apart from their ethical quality. God's Spirit works after His kind, and makes ours a holy spirit. There is an objective and subjective witness—the obverse and reverse of the medal (2 Tim. ii. 19). To be sealed by the Holy Spirit is, in St Paul's dialect, the same thing as to be *sanctified*; only, the phrase of this text brings out graphically the promissory aspect of sanctification, its bearing on our final redemption.[52]

When the sealing Spirit is called the Spirit *of promise*, does the expression look backward or forward? Is the apostle thinking of the past promise now fulfilled, or of some promise still to be fulfilled? The former, undoubtedly, is true. *The* promise (the article is significant[53]) is, in the words of Christ, "the promise of the Father." On the day of Pentecost St Peter pointed to the descent of the Holy Spirit as God's seal upon the Messiahship of Jesus, fulfilling what was promised to Israel for the last days. When this miraculous effusion was repeated in the household of Cornelius, the Jewish apostle saw its immense significance. He asked, "Can any one forbid water that these should be baptized, who have received the Holy Spirit as well as we?" (Acts x. 47). This was the predicted criterion of the Messianic times. Now it was *given*, and with an abundance beyond hope,—*poured out*, in the full sense of Joel's words, *upon all flesh.*

Now, if God has done so much—for this is the implied argument of verses 13, 14—He will surely accomplish the rest. The attainment of past hope is the warrant of present hope. He who gives us His own Spirit, will give us the fulness of eternal life. The earnest implies the sum. In the witness of the Holy Spirit there is for the Christian man the power of an endless life, a spring of courage and patience that can never fail.

II. But there are very definite conditions, upon which this assurance depends. "When you heard the word of truth, the gospel of your salvation"—there is the outward condition: "when you believed"—there is the inward and subjective qualification for the affixing of the seal of God to the heart.

How characteristic is this antithesis of *hearing* and *faith*![54] St Paul delights to ring the changes upon these terms. The gospel he carried about with him was a message from God to men, the good news about Jesus Christ. It needs, on the one hand, to be effectively uttered, proclaimed so as to be heard with the understanding; and, on the other hand, it must be trustfully received and obeyed. Then the due result follows. There is salvation,—conscious, full.

If they are to believe unto salvation, men must be made to *hear* the word of truth. Unless the good news reaches their ears and their heart, it is no good news to them. "How shall they believe in Him of whom they have not heard? how shall they hear without a preacher?" (Rom. x. 14). The light may be true, and the eyes clear and open; but there is no vision till both meet, till the illuminating ray falls on the sensitive spot and touches the responsive nerve. How many sit in darkness, groping and wearying for the light, ready for the message if there were any to speak it to them! Great would Paul's guilt have been, if when Christ called him to preach to the heathen, he had refused to go, if he had withheld the gospel of salvation from the multitudes waiting to receive it at his lips. Great also is our fault and blame, and heavy the reproach against the Church to-day, when with means in her hand to make Christ known to almost the whole world, she leaves vast numbers of men within her reach in ignorance of His message. She is not the proprietor of the Christian truth: it is God's gospel; and she holds it as God's trustee for mankind,—that through her "the message might be fully preached, and that all the nations might hear" (2 Tim. iv. 17). She has St Paul's programme in hand still to complete, and loiters over it.

The nature of the message constitutes our duty to proclaim it. It is "the word *of truth.*" If there be any doubt upon this, if our certainty of the Christian truth is shaken and we can no longer announce it with full conviction, our zeal for its propagation naturally declines. Scepticism chills and kills missionary fervour, as the breath of the frost the young growth of spring. At home and amongst our own people evangelistic agencies are supported by many who have no very decided personal faith, from secondary motives,—with a view to their social and reformatory benefits, out of philanthropic feeling and love to "the brother whom we have seen." The foreign missions of the Church, like the work of the Gentile apostle, gauge her real estimate of the gospel she believes and the Master she serves.

But if we have no sure word of prophecy to speak, we had better be silent. Men are not saved by illusion or speculation. Christianity did not begin by offering to mankind a legend for a gospel, or win the ear of the world for a beautiful romance. When the apostles preached Jesus and the resurrection, they declared what they knew. To have spoken otherwise, to have uttered cunningly devised fables or pious phantasies or conjectures of their own, would have been, in their view, to bear false witness against God. Before the hostile scrutiny of their fellow-men, and in prospect of the awful judgement of God, they testified the facts about Jesus Christ, the things that they had "heard, and seen with their eyes, and which their hands had handled concerning the word of life." They were as sure of these things as of their own being. Standing upon this ground and with this weapon of truth alone in their hands, they denounced "the wiles of error" and the "craftiness of men who lie in wait to deceive" (iv. 14).

And they could always speak of this word of truth, addressing whatsoever circle of hearers or of readers, as "the good news of *your salvation.*" The pronoun, as we have seen, is emphatic. The glory of Paul's apostolic mission was its universalism. His message was to every man he met. His latest writings glow with delight in the world-wide destination of his gospel.[55] It was his consolation that the Gentiles in multitudes received the Divine message to which his countrymen closed their ears. And he rejoiced in this the more, because he foresaw that ultimately the gospel would return to its native home, and at last amid "the fulness of the Gentiles all Israel would be saved" (Rom. xi. 13–32). At present Israel was not prepared to seek, while the Gentiles were seeking righteousness by the way of faith (Rom. ix. 30–33).

For it is upon this question of *faith* that the whole issue turns. Hearing is much, when one hears the word of truth and news of salvation. But faith is the point at which salvation becomes ours—no longer a possibility, an opportunity, but a fact: "in whom indeed, *when you believed,* you were sealed with the Holy Spirit." So characteristic is this act of the new life to which it admits, that St Paul is in the habit of calling Christians, without further qualification, simply *believers* ("those who believe," or "who believed"). Faith and the gift of the Holy Spirit are associated in his thoughts, as closely as Faith and Justification. "Did you receive the Holy Spirit when you believed?" was the question he put to the Baptist's disciples whom he found at Ephesus on first arriving there (Acts xix. 2). This was the test of the adequacy of their faith. He reminds the Galatians that they "received the Spirit from the hearing of faith," and tells them that in this way the blessing and the promise of Abraham were theirs already (Gal. iii. 2, 7, 14). Faith in the word of Christ admits the Spirit of Christ, who is in the word waiting to enter. Faith is the trustful surrender and expectancy of the soul towards God; it sets the heart's door open for Christ's incoming through the Spirit This was the order of things from the beginning of the new dispensation. "God gave to them," says St Peter of the first baptized Gentiles, "the like gift as He did also unto us, when we believed on the Lord Jesus Christ. The Holy Ghost fell on them, as on us at the beginning" (Acts xi. 15–18). Upon our faith in Jesus Christ, the Holy Spirit enters the soul and announces Himself by His message of adoption, crying in us to God, *Abba, Father* (Gal. iv. 6, 7).

In the chamber of our spirit, while we abide in faith, the Spirit of the Father and the Son dwells with us, witnessing to us of the love of God and leading us into all truth and duty and divine joy, instilling a deep and restful peace, breathing an energy that is a fire and fountain of life within the breast, which pours out itself in prayer and labour for the kingdom of God. The Holy Spirit is no mere gift to receive, or comfort to enjoy; He is an almighty Force in the believing soul and the faithful Church.

III. The end for which the seal of God was affixed to Paul's Gentile readers, along with their Jewish brethren in Christ, appears in the last verse, with which the Act of Praise terminates: "sealed," he says, "with the Holy Spirit, which is the earnest of our inheritance, *until the redemption of the possession.*"

The last of these words is the equivalent of the Old Testament phrase rendered in Exodus xix. 5, and elsewhere, "*a peculiar treasure* unto me"; in Deuteronomy vii. 6, etc., "a *peculiar* people" (*i.e.,* people of *possession*). The same Greek term is employed by the Septuagint translators in Malachi iii. 17, where our Revisers have substituted "a peculiar treasure" for the familiar, but misleading "jewels" of the older Version. St Peter in his first epistle (ii. 9, 10) transfers the title from the Jewish people to the new Israel of God, who are "an elect race, a royal priesthood, a holy nation, a people *for God's own possession.*" In that passage, as in this, the Revisers have inserted the word *God's* in order to signify whose possession the term signifies in Biblical use. In the other places in the New Testament where the same Greek noun occurs, [56] it retains its primary active force, and denotes "*obtaining* of the glory," etc., "*saving* of the soul." The word signifies not the possessing so much as the *acquiring* or *securing* of its object. The Latin Vulgate suitably renders this phrase, *in redemptionem acquisitions*,—"till the redemption of the acquisition."

God has "redeemed unto Himself a people"; He has "bought us with a price." His rights in us are both natural and *acquired*; they are redemptional rights, the recovered rights of the infinite love which in Jesus Christ saved mankind by extreme sacrifice from the doom of death eternal. This redemption "we have, in the remission of our trespasses" (ver. 7). But this is only the beginning. Those whose sin is cancelled and on whom God now looks with favour in Christ, are thereby redeemed and saved (ii. 5, 8).[57] They are within the kingdom of grace; they have passed out of death into life. They have but to persist in the grace into which they have entered, and all will be well. "Now," says the apostle to the Romans, "you are made free from sin and made servants to God; you have your fruit unto holiness, and the end eternal life."

Our salvation is come; but, after all, it is still to come. We find the apostle using the words "save" and "redeem" in this twofold sense, applying them both to the commencement and the consummation of the new life.[58] The last act, in Romans viii. 23, he calls "the redemption of the body." This will reinstate the man in the integrity of his twofold being as a son of God. Hence our bodily redemption is there called an *adoption*. For as Jesus Christ by His resurrection was "marked out [*or* instated] as Son of God in power" (Rom. i. 4), not otherwise will it be with His many brethren. Their reappearance in the new "body of glory" will be a "revelation" to the universe "of the sons of God."

But this last redemption—or rather this last act of the one redemption—like the first, is through the blood of the cross. Christ has borne for us in His death the entire penalty of sin; the remission of that penalty comes to us in two distinct stages. The shadow of death is lifted off from our spirits now, in the moment of forgiveness. But for reasons of discipline it remains resting upon our bodily frame. Death is a usurper and trespasser in the bounds of God's heritage. Virtually and in principle, he is abolished; but not in effect. "I will ransom them from the power of the grave,"[59] the Lord said of His Israel, with a meaning deeper than His prophet knew. When that is done, then God will have redeemed, in point of fact, those possessions in humanity which He so much prizes, that for their recovery He spared not His Son.

So long as mortality afflicts us, God cannot be satisfied on our account. His children are suffering and tortured; His people mourn under the oppression of the enemy. They sigh, and creation with them, under the burdensome and infirm tabernacle of the flesh, this body of our humiliation for which the hungry grave clamours. God's new estate in us is still encumbered with the liabilities in which the sin of the race involved us, with the "ills that flesh is heir to." But this mortgage—that we call, with a touching euphemism, *the debt of nature*—will at last be discharged. Soon shall we be free for ever from the law of sin and death. "And the ransomed of the Lord shall return and come with singing to Zion, and everlasting joy shall be upon their heads: they shall obtain gladness and joy, and sorrow and sighing shall flee away."

To God, as He looks down upon men, the seal of His Spirit upon their hearts anticipates this full emancipation. He sees already in the redeemed spirit of His children what will be manifest in their glorious heavenly form. The same token is to ourselves as believing men the "earnest of our inheritance." Note that at this point the apostle drops the "you" by which he has for several sentences distinguished between Jewish and Gentile brethren. He identifies them with himself and speaks of *"our* inheritance." This sudden resumption of the first person, the self-assertion of the filial consciousness in the writer breaking through the grammatical order, is a fine trait of the Pauline manner.
[60]

Arrhabon, the *earnest (fastening penny)*, is a Phœnician word of the market, which passed into Greek and Latin,—a monument of the daring pioneers of Mediterranean commerce. It denotes the part of the price given by a purchaser in making a bargain, or of the wages given by the hirer concluding a contract of service, by way of assurance that the stipulated sum will be forthcoming. Such pledge of future payment is at the same time a bond between those concerned, engaging each to his part in the transaction.

The earnest is the seal, and something more. It is an instalment, a *token in kind*, a foretaste of the feast to come. In the parallel passage, Romans viii. 23, the same earnest is called "the firstfruit of the Spirit." What the earliest sheaf is to the harvest, that the entrance of the Spirit of God into a human soul is to the glory of its ultimate salvation. The sanctity, the joy, the sense of recovered life is the same in kind then and now, differing only in degree and expression.

Of the "earnest of the Spirit" St Paul has spoken twice already, in 2 Corinthians i. 22 and v. 5, where he cites this inner witness to assure us, in the first instance, that God will fulfil to us His promises, "how many soever they be"; and in the second, that our mortal nature shall be "swallowed up of life"—assimilated to the living spirit to which it belongs—and that "God has wrought us for this very thing." These earlier sayings explain the apostle's meaning here. God has made us His sons, in accordance with His purpose formed in the depths of eternity (ver. 5). As sons, we are His heirs in fellowship with Christ, and already have received rich blessings out of this heritage (ver. 11). But the richest part of it, including that which concerns the bodily form of our life, is still unredeemed, notwithstanding that the price of its redemption is paid.

For this we wait till the time appointed of the Father,—the time when He will reclaim His heritage in us, and give us full possession of our heritage in Christ. We do not wait, as did the saints of former ages, ignorant of the Father's purpose for our future lot. "Life and immortality are brought to light through the gospel." We see beyond the chasm of death. We enjoy in the testimony of the Holy Spirit the foretaste of an eternal and glorious life for all the children of God—nay, the pledge that the reign of evil and death shall end throughout the universe.

With this hope swelling their hearts, the apostle's readers once more triumphantly join in the refrain: TO THE PRAISE OF HIS GLORY.

FOOTNOTES:

[47] Exod. xix. 3–6; Deut. iv. 20, 21; 1 Kings viii. 51, 53; Ps. lxxviii. 71, etc. With the above comp. Gen. xv. 8; Numb. xviii. 20; Jos. xiii. 33; Ps. xvi. 5.

[48] Ch. iv. 30. The "seal" of 2 Tim. ii. 19 has both the first and third of these meanings.

[49] Rom. iv. 11; 1 Cor. ix. 2; John iii. 33, vi. 27.

[50] Matt. xxvii. 66; Rev. v. 1, etc.

[51] Ch. ii. 11; comp. Rom. i. 28, 29; Gal. v, 5, 6; Phil. iii. 2, 3.

[52] Comp. Rom. viii. 9–11; 2 Cor. v. 1–5.

[53] Acts i. 4, ii. 33, 39, xiii. 32, xxvi. 6; Rom. iv. 13–20; Gal. iii. 14–29.

[54] See Rom. x. 14–18; Gal. iii. 2, 5; Col. i. 6, 23; 1 Thess. ii. 13; 2 Tim. i. 13.

[55] 1 Tim. ii. 1–7, iv. 10; Tit. ii. 11.

[56] 1 Thess. v. 9; 2 Thess. ii. 14; Heb. x. 39.

[57] Comp. Chapter VIII.

[58] For the former usage see, along with ver. 7 and ch. ii. 5, 8; Rom. iii, 24, x. 9; Titus iii. 5; 2 Tim. i. 9; Col. i. 14; Heb. ix. 15; for the latter, ch. iv. 30; Luke xxi. 28; Rom. v. 9, 10, viii. 23; Phil. ii. 12; 1 Thess. v. 8, 9; 2 Tim. ii. 10, iv. 18. It may be doubted whether St Paul ever uses these terms to denote present salvation or redemption without the final issue being also in his thoughts. Perhaps he would have called the redemption of ver. 7, in contrast with that of Rom. viii. 23, "the redemption of the spirit."

[59] Hosea xiii. 14; Isa. xxv. 8.

[60] The same incoherence occurs in Gal. iv. 5–7: "that *we* might receive the adoption of sons. And because *ye* are sons, God sent forth the Spirit of His Son into *our* hearts."

CHAPTER V.

FOR THE EYES OF THE HEART.

"For this cause I also, having heard of the faith in the Lord Jesus which is among you, and which *ye shew* toward all the saints, cease not to give thanks for you, making mention *of you* in my prayers:

"That the God of our Lord Jesus Christ, the Father of glory, may give unto you a spirit of wisdom and revelation in the knowledge of Him; having the eyes of your heart enlightened, that ye may know what is the hope of His calling, what the riches of the glory of His inheritance in the saints, and what the exceeding greatness of His power toward us who believe, according to that working of the might of His strength, which He wrought in the Christ, when He raised Him from the dead, and made Him to sit at His right hand in the heavenly *places*."—Eph. i. 15–20.

Because of this: because you have heard the glad tidings, and believing it have been sealed with the Holy Spirit (vv. 13, 14). *I too*: I your apostle, with so great an interest in your salvation, in return give thanks for you. Thus St Paul, having extolled to the uttermost God's counsel of redemption unfolded through the ages, claims to offer especial thanksgiving for the faith of those who belong to his Gentile province and are, directly or indirectly, the fruit of his own ministry (iii. 1–13).

The intermediate clause of verse 15, describing the readers' faith, is obscure. This form of expression occurs nowhere else in St Paul; but the construction is used by St Luke,—*e.g.*, in Acts xxi. 21: "All the Jews *which are among* the Gentiles," where it implies diffusion over a wide area. This being a circular letter, addressed to a number of Churches scattered through the province of Asia, of whose faith in many cases St Paul knew only by report, we can understand how he writes: "having heard of the faith that is [spread] amongst you."—*The love*, completing *faith* in the ordinary text (as in Col. i. 4), is relegated by the Revisers to the margin, upon evidence that seems conclusive. [61] The commentators, however, feel so strongly the harshness of this ellipsis that, in spite of the ancient witnesses, they read, almost with one consent,[62] "*your love* toward all the saints." The variation of the former clause prepares us, however, for something peculiar in this. In verse 13 we found St Paul's thought fixed on the decisive fact of his readers' *faith*. On this he still dwells lingeringly. The grammatical link needed between "faith" and "unto all the saints" is supplied in the Revised Version by *ye show*, after the analogy of Philemon 5. Perhaps it might be supplied as grammatically, and in a sense better suiting the situation, by *is come*. Then the co-ordinate prepositional phrases qualifying "faith" have both alike a local reference, and we paraphrase the clause thus: "since I heard of the faith in the Lord Jesus which

43

is spread amongst you, and whose report has reached all the saints."

We are reminded of the thanksgiving for the Roman Church, "that your faith is proclaimed throughout the whole world."[63] The success of the gospel in Asia gave encouragement to believers in Christ everywhere. St Paul loves in this way to link Church to Church, to knit the bonds of faith between land and land: in this letter most of all; for it is his catholic epistle, the epistle of the Church œcumenical.

In verse 16 we pass from praise to prayer. God is invoked by a double title peculiar to this passage, as "the God of our Lord Jesus Christ, the Father of glory." The former expression is in no way difficult. The apostle often speaks, as in verse 3, of "the God and Father of our Lord Jesus Christ": intending to qualify the Divine Fatherhood by another epithet, he writes for once simply of "*the God* of our Lord Jesus Christ." This reminds us of the dependence of the Lord Jesus upon the eternal Father, and accentuates the Divine sovereignty so conspicuous in the foregoing Act of Praise. Christ's constant attitude towards the Father was that of His cry of anguish on the cross, "My God, my God!" Yet He never speaks to men of *our* God. To us God is "the God of our Lord Jesus Christ," as He was to the men of old time "the God of Abraham and of Isaac and of Jacob."

The key to the designation *Father of glory* is in Romans vi. 4: "Christ was raised from the dead through *the glory of the Father.*" In the light of this august manifestation of God's power to save His lost sons in Christ, we are called to see light (vv. 19, 20). Its glory shines already about God's blessed name of Father, thrice glorified in the apostle's praise (vv. 3–14). The title is the counterpart of "the Father of compassions" in 2 Corinthians i. 3.

And now, what has the apostle to ask of the Father of men under these glorious appellations? He asks "a spirit of wisdom and revelation in the full-knowledge[64] of Him,—the eyes of your heart enlightened, in order that you may know," etc. This recalls the emphasis with which in verses 8 and 9 he set "wisdom and intelligence" amongst the first blessings bestowed by Divine grace upon the Church. It was the gift which the Asian Churches at the present juncture most needed; this is just now the burden of the apostle's prayers for his people.

The *spirit of wisdom and revelation* desired will proceed from the Holy Spirit dwelling in these Gentile believers (ver. 13). But it must belong to their own spirit and direct their personal mental activity, the spirit of revelation becoming "the spirit of their mind" (iv. 23). When St Paul asks for "a spirit of wisdom and *revelation,*" he desires that his readers may have amongst themselves a fountain of inspiration and share in the prophetic gifts diffused through the Church.[65] And "the knowledge—the full, deep knowledge of

God" is the sphere "in" which this richer inspiration and spiritual wisdom are exercised and nourished. "Philosophy, taking man for its centre, says, *Know thyself*: only the inspired word, which proceeds from God, has been able to say, *Know God*."[66]

The connexion of the first clause of verse 18 with the last of verse 17 is not very clear in St Paul's Greek; there is a characteristic incoherence of structure. The continuity of thought is unmistakable. He prays that through this inspired wisdom his readers may have their reason enlightened to see the grandeur and wealth of their religion. This is a vision for "the eyes of the heart." It is disclosed to the eye behind the eye, to the heart which is the true discerner.

> "The seeing eyes
> See best by the light in the heart that lies."

Yonder is an ox grazing in the meadow on a bright summer's day. Round him is spread the fairest landscape,—a broad stretch of herbage embroidered with flowers, the river gleaming in and out amongst the distant trees, the hills on both sides bounding the quiet valley, sunshine and shadows chasing each other as they leap from height to height. But of all this what sees the grazing ox? So much lush pasture and cool shade and clear water where his feet may plash when he has done feeding. In the same meadow there stands a poet musing, or a painter busy at his easel; and on the soul of that gifted man there descends, through eyes outwardly discerning no more than those of the beast at his side, a vision of wonder and beauty which will make all time richer. The eyes of the man's heart are opened, and the spirit of wisdom and revelation is given him in the knowledge of God's work in nature.

Like differences exist amongst men in regard to the things of religion. "So foolish was I and ignorant," says the Psalmist, speaking of his former dejection and unbelief, "I was as a beast before Thee!" There shall be two men sitting side by side in the same house of prayer, at the same gate of heaven. The one sees heaven opened; he hears the eternal song; his spirit is a temple filled with the glory of God. The other sees the place and the aspect of his fellow-worshippers; he hears the music of organ and choir, and the sound of some preacher's voice. But as for anything besides, any influence from another world, it is no more to him at that moment than is the music in the poet's soul or the colours on the painter's canvas to the ox that eateth grass.

It is not the strangeness and distance of Divine things alone that cause insensibility; their familiarity has the same effect. We know all this gospel so well. We have read it, listened to it, gone over its points of doctrine a hundred times. It is trite and easy to us as a worn glove. We discuss without a tremor of emotion truths the first whisper and dim promise of which once lifted men's souls into ecstasy, or cast them down into depths of shame and bewilderment so that they forgot to eat their bread. The awe of things eternal, the mystery of our faith, the Spirit of glory and of God rest on us no longer. So there come to be, as one hears it said, *gospel-hardened* hearers—and gospel-hardened preachers! The eyes see—and see not; the ears hear—and hear not; the lips speak without feeling; *the heart is waxen fat.* This is the nemesis of grace abused. It is the result that follows by an inevitable psychological law, where outward contact with spiritual truth is not attended with an inward apprehension and response. How do we need to pray, in handling these dread themes, for a true sense and savour of Divine things,—that there may be given, and ever given afresh to us "a spirit of wisdom and revelation in the knowledge of God."

Three things the apostle desires that his readers may see with the heart's enlightened eyes: the *hope to which God calls them*, the *wealth that He possesses in them*, and the *power which He is prepared to exert upon them as believing men.*

I. What, then, is our *hope* in God? What is the ideal of our faith? For what purpose has God called us into the fellowship of His Son? What is our religion going to do for us and to make of us?

It will bring us safe home to heaven. It will deliver us from the present evil world, and preserve us unto Christ's heavenly kingdom. God forbid that we should make light of "the hope laid up for us in the heavens," or cast it aside. It is an anchor of the soul, both sure and steadfast. But is it *the* hope of our calling? Is this what St Paul here chiefly signifies? We are very sure that it is not. But it is the one thing which stands for the hope of the gospel in many minds. "We trust that our sins are forgiven: we hope that we shall get to heaven!" The experience of how many Christian believers begins and ends there. We make of our religion a harbour of refuge, a soothing anodyne, an escape from the anguish of guilt and the fear of death; not a life-vocation, a grand pursuit. The definition we have quoted may suffice for the beginning and the end; but we need something to fill out that formula, to give body and substance, meaning and movement to the life of faith.

Let the apostle tell us what he regarded, for himself, as the end of religion, what was the object of his ambition and pursuit. "One thing I do," he writes to the Philippians, opening to them all his heart,—"One thing I do. I press towards the mark for the prize of my high calling of God in Christ Jesus." And what, pray, was that mark? —"that I may gain Christ and be found in Him!—that I may know Him, and the power of His resurrection and the fellowship of His sufferings, being conformed to His death, if by any means I may attain unto the final resurrection from the dead." Yes, Paul hopes for heaven; but he hopes for something else first, and most. It is through Christ that he sees heaven. To know Christ, to love Christ, to serve Christ, to follow Christ, to be like Christ, to be with Christ for ever!—that is what St Paul lived for. Whatever aim he pursues or affection he cherishes, Christ lies in it and reaches beyond it. In doing or in suffering, in his intellect and his heart, in his thoughts for himself or for others, Christ is all things to him and in all. When life is thus filled with Christ, heaven becomes, as one may say, a mere circumstance, and death but an incident upon the way,—in the soul's everlasting pursuit of Christ.

Behold, then, brethren, the hope of our calling. God could not call us to any destiny less or lower than this. It would have been unworthy of Him,—and may we not say, unworthy of ourselves, if we are in truth His sons? From eternity the Father of spirits has predestined you and me to be holy and without blemish before Him,—in a word, to be conformed to the image of His Son. Every other hope is dross compared to this.

II. Another vision for the heart's eyes, still more amazing than that we have seen: "what is," St Paul writes, "the riches of the glory of God's inheritance in the saints."

We saw, in considering the eleventh and fourteenth verses, how the apostle, in characteristic fashion, plays upon the double aspect of the *inheritance*, regarding it now as the heritage of the saints in God and again as His heritage in them. The former side of this relationship was indicated in the "hope of the Divine calling,"—which we live and strive for as it is promised us by God; and the latter comes out, by way of contrast, in this second clause. Verse 18 repeats in another way the antithesis of verse 14 between our inheritance and God's acquisition. We must understand that God sets great store by us His human children, and counts Himself rich in our affection and our service. How deeply it must affect us to know this, and to see the glory that in God's eyes belongs to His possession in believing men.

What presumption is all this, some one says. How preposterous to imagine that the Maker of the worlds interests Himself in atoms like ourselves,—in the ephemera of this insignificant planet! But moral magnitudes are not to be measured by a foot-rule. The mind which can traverse the immensities of space and hold them in its grasp, transcends the things it counts and weighs. As it is amongst earthly powers, so the law may hold betwixt sphere and sphere in the system of worlds, in the relations of bodies terrestrial and celestial to each other, that "God has chosen the weak things to put to shame the mighty, and the things that are not to bring to nought the things that are." Through the Church He is "making known to the potentates in the heavenly places His manifold wisdom" (iii, 10). The lowly can sing evermore with Mary in the Magnificat: "He that is mighty hath magnified me." If it be true that God spared not His Son for our salvation and has sealed us with the seal of His Spirit, if He chose us before the world's foundation to be His saints, He must set upon those saints an infinite value. We may despise ourselves; but He thinks great things of us.

And is this, after all, so hard to understand? If the alternative were put to some owner of wide lands and houses full of treasure: "Now, you must lose that fine estate, or see your own son lost and ruined! You must part with a hundred thousand pounds—or with your best friend!" there could be no doubt in such a case what the choice would be of a man of sense and worth, one who sees with the eyes of the heart. Shall we think less nobly of God than of a right-minded man amongst ourselves?—Suppose, again, that one of our great cities were so full of wealth that the poorest were housed in palaces and fared sumptuously every day, though its citizens were profligates and thieves and cowards! What would its opulence and luxury be worth? Is it not evident that *character* is the only possession of intrinsic value, and that this alone gives worth and weight to other properties? "The saints that are in the earth and the excellent" are earth's riches.

So far as we can judge of His ways, the great God who made us cares comparatively little about the upholstery and machinery of the universe; but He cares immensely about men, about the character and destiny of men. There is nothing in all that physical science discloses for God to *love*, nothing kindred to Himself. "Hast thou considered my servant Job?" the Hebrew poet pictures Him saying before heaven and hell!—"Hast thou considered my servant Job?—a perfect man and upright: there is none like him in the earth." How proud God is of a man like that, in a world like this. Who can tell the value that the Father of glory sets upon the tried fidelity of His humblest servant here on earth; the intensity with which He reciprocates the confidence of one timid, trembling human heart, or the simple reverence of one little child that lisps His awful name? "He *taketh pleasure* in them that fear Him, in those that hope in His mercy!" Beneath His feet all the worlds lie spread in their starry splendour, our sun with its train of planets no more than one glimmering spot of light amongst ten thousand. But amidst this magnificence, what is the sight that wins His tender fatherly regard? "To that man will I look, that is poor and of a contrite spirit, and that trembles at my word." Thus saith the High and Lofty One that inhabiteth eternity. The Creator rejoices in His works as at the beginning, the Lord of heaven and earth in His dominion. But these are not His "inheritance." That is in the love of His children, in the character and number of His saints. *We* are to be the praise of His glory.

Let us learn, then, to respect ourselves. Let us not take the world's tinsel for wealth, and spend our time, like the man in Bunyan's dream, scraping with "the muck-rake" while the crown of life shines above our head. The riches of a Church—nay, of any human community—lies not in its moneyed resources, but in the men and women that compose it, in their godlike attributes of mind and heart, in their knowledge, their zeal, their love to God and man, in the purity, the gentleness, the truthfulness and courage and fidelity that are found amongst them. These are the qualities which give distinction to human life, and are beautiful in the eyes of God and holy angels. "Man that is in honour and understandeth not, is like the beasts that perish."

III. One thing more we need to understand, or what we have seen already will be of little practical avail. We may see glorious visions, we may cherish high aspirations; and they may prove to be but the dreams of vanity. Nay, it is conceivable that God Himself might have wealth invested in our nature, a treasure beyond price, shipwrecked and sunk irrecoverably through our sin. What means exist for realizing this inheritance? what power is there at work to recover these forfeited hopes, and that glory of God of which we have come so miserably short?

The answer lies in the apostle's words: "That ye may know what is the exceeding greatness of His power toward us that believe,"—a power measured by "the energy of the might of His strength[67] which He wrought in the Christ, when He raised Him from the dead and set Him at His right hand in the heavenly places." This is the power that we have to count upon, the force that is yoked to the world's salvation and is at the service of our faith. Its energy has turned the tide and reversed the stream of nature—in the person of Jesus Christ and in the course of human history. It has changed death to life. Above all, it certifies the forgiveness of sin and releases us from its liabilities; it transforms the law of sin and death into the law of the Spirit of life in Christ Jesus.

We preachers hear it said sometimes: "You live in a speculative world. Your doctrines are ideal and visionary,—altogether too high for men as they are and the world as we find it. Human nature and experience, the coarse realities of life are all against you."

What would our objectors have said at the grave-side of Jesus? "The beautiful dreamer, the sublime idealist! He was too good for a world such as ours. It was sure to end like this. His ideas of life were utterly impracticable." So they would have moralized. "And the good prophet talked—strangest fanaticism of all—of rising again on the third day! One thing at least we know, that the dead are dead and gone from us. No, we shall never see Jesus or His like again. Purity cannot live in this infected air. The grave ends all hope for men." But, despite human nature and human experience, He has risen again, He lives for ever! That is the apostle's message and testimony to the world. For those "who believe" it, all things are possible. A life is within our reach that seemed far off as earth from heaven. *You* may become a perfect saint.

From His open grave Christ breathed on His disciples, and through them on all mankind, the Holy Spirit. This is the efficient cause of Christianity,—the Spirit that raised Jesus our Lord from the dead. The limit to its efficacy lies in the defects of our faith, in our failure to comprehend what God gave us in His Son. Is anything now too hard for the Lord? Shall anything be called impossible, in the line of God's promise and man's spiritual need? Can we put an arrest upon the working of this mysterious force, upon the Spirit of the new life, and say to it: Thus far shalt thou go, and no farther?

50

Look at Jesus where He was—the poor, tortured, wounded body, slain by our sins, lying cold and still in Joseph's grave: then lift up your eyes and see Him *where He is,*—enthroned in the worship and wonder of heaven! Measure by that distance, by the sweep and lift of that almighty Arm, the strength of the forces engaged to your salvation, the might of the powers at work through the ages for the redemption of humanity.

FOOTNOTES:

[61] See Westcott and Hort's *New Testament in Greek*, vol. ii., pp. 124, 125.

[62] Dr. Beet abides by the critical text. He solves the difficulty by giving πίστις a double sense: "the faith among you in the Lord Jesus, and the *faithfulness* towards all the saints." See his Commentary on *Ephesians, etc.*, pp. 284–6.

[63] In 1 Thess. i. 7–9; 2 Thess. i. 4, the same thought enters into Paul's thanksgiving; comp. 2 Cor. ix. 2.

[64] This is the emphatic ἐπίγνωσις, so frequent in the later epistles. See Lightfoot's *note* on Col. i. 9; or Cremer's *Lexicon to N.T. Greek*.

[65] See ch. iii. 3–5, iv. 11; and comp. 1 Cor. xiv. 26–40, etc.

[66] Adolphe Monod: *Explication de l'épître de S. Paul aux Éphésiens*. A deeply spiritual and suggestive Commentary.

[67] In this amplitude of expression there is no idle heaping up of words. The four synonyms for *power* have each a distinct force in the sentence. Δύναμις is *power* in general, as that which is able to effect some purpose; ἐνέργεια is *energy*, power in effective action and operation; κράτος is *might, mastery*, sovereign power,—in the New Testament used chiefly of the power of God; ἰσχύς is *force, strength*, power resident in some person and belonging to him. This is the order in which the words follow each other. Compare vi. 10 in the Greek.

THE DOCTRINE.

CHAPTER i. 20–iii. 13.

Ὑψηλῶν σφόδρα γέμει τῶν νοημάτων καὶ ὑπερόγκων. Ἃ γὰρ μηδαμοῦ σχέδον ἐφθέγξατο, ταῦτα ἐνταῦθά φησιν.

JOHN CHRYSOSTOM: *In epistolam ad Ephesios.*

CHAPTER VI.

WHAT GOD WROUGHT IN THE CHRIST.

"He raised Him from the dead, and made Him to sit at His right hand in the heavenly *places*, far above all rule, and authority, and power, and dominion, and every name that is named, not only in this world, but also in that which is to come: and He put all things in subjection under His feet, and Him He gave—the head over all things—to the Church which is His body,—the fulness of Him that filleth all in all."—EPH. i. 20–23.

The division that we make at verse 20, marking off at this point the commencement of the Doctrine of the epistle, may appear somewhat forced. The great doxology of the first half of the chapter is intensely theological; and the prayer which follows it, like that of the letter to the Colossians, melts into doctrine imperceptibly. The apostle teaches upon his knees. The things he has to tell his readers, and the things he has asked on their behalf from God, are to a great extent the same. Still the writer's attitude in the second chapter is manifestly that of teaching; and his doctrine there is so directly based upon the concluding sentences of his prayer, that it is necessary for logical arrangement to place these verses within the doctrinal section of the epistle.

The resurrection of Christ made men sensible that a new force of life had come into the world, of incalculable potency. This power was in existence before. In prelusive ways, it has wrought in the world from its foundation, and since the fall of man. By the incarnation of the Son of God it took possession of human flesh; by His sacrificial death it won its decisive triumph. But the virtue of these acts of Divine grace lay in their hiding of power, in the self-abnegation of the Son of God who emptied Himself and took a servant's form, and became obedient unto death.

With what a rebound did the "energy of the might of God's strength" put forth itself in Him, when once this sacrifice was accomplished! Even His disciples who had seen Jesus still the tempest and feed the multitude from a handful of bread and call back the spirit to its mortal frame, had not dreamed of the might of Godhead latent in Him, until they beheld Him risen from the dead. He had promised this in words; but they understood His words only when they saw the fact, when He actually stood before them "alive after His passion." The scene of Calvary—the cruel sufferings of their Master, His helpless ignominy and abandonment by God, the malignant triumph of his enemies—gave to this revelation an effect beyond measure astonishing and profound in its impression. From the stupor of grief and despair they were raised to a boundless hope, as Jesus rose from the death of the cross to glorious life and Godhead.

Of the same nature was the effect produced by His manifestation to Paul himself. The Nazarene prophet known to Saul by report as an attractive teacher and worker of miracles, had made enormous pretensions, blasphemous if they were not true. He put Himself forward as the Messiah and the very Son of God! But when brought to the test, His power utterly failed. God disowned and forsook Him; and He "was crucified of weakness." His followers declared, indeed, that He had returned from the grave. But who could believe them, a handful of Galilean enthusiasts, desperately clinging to the name of their disgraced leader! If He has risen, why does He not show Himself to others? Who can accept a crucified Messiah? The new faith is a madness, and an insult to our common Judaism! Such were Saul's former thoughts of the Christ. But when his challenge was met and the Risen One confronted him in the way to Damascus, when from that Form of insufferable glory there came a voice saying, "I am Jesus, whom thou persecutest!" it was enough. Instantly the conviction penetrated his soul, "He liveth by the power of God." Saul's previous reasonings against the Messiahship of Jesus by the same rigorous logic were now turned into arguments for Him.

It is "*the* Christ," let us observe, in whom God "wrought raising Him from the dead": the Christ of Jewish hope (ver. 12), the centre and sum of the Divine counsel for the world (ver. 10),[68] the Christ whom in that moment never to be forgotten the humbled Saul recognized in the crucified Nazarene.

The demonstration of the power of Christianity Paul had found in the resurrection of Jesus Christ. The power which raised Him from the dead is the working energy of our faith. Let us see what this mysterious power wrought in the Redeemer Himself; and then we will consider how it bears upon us. There are two steps indicated in Christ's exaltation: He was raised *from the death of the cross to new life amongst men*; and again from the world of men He was raised *to the throne of God in heaven*. In the enthronement of Jesus Christ at the Father's right hand, verses 22, 23 further distinguish two separate acts: there was conferred on Him *a universal Lordship*; and He was made specifically *Head of the Church*, being given to her for her Lord and Life, He who contains the fulness of the Godhead. Such is the line of thought marked out for us.

I. God raised the Christ from the dead.

This assertion is the corner-stone of St Paul's life and doctrine, and of the existence of Christendom. Did the event really take place? There were Christians at Corinth who affirmed, "There is no resurrection of the dead." And there are followers of Jesus now who with deep sadness confess, like the author of *Obermann once more*:

"Now He is dead! Far hence He lies

54

In the lorn Syrian town;
And on His grave, with shining eyes,
The Syrian stars look down."

If we are driven to this surrender, compelled to think that it was an apparition, a creation of their own passionate longing and heated fancy that the disciples saw and conversed with during those forty days, an apparition sprung from his fevered remorse that arrested Saul on the Damascus road—if we no longer believe in Jesus and the resurrection, it is in vain that we still call ourselves Christians. The foundation of the Christian creed is struck away from under our feet. Its spell is broken; its energy is gone.

Individual men may and do continue to believe in Christ, with no faith in the supernatural, men who are sceptics in regard to His resurrection and miracles. They believe in Himself, they say, not in His legendary wonders; in His character and teaching, in His beneficent influence—in the *spiritual* Christ, whom no physical marvel can exalt above His intrinsic greatness. And such trust in Him, where it is sincere, He accepts for all that it is worth, from the believer's heart. But this is not the faith that saved Paul, and built the Church. It is not the faith which will save the world. It is the faith of compromise and transition, the faith of those whose conscience and heart cling to Christ while their reason gives its verdict against Him. Such belief may hold good for the individuals who profess it; but it must die with them. No skill of reasoning or grace of sentiment will for long conceal its inconsistency. The plain, blunt sense of mankind will decide again, as it has done already, that Jesus Christ was either a blasphemer, or He was the Son of the eternal God; either He rose from the dead in very truth, or His religion is a fable. Christianity is not bound up with the infallibility of the Church, whether in Pope or Councils, nor with the inerrancy of the letter of Scripture: it stands or falls with the reality of the facts of the gospel, with the risen life of Christ and His presence in the Spirit amongst men.

The fact of Christ's resurrection is one upon which modern science has nothing new to say. The law of death is not a recent discovery. Men were as well aware of its universality in the first century as they are in the nineteenth, and as little disposed as we are ourselves to believe in the return of the dead to bodily life. The stark reality of death makes us all sceptics. Nothing is clearer from the narratives than the utter surprise of the friends of Jesus at His reappearance, and their complete unpreparedness for the event. They were not eager, but "*slow* of heart to believe." Their very love to the Master, as in the case of Thomas, made them fearful of self-deception. It is a shallow and an unjust criticism that dismisses the disciples as interested witnesses and predisposed to faith in the resurrection of their dead Master. Should we be thus credulous in the case of our best-beloved dead? The instinctive feeling that meets any thought of the kind, after the fact of death is once certain, is rather that of deprecation and aversion, such as Martha expressed when Jesus went to call her brother from his grave. In all the long record of human imposture and illusion, no resurrection story has ever found general credence outside of the Biblical revelation. No system of faith except our own has ever been built on the allegation that a dead man rose from the grave.

Christ's was not the only resurrection; but it is the only *final* resurrection. Lazarus of Bethany left his tomb at the word of Jesus, a living man; but he was still a mortal man, doomed to see corruption. He returned from the grave on this side, as he had entered it, "bound hand and foot with grave-clothes." Not so with the Christ. He passed through the region of death and issued on the immortal side, escaped from the bondage of corruption. Therefore He is called the "firstfruits" and "the firstborn *out of* the dead."[69] Hence the alteration manifest in the risen form of Jesus. He was "changed," as St Paul conceives those will be who await on earth their Lord's return (1 Cor. xv. 51). The mortal in Him was swallowed up of life. The corpse that was laid in Joseph's tomb was there no longer. From it another body has issued, recognized for the same person by look and voice and movement, but indescribably transfigured. Visible and tangible as the body of the Risen One was—"Handle me, and see," He said—it was superior to material limitations; it belonged to a state whose laws transcend the range of our experience, in which the body is the pliant instrument of the animating spirit. From the Person of the risen Saviour the apostle formed his conception of the "spiritual body," the "house from heaven" with which, as he teaches, each of the saints will be clothed—the wasted form that we lay down in the grave being transformed into the semblance of His "body of glory, according to the mighty working whereby He is able to subdue all things to Himself" (Phil. iii. 20, 21).

The resurrection of the Christ inaugurated a new order of things. It was like the appearance of the first living organism amidst dead matter, or of the first rational consciousness in the unconscious world. He "is," says the apostle, the "beginning, first-begotten out of the dead" (Col. i. 18). With the harvest filling our granaries, we cease to wonder at the firstfruits; and in the new heavens and earth Christ's resurrection will seem an entirely natural thing. Immortality will then be the normal condition of human existence.

That resurrection, nevertheless, did homage to the fundamental law of science and of reason, that every occurrence, ordinary or extraordinary, shall have an adequate cause. The event was not more singular and unique than the nature of Him to whom it befell. Looking back over the Divine life and deeds of Jesus, St Peter said: "It was not possible that He should be holden of death."

How unfitting and repugnant to thought, that the common death of all men should come upon Jesus Christ! There was that in His Person, in its absolute purity and godlikeness, which repelled the touch of corruption. He was "marked out," writes our apostle, "as Son of God, *according to His spirit of holiness*, by His resurrection from the dead" (Rom. i. 4). These two signs of Godhead agree in Jesus; and the second is no more superhuman than the first. For Him the supernatural was natural. There was a mighty working of the being of God latent in Him, which transcended and subdued to itself the laws of our physical frame, even more completely than they do the laws and conditions of the lower realms of nature.

II. The power which raised Jesus our Lord from the dead could not leave Him in the world of sin and death. Lifting Him from hades to earth, by another step it exalted the risen Saviour above the clouds, and *seated Him at God's right hand in the heavens.*

The forty days were a halt by the way, a condescending pause in the operation of the almighty power that raised Him. "I ascend," He said to the first that saw Him,—"I ascend to my Father and your Father, to my God and your God." He must see His own in the world again; He must "show Himself alive after His passion by infallible proofs," that their hearts may be comforted and knit together in the assurance of faith, that they may be prepared to receive His Spirit and to bear their witness to the world. Then He will ascend up where He was before, returning to the Father's bosom. It was impossible that a spiritual body should tarry in a mortal dwelling; impossible that the familiar relations of discipleship should be resumed. No new follower can now ask of Him, "Rabbi, where dwellest Thou," under what roof amid the homes of men? For He dwells with those that love Him always and everywhere, like the Father (John xiv. 23). From this time Christ will not be known after the flesh, but as the "Lord of the Spirit" (2 Cor. iii. 18).

"In the heavenlies" now abides the Risen One. This expression, so frequent in the epistle as to be characteristic of it,[70] denotes not locality so much as condition and sphere. It speaks of the bright and deathless world of God and the angels, of which the sky has always been to men the symbol. Thither Christ ascended in the eyes of His apostles on the fortieth day from His rising. Once before His death its brightness for a moment had irradiated His form upon the Mount of Transfiguration. Clad in the like celestial splendour He showed Himself to His future apostle Paul, as to one born out of due time, to make him His minister and witness. Since then, of all the multitudes that have loved His appearing, no other has looked upon Him with bodily eyes. He dwells with the Father in light unapproachable.

But rest and felicity are not enough for Him. Christ sits at the right hand of power, that He may *rule*. In those heavenly places, it seems, there are thrones higher and lower, names more or less eminent, but His stands clear above them all. In the realms of space, in the epochs of eternity there is none to rival our Lord Jesus, no power that does not owe Him tribute. God "hath put all things under His feet." *The Christ*, who died on the cross, who rose in human form from the grave, is exalted to share the Father's glory and dominion, is filled with God's own fulness, and made without limitation or exception "Head over all things."

In his enumeration of the angelic orders in verse 21, the apostle follows the phraseology current at the time, without giving any precise dogmatic sanction to it. The epistle to the Colossians furnishes a somewhat different list (ch. i. 16); and in 1 Corinthians xv. 24 we find the "principality, dominion, and power" without the "lordship." As Lightfoot says,[71] St Paul "brushes away all these speculations" about the ranks and titles of the angels, "without inquiring how much or how little truth there may be in them…. His language shows a spirit of impatience with this elaborate angelology." There is, perhaps, a passing reproof conveyed by this sentence to the "worshipping of the angels" inculcated at the present time in Colossæ, to which other Asian Churches may have been drawn. "Paul's faith saw the Risen and Rising One passing through and beyond and above successive ranks of angelic powers, until there was in heaven no grandeur which He had not left behind. Then, after naming heavenly powers known to him, he uses a universal phrase covering 'not only' those known by men living on earth 'in the' present 'age, but also' those names which will be needed and used to describe men and angels throughout the eternal future" (Beet).

The apostle appropriates here two sentences of Messianic prophecy, from Psalms cx. and viii. The former was addressed to the Lord's Anointed, the King-Priest enthroned in Zion: "Sit thou on my right hand, until I make thine enemies thy footstool!" The latter text describes man in his pristine glory, as God formed him after His likeness and set him in command over His creation. This saying St Paul applies, with an unbounded scope, to the God-man raised from the dead, Founder of the new creation: "Thou madest Him to have dominion over the works of Thy hands; Thou hast put all things under His feet." To the former of these passages St Paul repeatedly alludes; indeed, since our Lord quoted it in this sense, it became the standing designation of His heavenly dignity.[72] The words of Psalm viii. are brought in evidence again in Hebrews ii. 5–10, and expounded from a somewhat different standpoint. As the writer of the other epistle shows, this coronation belongs to the human race, and it falls to the Son of man to win it. St Paul in quoting the same Psalm is not insensible of its human reference. It was a prophecy for Jesus and His brethren, for Christ and the Church. So it forms a natural transition from the thought of Christ's dominion over the universe (ver. 21) to that of His union with the Church (ver. 22*b*).

III. The second clause of verse 22 begins with an emphasis upon the *object* which the English Version fails to recognize: "and *Him* He gave"—the Christ exalted to universal authority—"*Him* God gave, Head over all things [as He is], to the Church which is His body,—the fulness of Him who fills all things in all."

At the topmost height of His glory, with thrones and princedoms beneath His feet, *Christ is given to the Church!* The Head over all things, the Lord of the created universe, He—and none less or lower—is the Head of redeemed humanity. For the Church "is His body" (this clause is interjected by way of explanation): she is the vessel of His Spirit, the organic instrument of His Divine-human life. As the spirit belongs to its body, by the like fitness the Christ in His surpassing glory is the possession of the community of believing men. The body claims its head, the wife her husband. No matter where Christ is, however high in heaven, He belongs to us. Though the Bride is lowly and of poor estate, He is hers! and she knows it, and holds fast His heart. She recks little of the people's ignorance and scorn, if their Master is her affianced Lord, and she the best-beloved in His eyes.

How rich is this gift of the Father to the Church in the Son of His love, the concluding words of the paragraph declare: "Him He gave ... to the Church ... [gave] the fulness of Him that fills all in all." In the risen and enthroned Christ God bestowed on men a gift in which the Divine plenitude that fills creation is embraced. For this last clause, it is clear to us, does not qualify "the Church which is His body," and expositors have needlessly taxed their ingenuity with the incongruous apposition of "body" and "fulness"; it belongs to the grand Object of the foregoing description, to "the Christ" whom God raised from the dead and invested with His own prerogatives. The two separate designations, "Head over all things" and "Fulness of the All-filler," are parallel, and alike point back to *Him* who stands with a weight of gathered emphasis—heaped up from verse 19 onwards—at the front of this last sentence (ver. 22*b*). There has been nothing to prepare the reader to ascribe the august title of the *pleroma*, the Divine fulness, to the Church—enough for her, surely, if she is His body and He God's gift to her—but there has been everything to prepare us to crown the Lord Jesus with this glory. To that which God had wrought in Him and bestowed on Him, as previously related, verse 23 adds something more and greater still; for it shows what God makes the Christ to be, not to the creatures, to the angels, to the Church, *but to God Himself!*[73]

Our text is in strict agreement with the sayings about "the fulness" in

Colossians i. 15–20 and ii. 9, 10; as well as with the later references of this epistle, in chapter iii. 19, iv. 13; and with John i. 16. This title belongs to Christ as God is in Him and communicates to Him all Divine powers. It was, in the apostle's view, a new and distinct act by which the Father bestowed on the incarnate Son, raised by His power from the dead, the functions of Deity. Of this glory Christ had of His own accord "emptied Himself" in becoming man for our salvation (Phil. ii. 6, 7). Therefore when the sacrifice was effected and the time of humiliation past, it "was the Father's pleasure that all the fulness should make its dwelling in Him" (Col. i. 19). At no point did Christ exalt Himself, or arrogate the glory once renounced. He prayed, when the hour was come: "Now, Father, *glorify Thou me* with Thine own self, with the glory which I had with Thee before the world was." It was for the Father to say, as He raised and enthroned Him: "Thou art my Son; I to-day have begotten Thee!" (Acts xiii. 33).

Again there was poured into the empty, humbled and impoverished form of the Son of God the brightness of the Father's glory and the infinitude of the Father's authority and power. The majesty that He had foregone was restored to Him in undiminished measure. But how great a change meanwhile in Him who received it! This plenitude devolves not now on the eternal Son in His pure Godhead, but on the Christ, the Head and Redeemer of mankind. God who fills the universe with His presence, with His cherishing love and sustaining power, has conferred the fulness of all that He is upon our Christ. He has given Him, so replenished and perfected, to the body of His saints, that He may dwell and work in them for ever.

FOOTNOTES:

[68] See the note upon this definite article on p. 47.

[69] Πρωτότοκος ἐκ τῶν νεκρῶν, Col. i. 18: comp. Rom. vi. 13, x. 7, for the force of the preposition. Hence the peculiar ἐξανάστασιν τὴν ἐκ νεκρῶν of Phil. iii. 10, 11,—the *out-and-out* resurrection, which will utterly remove us from the sphere of death.

[70] Ver. 3, ch. ii. 6, iii. 10, vi. 12; nowhere else in the New Testament. Comp., however, 1 Cor. xv. 40, 48; Phil. ii. 10; Heb. viii. 5, ix. 23, xi. 16, xii. 22, where the adjective has the same kind of use.

[71] *Note* on Col. i. 16.

[72] Matt. xxii. 41–46, also in Mark and Luke; Acts ii. 34, 35; Rom. viii. 34; Col. iii. 1; Heb. i. 13; 1 Peter iii. 22, etc.

[73] The reader of the Old Testament, unless otherwise advertized, must inevitably have referred the words *who filleth all things in all* to the Supreme God. See Jer. xxiii. 24; Isai. vi. 1, 3; Hag. ii. 7; Ps. xxxiii. 5, etc.; Exod. xxxi. 3. "That filleth all in all" is an attribute belonging to "the same God, that worketh all in all" (1 Cor. xii. 6). Comp. iv. 6.

CHAPTER VII.

FROM DEATH TO LIFE.

"And you *did He quicken*, when ye were dead through your trespasses and sins, wherein aforetime ye walked according to the course of this world, according to the prince of the power of the air, of the spirit that now worketh in the sons of disobedience; among whom we also all once lived in the lusts of our flesh, doing the desires of the flesh and of the mind, and were by nature children of wrath, even as the rest:—but God, being rich in mercy, for His great love wherewith He loved us, even when we were dead through our trespasses, quickened us together with the Christ (by grace have ye been saved), and raised us up together and made us to sit together in the heavenly *places* in Christ Jesus."—Eph. ii. 1–6.

We pass by a sudden transition, just as in Colossians i. 21, 22, from the thought of that which God wrought in Christ Himself to that which He works through Christ in believing men. So God raised, exalted, and glorified His Son Jesus Christ (i. 19–23)—*and you*! The finely woven threads of the apostle's thought are frequently severed, and awkward chasms made in the highway of his argument by our chapter and verse divisions. The words inserted in our Version (*did He quicken*) are borrowed by anticipation from verse 5; but they are more than supplied already in the foregoing context. "The same almighty Hand that was laid upon the body of the dead Christ and lifted Him from Joseph's grave to the highest seat in heaven, is now laid upon your soul. It has raised *you* from the grave and death of sin to share by faith His celestial life."

The apostle, in verse 3, pointedly includes amongst the "dead in trespasses and sins" himself and his Jewish fellow-believers as they "once lived," when they obeyed the motions and "volitions of the flesh," and so were "by birth" not children of favour, as Jews presumed, but "children of anger, even as the rest."[74]

This passage gives us a sublime view of the event of our conversion. It associates that change in us with the stupendous miracle which took place in our Redeemer. The one act is a continuation of the other. There is an acting over again in us of Christ's crucifixion, resurrection and ascension, when we realize through faith that which was done for mankind in Him. At the same time, the redemption which is in Christ Jesus is no mere legacy, to be received or declined; it is not something done once for all, and left to be appropriated passively by our individual will. It is a "*power* of God unto salvation," unceasingly operative and effective, that works "of faith and *unto faith*" that summons men to faith, challenging human confidence wherever its message travels and awakening the spiritual possibilities dormant in our nature.

It is a supernatural force, then, which is at work upon us in the word of Christ. It is a resurrection-power, that turns death into life. And it is a power instinct with love. The love which went out towards the slain and buried Jesus when the Father stooped to raise Him from the dead, bends over us as we lie in the grave of our sins, and exerts itself with a might no less transcendent, that it may raise us from the dust of death to sit with Him in the heavenly places (vv. 4–6).

Let us look at the two sides of the change effected in men by the gospel—at the death they leave, and the life into which they enter. Let us contemplate the task to which this unmatched power has set itself.

I. *You that were dead*, the apostle says.

Jesus Christ came into a dead world—He the one living man, alive in body, soul, and spirit—alive to God in the world. He was, like none besides, aware of God and of God's love, breathing in His Spirit, "living not by bread alone, but by every word that proceeded from His mouth." "This," He said, "is life eternal." If His definition was correct, if it be life to know God, then the world into which Christ entered by His human birth, the world of heathendom and Judaism, was veritably dying or dead—"dead indeed unto God."

Its condition was visible to discerning eyes. It was a world rotting in its corruption, mouldering in its decay, and which to His pure sense had the moral aspect and odour of the charnel-house. We realize very imperfectly the distress, the inward nausea, the conflict of disgust and pity which the fact of being in such a world as this and belonging to it caused in the nature of Jesus Christ, in a soul that was in perfect sympathy with God. Never was there loneliness such as His, the solitude of life in a region peopled with the dead. The joy which Christ had in His little flock, in those whom the Father had given Him out of the world, was proportionately great. In them He found companionship, teachableness, signs of a heart awakening towards God— men to whom life was in some degree what it was to Him. He had come, as the prophet in his vision, into "the valley full of dry bones," and He "prophesied to these slain, that they might live." What a comfort to see, at His first words, a shaking in the valley,—to see some who stirred at His voice, who stood upon their feet and gathered round Him—not yet a great army, but a band of living men! In their breasts, inspired from His, was the life of the future. "I am come," He said, "that they might have life." It was the work of Jesus Christ to breathe His vital spirit into the corpse of humanity, to reanimate the world.

When St Paul speaks of his readers in their heathen condition as "dead," it is not a figure of speech. He does not mean that they were like dead men, that their state resembled death; "nor only that they were in peril of death; but he signifies a real and present death" (Calvin). They were, in the inmost sense and truth of things, *dead men*. We are twofold creatures, two-lived,—spirits cased in flesh. Our human nature is capable, therefore, of strange duplicities. It is possible for us to be alive and flourishing upon one side of our being, while we are paralyzed or lifeless upon the other. As our bodies live in commerce with the light and air, in the environment of house and food and daily exercise of the limbs and senses under the economy of material nature, so our spirits live by the breath of prayer, by faith and love towards God, by reverence and filial submission, by communion with things unseen and eternal. "With Thee," says the Psalmist to his God, "is the fountain of life: in Thy light we see light." We must daily resort to that fountain and drink of its pure stream, we must faithfully walk in that light, or there is no such life for us. The soul that wants a true faith in God, wants the proper spring and principle of its being. It sees not the light, it bears not the voices, it breathes not the air of that higher world where its origin and its destiny lie.

The man who walks the earth a sinner against God, becomes by the act and fact of his transgression a dead man. He has imbibed the fatal poison; it runs in his veins. The doom of sin lies on his unforgiven spirit. He carries death and judgement about with him. They lie down with him at night and wake with him in the morning; they take part in his transactions; they sit by his side in the feast of life. His works are "dead works"; his joys and hopes are all shadowed and tainted. Within his living frame he bears a coffined soul. With the machinery of life, with the faculties and possibilities of a spiritual being, the man lies crushed under the activity of the senses, wasted and decaying for want of the breath of the Spirit of God. In its coldness and powerlessness— too often in its visible corruption—his nature shows the symptoms of advancing death. It is dead as the tree is dead, cut off from its root; as the fire is dead, when the spark is gone out; dead as a man is dead, when the heart stops.

As it is with the departed saints sleeping in Christ,—"put to death, indeed, in the flesh, but living in the spirit,"—so by a terrible inversion with the wicked in this life. They are put to death, indeed, in the spirit, while they live in the flesh. They may be and often are powerfully alive and active in their relations to the world of sense, while on the unseen and Godward side utterly paralyzed. Ask such a man about his business or family concerns; touch on affairs of politics or trade,—and you deal with a living mind, its powers and susceptibilities awake and alert. But let the conversation pass to otherthemes; sound him on questions of the inner life; ask him what he thinks of Christ, how he stands towards God, how he fares in the spiritual conflict,—and you strike a note to which there is no response. You have taken him out of his element. He is a practical man, he tells you; he does not live in the clouds, or hunt after shadows; he believes in hard facts, in things that he can grasp and handle. "The natural man perceiveth not the things of the Spirit of God. They are foolishness to him." They are pictures to the eye of the blind, heavenly music to the stone-deaf.

And yet that hardened man of the world—starve and ignore his own spirit and shut up its mystic chambers as he will—cannot easily destroy himself. He has not extirpated his religious nature, nor crushed out, though he has suppressed, the craving for God in his breast. And when the callous surface of his life is broken through, under some unusual stress, some heavy loss or the shock of a great bereavement, one may catch a glimpse of the deeper world within of which the man himself was so little conscious. And what is to be seen there? Haunting memories of past sin, fears of a conscience fretted already by the undying worm, forms of weird and ghostly dread flitting amid the gloom and dust of death through that closed house of the spirit,—

"The bat and owl inhabit here:
    The snake nests on the altar stone:
The sacred vessels moulder near:
    The image of the God is gone!"

In this condition of death the word of life comes to men. It is the state not of heathendom alone; but of those also, favoured with the light of revelation, who have not opened to it the eyes of the heart, of all who are "doing the desires of the flesh and the thoughts"—who are governed by their own impulses and ideas and serve no will above the world of sense.[75] Without distinction of birth or formal religious standing, "all" who thus live and walk are dead while they live. Their *trespasses and sins* have killed them. From first to last Scripture testifies: "Your sins have separated between you and your God." We find a hundred excuses for our irreligion: there is the cause. There is nothing in the universe to separate any one of us from the love and fellowship of his Maker but his own unforsaken sin.

It is true, there are other hindrances to faith, intellectual difficulties of great weight and seriousness, that press upon many minds. For such men Christ has all possible sympathy and patience. There is a real, though hidden faith that "lives in honest doubt." Some men have more faith than they suppose, while others certainly have much less. One has a name to live, and yet is dead; another, perchance, has a name to die, and yet is alive to God through Jesus Christ. There are endless complications, self-contradictions, and misunderstandings in human nature. "Many are first" in the ranks of religious profession and notoriety, "which shall be last, and the last first." We make the largest allowance for this element of uncertainty in the line that bounds faith from unfaith; "The Lord knoweth them that are His." No intellectual difficulty, no mere misunderstanding, will ultimately or for long separate between God and the soul that He has made.

It is *antipathy* that separates. "They did not like to retain God in their knowledge"; that is Paul's explanation of the ungodliness and vice of the ancient world. And it holds good still in countless instances. "Numbers in this bad world talk loudly against religion in order to encourage each other in sin, because they need encouragement. They know that they ought to be other than they are; but are glad to avail themselves of anything that looks like argument, to overcome their consciences withal" (Newman). The fashionable scepticism of the day too often conceals an inner revolt against the moral demands of the Christian life; it is the pretext of a carnal mind, which is "enmity against God, because it is not subject to His law." Christ's sentence upon unbelief as He knew it was this: "Light is come into the world; and men love darkness rather than light, because their deeds are evil." So said the keenest and the kindest judge of men. If we are refusing Him our faith, let us be very sure that this condemnation does not touch ourselves. Is there no passion that bribes and suborns the intellect? no desire in the soul that dreads His entrance? no evil deeds that shelter themselves from His accusing light?

When the apostle says of his Gentile readers that they "once walked in the way of the age, according to the course of this world,[76] according to the prince of the power of the air," the former part of his statement is clear enough. The age in which he lived was godless to the last degree; the stream of the world's life ran in turbid course toward moral ruin. But the second clause is obscure. The "prince" (or "ruler") who guides the world along its career of rebellion is manifestly Satan, the spirit of darkness and hate whom St Paul entitles "the god of this world" (2 Cor. iv. 4), and in whom Jesus recognized, under the name of "the prince of the world," His great antagonist (John xiv. 30).

But what has this spirit of evil to do with "the air"? The Jewish rabbis supposed that the terrestrial atmosphere was Satan's abode, that it was peopled by demons flitting about invisibly in the encompassing element. But this is a notion foreign to Scripture—certainly not contained in chapter vi. 12 —and, in its bare physical sense, without point or relevance to this passage. There follows in immediate apposition to "the domain of the air, *the spirit* that now works in the sons of disobedience." Surely, *the air* here partakes (if it be only here) of the figurative significance of *spirit* (i.e. *breath*). St Paul refines the Jewish idea of evil spirits dwelling in the surrounding atmosphere into an ethical conception of *the atmosphere of the world*, as that from which the sons of disobedience draw their breath and receive the spirit that inspires them. Here lies, in truth, the dominion of Satan. In other words, Satan constituted the *Zeitgeist*.

As Beck profoundly remarks upon this text:[77] "The Power of the air is a fitting designation for the prevailing spirit of the times, whose influence spreads itself like a miasma through the whole atmosphere of the world. It manifests itself as a contagious nature-power; and a *spiritus rector* works within it, which takes possession of the world of men, alike in individuals and in society, and assumes the direction of it. The form of expression here employed is based on the conception of evil peculiar to Scripture. In Scripture, evil and the principle of evil are not conceived in a purely spiritual way; nor could this be the case in a world of fleshly constitution, where the spiritual has the sensuous for its basis and its vehicle. Spiritual evil exists as a power immanent in cosmical nature."[78] Concerning great tracts of the earth, and large sections even of Christianized communities, we must still confess with St John: "The world lieth in the Evil One." The air is impregnated with the infection of sin;[79] its germs float about us constantly, and wherever they find lodgement they set up their deadly fever. Sin is the malarial poison native to our soil; it is an epidemic that runs its course through the entire "age of this world."

Above this feverous, sin-laden atmosphere the apostle sees God's anger brooding in threatening clouds. For our trespasses and sins are, after all, not forced on us by our environment. Those offences by which we provoke God, lie in our nature; they are no mere casual acts, they belong to our bias and disposition. Sin is a constitutional malady. There exists a bad element in our human nature, which corresponds but too truly to the course and current of the world around us. This the apostle acknowledges for himself and his law-honouring Jewish kindred: "We were by nature children of wrath, even as the rest." So he wrote in the sad confession of Romans vii. 14–23: "I see a different law in my members, warring against the law of my mind and bringing me into captivity to the law of sin which is in my members."

It is upon this "other law," the contradiction of His own, upon the sinfulness beneath the sin, that God's displeasure rests. Human law notes the overt act: "the Lord looketh upon the heart." There is nothing more bitter and humiliating to a conscientious man than the conviction of this penetrating Divine insight, this detection to himself of his incurable sin and the hollowness of his righteousness before God. How it confounds the proud Pharisee to learn that he *is* as other men are,—and even as this publican!

"The sons of disobedience" must needs be "children of wrath." All sin, whether in nature or practice, is the object of God's fixed displeasure. It cannot be matter of indifference to our Father in heaven that His human children are disobedient toward Himself. Children of His favour or anger we are each one of us, and at every moment. We "keep His commandments, and abide in His love"; or we do not keep them, and are excluded. It is His smile or frown that makes the sunshine or the gloom of our inner life. How strange that men should argue that God's love forbids His wrath! It is, in truth, the cause of it. I could neither love nor fear a God who did not care enough about me to be angry with me when I sin. If my child does wilful wrong, if by some act of greed or passion he imperils his moral future and destroys the peace and well-being of the house, shall I not be grieved with him, with an anger proportioned to the love I bear him? How much more shall your heavenly Father—how much more justly and wisely and mercifully!

St Paul feels no contradiction between the words of verse 3 and those that follow. The same God whose wrath burns against the sons of disobedience while they so continue, is "rich in mercy" and "loved us even when we were dead in our trespasses!" He pities evil men, and to save them spared not His Son from death; but Almighty God, the Father of glory, hates and loathes the evil that is in them, and has determined that if they will not let it go they shall perish with it.

II. Such was the death in which Paul and his readers once had lain. But God in His "great love" has *made them to live* along with the Christ."

How wonderful to have witnessed a resurrection: to see the pale cheek of the little maid, Jairus' daughter, flush again with the tints of life, and the still frame begin to stir, and the eyes softly open—and she looks upon the face of Jesus! or to watch Lazarus, four days dead, coming out of his tomb, slowly, and as one dreaming, with hands and feet bound in the grave-clothes. Still more marvellous to have beheld the Prince of Life at the dawn of the third day issue from Joseph's grave, bursting His prison-gates and stepping forth in new-risen glory as one refreshed from slumber.

But there are things no less divine, had we eyes for their marvel, that take place upon this earth day by day. When a human soul awakes from its trespasses and sins, when the love of God is poured into a heart that was cold and empty, when the Spirit of God breathes into a spirit lying powerless and buried in the flesh, there is as true a rising from the dead as when Jesus our Lord came out from His sepulchre. It was of this spiritual resurrection that He said: "The hour cometh, and now is, when the dead shall hear the voice of the Son of God, and they that hear shall live." Having said that, He added, concerning the bodily resurrection of mankind: "Marvel not at this; for the hour cometh, in which all that are in the tombs shall hear His voice, and shall come forth!" The second wonder only matches and consummates the first (John v. 24–28).

"This is life eternal, to know God the Father,"—the life, as the apostle elsewhere calls it, that is "life indeed." It came to St Paul by a new creation, when, as he describes it, "God who said, Light shall shine out of darkness, shined in our hearts, to give the light of the knowledge of His glory in the face of Jesus Christ." We are born again—the God-consciousness is born within us: an hour mysterious and decisive as that in which our personal consciousness first emerged and the soul knew itself. Now it knows God. Like Jacob at Peniel it says: "I have seen God face to face; and my life is preserved." God and the soul have met in Christ—and are reconciled.

The words the apostle uses—*gave us life—raised us up—seated us in the heavenly places*—embrace the whole range of salvation. "Those united with Christ are through grace delivered from their state of death, not only in the sense that the resurrection and exaltation of Christ redound to their benefit as Divinely imputed to them; but by the life-giving energy of God they are brought out of their condition of death into a new and actual state of life. The act of grace is an act of the Divine power and might, not a mere judicial declaration" (Beck). This comprehensive action of the Divine grace upon believing men takes place by a constant and constantly deepening union of the soul with Christ. This is well expressed by A. Monod: "The entire history of the Son of man is reproduced in the man who believes in Him, not by a simple moral analogy, but by a spiritual communication which is the true secret of our justification as well as of our sanctification, and indeed of our whole salvation."

There is no repetition in the three verbs employed, which are alike extended by the Greek preposition *with* (*syn*). The first sentence (raised us up *with the Christ*) virtually includes everything; it shows us one with Christ who lives evermore to God. The second sentence gathers into its scope all believers— the *you* of verse 1 and the *we* of verse 3: "He raised us up together, and together made us sit in the heavenly places in Christ Jesus." Nothing is more characteristic of our epistle than this turn of thought. To the conception of our *union with Christ* in His celestial life, it adds that of our *union with each other in Christ* as sharers in common of that life. Christ "reconciles us in one body unto God" (ver. 16). We sit not alone, but together in the heavenly places. This is the fulness of life; this completes our salvation.

FOOTNOTES:

[74] For the antithesis of "you" and "we," comp. vv. 11–18, ch. i, 12, 13; also Rom. iii. 19, 23 (*For there is no distinction*), Gal. ii. 15.

[75] Ποιοῦντες τὰ θελήματα τῆς σαρκὸς καὶ τῶν διανοιῶν (ver. 3).

[76] Perhaps this double rendering may bring out the force of κατὰ τὸν αἰῶνα τοῦ κόσμου τούτου.

[77] In the posthumous *Erklärung des Briefes Pauli an die Epheser*—a valuable exposition, marked by Beck's theological acumen and lucidity.

[78] The φύσει of verse 3 thus corresponds to the ἐξουσία τοῦ ἀέρος of verse 2. "Sin entered into *the world*" (κόσμος), Rom. v. 12, which signifies more than the nature of individual men.

[79] I John iii. 8; comp. John viii. 41–44.

CHAPTER VIII.

SAVED FOR AN END.

"That in the ages to come He might show the exceeding riches of His grace in kindness toward us in Christ Jesus. For by grace have ye been saved through faith; and that not of yourselves, *it is* the gift of God: not of works, that no man should glory. For we are His workmanship, created in Christ Jesus for good works, which God afore prepared that we should walk in them."—Eph. ii. 7–10.

The plan which God has formed for men in Christ is of great dimensions every way,—in its length no less than in its breadth and height. He "raised us up and seated us together [Gentiles with Jews] in the heavenly places in Christ Jesus, that *in the ages which are coming on* He might show the surpassing riches of His grace." All the races of mankind and all future ages are embraced in the redeeming purpose, and are to share in its boundless wealth. Nor are the ages past excluded from its operations. God "afore prepared the good works in which" He summons us to walk. The highway of the new life has been in building since time began.

Thus large and limitless is the range of "the purpose and grace given us in Christ Jesus before times eternal" (2 Tim. i. 9). But what strikes us most in this passage is the exuberance of the grace itself. Twice over the apostle exclaims, "By grace you are saved": once in verse 5, in an eager, almost jealous parenthesis, where he hastens to assure the readers of their deliverance from the fearful condition just described (vv. 1–3, 5). Again, deliberately and with full definition he states the same fact, in verse 8: "For by grace you are saved, through faith; and this is not of yourselves, it is the gift of God. It does not come of works, to the end that none may boast."

These words place us on familiar ground. We recognize the Paul of Galatians and Romans, the dialect and accent of the apostle of salvation by faith. But scarcely anywhere do we find this wonder-working grace so affluently described. "God being rich in mercy, for the great love wherewith He loved us —the exceeding riches of His grace, shown in kindness toward us—the gift of God." *Mercy, love, kindness, grace, gift*: what a constellation is here! These terms present the character of God in the gospel under the most delightful aspects, and in vivid contrast to the picture of our human state outlined in the beginning of the chapter.

Mercy denotes the Divine pitifulness towards feeble, suffering men, akin to those "compassions of God" to which the apostle repeatedly appeals.[80] It is a constant attribute of God in the Old Testament, and fills much the same place

70

there that grace does in the New. "Of mercy and judgement" do the Psalmists sing—of mercy most. Out of the thunder and smoke of Sinai He declared His name: "Jehovah, a God full of compassion and gracious, slow to anger, and plenteous in mercy and truth, keeping mercy for thousands." The dread of God's justice, the sense of His dazzling holiness and almightiness threw His mercy into bright relief and gave to it an infinite preciousness. It is the contrast which brings in "mercy" here, in verse 4, by antithesis to "wrath" (ver. 3).[81] These qualities are complementary. The sternest and strongest natures are the most compassionate. God is *"rich* in mercy." The wealth of His Being pours itself out in the exquisite tendernesses, the unwearied forbearance and forgivingness of His compassion towards men. The Judge of all the earth, whose hate of evil is the fire of hell, is gentler than the softest-hearted mother,—rich in mercy as He is grand and terrible in wrath.

God's mercy regards us as we are weak and miserable: His *love* regards us as we are, in spite of trespass and offence, His offspring,—objects of "much love" amid much displeasure, "even when we were dead through our trespasses." What does the story of the prodigal son mean but this? and what Christ's great word to Nicodemus (John iii. 16)?—*Grace* and *kindness* are love's executive. Grace is love in administration, love counteracting sin and seeking our salvation. Christ is the embodiment of grace; the cross its supreme expression; the gospel its message to mankind; and Paul himself its trophy and witness.[82] The "overpassing riches" of grace is that affluence of wealth in which through Christ it "superabounded" to the apostolic age and has outdone the magnitude of sin (Rom. v. 20), in such measure that St Paul sees future ages gazing with wonder at its benefactions to himself and his fellow-believers. Shown "in *kindness* toward us," he says,—in a condescending fatherliness, that forgets its anger and softens its old severity into comfort and endearment. God's kindness is the touch of His hand, the accent of His voice, the cherishing breath of His Spirit. Finally, this generosity of the Divine grace, this infinite goodwill of God toward men, takes expression in *the gift*—the gift of Christ, the gift of righteousness (Rom. v. 15–18), the gift of eternal life (Rom. vi. 23); or—regarded, as it is here, in the light of experience and possession—*the gift of salvation.*

The opposition of *gift* and *debt*, of gratuitous salvation through faith to salvation earned by works of law, belongs to the marrow of St Paul's divinity. The teaching of the great evangelical epistles is condensed into the brief words of verses 8 and 9. The reason here assigned for God's dealing with men by way of gift and making them absolutely debtors—"lest any one should boast"—was forced upon the apostle's mind by the stubborn pride of legalism; it is stated in terms identical with those of the earlier letters. Men will glory in their virtues before God; they flaunt the rags of their own righteousness, if any such pretext, even the slightest, remains to them. We sinners are a proud race, and our pride is oftentimes the worst of our sins. Therefore God humbles us by His compassion. He makes to us a free gift of His righteousness, and excludes every contribution from our store of merit; for if we could supply anything, we should inevitably boast as though all were our own. We must be content to receive mercy, love, grace, kindness—everything, without deserving the least fraction of the immense sum. How it strips our vanity; how it crushes us to the dust—"the weight of pardoning love!"

Concerning the office of *faith* in salvation we have already spoken in Chapter IV.[83] It is on the objective fact rather than the subjective means of salvation that the apostle lays stress in this passage. His readers do not seem to have realized sufficiently what God has given them and the greatness of the salvation already accomplished. They measured inadequately the power which had touched and changed their lives (i. 19). St Paul has shown them the depth to which they were formerly sunk, and the height to which they have been raised (vv. 1–6). He can therefore assure them, and he does it with redoubled emphasis: "You *are saved*; By grace you are saved men!"[84] Not, "You will be saved"; nor, "You were saved"; nor, "You are in course of salvation,"—for salvation has many moods and tenses,—but, in the perfect passive tense, he asserts the glorious accomplished *fact*. With the same reassuring emphasis in chapter i. 7 he declared, "We have redemption in His blood, the forgiveness of our trespasses."

Here is St Paul's doctrine of Assurance. It was laid down by Christ Himself when He said: "He that believeth on the Son of God hath eternal life." This sublime confidence is the ruling note of St John's great epistle: "We know that we are in Him.... We know that we have passed out of death into life.... This is the victory that overcometh the world, even our faith." It was this confidence of present salvation that made the Church irresistible. With its foundation secure, the house of life can be steadily and calmly built up. Under the shelter of the full assurance of faith, in the sunshine of God's love felt in the heart, all spiritual virtues bloom and flourish. But with a faith hesitant, distracted, that is sure of no doctrine in the creed and cannot plant a firm foot anywhere, nothing prospers in the soul or in the Church. Oh for the clear accent, the ringing, joyous note of apostolic assurance! We want a faith not loud, but deep; a faith not born of sentiment and human sympathy, but that comes from the vision of the living God; a faith whose rock and corner-stone is neither the Church nor the Bible, but Christ Jesus Himself.

Greatly do we need, like the Asian disciples of Paul and John, to "assure our hearts" before God. With death confronting us, with the hideous evil of the world oppressing us; when the air is laden with the contagion of sin; when the faith of the strongest wears the cast of doubt; when the word of promise shines dimly through the haze of an all-encompassing scepticism and a hundred voices say, in mockery or grief, Where is now thy God? when the world proclaims us lost, our faith refuted, our gospel obsolete and useless,— then is the time for the Christian assurance to recover its first energy and to rise again in radiant strength from the heart of the Church, from the depths of its mystic life where it is hid with Christ in God.

You are saved! cries the apostle; not forgetting that his readers have their battle to fight, and many hazards yet to run (vi. 10–13). But they hold the earnest of victory, the foretaste of life eternal. In spirit they sit with Christ in the heavenly places. Pain and death, temptation, persecution, the vicissitudes of earthly history, by these God means to perfect that which He has begun in His saints—"if you continue in the faith, grounded and firm" (Col. i. 23). That condition is expressed, or implied, in all assurance of final salvation. It is a condition which excites to watchfulness, but can never cause misgiving to a loyal heart. God is for us! He justifies us, and counts us His elect. Christ Jesus who died is risen and seated at the right hand of God, and there intercedes for us. *Quis separabit?*[85]

This is the epistle of the Church and of humanity. It dwells on the grand, objective aspects of the truth, rather than upon its subjective experiences. It does not invite us to rest in the comforts and delights of grace, but to lift up our eyes and see whither Christ has translated us and what is the kingdom that we possess in Him. God "quickened us together with the Christ": He "raised us up, He made us to sit *in the heavenly places in Christ Jesus.*" Henceforth "our citizenship is in heaven" (Phil. iii. 20).

This is the inspiring thought of the third group of St Paul's epistles; we heard it in the first note of his song of praise (i. 3). It supplies the principle from which St Paul unfolds the beautiful conception of the Christian life contained in the third chapter of the companion letter to the Colossians: "Your life is hid with the Christ in God"; therefore "seek the things that are above, where He is." We live in two worlds at once. Heaven lies about us in this new mystic childhood of our spirit. There our names are written; thither our thoughts and hopes resort. Our treasure is there; our heart we have lodged there, with Christ in God. *He* is there, the Lord of the Spirit, from whom we draw each moment the life that flows into His members. In the greatness of His love conquering sin and death, time and space, He is with us to the world's end. May we not say that we, too, are with Him and shall be with Him always? So we reckon in the logic of our faith and at the height of our high calling, though the soul creeps and drudges upon the lower levels.

> "With Him we are gone up on high,
> Since He is ours and we are His;
> With Him we reign above the sky,
> We walk upon our subject seas!"

In his lofty flights of thought the apostle always has some practical and homely end in view. The earthly and heavenly, the mystical and the matter-of-fact were not distant and repugnant, but interfused in his mind. From the celestial heights of the life hidden with Christ in God (ver. 6), he brings us down in a moment and without any sense of discrepancy to the prosaic level of "good works" (ver. 10). The love which viewed us from eternity, the counsels of Him who works all things in all, enter into the humblest daily duties.

Grace, moreover, sets us great tasks. There should be something to show in deed and life for the wealth of kindness spent upon us, some visible and commensurate result of the vast preparations of the gospel plan. Of this result the apostle saw the earnest in the work of faith wrought by his Gentile Churches.

St Paul was the last man in the world to undervalue human effort, or disparage good work of any sort. It is, in his view, the end aimed at in all that God bestows on His people, in all that He Himself works in them. Only let this end be sought in God's way and order. Man's doings must be the fruit and not the root of his salvation. "Not *of* works," but "*for* good works" were believers chosen. "This little word *for*" says Monod, "reconciles St Paul and St James better than all the commentators." God has not raised us up to sit idly in the heavenly places lost in contemplation, or to be the useless pensioners of grace. He sends us forth to "walk in the works, prepared for us,"—equipped to fight Christ's battles, to till His fields, to labour in the service of building His Church.

The "workmanship" of our Version suggests an idea foreign to the passage. The apostle is not thinking of the Divine art or skill displayed in man's creation; but of the simple fact that "God made man" (Gen. i. 27). "We are His *making*, created in Christ Jesus." The "preparation" to which he refers in verse 10 leads us back to that primeval election of God's sons in Christ for which we gave thanks at the outset (i. 3). There are not two creations, the second formed upon the ruin and failure of the first; but one grand design throughout. Redemption is creation re-affirmed. The new creation, as we call it, restores and consummates the old. When God raised His Son from the dead, He vindicated His original purpose in raising man from the dust a living soul. He has not forsaken the work of His hands nor forgone His original plan, which took account of all our wilfulness and sin. God in making us

74

meant us to do good work in His world. From the world's foundation down to the present moment He who worketh all in all has been working for this end —most of all in the revelation of His grace in Jesus Christ.

Far backward in the past, amid the secrets of creation, lay the beginnings of God's grace to mankind. Far onward in the future shines its lustre revealed in the first Christian age. The apostle has gained some insight into those "times and seasons" which formerly were veiled from him. In his earliest letters, to the Thessalonians and Corinthians, St Paul echoes our Lord's warning, never out of season, that we should "watch, for the hour is at hand." *Maran atha* is his watchword: "Our Lord cometh; the time is short." Nor does that note cease to the end. But when in this epistle he writes of "the ages that are coming on," and of "all the generations of the age of the ages" (iii. 21), there is manifestly some considerable period of duration before his eyes. He sees something of the extent of the world's coming history, something of the magnitude of the field that the future will afford for the unfolding of God's designs.

In those approaching æons he foresees that the apostolic dispensation will play a conspicuous part. Unborn ages will be blessed in the blessing now descending upon Jews and Gentiles through Christ Jesus. So marvellous is the display of God's kindness toward them, that all the future will pay homage to it. The overflowing wealth of blessing poured upon St Paul and the first Churches had an end in view that reached beyond themselves, an end worthy of the Giver, worthy of the magnitude of His plans and of His measureless love. If all this was theirs—this fulness of God exceeding the utmost they had asked or thought—it is because God means to convey it through them to multitudes besides! There is no limit to the grace that God will impart to men and to Churches who thus reason, who receive His gifts in this generous and communicative spirit. The apostolic Church chants with Mary at the Annunciation: "For, behold, from henceforth all generations shall call me blessed!"

Never was any prediction better fulfilled. This spot of history shines with a light before which every other shows pale and commonplace. The companions of Jesus, the humble fraternities of the first Christian century have been the object of reverent interest and intent research on the part of all centuries since. Their history is scrutinized from all sides with a zeal and industry which the most pressing subjects of the day hardly command. For we feel that these men hold the secret of the world's life. The key to the treasures we all long for is in their hands. As time goes on and the stress of life deepens, men will turn with yet fonder hope to the age of Jesus Christ. "And many nations will say: Come, and let us go up to the mountain of the Lord, to the house of the God of Jacob. And He will teach us of His ways; and we will walk in His paths."

The stream will remember its fountain; the children of God will gather to their childhood's home. The world will hear the gospel in the recovered accents of its prophets and apostles.

FOOTNOTES:

[80] Rom. xii. 1; 2 Cor. i. 3; Phil. i. 8, ii. 1; comp. Luke i. 78. The οἰκτιρμοὶ τοῦ Θεοῦ, σπλάγχνα καὶ οἰκτιρμοί, rendered in our Version "mercies of God," denotes something even more affecting,—God's sense of the woefulness of human life,—"the pitying tenderness Divine."

[81] Comp. Rom. ix. 22, 23.

[82] On *grace*, comp. *The Epistle to the Galatians* (Expositor's Bible), Chapter X.

[83] Compare also, on Faith, *The Epistle to the Galatians* (Expositor's Bible), Chapters X.–XII. and XV.

[84] Ἐστὲ σεσωσμένοι: for the peculiar emphasis of this form of the verb, implying a settled fact, an assured state, compare ver. 12, ἦτε ... ἀπηλλοτριωμένοι; Col. ii. 10; Gal. ii. 11, iv. 3; 2 Cor. iv. 3, etc.

[85] Rom. viii. 31–39; comp. vv. 9–17; also 1 Thess. v. 23, 24; 2 Thess. iii. 3–5; 1 Cor. i. 4–9; Phil. i. 6, iii. 13, 14; 2 Tim. i. 12, iv. 18, for St Paul's doctrine of Assurance.

CHAPTER IX.

THE FAR AND NEAR.

"Wherefore remember, that aforetime ye, the Gentiles in the flesh, who are called Uncircumcision by that which is called Circumcision in the flesh, made by hands; that ye were at that time separate from Christ, being aliens from the commonwealth of Israel, and strangers from the covenants of promise, having no hope, and without God in the world: but now in Christ Jesus ye who sometime were far off are made nigh in the blood of Christ."— EPH. ii. 11–13.

The apostle's *Wherefore* sums up for his readers the record of their salvation rehearsed in the previous verses. "You were buried in your sins, sunk in their corruption, ruined by their guilt, living under God's displeasure and in the power of Satan. All this has passed away. The almighty Hand has raised you with Christ into a heavenly life. God has become your Father; His love is in your heart; by the strength of His grace you are enabled to walk in the way marked out for you from your creation. *Wherefore remember*: think of what you were, and of what you are!"

To such recollections we do well to summon ourselves. The children of grace love to recall, and on fit occasions recount for God's glory and the help of their fellows, the way in which God led them to the knowledge of Himself. In some the great change came suddenly. He "made speed" to save us. It was a veritable resurrection, as signal and unlooked for as the rising of Christ from the dead. By a swift passage we were "translated from the power of darkness into the kingdom of the Son of His love." Once living without God in the world, we were arrested by a strange providence—through some overthrow of fortune or shock of bereavement, or by a trivial incident touching unaccountably a hidden spring in the mind—and the whole aspect of life was altered in a moment. We saw revealed, as by a lightning flash at night, the emptiness of our own life, the misery of our nature, the folly of our unbelief, the awful presence of *God*—God whom we had forgotten and despised! We sought, and found His mercy. From that hour the old things passed away: we lived who had been dead,—made alive to God through Jesus Christ.

This instant conversion, such as Paul experienced, this sharp and abrupt transition from darkness to light, was common in the first generation of Christians, as it is wherever religious awakening takes place in a society that has been largely dead to God. The advent of Christianity in the Gentile world was much after this fashion,—like a tropical sunrise, in which day leaps on the earth full-born. This experience gives a stamp of peculiar decision to the convictions and character of its subjects. The change is patent and palpable;

no observer can fail to mark it. And it burns itself into the memory with an ineffaceable impression. The violent throes of such a spiritual birth cannot be forgotten.

But if our entrance into the life of God was gradual, like the dawn of our own milder clime, where the light steals by imperceptible advances upon the darkness—if the glory of the Lord has thus risen upon us, our certainty of its presence may be no less complete, and our remembrance of its coming no less grateful and joyous. One leaps into the new life by a single eager bound; another reaches it by measured, thoughtful steps: but both are *there*, standing side by side on the common ground of salvation in Christ. Both walk in the same light of the Lord, that floods the sky from east to west. The recollections which the latter has to cherish of the leading of God's kindly light—how He touched our childish thought, and checked gently our boyish waywardness, and mingled reproof with the first stirrings of passion and self-will, and wakened the alarms of conscience and the fears of another world, and the sense of the beauty of holiness and the shame of sin,—

> "Shaping to truth the froward will
> Along His narrow way,"—

such remembrances are a priceless treasure, that grows richer as we grow wiser. It awakens a joy not so thrilling nor so prompt in utterance as that of the soul snatched like a brand from the burning, but which passes understanding. Blessed are the children of the kingdom, those who have never roamed far from the fold of Christ and the commonwealth of Israel, whom the cross has beckoned onwards from their childhood. But however it was—by whatever means, at whatever time it pleased God to call you from darkness to His marvellous light, *remember*.

But we must return to Paul and his Gentile readers. The old death in life was to them a sombre reality, keenly and painfully remembered. In that condition of moral night out of which Christ had rescued them, Gentile society around them still remained. Let us observe its features as they are delineated in contrast with the privileges long bestowed on Israel. The Gentile world was *Christless, hopeless, godless*. It had no share in the Divine polity framed for the chosen people; the outward mark of its uncircumcision was a true symbol of its irreligion and debasement.

Israel had a *God*. Besides, there were only "those who are called gods." This was the first and cardinal distinction. Not their race, not their secular calling, their political or intellectual gifts, but their faith formed the Jews into a nation. They were "the people of God," as no other people has been—of *the* God, for theirs was "the true and living God"—Jehovah, the I AM, the One, the Alone. The monotheistic belief was, no doubt, wavering and imperfect in the mass of the nation in early times; but it was held by the ruling minds amongst them, by the men who have shaped the destiny of Israel and created its Bible, with increasing clearness and intensity of passion. "All the gods of the nations are idols—vapours, phantoms, nothings!—but Jehovah made the heavens." It was the ancestral faith that glowed in the breast of Paul at Athens, amidst the fairest shrines of Greece, when he "saw the city wholly given to idolatry"—man's highest art and the toil and piety of ages lavished on things that were no gods; and in the midst of the splendour of a hollow and decaying Paganism he read the confession that God was "unknown."

Ephesus had her famous goddess, worshipped in the most sumptuous pile of architecture that the ancient world contained. Behold the proud city, "temple-keeper of the great goddess Artemis," filled with wrath! Infuriate Demos flashes fire from his thousand eyes, and his brazen throat roars hoarse vengeance against the insulters of "her magnificence, whom all Asia and the world worshippeth"! Without God—*atheists*, in fact, the apostle calls this devout Asian population; and Artemis of Ephesus, and Athené, and Cybelé of Smyrna, and Zeus and Asclepius of Pergamum, though all the world worship them, are but "creatures of art and man's device."

The Pagans retorted this reproach. "Away with *the atheists!*" they cried, when Christians were led to execution. Ninety years after this time the martyr Polycarp was brought into the arena before the magistrates of Asia and the populace gathered in Smyrna at the great Ionic festival. The Proconsul, wishing to spare the venerable man, said to him: "Swear by the Fortune of Cæsar; and say, Away with the atheists!" But Polycarp, as the story continues, "with a grave look gazing on the crowd of lawless Gentiles in the stadium and shaking his hand against them, then groaning and looking up to heaven, said, *Away with the atheists!*" Pagan and Christian were each godless in the eyes of the other. If visible temples and images, and the local worship of each tribe or city made a god, then Jews and Christians had none: if God was a Spirit— One, Holy, Almighty, Omnipresent—then polytheists were in truth atheists; their many gods, being many, were no gods; they were idols,—*eidola*, illusive shows of the Godhead.

The more thoughtful and pious among the heathen felt this already. When the apostle denounced the idols and their pompous worship as "these vanities," his words found an echo in the Gentile conscience. The classical Paganism held the multitude by the force of habit and local pride, and by its sensuous and artistic charms; but such religious power as it once had was gone. In all directions it was undermined by mystic Oriental and Egyptian rites, to which men resorted in search of a religion and sick of the old fables, ever growing more debased, that had pleased their fathers. The majesty of Rome in the person of the Emperor, the one visible supreme power, was seized upon by the popular instinct, even more than it was imposed by state policy, and made to fill the vacuum; and temples to Augustus had already risen in Asia, side by side with those of the ancient gods.

In this despair of their ancestral religions many piously disposed Gentiles turned to Judaism for spiritual help; and the synagogue was surrounded in the Greek cities by a circle of earnest proselytes. From their ranks St Paul drew a large proportion of his hearers and converts. When he writes, "Remember that you were at that time *without God*," he is within the recollection of his readers; and they will bear him out in testifying that their heathen creed was dead and empty to the soul. Nor did philosophy construct a creed more satisfying. Its gods were the Epicurean deities who dwell aloof and careless of men; or the supreme Reason and Necessity of the Stoics, the *anima mundi*, of which human souls are fleeting and fragmentary images. "Deism finds God only in heaven; Pantheism, only on earth; Christianity alone finds Him both in heaven and on earth" (Harless). The Word made flesh reveals *God in the world*.

When the apostle says "without God *in the world*," this qualification is both reproachful and sorrowful. To be without God in the world that He has made, where His "eternal power and Godhead" have been visible from creation, argues a darkened and perverted heart.[86] To be without God in the world is to be in the wilderness, without a guide; on a stormy ocean, without harbour or pilot; in sickness of spirit, without medicine or physician; to be hungry without bread, and weary without rest, and dying with no light of life. It is to be an orphaned child, wandering in an empty, ruined house.

In these words we have an echo of Paul's preaching to the Gentiles, and an indication of the line of his appeals to the conscience of the enlightened pagans of his time. The despair of the age was darker than the human mind has known before or since. Matthew Arnold has painted it all in one verse of those lines, entitled *Obermann once more*, in which he so perfectly expresses the better spirit of modern scepticism.

"On that hard Pagan world disgust
    And secret loathing fell
Deep weariness and sated lust
    Made human life a hell."

The saying by which St Paul reproved the Corinthians, "Let us eat and drink, for to-morrow we die," is the common sentiment of pagan epitaphs of the time. Here is an extant specimen of the kind: "Let us drink and be merry; for we shall have no more kissing and dancing in the kingdom of Proserpine. Soon shall we fall asleep, to wake no more." Such were the thoughts with which men came back from the grave-side. It is needless to say how depraving was the effect of this hopelessness. At Athens, in the more religious times of Socrates, it was even considered a decent and kindly thing to allow a criminal condemned to death to spend his last hours in gross sensual indulgence. There is no reason to suppose that the extinction of the Christian hope of immortality would prove less demoralizing. We are "saved by hope," said St Paul: we are ruined by despair. Pessimism of creed for most men means pessimism of conduct.

Our modern speech and literature and our habits of feeling have been for so many generations steeped in the influence of Christ's teaching, and it has thrown so many tender and hallowed thoughts around the state of our beloved dead, that it is impossible even for those who are personally without hope in Christ to realize what its general decay and disappearance would mean. To have possessed such a treasure, and then to lose it! to have cherished anticipations so exalted and so dear,—and to find them turn out a mockery! The age upon which this calamity fell would be of all ages the most miserable.

The hope of Israel which Paul preached to the Gentiles was a hope for the world and for the nations, as well as for the individual soul. "The commonwealth [or *polity*] of Israel" and "the covenants of promise" guaranteed the establishment of the Messianic kingdom upon earth. This expectation took amongst the mass of the Jews a materialistic and even a revengeful shape; but in one form or other it belonged, and still belongs to every man of Israel. Those noble lines of Virgil in his fourth Eclogue[87]—like the words of Caiaphas, an unintended Christian prophecy—which predicted the return of justice and the spread of a golden age through the whole world under the rule of the coming heir of Cæsar, had been signally belied by the imperial house in the century that had elapsed. Never were human prospects darker than when the apostle wrote as Nero's prisoner in Rome. It was an age of crime and horror. The political world and the system of pagan society seemed to be in the throes of dissolution. Only in "the commonwealth of Israel" was there a light of hope and a foundation for the future of mankind; and of this in its wisdom the world knew nothing.

The Gentiles were "alienated from the commonwealth of Israel,"—that is to say, treated as aliens and made such by their exclusion. By the very fact of Israel's election, the rest of mankind were shut out of the visible kingdom of God. They became mere *Gentiles*, or *nations*,—a herd of men bound together only by natural affinity, with no "covenant of promise," no religious constitution or destiny, no definite relationship to God, Israel being alone the acknowledged and organized "*people* of Jehovah."

These distinctions were summed up in one word, expressing all the pride of the Jewish nature, when the Israelites styled themselves "the Circumcision." The rest of the world—Philistines or Egyptians, Greeks, Romans, or Barbarians, it mattered not—were "the Uncircumcision." How superficial this distinction was in point of fact, and how false the assumption of moral superiority it implied in the existing condition of Judaism, St Paul indicates by saying, "those who are *called* Uncircumcision by that which is *called* Circumcision, in flesh, wrought by human hands." In the second and third chapters of his epistle to the Romans he exposed the hollowness of Jewish sanctity, and brought his fellow-countrymen down to the level of those "sinners of the Gentiles" whom they so bitterly despised.

The destitution of the Gentile world is put into a single word, when the apostle says: "You were at that time *separate from Christ*"—without a Christ, either come or coming. They were deprived of the world's one treasure,—shut out, as it appeared, for ever[88] from any part in Him who is to mankind all things and in all.—*Once far off!*

"But now in Christ Jesus ye were *made nigh*." What is it that has bridged the distance, that has transported these Gentiles from the wilderness of heathenism into the midst of the city of God? It is "the blood of Christ." The sacrificial death of Jesus Christ transformed the relations of God to mankind, and of Israel to the Gentiles. In Him God reconciled not a nation, but "a world" to Himself (2 Cor. v. 19). The death of the Son of man could not have reference to the sons of Abraham alone. If sin is universal and death is not a Jewish but a human experience, and if one blood flows in the veins of all our race, then the death of Jesus Christ was a universal sacrifice; it appeals to every man's conscience and heart, and puts away for each the guilt which comes between his soul and God.

When the Greeks in Passion week desired to see Him, He exclaimed: "I, if I be lifted up from the earth, will draw *all* unto me." The cross of Jesus was to draw humanity around it, by its infinite love and sorrow, by the perfect apprehension there was in it of the world's guilt and need, and the perfect submission to the sentence of God's law against man's sin. So wherever the gospel was preached by St Paul, it won Gentile hearts for Christ. Greek and Jew found themselves weeping together at the foot of the cross, sharing one forgiveness and baptized into one Spirit.

The union of Caiaphas and Pilate in the condemnation of Jesus and the mingling of the Jewish crowd with the Roman soldiers at His execution were a tragic symbol of the new age that was coming. Israel and the Gentiles were accomplices in the death of the Messiah—the former of the two the more guilty partner in the counsel and deed. If this Jesus whom they slew and hanged on a tree was indeed the Christ, God's chosen, then what availed their Abrahamic sonship, their covenants and law-keeping, their proud religious eminence? They had killed their Christ; they had forfeited their calling. His blood was on them and on their children.

Those who seemed nigh to God, at the cross of Christ were found far off,— that both together, the far and the near, might be reconciled and brought back to God. "He shut up all unto disobedience, that He might have mercy upon all."

FOOTNOTES:

[86] Rom. i. 19–23; comp. John i. 10: "He [the true Light] was *in the world*, and the world knew Him not."

[87]

> Magnus ab integro sæclorum nascitur ordo.
> Jam redit et Virgo, redeunt Saturnia regna;
> Jam nova progenies cœlo demittitur alto.
> Tu modo nascenti puero, quo ferrea primum
> Desinet, ac toto surget gens aurea mundo,
> Casta, fave, Lucina.

[88] Observe the perfect participle ἀπηλλοτριωμένοι, which signifies an abiding fact or fixed condition. Similar is the turn of expression in ch. iii. 9, and in Col. i. 26, Rom. xvi. 25, Matt. xiii. 35.

CHAPTER X.

THE DOUBLE RECONCILIATION.

"For He is our peace, who made both one, and brake down the middle wall of partition, having abolished in His flesh the enmity, *even* the law of commandments *contained* in ordinances, that He might create in Himself of the twain one new man, *so* making peace; and might reconcile them both in one body unto God through the cross, having slain the enmity thereby: and He came and preached good tidings of peace to you that were far off, and peace to them that were nigh: for through Him we both have our access in one Spirit unto the Father."—EPH. ii. 14–18.

Peace, peace—to the far off, and to the near! Such was God's promise to His scattered people in the times of the exile (Isai. lvii. 19). St Paul sees that peace of God extending over a yet wider field, and terminating a longer and sadder banishment than the prophet had foreseen. Christ is "our peace"—not for the divided members of Israel alone, but for all the tribes of men. He brings about a universal pacification.

There were two distinct, but kindred enmities to be overcome by Christ, in preaching to the world His good tidings of peace (ver. 17). There was the hostility of Jew and Gentile, which was removed in its cause and principle when Christ "in His flesh" (by His incarnate life and death) "abolished the law of commandments in decrees"—*i.e.*, the law of Moses as it constituted a body of external precepts determining the way of righteousness and life. This abolition of the law by the evangelical principle "dissolved the middle wall of partition." The occasion of quarrel between Israel and the world was destroyed; the barrier disappeared that had for so long fenced off the privileged ground of the sons of Abraham (vv. 14, 15). But behind this human enmity, underneath the feud and rancour existing between the Jews and the nations, there lay the deeper quarrel of mankind with God. Both enmities centred in the law; both were slain by one stroke, in the reconciliation of the cross (ver. 16).

The Jewish and Gentile peoples formed two distinct types of humanity. Politically, the Jews were insignificant and had scarcely counted amongst the great powers of the world. Their religion alone gave them influence and importance. Bearing his inspired Scriptures and his Messianic hope, the wandering Israelite confronted the vast masses of heathenism and the splendid and fascinating classical civilization with the proudest sense of his superiority. To his God he knew well that one day every knee would bow and every tongue confess. The circumstances of the time deepened his isolation and aggravated to internecine hate his spite against his fellow-men, the *adversus omnes alios hostile odium* stigmatized by the incisive pen of Tacitus. Within three years of the writing of this letter the Jewish war against Rome broke out, when the enmity culminated in the most appalling and fateful overthrow recorded in the pages of history. Now, it is this enmity at its height —the most inveterate and desperate one can conceive—that the apostle proposes to reconcile; nay, that he sees already slain by the sacrifice of the cross, and within the brotherhood of the Christian Church. It was slain in the heart of Saul of Tarsus, the proudest that beat in Jewish breast.

In his earlier writings the apostle has been concerned chiefly to guard the position and rights of the two parties within the Church. He has abundantly maintained, especially in the epistle to the Galatians, the claims of Gentile believers in Christ against Judaic assumptions and impositions. He has defended the just prerogative of the Jew and his hereditary sentiments from the contempt to which they were sometimes exposed on the part of the Gentile majority.[89] But now that this has been done, and that Gentile liberties and Jewish dignity have been vindicated and safeguarded on both sides, St Paul advances a step further: he seeks to amalgamate the Jewish and Gentile section of the Church, and to "make of the twain one new man, so making peace." This, he declares, was the end of Christ's mission; this a chief purpose of His atoning death. Only by such union, only through the burying of the old enmity slain on the cross, could His Church be built up to its completeness. St Paul would have Gentile and Jewish believers everywhere forget their differences, efface their party lines, and merge their independence in the oneness of the all-embracing and all-perfecting Church of Jesus Christ, God's habitation in the Spirit. Instead of saying that a catholic ideal like this belongs to a later and post-apostolic age, we maintain, on the contrary, that a catholic mind like St Paul's, under the conditions of his time, could not fail to arrive at this conception.

It was his confidence in the victory of the cross over all strife and sin that sustained St Paul through these years of captivity. As he looks out from his Roman prison, under the shadow of Nero's palace, the future is invested with a radiance of hope that makes the heart of the chained apostle exult within him. The world is lost, to all outward seeming: he knows it is saved! Jew and Gentile are about to close in mortal conflict: he proclaims peace between them, assured of their reconcilement, and knowing that in their reunion the salvation of human society is assured.

The enmity of Jew and Gentile was representative of all that divides mankind. In it were concentrated most of the causes by which society is rent asunder. Along with religion, race, habits, tastes and culture, moral tendencies, political aspirations, interests of trade, all helped to widen the breach. The

85

cleavage ran deep into the foundations of life; the enmity was the growth of two thousand years. It was not a case of local friction, nor a quarrel arising from temporary causes. The Jew was ubiquitous, and everywhere was an alien and an irritant to Gentile society. No antipathy was so hard to subdue. The grace that conquers it, can and will conquer all enmities.

St Paul's view embraced, in fact, a world-wide reconcilement. He contemplates, as the Hebrew prophets themselves did, the fraternization of mankind under the rule of the Christ. After this scale he laid down the foundation of the Church, "wise master-builder" that he was. It was destined to bear the weight of an edifice in which all the races of men should dwell together, and every order of human faculty should find its place. His thoughts were not confined within the Judaic antithesis. "There is no Jew and Greek," he says in another place; yes, and "no barbarian, Scythian, bondman, freeman, male or female. Ye are all one in Christ Jesus."[90] Birth, rank, office in the Church, culture, even sex are minor and subordinate distinctions, merged in the unity of redeemed souls in Christ. That which He "creates in Himself of the twain" is *one new man*—one incorporate humanity, neither Jew nor Gentile, Englishman nor Hindu, priest nor layman, male nor female; but simply *man*, and *Christian*.

At the present time we are better able to enter into these views of the apostle than at any intervening period of history. In his day almost the whole visible world, lying round the Mediterranean shores, was brought under the government and laws of Rome. This fact made the establishment of one religious polity a thing quite conceivable. The Roman empire did not, as it proved, allow Christianity to conquer it soon enough and to leaven it sufficiently to save it. That huge construction, the mightiest fabric of human polity, fell and covered the earth with its ruins. In its fall it reacted disastrously upon the Church, and has bequeathed to it the corrupt and despotic unity of Papal Rome. Now, in these last days, the whole world is opened to the Church, a world stretching far beyond the horizon of the first century. Science and Commerce, those two strong-winged angels and giant ministers of God, are swiftly binding the continents together in material ties. The peoples are beginning to realize their brotherhood, and are feeling their way in many directions towards international union; while in the Churches a new, federal catholicity is taking shape, that must displace the false catholicism of external uniformity and the disastrous absolutism inherited from Rome. The spread of European empire and the marvellous expansion of our English race are carrying forward the world's unification with enormous strides,—towards some end or other. What end is this to be? Is the kingdom of the world about to become the kingdom of our Lord and His Christ? and are the nations preparing to be "reconciled in one body unto God"?

If Christendom were worthy of her Master and her name, this question would be answered with no doubtful affirmative. The Church is well able, if she were prepared, to go up and possess the whole earth for her Lord. The way is open; the means are in her hand. Nor is she ignorant, nor wholly negligent of her opportunity and of the claims that the times impose upon her. She is putting forth new strength and striving to overtake her work, notwithstanding the weight of ignorance and sloth that burdens her. Soon the reconciling cross will be planted on every shore, and the praises of the Crucified sung in every human language.

But there are dark as well as bright auguries for the future. The advance of commerce and emigration has been a curse and not a blessing to many heathen peoples. Who can read without shame and horror the story of European conquest in America? And it is a chapter not yet closed. Greed and injustice still mark the dealings of the powerful and civilized with the weaker races. England set a noble example in the abolition of negro slavery; but she has since inflicted, for purposes of gain, the opium curse on China, putting poison to the lips of its vast population. Under our Christian flags fire-arms are imported, and alcohol, amongst tribes of men less able than children to resist their evils. Is this "preaching peace to those far off"? It is likely that the commercial profits made in the destruction of savage races as yet exceed all that our missionary societies have spent in saving them. One of these days Almighty God may have a stern reckoning with modern Europe about these things. "When He maketh inquisition for blood, He will remember."

And what shall we say of ourselves at home, in our relation to this great principle of the apostle? The old "middle wall of partition," the temple-barrier that sundered Jew and Gentile, is "broken down,"—visibly levelled by the hand of God when Jerusalem fell, as it had been virtually and in its principle destroyed by the work of Christ. But are there no other middle walls, no barriers raised within the fold of Christ? The rich man's purse, and the poor man's penury; aristocratic pride, democratic bitterness and jealousy; knowledge and refinement on the one hand, ignorance and rudeness on the other—how thick the veil of estrangement which these influences weave, how high the party walls which they build in our various Church communions!

It is the duty of the Church, as she values her existence, with gentle but firm hands to pull down and to keep down all such partitions. She cannot abolish the natural distinctions of life. She cannot turn the Jew into a Gentile, nor the Gentile into a Jew. She will never make the poor man rich in this world, nor the rich man altogether poor. Like her Master, she declines to be "judge or divider" of our secular inheritance. But she can see to it that these outward distinctions make no difference in her treatment of the men as men. She can combine in her fellowship all grades and orders, and teach them to understand and respect each other. She can soften the asperities and relieve many of the hardships which social differences create. She can diffuse a healing and purifying influence upon the contentions of society around her.

Let us labour unweariedly for this, and let our meeting at the Lord's table be a symbol of the unreserved communion of men of all classes and conditions in the brotherhood of the redeemed sons of God. *"He* is our peace"; and if He is in our hearts, we must needs be sons of peace. "Behold the secret of all true union! It is not by others coming to us, nor by our going over to them; but it is by both them and ourselves coming to Christ" that peace is made (Monod).

Thus within and without the Church the work of atonement will advance, with Christ ever for its preacher (ver. 17). He speaks through the words and the lives of His ten thousand messengers,—men of every order, in every age and country of the earth. The leaven of Christ's peace will spread till the lump is leavened. God will accomplish His purpose of the ages, whether in our time, or in another worthier of His calling. His Church is destined to be the home of the human family, the universal liberator and instructor and reconciler of the nations. And Christ shall sit enthroned in the loyal worship of the federated peoples of the earth.

But the question remains: What is the foundation, what the warrant of this grand idealism of the apostle Paul? Many a great thinker, many an ardent reformer before and since has dreamed of some such millennium as this. And their enthusiastic plans have ended too often in conflict and destruction. What surer ground of confidence have we in Paul's undertaking than in those of so many gifted visionaries and philosophers? The difference lies here: his expectation rests on the word and character of God; his instrument of reform is the cross of Jesus Christ.

God is the centre of His own universe. Any reconciliation that is to stand, must include Him first of all. Christ reconciled Jew and Gentile "both in one body *to God."* There is the meeting point, the true focus of the orbit of human life, that can alone control its movements and correct its wild aberrations. Under the shadow of His throne of justice, in the arms of His fatherly love, the kindreds of the earth will at last find reconciliation and peace. Humanitarian and secularist systems make the simple mistake of ignoring the supreme Factor in the scheme of things; they leave out the All in all.

"Be ye *reconciled to God,"* cries the apostle. For Almighty God has had a great quarrel with this world of ours. The hatred of men towards each other is rooted in the "carnal mind which is enmity against God." The "law of commandments contained in ordinances," in whose possession the Jew boasted over the lawless and profane Gentile, in reality branded both as culprits.

The secret disquiet and dread lurking in man's conscience, the pangs endured in his body of humiliation, the groaning frame of nature declare the world unhinged and out of course. Things have gone amiss, somehow, between man and his Creator. The face of the earth and the field of human history are scarred with the thunderbolts of His displeasure. God, the Father of our Lord Jesus Christ and the King of the ages, is not the amiable, almighty Sentimentalist that some pious people would make Him out to be. The men of the Bible felt and realized, if we do not, the grave and tremendous import of the Lord's controversy with all flesh. He is unceasingly at war with the sins of men. "God is *love*"—oh yes; but then He is also "a consuming fire"! There is no anger so crushing as the anger of love, for there is none so just; no wrath to be feared like "the wrath of the Lamb." God is not a man, weak and passionate, whom a spark of anger might set all on fire, burning out His justice and compassion. "In His wrath He remembers mercy." Within that infinite nature there is room for an absolute loathing and resentment towards sin, in consistence with an immeasurable pity and yearning towards His sinful children. Hence the cross of our Lord Jesus Christ.

Look at it from what side you will (and it has many sides), propound it in what terms you may (and it translates itself anew into the dialect of every age), you must not explain the cross of Christ away nor cause its offence to cease. "The atonement has always been a scandal and a folly to those who did not receive it; it has always contained something which to formal logic is false and to individualistic ethics immoral; yet in that very element which has been branded as immoral and false, has always lain the seal of its power and the secret of its truth." The Holy One of God, the Lamb without spot and blemish, He died by His own consent a sinner's death. That sacrifice, undergone by the Son of God and Son of man dying as man for men, in love to His race and in obedience to the Divine will and law, gave an infinite satisfaction to God in His relation to the world, and there went up to the Divine throne from the anguish of Calvary a "savour of sweet smell." The moral glory of the act of Jesus Christ in dying for His guilty brethren outshone its horror and disgrace; and it redeemed man's lost condition, and clothed human nature with a new character and aspect in the eyes of God Himself. "Now therefore there is no more condemnation to them that are in Christ Jesus." The mercy of God, if we may so say, is set free to act in forgiveness and restoration, without any compromise of justice and inflexible law. No peace without this: no peace that did not *satisfy God*, and satisfy that law, deep as the deepest in God, that binds suffering to wrong-doing and death to sin.

Perhaps you say: This is immoral, surely, that the just should suffer for the unjust; that one commits the offence, and another bears the penalty.—Stay a moment: that is only half the truth. We are more than individuals; we are members of a race; and vicarious suffering runs through life. Our sufferings and wrong-doings bind the human family together in an inextricable web. We are *communists in sin and death*. It is the law and lot of our existence. And Christ, the Lord and centre of the race, has come within its scope. He bound Himself to our sinking fortunes. He became co-partner in our lost estate, and has redeemed it to God by His blood. If He was true and perfect man, if He was the creative Head and Mediator of the race, the eternal Firstborn of many brethren, He could do no other. He who alone had the right and the power, —"*One* died for all." He took upon His Divine heart the sin and curse of the world, He fastened it to His shoulders with the cross; and He bore it away from Caiaphas' hall and Pilate's judgement-seat, away from guilty Jerusalem; He took away the sin of the world, and expiated it once for all. He quenched in His blood the fires of wrath and hate it kindled. He slew *the enmity* thereby.

Still, we are individuals, as you said, not lost after all in the world's solidarity. Here your personal right and will must come in. What Christ has done for you is yours, so far as you accept it. He has died your death beforehand, trusting that you would not repudiate His act, that you would not let His blood be spilt in vain. But He will never force His mediation upon you. He respects your freedom and your manhood. Do you now endorse what Jesus Christ did on your behalf? Do you renounce the sin, and accept the sacrifice? Then it is yours, from this moment, before the tribunal of God and of conscience. By the witness of His Spirit you are proclaimed a forgiven and reconciled man. Christ crucified is yours—if you will have Him, if you will identify your sinful self with the sinless Mediator, if as you see Him lifted up on the cross you will let your heart cry out, "Oh my God, He dies for *me!*"

Coming "in one Spirit to the Father," the reconciled children join hands again with each other. Social barriers, caste feelings, family feuds, personal quarrels, national antipathies, alike go down before the virtue of the blood of Jesus.

> "Neither passion nor pride
> His cross can abide,
> But melt in the fountain that streams from His side!"

"Beloved," you will say to the man that hates or has wronged you most, —"Beloved, if God so loved us, we ought also to love one another." In these simple words of the apostle John lies the secret of universal peace, the hope of the fraternization of mankind. Nations will have to say this one day, as well as men.

FOOTNOTES:

[89] See to this effect such passages as Rom. i. 16 (*to the Jew first*), ix. 4, 5; and especially xi. 13–32.

[90] Gal. iii. 28; Col. iii. 11. Comp. John x. 16, xi. 52. See *The Epistle to the Galatians* (Expositor's Bible), Chapter XV.

CHAPTER XI.

GOD'S TEMPLE IN HUMANITY.

"So then ye are no more strangers and sojourners, but ye are fellow-citizens with the saints and of the household of God, being built upon the foundation of the apostles and prophets, Christ Jesus Himself being the chief corner stone; in whom each several building, fitly framed together, groweth into a holy temple in the Lord; in whom ye also are builded together for a habitation of God in the Spirit."—EPH. ii. 19–22.

Not unfrequently it is the last word or phrase of the paragraph that gives us the clue to St Paul's meaning and discloses the point at which he has aimed all along. So in this instance. "For a habitation of God in the Spirit": behold the goal of God's ways with mankind! For this end the Divine grace has wrought through countless ages and has made its great sacrifice. For this end Jew and Gentile are being gathered into one and compacted into a new humanity.

I. The Church is a house built for an *Occupant*. Its quality and size, and the mode of its construction are determined by its destination. It is built to suit the great Inhabitant, who says concerning the new Zion as He said of the old in figure: "This is my rest for ever! Here will I dwell, for I have desired it." God, who is spirit, cannot be satisfied with the fabric of material nature for His temple, nor does "the Most High dwell in houses made by men's hands." He seeks our spirit for His abode, and

"Doth prefer
Before all temples the upright heart and pure."

In the collective life and spirit of humanity God claims to reside, that He may fill it with His glory and His love. "Know you not," cries the apostle to the once debased Corinthians, "that you are God's temple, and that the Spirit of God dwells in you?"

Nothing that is bestowed upon man terminates in himself. The deliverance of Jewish and Gentile believers from their personal sins, their re-instatement into the broken unity of mankind and the destruction in them of their old enmities, of the antipathies generated by their common rebellion against God—these great results of Christ's sacrifice were means to a further end. "Hallowed be Thy name" is our first petition to the Father in heaven; "Glory to God in the highest" is the key-note of the angels' song, that runs through all the harmonies of "peace on earth," through every strain of the melody of life. Religion is the mistress, not the handmaid in human affairs. She will never consent to become a mere ethical discipline, an instrument and subordinate stage in social evolution, a ladder held for men to climb up into their self-sufficiency.

The old temptation of the Garden, "Ye shall be as gods," has come upon our age in a new and fascinating form, "You shall be as gods," it is whispered: "nay, you *are* God, and there is no other. The supernatural is a dream. The Christian story is a fable. There is none to fear or adore above yourselves!" Man is to worship his collective self, his own humanity. "I am the Lord thy

93

God," the great idol says, "that brought thee up out of animalism and savagery, and me only shalt thou serve!—Love and faithful service to one's kind, a holy passion for the welfare of the race, for the relief of human ignorance and poverty and pain, this is the true religion; and you need no other. Its obligation is instinctive, its benefits immediate and palpable; and it gives a consecration to individual life that dignifies and chastens, while it calls into exercise all our faculties."

Yes, we willingly admit, such human service is "religion pure and undefiled, *before our God and Father.*" If service is rendered to our kind as worship to the Father of men; if we reverence in each man the image of God and the shrine of His Spirit; if we are seeking to cleanse and adorn in men the temple where the Most High shall dwell, the humblest work done for our fellows' good is done for Him. The best human charity is rendered for the love of God. "Thou shalt love the Lord thy God with all thy heart, mind, soul, and strength. This," said Jesus, "is the first and great commandment. And the second is *like unto it*: Thou shalt love thy neighbour as thyself. On these two commandments hang all the law and the prophets." On these two hangs the welfare of men and nations.

But the first commandment must come first. The second law of Jesus never has been or will be kept to purpose without the first. Humanitarian sentiments, dreams of universal brotherhood, projects of social reform, may seem for the moment to gain by their independence of religion a certain zest and emphasis; but they are without root and vitality. Their energy fails, or spends itself in revolt; their glow declines, their purity is stained. The leaders and first enthusiasts trained in the school of Christ, whose spirit, in vain repudiated, lives on in them, find themselves betrayed and alone. The coarse selfishness and materialism of the human heart win an easy triumph over a visionary altruism. "Without me," says Jesus Christ, "ye can do nothing."

In the light of God's glory man learns to reverence his nature and understand the vocation of his race. The love of God touches the deep and enduring springs of human action. The kingdom of Christ and of God commands an absolute devotion; its service inspires unfaltering courage and invincible patience. There is a grandeur and a certainty, of which the noblest secular aims fall short, in the hopes of those who are striving together for the faith of the gospel, and who work to build human life into a dwelling-place for God.

II. God's temple in the Church of Jesus Christ, while it is one, is also manifold. "In whom *each several building* [or *every part of the building*[91]], while it is compacted together, grows into a holy temple in the Lord."

The image is that of an extensive pile of buildings, such as the ancient temples commonly were, in process of construction at different points over a wide area. The builders work in concert, upon a common plan. The several parts of the work are adjusted to each other; and the various operations in process are so harmonized, that the entire construction preserves the unity of the architect's design. Such an edifice was the apostolic Church—one, but of many parts—in its diverse gifts and multiplied activities animated by one Spirit and directed towards one Divine purpose.

Jerusalem, Antioch, Ephesus, Corinth, Rome—what a various scene of activity these centres of Christian life presented! The Churches founded in these great cities must have differed in many features. Even in the communities of his own province the apostle did not, so far as we can judge, impose a uniform administration. St Peter and St Paul carried out their plans independently, only maintaining a general understanding with each other. The apostolic founders, inspired by one and the self-same Spirit, could labour at a distance, upon material and by methods extremely various, with entire confidence in each other and with an assurance of the unity of result which their teaching and administration would exhibit. The many buildings rested on the one foundation of the apostles. "Whether it were I or they," says our apostle, "so we preach, and so you believed." Where there is the same Spirit and the same Lord, men do not need to be scrupulous about visible conformity. Elasticity and individual initiative admit of entire harmony of principle. The hand may do its work without irritating and obstructing the eye; and the foot run on its errands without mistrusting the ear.

Such was the catholicism of the apostolic age. The true reading of verse 21, as it is restored by the Revisers, is an incidental witness to the date of the epistle. A churchman of the second century, writing under Paul's name in the interests of catholic unity as it was then understood, would scarcely have penned such a sentence without attaching to the subject the definite article: he must have written "all the building," as the copyists from whom the received text proceeds very naturally have done. From that time onwards, as the system of the ecclesiastical hierarchy was developed, external unity was more and more strictly imposed. The original "diversity of operations" became a rigid uniformity. The Church swallowed up the Churches. Finally, the spiritual bureaucracy of Rome gathered all ecclesiastical power into one centre, and placed the direction of Western Christendom in the hands of a single priest, whom it declared to be the Vicar of Jesus Christ and endowed with the Divine attribute of infallibility.

Had not Jerusalem been overthrown and its Church destroyed, the hierarchical movement would probably have made that city, rather than Rome, its centre. This was in fact the tendency, if not the express purpose of the Judaistic party in the Church. St Paul had vindicated in his earlier epistles the freedom of the

Gentile Christian communities, and their right of non-conformity to Jewish usage. In the words "each several building, fitly framed together," there is an echo of this controversy. The Churches of his mission claim a standing side by side with those founded by other apostles. For himself and his Gentile brethren he seems to say, in the presence of the primitive Church and its leaders: "As they are Christ's, so also are we."

The co-operation of the different parts of the body of Christ is essential to their collective growth. Let all Churches beware of crushing dissent. Blows aimed at our Christian neighbours recoil upon ourselves. Undermining their foundation, we shake our own. Next to positive corruption of doctrine and life, nothing hinders so greatly the progress of the kingdom of God as the claim to exclusive legitimacy made on behalf of ancient Church organizations. Their representatives would have every part of God's temple framed upon one pattern. They refuse a place on the apostolic foundation to all Churches, however numerous, however rich in faith and good works, however strong the historical justification for their existence, however clear the marks they bear of the Spirit's seal, which do not conform to the rule they themselves have received. Their rites and ministry, they assert, are those alone approved by Christ and authorized by His apostles, within a given area. They refuse the right hand of fellowship to men who are doing Christ's work by their side; they isolate their flocks, as far as possible, from intercourse with the Christian communities around them.

This policy on the part of any Christian Church, or Church party, is contrary to the mind of Christ and to the example of His apostles. Those who hold aloof from the comity of the Churches and prevent the many buildings of God's temple being fitly framed together, must bear their judgement, whosoever they be. They prefer conquest to peace, but that conquest they will never win; it would be fatal to themselves. Let the elder sister frankly allow the birthright of the younger sisters of Christ's house in these lands, and be our example in justice and in charity. Great will be her honour; great the glory won for our common Lord.

"Every building fitly framed together *groweth into a holy temple* in the Lord." The subject is distributive; the predicate collective. The parts give place to the whole in the writer's mind. As each several piece of the structure, each cell or chapel in the temple, spreads out to join its companion buildings and adjusts itself to the parts around it, the edifice grows into a richer completeness and becomes more fit for its sacred purpose. The separate buildings, distant in place or historical character, approximate by extension, as they spread over the unoccupied ground between them and as the connecting links are multiplied. At last a point is reached at which they will become continuous.

Growing into each other step by step and forming across the diminishing distance a web of mutual attachment constantly thickening, they will insensibly, by a natural and vital growth, become one in visible communion as they are one in their underlying faith.

When each organ of the body in its own degree is perfect and holds its place in keeping with the rest, we think no longer of their individual perfection, of the charm of this feature or of that; they are forgotten in the beauty of the perfect frame. So it will be in the body of Christ, when its several communions, cleansed and filled with His Spirit, each honouring the vocation of the others, shall in freedom and in love by a spontaneous movement be gathered into one. Their strength will then be no longer weakened and their spirit chafed by internal conflict. With united forces and irresistible energy, they will assail the kingdom of darkness and subjugate the world to Christ.

For this consummation our Saviour prayed in the last hours before His death: "that they all may be one, as Thou, Father, art in me and I in Thee, that they also may be in us, that the world may believe that Thou didst send me" (John xvii. 21). Did He fear that His little flock of the Twelve would be parted by dissensions? Or did He not look onward to the future, and see the "offences that must come," the alienations and fierce conflicts that would arise amongst His people, and the blood that would be shed in His name? Yet beyond these divisions, on the horizon of the end of the age, He foresaw the day when the wounds of His Church would be healed, when the sword that He had brought on the earth would be sheathed, and through the unity of faith and love in His people all mankind would at last come to acknowledge Him and the Father who had sent Him.

III. To appearance, we are many rather than one who bear the name of Christ. But we are one notwithstanding, if below the variety of superstructure our faith rests upon the witness of the apostles, and the several buildings have Christ Jesus Himself for chief corner-stone. The *one foundation* and the *one Spirit* constitute the unity of God's temple in the Church.

"The apostles and prophets" are named as a single body, *the prophets* being doubtless, in this passage and in chapters iii. 5 and iv. 11, the existing prophets of the apostolic Church, whose inspired teaching supplemented that of the apostles and helped to lay down the foundation of revealed truth. That foundation has been, through the providence of God, preserved for later ages in the Scriptures of the New Testament, on which the faith of Christians has rested ever since. Such a prophet Barnabas was in the first days (Acts xiii. 1), and such was the unknown, but deeply inspired writer of the epistle to the Hebrews; such prophets, again, were SS. Mark and Luke, the Evangelists. Prophecy was not a stated gift of office. Just as there were "teachers" in the early Church whose knowledge and eloquence did not entitle them to bear rule, so prophecy was frequently exercised by private persons and carried with it no such official authority as belonged in the highest degree to the apostles.

It is thought surprising that St Paul should write thus, in so general and distant a fashion, of the order to which he belonged (comp. iii. 5). This, it is said, is the language of a later generation, which looks back with reverence to the inspired Founders. But this letter is written, as we observed at the outset, from a peculiarly objective and impersonal standpoint. It differs in this respect from other epistles of St Paul. He is addressing a number of Churches, with some of which his personal relations were slight and distant. He is contemplating the Church in its most general character. He is not the only founder of Churches; he is one of a band of colleagues, working in different regions. It is natural that he should use the plural here. He sets his successors an example of the recognition due to fellow-labourers whose work bears the seal of Christ's Spirit.

These men have laid *the foundation*—Peter and Paul, John and James, Barnabas and Silas, and the rest. They are our spiritual progenitors, the fathers of our faith. We see Jesus Christ through their eyes; we read His teaching, and catch His Spirit in their words. Their testimony, in its essential facts, stands secure in the confidence of mankind. Nor was it their word alone, but the men themselves—their character, their life and work—laid for the Church its historical foundation. This "glorious company of the apostles" formed the first course in the new building, on whose firmness and strength the stability of the entire structure depends. Their virtues and their sufferings, as well as the revelations made through them, have guided the thoughts and shaped the life of countless multitudes of men, of the best and wisest men in all ages since. They have fixed the standard of Christian doctrine and the type of Christian character. At our best, we are but imitators of them as they were of Christ.

In regard to the chief part of their teaching, both as to its meaning and authority, the great bulk of Christians in all communions are agreed. The keen disputes which engage us upon certain points, testify to the cardinal importance which is felt on all hands to attach to the words of Christ's chosen apostles. Their living witness is in our midst. The self-same Spirit that wrought in them, works amongst men and dwells in the communion of saints. He still reveals the things of Christ, and guides into truth the willing and obedient.

So "the firm foundation of God standeth"; though men, shaken themselves, seem to see it tremble. On that basis we may labour confidently and loyally, with those amongst whom the Master has placed us. Some of our fellow-workmen disown and would hinder us: that shall not prevent us from rejoicing in their good work, and admiring the gold and precious stones that they contribute to the fabric. The Lord of the temple will know how to use the labour of His many servants. He will forgive and compose their strife, who are jealous for His name. He will shape their narrow aims to His larger purposes. Out of their discords He will draw a finer harmony. As the great house grows to its dimensions, as the workmen by the extension of their labours come nearer to each other and their sectional plans merge in Christ's great purpose, reproaches will cease and misunderstandings vanish. Over many who followed not with us and whom we counted but as "strangers and sojourners," as men whose place within the walls of Zion was doubtful and unauthorized, we shall hereafter rejoice with a joy not unmixed with self-upbraiding, to find them in the fullest right our fellow-citizens amongst the saints and of the household of God.

The Holy Spirit is the supreme Builder of the Church, as He is the supreme witness to Jesus Christ (John xv. 26, 27). The words *in the Spirit*, closing the verse with solemn emphasis, denote not the mode of God's habitation—that is self-evident—but the agency engaged in building this new house of God. With one "chief corner-stone" to rest upon and one Spirit to inspire and control them, the apostles and prophets laid their foundation and the Church was "builded together" for a habitation of God. Hence its unity. But for this sovereign influence the primitive founders of Christianity, like later Church leaders, would have fallen into fatal discord. Modern critics, reasoning upon natural grounds and not understanding the grace of the Holy Spirit, assume that they did thus quarrel and contend. Had this been so, no foundation could ever have been laid; the Church would have fallen to pieces at the very beginning.

In the hands of these faithful and wise stewards of God's dispensation, "the stone which the builders rejected was made the head of the corner." Their work has been tried by fire and by flood; and it abides. The rock of Zion stands unworn by time, unshaken by the conflict of ages,—amidst the movements of history and the shifting currents of thought the one foundation for the peace and true welfare of mankind.

FOOTNOTES:

[91] Πᾶσα οἰκοδομή, according to the well-established critical reading. For πᾶς without the article, implying a various whole, compare πάσης κτίσεως in Col. i. 15; πᾶσα γραφή, 2 Tim. iii. 16; ἐν πάσῃ ἀναστροφῇ, 1 Peter i. 15; and Θεὸς πάσης χάριτος, 1 Peter v. 10.

CHAPTER XII.

THE SECRET OF THE AGES.

"For this cause I Paul, the prisoner of Christ Jesus in behalf of you Gentiles,—if so be that ye have heard of the dispensation of that grace of God which was given me toward you; how that by revelation was made known unto me the mystery (as I wrote afore in few words, whereby, when ye read, ye can perceive my understanding in the mystery of Christ), which in other generations was not made known unto the sons of men, as it hath now been revealed unto His holy apostles and prophets in the Spirit; *to wit*, that the Gentiles are fellow-heirs, and fellow-members of the body, and fellow-partakers of the promise in Christ Jesus through the gospel, whereof I was made a minister, according to the gift of that grace of God which was given me according to the working of His power. Unto me, who am less than the least of all saints, was this grace given, to preach unto the Gentiles the unsearchable riches of Christ; and to bring to light what is the dispensation of the mystery which from all ages hath been hid in God who created all things."—EPH. iii. 1–9.

Verses 2–13 are in form a parenthesis. They interrupt the prayer which appears to be commencing in the first verse and is not resumed until verse 14. This intervening period is parenthetical, however, in appearance more than in reality. The matter it contains is so weighty and so essential to the argument and structure of the epistle, that it is impossible to treat it as a mere *aside*. The writer intends, at the pause which occurs after the paragraph just concluded (ii. 22), to interpose a few words of prayer before passing on to the next topic. But in the act of doing so, this subject of which his mind is full—viz., that of his own relation to God's great purpose for mankind—forces itself upon him; and the prayer that was on his lips is pent up for a few moments longer, until it flows forth again, in richer measure, in verses 14–19.

Like chapter i. 3–14, this passage is an extreme instance of St Paul's amorphous style. His sentences are not composed; they are spun in a continuous thread, an endless chain of prepositional, participial, and relative adjuncts. They grow under our eyes like living things, putting forth new processes every moment, now in this and now in that direction. Within the main parenthesis we soon come upon another parenthesis including verses 3*b* and 4 ("as I wrote afore," etc.); and at several points the grammatical connexion is uncertain. In its general scope, this intricate sentence resolves itself into a statement of *what God has wrought in the apostle* toward the accomplishment of His great plan. It thus completes the exposition given already of that which *God wrought in Christ for the Church*, and that which *He has wrought through Christ in Gentile believers* in fulfilment of the same end.

Verses 1–9 speak (1) of the mystery itself—God's gracious intention toward the human race, unknown in earlier times; and (2) of the man to whom, above others, it was given to make known the secret.

I. *The mystery* is defined twice over. First, it consists in the fact that "in Christ Jesus through the gospel the Gentiles are co-heirs and co-incorporate and co-partners in the promise" (ver. 6); and secondly, it is "the unsearchable riches of Christ" (ver. 8). The latter phrase gathers to a point what is diversely expressed in the former.

Christ is, to St Paul, the centre and the sum of the mysteries of Divine truth, of the whole enigma of existence. In the parallel epistle he calls Him "the mystery of God—in whom are all the treasures of wisdom and knowledge hidden" (Col. ii. 2, 3: R.V.). The mystery of God, discovered in Christ, was hidden out of the sight and reach of previous times. Now, by the preaching of the gospel, it is made the common property of mankind (Col. i. 25–28).

In close connexion with these statements, St Paul speaks there, as he does here, of his own heavy sufferings endured on this account and the joy they gave him. He is the instrument of a glorious purpose worthy of God; he is the mouthpiece of a revelation waiting to be spoken since the world began, that is addressed to all mankind and interests heaven along with earth. The greatness of his office is commensurate with the greatness of the truth given him to announce.

The mystery, as we have said, consists in *Christ*. This we learned from chapter i. 4, 5, and 9, 10. In Christ the Eternal lodged His purpose and laid His plans for the world. It is His fulness that the fulness of the times dispenses. The Old Testament, the reservoir of previous revelation, had Him for its close-kept secret, "held in silence through eternal times" (Rom. xvi. 25–27). The drift of its prophecies, the focus of its converging lights, the veiled magnet towards which its spiritual indications pointed, was "Christ." He "was the spiritual rock that followed" Israel in its wanderings, from whose springs the people drank, as it answered to the touch of one and now another of the holy men of old. The revelation of Jesus Christ gives unity, substance, and meaning to the history of Israel, which is otherwise a pathway without goal, a problem without solution. Priest and prophet, law and sacrifice; the kingly Son of David, and the suffering Servant of Jehovah; the Seed of the woman with bruised foot bruising the serpent's head; the Lord whom His people seek, suddenly coming to His temple; the Stone hewn from the mountains without hands, that grows till it fills the earth—the manifold representations of Israel's ideal, centre in the Lord Jesus Christ. The lines of the great figure drawn on the canvas of prophecy—disconnected as they seemed and without a plan, giving rise to a thousand dreams and speculations

—are filled out and drawn into shape and take life and substance in Him. They are found to be parts of a consistent whole, sketches and studies of this fragment or of that belonging to the consummate Person and the comprehensive plan manifest in the revelation of Jesus Christ.

But while Christ gathers into Himself the accumulated wealth of former revelation, His fulness is not measured thereby or exhausted. He solves the problems of the past; He unseals the ancient mysteries. But He creates new and deeper problems, some explained in the continued teaching of His Spirit and His providence, others that remain, or emerge from time to time to tax the faith and understanding of His Church. There are the mysteries surrounding His own Person, with which the Greek Church struggled long—His eternal Sonship, His pre-incarnate relation to mankind and the creatures, the final outcome of the mediatorial reign and its subordination to the absolute sovereignty of God. These depths St Paul sounded with his plummet; but he found them unfathomable. Theological science has explored and defined them, and illuminated them on many sides, but cannot reach to their inmost mystery. Then there is the problem of the atonement, with all the cognate difficulties touching the origin of sin, its heredity and its personal guilt, touching the adjustment of law and grace, the method of justification, the extent and efficacy of Christ's redeeming work, touching the future destiny and eternal state of souls. Another class of questions largely occupies the minds of thoughtful men to-day. They are studying the relation of Christ and His Church to nature and the outward world, the bearings of Christian truth upon social conditions, the working of the Spirit of God in communities, and the place of man's collective life in the progress and upbuilding of the kingdom of Christ.

For such inquiries the Spirit of wisdom and revelation is given to those who humbly seek His light. He is given afresh in every age. Out of Christ's unsearchable riches ever-new resources are forthcoming at His Church's need, new treasures lying hidden in the old for him who can extract them. But His riches, however far they are investigated, remain unsearchable, and inexhaustible however largely drawn upon. God's ways may be tracked further and further in each generation; they will remain to the end, as they were to the mind of Paul at the limit of his bold researches, "past finding out." The inspired apostle confesses himself a child in Divine learning: "We know in part," he says, "we prophesy in part." Oh the depths of "hidden wisdom" unimagined now, that are in store for us in Christ, "foreordained before the worlds unto our glory!"

The particular aspect of the mystery of Christ with which the apostle is concerned, is that of His relationship to the Gentile world. "The grace of

God," he says in verse 2, "was given me *for you*." Such is "the dispensation" in which God is now engaged. Upon this lavish and undreamed-of scale He is dealing forth salvation to men. St Paul describes this revelation of God's goodness to the Gentiles by three parallel but distinct terms in verse 6. They "are fellow-heirs"—a word that carries us back to chapter i. 11–13, and assures the Gentile readers of their final redemption and heavenly glory.[92] They "are of the same body"—which sums up all that we have learnt from chapter ii. 11–22. And they "are fellow-partakers of the promise"—receiving upon a footing of equal privilege with Jewish believers the gift of the Spirit and the blessings promised to Israel in the Messianic kingdom.

In virtue of the dispensation committed to him, St Paul formally proclaims the incorporation of the Gentiles into the body of Christ, their investiture with the franchise of faith. The forgiveness of sins is theirs, the light of God's smile, the breath of His Spirit, the worship and fellowship of His Church, the tasks and honours of His service. The incarnation of Christ is theirs; His life, teaching, and miracles; His cross is theirs, His resurrection and ascension, and His second coming, and the glories of His heavenly kingdom—all made their own on the bare condition of a penitent and obedient faith. The past is theirs —is ours, along with the present and the future. The God of Israel is our God. Abraham is our father, though his sons after the flesh acknowledge us not. Their prophets prophesied of the grace that should come unto us. Their poets sing the songs of Zion to Gentile peoples in a hundred tongues. They lead our prayers and praises. In their words we find expression for our heart-griefs and joys. At the wedding-feast or by the grave-side, amidst "the multitude that keep holy day" and in "dry lands" where the soul thirsts for God's ordinances, we carry the Psalmists with us and the teachers of Israel.

What a boundless wealth we Gentiles, taught by Jesus Christ, have discovered in the Jewish Bible! When will the Jewish people understand that their greatness is in Him, that the light which lightens the Gentiles is their true glory? When will they accept their part in the riches of which they have made all the world partakers? The mystery of our participation in their Christ has now been "revealed to the sons of men" long enough. Is it not time that they themselves should see it, that the veil should be lifted from the heart of Israel? The disclosure was in the first instance so astounding, so contrary to their cherished expectations, that one can scarcely wonder if it was at first rejected. But God the King of the ages has been asserting and re-asserting the fact in the course of history ever since. How vain to fight against Him! how useless to deny the victory of the Nazarene!

II. But there was in Israel an election of grace,—men of unveiled heart to whom the mystery of ages was disclosed. "The secret of Jehovah is with them that fear Him, and He will show them His covenant." Such is the rule of revelation. To the like effect Christ said: "The pure in heart shall see God. He that willeth to do His will shall know of the doctrine."

The light of God's universal love had come into the world; but where it fell on cold or impure hearts, it shone in vain. The mystery "was made manifest to His *saints*," writes the apostle in Colossians i. 26. So in this passage: "revealed to His *holy* apostles and prophets in the Spirit." The pure eye sees the true light. This was the condition which made it possible for Paul himself and his partners in the gospel to be the bearers of this august revelation. It needed sincere and devoted men, willing to be taught of God, willing to surrender every prejudice and the preconceptions of flesh and blood, in order to receive and convey to the world thoughts of God so much larger and loftier than the thoughts of men. To such men—true disciples, loyal at all costs to God and truth, holy and humble of heart—Jesus Christ gave His great commission and bade them "go and make disciples of all the nations."

The secret was further disclosed to Peter, when he was taught at the house of Cornelius "not to call any man common or unclean." He saw, and the Church of Jerusalem saw and confessed that God "gave the like gift" to uncircumcised Gentiles as to themselves and had "purified their hearts by faith." Many prophetic voices, unrecorded, confirmed this revelation. Of all this Paul is thinking here. It is to his predecessors in the knowledge of the truth rather than to himself that he refers when he speaks of "holy apostles and prophets" in verse 5. His readers would naturally turn to them in coming to this plural expression. The original apostles of Jesus and witnesses of His truth first attested the doctrine of universal grace; and that they did so was a fact of vital importance to Paul and the Gentile Church. The significance of this fact is shown by the stress which is laid upon it and the prominence given to it in the narrative of the Acts of the Apostles.

The apostle frequently alludes to revelations made to himself; he never claims that this chief matter was *revealed* personally to himself. It was an open secret when Saul entered the Church. "Whereof," he says, in verse 7, "I *became minister*"; again, "to me was this grace given, to *preach to the Gentiles* Christ's unsearchable riches." The leaders of the Jewish Christian Church knew well that their message was meant for all the world. But the abstract knowledge of a truth is one thing; the practical power to realize it is another. Until the new apostle came upon the field, there was no man ready for this great task and equal to it. It was at this crisis that Paul was raised up. Then "it pleased God to reveal His Son" in him, that he might "preach Him among the Gentiles."

The effect of this summons upon Paul himself was overwhelming, and continued to be so till the end of life. The immense favour humbles him to the dust. He strains language, heaping comparative upon superlative, to describe his astonishment as the import of his mission unfolds itself: "To me, less than the least of all the saints, was this grace given." That Saul the Pharisee and the persecutor, the most unworthy and most unlikely of men, should be the chosen vessel to bear Christ's riches to the Gentile world, how shall he sufficiently give thanks for this! how express his wonder at the unfathomable wisdom and goodness that the choice displays in the mind of God! But we can see well that this choice was precisely the fittest. A Hebrew of the Hebrews, steeped in Jewish traditions and glorying in his sacred ancestry, none knew better than the apostle Paul how rich were the treasures stored in the house of Abraham that he had to make over to the Gentiles. A true son of that house, he was the fittest to lead in the aliens, to show them its precious things and make them at home within its walls.

To himself the office was an unceasing delight. The universalism of the gospel—a commonplace of our modern rhetoric—had burst upon his mind in its unspoilt freshness and undimmed splendour. He is sailing out into an undiscovered ocean, with a boundless horizon. A new heaven and earth are opened to him in the revelation that the Gentiles are partakers of the promise in Christ Jesus. He is entranced, as he writes, with the largeness of the Divine purpose, with the magnificent sweep and scope of the designs of grace. These verses give us the warm and genuine impression made upon the hearts of its first recipients by the disclosure of the universal destination of the gospel of Christ.

St Paul's work, in carrying out the dispensation of this mystery, was twofold. It was both external and internal. He was a "herald and apostle"; he was also "teacher of the Gentiles in faith and truth" (1 Tim. ii. 7). He had in the former capacity to carry the good tidings from one end to the other of the Roman empire, to spread it abroad as far as his feet could travel and his voice reach, and thus "to fulfil the gospel of Christ." But there was another, mental task, as necessary and still more difficult, which likewise fell to his lot. He had to *think out* the gospel. It was his office to unfold and apply it to the wants of a new world, to solve by its aid the problems that confronted him as evangelist and pastor,—questions that contained the seed and beginning of the intellectual difficulties of the Church in future times. He had to free the gospel from the swaddling-bands of Judaism, to emancipate the spirit from the letter of a mechanical and legal interpretation. On the other hand, he had equally to guard the truth as it is in Jesus from the dissolving influences of Gentile scepticism and theosophy. Fighting his way through fierce and incessant opposition on both sides, the apostle Paul led the mind of the Church onwards and guides it still in the faith and knowledge of the Son of God. These noble epistles are the fruit and record of St Paul's theological work. Through them he has left a deeper mark on the conscience of the world than any one man besides, except the Master of truth who was more than man.

The apostle was not unaware of the vast influence he now possessed, and that must accrue to him in the future from the transcendent interest of the doctrines committed to his charge. There is no false modesty about this splendidly gifted man. It is his not only to "preach to the Gentiles the good news of Christ's unsearchable riches"; but more than that, "to bring to light what is the administration of the mystery that has been hidden away from the ages in God who created all things." The great secret was out while Saul of Tarsus was still a persecutor and blasphemer. But as to the *management* and *dispensation* of the mystery, the practical handling of it, as to the mode and way in which God would convey and apply it to the world at large, and as to the bearings and consequences of this momentous truth,—the apostle Paul, and no one but he, had all this to expound and set in order. He was, in fact, the architect of Christian doctrine.

Theologically, Peter and John himself were Paul's debtors; and are included amongst the "all men" of verse 9 (if this reading of the text is correct). St John had, it is true, a more direct intuition into the mind of Christ and rose to an even loftier height of contemplation; but the labours and the logic of St Paul provided the field into which he entered in his ripe old age spent at Ephesus. John, who absorbed and assimilated everything that belonged to Christ and found for everything its principle and centre in the Master of his youth—"the way, the truth, and the life"—passed through the school of Paul. With the rest, he learnt through the new apostle to see more perfectly "what is the dispensation of the mystery hidden from the ages in God."

Well persuaded is our apostle that all readers of this letter in the Asian towns, if they have not known it before, will now "perceive" his "understanding in the mystery of Christ." All ages have discerned it since. And the ages to come will measure its value better than we can do now.

FOOTNOTES:

[92] See Gal. iii. 7, v. 5; Rom. viii. 14–25; 1 Peter i. 4, 5.

CHAPTER XIII.

EARTH TEACHING HEAVEN.

"To the intent that now unto the principalities and powers in the heavenly *places* might be made known through the Church the manifold wisdom of God, according to the purpose of the ages which He formed in the Christ, *even* Jesus our Lord: in whom we have boldness and access in confidence through our faith in Him. Wherefore I ask that ye faint not at my tribulations for you, which are your glory."—Eph. iii. 10–13.

The mystery hidden since the ages began, in God who created all things: so the last paragraph concluded. The added phrase "through Jesus Christ" is a comment of the pious reader, that has been incorporated in the received text; but it is wanting in the oldest copies, and is out of place. The apostle is not concerned with the prerogatives of Christ, but with the scope of the Christian economy. He is displaying the breadth and grandeur of the dispensation of grace, the infinite range of the Divine plans and operations of which it forms the centre. Its secret was cherished in the Eternal Mind. Its foundations are laid in the very basis of the world. And the disclosure of it now being made brings new light and wisdom to the powers of the celestial realms.

"There is nothing covered," said Jesus, "which shall not be revealed, and hidden which shall not be known." The mysteries which God sets before His intelligent creatures, are promises of knowledge; they are drafts, to be honoured in due time, upon the treasures of wisdom hidden in Christ. So this great secret of the destiny of the Gentile world was "from all ages hidden, in order that now through the Church it might be made known," and by its means God's wisdom, to these sublime intelligences. This intention was a part of the "plan of the ages" formed in Christ (ver. 11). God designed by our redemption to bless higher races along with our own. The elder sons of God, those "morning stars" of creation, are schooled and instructed by what is transpiring here upon earth.

To some this will appear to be mere extravagance. They see in such expressions the marks of an unrestrained enthusiasm, of theological speculation pushed beyond its limits and unchecked by any just knowledge of the physical universe. This censure would be plausible and it might seem that the apostle had extended the mission of the gospel beyond its province, were it not for what he says in verse 11: This "purpose of the ages" God "made in *the Christ, even Jesus our Lord*." Jesus Christ links together angels and men. He draws after Him to earth the eyes of heaven. Christ's coming to this world and identification with it unite to it enduringly the great worlds above us. The scenes enacted upon this planet and the events of its religious history have sent their shock through the universe. The incarnation of the Son of God gives to human life a boundless interest and significance. It is idle to oppose to this conviction the fact of the littleness of the terrestrial globe. Spiritual and physical magnitudes are incommensurable. You cannot measure a man's soul by the size of his dwelling-house. Science teaches us that the most powerful forces may exist and operate within the narrowest space. A microscopic cell may contain the potential life of a world. If our earth is but a grain of sand to the astronomer, it has been the home of Godhead. It is the world for which God spared not to give His own Son!

Here, then, lies the centre of the apostle's thoughts in this paragraph: *God's all-comprehending purpose in Christ*. The magnitude and completeness of this plan are indicated by the fact that it embraces in its purview *the angelic powers and their enlightenment*. So understanding it, our *human faith gains confidence and courage* (vv. 12, 13).

I. The textual critics restore the definite article which later copyists had dropped before the word *Christ* in verse 11. We have already remarked the frequency of "the Christ" in this epistle.[93] Once besides this peculiar combination of the names of our Saviour occurs—in Colossians ii. 6, where Lightfoot renders it *the Christ, even Jesus the Lord*. So it should be rendered in this place. St Paul sets forth the purpose of "God who created all things." He is looking back through "the ages" during which the Divine plan was kept secret. God was all the time designing His work of mercy, pointing meanwhile the hopes of men by token and promise to the Coming One. The Messiah was the burden of those prophetic ages. That inscrutable Christ of the Old Testament, the veiled mystery of Jewish hope, stands manifested before us and challenges our faith in the glorious person of "Jesus our Lord." This singular turn of expression identifies the ideal and the real, the promise and fulfilment, the dream of Old Testament prophecy and the fact of New Testament history. For Jesus our Lord is the very Christ to whom the generations before His coming looked forward out of their twilight with wistful expectancy.

Not without meaning is He called "Jesus *our Lord*." The "principalities and powers" of the heavenly places are in our view (ver. 10). These potentates some of the Asian Christians were fain to worship. "See ye do it not," Paul seems to say. "Jesus, the Christ of God, is alone our Lord; not these. He is our Lord *and theirs* (i. 21, 22). As our Lord He commands their homage, and gives them lessons through His Church in God's deep counsels." Everything that the apostle says tends to exalt our Redeemer and to enhance our confidence in Him. His position is central and supreme, in regard alike to the ages of time and the powers of the universe. In His hand is the key to all mysteries. He is the Alpha and Omega, the beginning, middle, and end of God's ways. He is the centre of Israel, Israel of the world and the human ages; while the world of men is bound through Him to the higher spheres of being, over which He too presides.

There is a splendid intellectual courage, an incredible boldness and reach of thought in St Paul's conception of the sovereignty of Christ. Remember that He of whom these things are said, but thirty years before died a felon's death in the sight of the Jewish people. It is not *our* Lord Jesus Christ, whose name is hallowed by the lips of millions and glorified by the triumphs of centuries upon centuries past, but the Nazarene with the obscurity of His life and the cruel shame of Calvary fresh in the recollection of all men. With what immense force had the facts of His glorification wrought upon men's minds— His resurrection and ascension, the witness of His Spirit and the virtue of His gospel—for it to be possible to speak of Him thus, within a generation of His death! While "the foolishness of preaching" such a Christ and the weakness in which He was crucified were patent to all eyes, unrelieved by the influence of time and the glamour of success, how was it that the first believers raised Jesus to this limitless glory and dominion? It was through the conviction, certified by outward fact and inward experience, that "He liveth by the power of God." Thus Peter on the day of Pentecost: "By the right hand of God exalted, He hath shed forth this which ye now see and hear." The resurrection from the dead, the demonstration of the Spirit proved Jesus Christ to be that which He had claimed to be, the Saviour of men and the eternal Son of God.

The supremacy here assigned to Christ is a consequence of the exaltation described at the close of the first chapter. There we see the height, here the breadth and length of His dominion. If He is raised from the grave so high that all created powers and names are beneath His feet, we cannot wonder that the past ages were employed in preparing His way, that the basis of His throne lies in the foundation of the world.

II. The universe is one. There is a solidarity of rational and moral interests amongst all intelligences. Granting the existence of such beings as the angels of Scripture, we should expect them to be profoundly concerned in the redeeming work of Christ. They are the "watchers" and "holy ones" spoken of by the later Isaiah and Daniel, whom the Lord has "set upon the walls of Jerusalem" and who survey the affairs of nations. Such was "the angel who talked" with Zechariah in his vision, and whom the prophet overheard pleading for Jerusalem. In the Apocalypse, again, we find the angels acting as God's unseen executive. We decline to believe that these superhuman creatures are nothing more than apocalyptic machinery, that they are creations of fancy employed to give a livelier aspect to spiritual truth. "Cannot I pray to my Father, and He shall presently give me more than twelve legions of angels?" So Jesus said, in the most solemn hour of His life. And who can forget His tender words concerning the little children, whose "angels do always behold the face of my Father who is in heaven"?

The apostle Paul, who denounces "worship of the angels" in the fellow epistle to this, earnestly believed in their existence and their interest in human affairs. If he did not write the words of Hebrews i. 14, he certainly held that "they are ministering spirits sent forth to do service for the sake of them that shall inherit salvation." Most clearly is their relationship to the Church affirmed by the words of the revealing angel to the apostle John: "I am a fellow-servant with thee and with thy brethren the prophets, and with them that keep the words of this book."

Christ's service is the high school of wisdom for the universe. These princes of heaven win by their ministry to Christ and His Church a great reward. Their intelligence, however lofty its range, is finite. Their keen and burning intuition could not penetrate the mystery of God's intentions toward this world. The revelations of the latter days—the incarnation, the cross, the publication of the gospel, the outpouring of the Spirit—were full of surprises to the heavenly watchers. They sang at Bethlehem; they hid their faces and shrouded heaven in blackness at the sight of Calvary. They bent down with eager observation and searching thought "desiring to look into" the things made known to men (1 Peter i. 12),—close and sympathetic students of the Church's history. The apostle felt that there were other eyes bent upon him than those of his fellow-men, and that he was acting in a grander arena than the visible world. "We are a spectacle," he says, "*to angels* and to men." So he enjoins faithfulness on Timothy, and with Timothy on all who bear the charge of the gospel, "before God and Christ Jesus, and the elect angels." What is public opinion, what the applause or derision of the crowd, to him who lives and acts in the presence of these august spectators?

"Through the Church," we are told, the angels of God are "now" having His "manifold wisdom made known" to them. It is not from the abstract scheme of salvation, from the theory or theology of the Church that they get this education, but through the living Church herself. The Saviour's mission to earth created a problem for them, the development of which they follow with the most intense and sympathetic interest. With what solicitude they watch the conflict between good and evil and the varying progress of Christ's kingdom amongst men! Many things, doubtless, that engage our attention and fill a large space in our Church records, are of little account with them; and much that passes in obscurity, names and deeds unchronicled by fame, are written in heaven and pondered in other spheres. No brave and true blow is struck in Christ's battle, but it has the admiration of these high spectators. No advance is made in character and habit, in Christian intelligence and efficiency and the application of the gospel to human need, but they notice and approve. When the cause of the Church and the salvation of mankind go forward, when righteousness and peace triumph, the morning stars sing together and the sons of God shout for joy. The joy that there is in the presence of the angels of God over the repenting sinner, is not the joy of sympathy or pity only; it is the delight of growing wisdom, of deepening insight into the ways of God, into the heart of the Father and the love that passes knowledge.

One would suppose from what the apostle hints, that our world presents a problem unique in the kingdom of God, one which raises questions more complicated and crucial than have elsewhere arisen. The heavenly princedoms are learning through the Church "the *manifold* wisdom of God." His love, in its pure essence, those happy and godlike beings know. They have lived for ages in its unclouded light. His power and skill they may see displayed in proportions immensely grander than this puny globe of ours presents. God's justice, it may be, and the thunders of His law have issued forth in other regions clothed with a splendour of which the scenes of Sinai were but a faint emblem. It is in the combination of the manifold principles of the Divine government that the peculiarity of the human problem appears to lie. The delicate and continuous balancing of forces in God's plan of dealing with this world, the reconciliation of seeming incompatibilities, the issue found from positions of hopeless contradiction, the accord of goodness with severity, of inflexible rectitude and truth with fatherly compassion, afford to the greatest minds of heaven a spectacle and a study altogether wonderful. So amongst ourselves the child of a noble house, reared in cultured ease and shielded from moral peril, in visiting the homes of poverty in the crowded city finds a new world opened to him, that can teach him Divine lessons if he has the heart to learn. His mind is awakened, his sympathies enriched. He hears the world's true voice, "the still, sad music of humanity." He measures the heights and depths of man's nature. A host of questions are thrust upon him, whose urgency he had scarcely guessed; and wide ranges of truth are lighted up for him, which before were distant and unreal. The highest have ever to learn from the lowest in Christ's school, the seeming-wise from the simple; even the pure and good, from contact with the fallen whom they seek to save.

And "the principalities and the powers in the heavenly places" are, it seems, willing to learn from those below them. As they traced the course of human history in those "eternal times" during which the mystery lay wrapped in silence, the angel watchers were too wise to play the sceptic, too cautious to

111

criticize an unfinished plan and arraign a justice they could not yet understand. With a dignified patience they waited the uplifting of the curtain and the unravelling of the entangled plot. They looked for the coming of the Promised One. So in due time they witnessed and, for their reward, assisted in His manifestation. With the same docility these high sharers of our theological inquiries still wait to see the end of the Lord and to take their part in the dénouement of the time-drama, in the revelation of the sons of God. Let us copy their long patience. God has not made us to mock us. "What thou knowest not now," said the great Revealer, the Master of all mysteries, to His disciple, "thou shalt know hereafter."

These wise elder brothers of ours, rich in the lore of eternity, foresee the things to come as we cannot do. They are far above the smoke and dust of the earthly conflict. The doubts that shake the strongest souls amongst us, the cries of the hour which confuse and deceive us, do not trouble them. They behold us in our weakness, our fears and our divisions; but they also look on Him who "sits expecting till His enemies are made His footstool." They see how calmly He sits, how patiently expectant, while the sound of clashing arms and the rage and tumult of the peoples go up from the earth. They mark the steadiness with which through century after century, in spite of refluent waves, the tide of mercy rises, and still rises on the shores of earth. Thrones, systems, civilizations have gone down; one after another of the powers that strove to crush or to corrupt Christ's Church has disappeared; and still the name of Jesus lives and spreads. It has traversed every continent and sea; it stands at the head of the living and moving forces of the world. Those who come nearest to the angelic point of view, and judge of the progress of things not by the froth upon the surface but by the trend of the deeper currents, are the most confident for the future of our race. The kingdom of Satan will not fall without a struggle—a last struggle, perhaps more furious than any in the past—but it is doomed, and waning to its end. So far has the kingdom of Christ advanced, so mightily does the word of God grow and prevail in the earth, that faith may well assure itself of the promised triumph. Soon we shall shout: "Alleluia! The Lord God Omnipotent reigneth!"

III. Suddenly, according to his wont, the apostle drops down from the heights of contemplation to the level of ordinary fact. He descends in verse 12 from the thought of the eternal purpose and the education of the angels to the struggling Church. The assurance of its life in the Spirit corresponds to the grandeur of that Divine order to which it belongs. "In whom," he says—in this Christ, the revealed mystery of ages past, the Teacher of angels and archangels—"we have our freedom and confident access to God through faith in Him."

If it be "Jesus our Lord" to whom these attributes belong, and He is not ashamed of us, well may we draw near with *confidence* to the Father, unashamed in the presence of His holy angels. We have no need to be abashed, if we approach the Divine Majesty with a true faith in Christ. His name gives the sinner access to the holiest place. The cherubim sheathe their swords of flame. The heavenly warders at this passport open the golden gates. We "come unto Mount Sion, the city of the living God, and to an innumerable company of angels." Not one of these mightinesses and ancient peers of heaven, not Gabriel or Michael himself, would wish or dare to bar our entrance.

"We *have* boldness and access," says the apostle, as in chapter i. 7: "We have redemption in His blood." He insists upon the conscious fact. This freedom of approach to God, this sonship of faith, is no hope or dream of what may be; it is a present reality, a filial cry heard in a multitude both of Gentile and Jewish hearts (comp. ii. 18).

This sentence exhibits the richness of synonyms characteristic of the epistle. There is *boldness* and *access*, *confidence* as well as *faith*. The three former terms Bengel nicely distinguishes: "libertatem *oris* in orando," and "admissionem in fiducia *in re*, et *corde*"—freedom of *speech* (in prayer), of *status*, and of *feeling*. The second word (as in chapter ii. 18 and Romans v. 2) appears to be active rather than passive in its force, denoting *admittance* rather than *access*. So that while the former of the parallel terms (*boldness*) describes the liberty with which the new-born Church of the redeemed address themselves to God the Father and the unchecked freedom of their petitions, the latter (*admittance*) takes us back to the act of Christ by which He introduced us to the Father's presence and gave us the place of sons in the house. Being thus admitted, we may come with confidence of heart, though we be less than the least of saints. Accepted in the Beloved, we are within our right if we say to the Father:—

"Yet in Thy Son divinely great,
We claim Thy providential care.
Boldly we stand before Thy seat;
Our Advocate hath placed us there!"

"Wherefore," concludes the imprisoned apostle, "I beg you not to lose heart at my afflictions for you." Assuredly Paul did not pray that *he* should not lose heart, as some interpret his meaning. But he knew how his friends were fretting and wearying over his long captivity. Hence he writes to the Philippians: "I would have you know that the things which have happened to me have turned out rather to the furtherance of the gospel." Hence, too, he assures the Colossians earnestly of his joy in suffering for their sake (ch. i. 24).

The Church was fearful for Paul's life and distressed by his prolonged sufferings. It missed his cheering presence and the inspiration of his voice. But if the Church is so dear to God as the pages of this letter show, and grounded in His eternal purposes, then let all friends of Christ take courage. The ark freighted with such fortunes cannot sink. St Paul is a martyr for Christ, and for Gentile Christendom! Every stroke that falls upon him, every day added to the months of his imprisonment helps to show the worth of the cause he has espoused and gives to it increased lustre: "my afflictions for you, which are your glory."

Those that love him should *boast* rather than grieve over his afflictions. "We make our boast in you amongst the Churches of God," he wrote to the distressed Thessalonians (2 Ep. i. 4), "for your patience and faith in all your persecutions and afflictions"; so he would have the Churches think of him. When good men suffer in a good cause, it is not matter for pity and dread, but rather for a holy pride.

FOOTNOTES:

[93] See note on p. 47; also pp. 83, 189.

PRAYER AND PRAISE.

CHAPTER iii. 14–21.

Τὸ ὑπερέχον τῆς γνώσεως Χριστοῦ Ἰησοῦ τοῦ Κυρίου μου.—PHIL. iii. 8.

CHAPTER XIV.

THE COMPREHENSION OF CHRIST.

"For this cause I bow my knees unto the Father, from whom every family in heaven and upon earth is named, that He would grant you, according to the riches of His glory, that ye may be strengthened with power through His Spirit in the inward man; that the Christ may dwell in your hearts through faith; to the end that ye, being rooted and grounded in love, may be strong to comprehend with all the saints what is the breadth and length and height and depth."—EPH. iii. 14–18.

In verse 14 the prayer is resumed which the apostle was about to offer at the beginning of the chapter, when the current of his thoughts carried him away. The supplication is offered "for this cause" (vv. 1, 14),—it arises out of the teaching of the preceding pages. Thinking of all that God has wrought in the Christ, and has accomplished by means of His gospel in multitudes of Gentiles as well as Jews, reconciling them to Himself in one body and forming them together into a temple for His Spirit, the apostle bows his knees before God on their behalf. So much he had in mind, when at the end of the second chapter he was in act to pray for the Asian Christians that they might be enabled to enter into this far-reaching purpose. Other aspects of the great design of God rose upon the writer's mind before his prayer could find expression. He has told us of his own part in disclosing it to the world, and of the interest it excites amongst the dwellers in heavenly places,—thoughts full of comfort for the Gentile believers troubled by his imprisonment and continued sufferings. These further reflections add new meaning to the "For this cause" repeated from verse 1.

The prayer which he offers here is no less remarkable and unique in his epistles than the act of praise in chapter i. Addressing himself to God as the Father of angels and of men, the apostle asks that He will endow the readers in a manner corresponding to *the wealth of His glory*—in other words, that the gifts He bestows may be worthy of the universal Father, worthy of the august character in which God has now revealed Himself to mankind. According to this measure, St Paul beseeches for the Church, in the first instance, two gifts, which after all are one,—viz., *the inward strength of the Holy Spirit* (ver. 16), and *the permanent indwelling of Christ* (ver. 17). These gifts he asks on his readers' behalf with a view to their gaining two further blessings, which are also one,—viz., *the power to understand the Divine plan* (ver. 18) as it has been expounded in this letter, and so *to know the love of Christ* (ver. 19). Still, beyond these there rises in the distance a further end for man and the Church: *the reception of the entire fulness of God.* Human desire and thought thus reach their limit; they grasp at the infinite.

In this Chapter we will strive to follow the apostle's prayer to the end of the eighteenth verse, where it arrives at its chief aim and touches the main thought of the epistle, expressing the desire that all believers may have power to realize the full scope of the salvation of Christ in which they participate.

Let us pause for a moment to join in St Paul's invocation: "I bow my knees to the Father, of whom [not *the whole family*, but] *every family* in heaven and upon earth is named." The point of St Paul's original phrase is somewhat lost in translation. The Greek word for *family* (*patria*) is based on that for *father* (*pater*). A distinguished father anciently gave his name to his descendants; and this paternal name became the bond of family or tribal union, and the title which ennobled the race. So we have "the sons of Israel," the "sons of Aaron" or "of Korah"; and in Greek history, the Atridæ, the Alcmæonidæ, who form a family of many kindred households—a *clan*, or *gens*, designated by their ancestral head. Thus Joseph (in Luke ii. 4) is described as "being of the house and family [*patria*] of David"; and Jesus is "the Son of David." Now Scripture speaks also of *sons of God*; and these of two chief orders. There are those "in heaven," who form a race distinct from ourselves in origin— divided, it may be, amongst themselves into various orders and dwelling in their several homes in the heavenly places.

Of these are "the sons of God" whom the Book of Job pictures appearing in the Divine court and forming a "family in heaven." When Christ promises (Luke xx. 36) that His disciples in their immortal state will be "equal to the angels," because they are "sons of God," it is implied that the angels are already and by birthright sons of God. Hence in Hebrews xii. 22, 23 the angels are described as "the festal gathering and assembly of *the firstborn* enrolled in heaven." We, the sons of Adam, with our many tribes and kindreds, through Jesus Christ our Elder Brother constitute a new family of God. God becomes our Name-father, and permits us also to call ourselves His sons through faith. Thus the Church of believers in the Son of God constitutes the "family on earth named" from the same Father who gave His name to the holy angels, our wise and strong and brilliant elder brothers. They and we are alike God's offspring. Heaven and earth are kindred spheres.

This passage gives to God's Fatherhood the same extension that chapter i. 21 has given to Christ's Lordship. Every order of creaturely intelligence acknowledges God for the Author of its being, and bows to Christ as its sovereign Lord. In God's name of Father the entire wealth of love that streams forth from Him through endless ages and unmeasured worlds is hidden; and in the name of sons of God there is contained the blessedness of all creatures that can bear His image.

I. What, therefore, shall the universal Father be asked to give to His needy children upon earth? They have newly learnt His name; they are barely recovered from the malady of their sin, fearful of trial, weak to meet temptation. *Strength* is their first necessity: "I bow my knees to the Father of heaven and earth, praying that He may grant you, according to the riches of His glory, to be strengthened by the entering of the Spirit into your inward man." The apostle asked them in verse 13, in view of the greatness of his own calling, to be of good courage on his account; now he entreats God so to reveal to them His glory and to pour into their hearts His Spirit, that no weakness and fear may remain in them. The *strengthening* of which he speaks is the opposite of the *faintness of heart*, the failure of courage deprecated in verse 13. Using the same word, the apostle bids the Corinthians "Quit themselves like men, *be strong*" (1 Ep. xvi. 13). He desires for the Asian believers a manful heart, the strength that meets battle and danger without quailing.

The source of this strength is not in ourselves. We are to be "strengthened *with* [or *by*] *power*,"—by "the power" of God "working in us" (ver. 20), the very same "power, exceeding great," that raised Jesus our Lord from the dead (i. 19). This superhuman might of God operating in men is always referred to the Holy Spirit: "by power made strong," he says, "*through the Spirit*." Nothing is more familiar in Scripture than the conception of the indwelling Spirit of God as the source of moral strength. The special power that belongs to the gospel Christ ascribes altogether to this cause. "Ye shall receive power," He said to His disciples, "after that the Holy Spirit is come upon you." Hence is derived the vigour of a strong faith, the valour of the good soldier of Christ Jesus, the courage of the martyrs, the cheerful and indomitable patience of multitudes of obscure sufferers for righteousness' sake. There is a great truth expressed when we describe a brave and enterprising man as a *man of spirit*. All high and commanding qualities of soul come from this invisible source. They are inspirations. In the human will, with its *vis vivida*, its elasticity and buoyancy, its steadfastness and resolved purpose, is the highest type of force and the image of the almighty Will. When that will is animated and filled with "the Spirit," the man so possessed is the embodiment of an inconceivable power. Firm principle, hope and constancy, self-mastery, superiority to pleasure and pain,—all the elements of a noble courage are proper to the man of the Spirit. Such power is not neutralized by our infirmities; it asserts itself under their limiting conditions and makes them its contributories. "My grace is sufficient for thee," said Christ to His disabled servant; "for power is perfected in weakness." In privation and loneliness, in old age and bodily decay, the strength of God in the human spirit shines with its purest lustre. Never did St Paul rise to such a height of moral ascendency as at the time when he was "smitten down" and all but destroyed by persecution and affliction. "That the excellency of the power," he says, "may be of God, and not from ourselves" (2 Cor. iv. 7–11).

The apostle points to "the inner man" as the seat of this invigoration, thinking perhaps of its secrecy. While the world buffets and dismays the Christian, new vigour and joy are infused into his soul. The surface waters and summer brooks of comfort fail; but there opens in the heart a spring fed by the river of life proceeding from the throne of God. Beneath the toil-worn frame, the mean attire and friendless condition of the prisoner Paul—a mark for the world's scorn—there lives a strength of thought and will mightier than the empire of the Cæsars, a power of the Spirit that is to dominate the centuries to come. Of this omnipotent power dwelling in the Church of God, the apostle prays that every one of his readers may partake.

II. Parallel to the first petition, and in substance identical with it, is the second: "that the Christ may make His dwelling through faith in your hearts." Such, it seems to us, is the relation of verses 16 and 17. Christ's residence in the heart is to be viewed neither as the result, nor the antecedent of the strength given by the Spirit to the inward man: the two are simultaneous; they are the same things seen in a varying light.

We observe in this prayer the same vein of Trinitarian thought which marks the doxology of chapter i., and other leading passages in this epistle.[94] The Father, the Spirit, and the Christ are unitedly the object of the apostle's devout supplication.

As in the previous clause, the verb of verse 17 bears emphasis and conveys the point of St Paul's entreaty; he asks that "the Christ may *take up His abode*,—may *settle* in your hearts." The word signifies to *set up one's house* or *make one's home* in a place, by way of contrast with a temporary and uncertain sojourn (comp. ii. 19). The same verb in Colossians ii. 9 asserts that in Christ "*dwells* all the fulness of the Godhead"; and in Colossians i. 19 it declares, used in the same tense as here, how it was God's "pleasure that all the fulness should *make its dwelling* in Him" now raised from the dead, who had emptied and humbled Himself to fulfil the purpose of the Father's love. So it is desired that Christ should take His seat within us. He is never again to stand at the door and knock, nor to have a doubtful and disputed footing in the house. Let the Master come in, and claim His own. Let Him become the heart's fixed tenant and full occupier. Let Him, if He will thus condescend, make Himself at home within us and there rest in His love. For He promised: "If any man love me, my Father will love him; and we will come unto him, and make our abode with him."

119

And "*the* Christ," not Christ alone. Why does the apostle say this? There is a reason for the definite article, as we have found elsewhere.[95] The apostle is asking for his Asian brethren something beyond that possession of Christ which belongs to every true Christian,—more even than the permanence and certainty of this indwelling indicated by the verb. "The Christ" is Christ in the significance of His *name*. It is Christ not only possessed, but understood,—Christ realized in the import of His work, in the light of His relationship to the Father and the Spirit, and to men. It is the Christ of the Church and the ages—known and accepted for all this—that St Paul would fain have dwelling in the heart of each of his Gentile disciples. He is endeavouring to raise them to an adequate comprehension of the greatness of the Redeemer's person and offices; he longs to have their minds possessed by his own views of Christ Jesus the Lord.

The heart, in the language of the Bible, never denotes the emotional nature by itself. The antithesis of "heart and head," the divorce of feeling and understanding in our modern speech is foreign to Scripture. The heart is our interior, conscious self—thought, feeling, will in their personal unity. It needs the whole Christ to fill and rule the whole heart,—a Christ who is the Lord of the intellect, the Light of the reason, no less than the Master of the feelings and desires.

The difference in significance between "Christ" or "Christ Jesus" and "the Christ" in such a sentence as this, is not unlike the difference between "Queen Victoria" and "the Queen." The latter phrase brings Her Majesty before us in the grandeur and splendour of her Queenship. We think of her vast dominion, of her line of royal and famous ancestry, of her beneficent and memorable reign. So, to know the Christ is to apprehend Him in the height of His Godhead, in the breadth of His humanity, in the plenitude of His nature and His powers. And this is the object to which the teaching and the prayers of St Paul for the Churches at the present time are directed. Understanding in this larger sense the indwelling of the Christ for which he prays, we see how naturally his supplication expands into the "height and depth" of the ensuing verse.

But however large the mental conception of Christ that St Paul desires to impart to us, it is to be grasped "through faith." All real understanding and appropriation of Christ, the simplest and the most advanced, come by this channel,—through the faith of the heart in which knowledge, will and feeling blend in that one act of trustful apprehension of the truth concerning Jesus Christ by which the soul commits itself to Him.

How much is contained in this petition of the apostle that we need to ask for ourselves, Christ Jesus dwells now as then in the hearts of all who love Him.

But how little do we know our heavenly Guest! how poor a Christ is ours, compared to the Christ of Paul's experience! how slight and empty a word is His name to multitudes of those who bear it! If men have once attained a sense of His salvation, and are satisfied of their interest in His atonement and their right to hope for eternal life through Him, their minds are at rest. They have accepted Christ and received what He has to give them; they turn their attention to other things. They do not love Christ enough to study Him. They have other mental interests,—scientific, literary, political or industrial; but the knowledge of Christ has no intellectual attraction for them. With St Paul's passionate ardour, the ceaseless craving of his mind to "know Him," these complacent believers have no sympathy whatever. This, they think, belongs only to a few, to men of metaphysical bias or of religious genius like the great apostle. Theology is regarded as a subject for specialists. The laity, with a lamentable and disastrous neglect, leave the study of Christian doctrine to the ministry. The Christ cannot take His due place in His people's heart, He will not reveal to them the wealth of His glory, while they know so little and care to know so little of Him. How many can be found, outside the ranks of the ordained, that make a sacrifice of other favourite pursuits to meditate on Christ? what prosperous merchant, what active man of affairs is there who will spare an hour each day from his other gains "for the excellency of the knowledge of Christ Jesus my Lord"?—"If at the present time the religious life of the Church is languid, and if in its enterprises there is little of audacity and vehemence, a partial explanation is to be found in that decline of intellectual interest in the contents of the Christian Faith which has characterized the last hundred or hundred and fifty years of our history."[96]

It is a knowledge that when pursued grows upon the mind without limit. St Paul, who knew so much, for that reason felt that all he had attained was but in the bud and beginning. "The Christ" is a subject infinite as nature, large and wide as history. With our enlarged apprehension of Him, the heart enlarges in capacity and moral power. Not unfrequently, the study of Christ in Scripture and experience gives to unlettered men, to men whose mind before their conversion was dull and uninformed, an intellectual quality, a power of discernment and apprehension that trained scholars might envy. By such thoughtful, constant fellowship with Him the vigour of spirit and courage in affliction are sustained, that the apostle first asked from God on behalf of his anxious Gentile friends.

III. The prayers now offered might suffice, if St Paul were concerned only for the individual needs of those to whom he writes and their personal advancement in the new life. But it is otherwise. *The Church* fills his mind. Its lofty claims at every turn he has pressed on our attention. This is God's holy temple and the habitation of His Spirit; it is the body in which Christ dwells, the bride that He has chosen. The Church is the object that draws the eyes of heaven; through it the angelic powers are learning undreamed-of lessons of God's wisdom. Round this centre the apostle's intercession must needs revolve. When he asks for his readers added strength of heart and a richer fellowship with Christ, it is in order that they may be the better able to enter into the Church's life and to apprehend God's great designs for mankind.

This object so much absorbs the writer's thoughts and has been so constantly in view from the outset, that it does not occur to him, in verse 18, to say precisely *what* that is whose "breadth and length and height and depth" the readers are to measure. The vast building stands before us and needs not to be named; we have only not to look away from it, not to forget what we have been reading all this time. It is *God's plan for the world in Christ*; it is the purpose of the ages realized in the building of His Church. This conception was so impressive to the original readers and has held their attention so closely since the apostle unfolded it in the course of the second chapter, that they would have no difficulty in supplying the ellipsis which has given so much trouble to the commentators since.

If we are asked to interpret the four several magnitudes that are assigned to this building of God, we may say with Hofmann[97]: "It stretches *wide* over all the world of the nations, east and west. In its *length*, it reaches through all time unto the end of things. In *depth*, it penetrates to the region where the faithful sleep in death [comp. iv. 9]. And it rises to heaven's *height*, where Christ lives." In the like strain Bernardine à Piconio, most genial and spiritual of Romanist interpreters: "*Wide* as the furthest limits of the inhabited world, *long* as the ages of eternity through which God's love to His people will endure, *deep* as the abyss of misery and ruin from which He has raised us, *high* as the throne of Christ in the heavens where He has placed us." Such is the commonwealth to which we belong, such the dimensions of this city of God built on the foundation of the apostles,—"that lieth four-square."

Do we not need to be *strong*—to "gain full strength," as the apostle prays, in order to grasp in its substance and import this immense revelation and to handle it with practical effect? Narrowness is feebleness. The greatness of the Church, as God designed it, matches the greatness of the Christ Himself. It needs a firm spiritual faith, a far-seeing intelligence, and a charity broad as the love of Christ to comprehend this mystery. From many believing eyes it is still hidden. Alas for our cold hearts, our weak and partial judgements! alas for the materialism that infects our Church theories, and that limits God's free grace and the sovereign action of His Spirit to visible channels and ministrations "wrought by hand." Those who call themselves Churchmen and Catholics contradict the titles they boast when they bar out their loyal

Christian brethren from the covenant rights of faith, when they deny churchly standing to communities with a love to Christ as warm and fruitful in good works, a gospel as pure and saving, a discipline at least as faithful as their own. Who are we that we dare to forbid those who are doing mighty works in the name of Christ, because they follow not with us? When we are fain to pull down every building of God that does not square with our own ecclesiastical plans, we do not apprehend "what is the breadth!"

We draw close about us the walls of Christ's wide house, as if to confine Him in our single chamber. We call our particular communion "the Church," and the rest "the sects"; and disfranchise, so far as our word and judgement go, a multitude of Christ's freemen and God's elect, our fellow-citizens in the New Jerusalem—saints, some of them, whose feet we well might deem ourselves unworthy to wash. A Church theory that leads to such results as these, that condemns Nonconformists to be strangers in the House of God, is self-condemned. It will perish of its own chillness and formalism. Happily, many of those who hold the doctrine of exclusive Roman or Anglican, or Baptist or Presbyterian legitimacy, are in feeling and practice more catholic than in their creed.

"With *all* the saints" the Asian Christians are called to enter into St Paul's wider view of God's work in the world. For this is a collective idea, to be shared by many minds and that should sway all Christian hearts at once. It is the collective aim of Christianity that St Paul wants his readers to understand, its mission to save humanity and to reconstruct the world for a temple of God. This is a calling for *all the saints*; but only for *saints*,—for men devoted to God and renewed by His Spirit. It was "revealed to His *holy* apostles and prophets" (ver. 5); and it needs men of the same quality for its bearers and interpreters.

But the first condition for this largeness of sympathy and aim is that stated at the beginning of the verse, thrown forward there with an emphasis that almost does violence to grammar: "in love being fast rooted and grounded." Where Christ dwells abidingly in the heart, love enters with Him and becomes the ground of our nature, the basis on which our thought and action rest, the soil in which our purposes grow. *Love* is the mark of the true Broad Churchman in all Churches, the man to whom Christ is all things and in all, and who, wherever he sees a Christlike man, loves him and counts him a brother.

When such love to Christ fills all our hearts and penetrates to their depths, we shall have strength to shake off our prejudices, strength to master our intellectual difficulties and limitations. We shall have the courage to adopt Christ's simple rule of fellowship: "Whosoever shall do the will of my Father who is in heaven, he is my brother, and sister, and mother."

FOOTNOTES:

[94] See ch. i. 17, ii. 18, 22, and especially ch. iv. 4–6.

[95] See pp. 47, 83, 169.

[96] *Lectures on Ephesians*, pp. 235–8. No one who has read Dr. R. W. Dale's noble Lectures on this epistle, can write upon the same subject without being deeply in his debt.

[97] *Der Brief Pauli an die Epheser*, p. 138. Hofmann is one of those writers from whom one constantly learns, although one must as often differ from him as agree with him.

CHAPTER XV.

KNOWING THE UNKNOWABLE.

"[I pray] that ye, being rooted and grounded in love, may be strong to comprehend with all
the saints what is the breadth and length and height and depth, and to know the love of Christ
which passeth knowledge, that ye may be filled unto all the fulness of God."—EPH. iii. 17–
19.

We were compelled to pause before reaching the end of the apostle's
comprehensive prayer. But we must not let slip the thread of its connexion.
Verse 19 is the necessary sequel and counterpart of verse 18. The catholic
love which embraces "all the saints" and "comprehends" in its wide
dimensions the extent of the Redeemer's kingdom, admits us to a deeper
knowledge of Christ's own love. The breadth and length, the height and depth
of the work of Christ in men and the ages give us a worthier conception of the
love that inspired and sustains it. "In the Church" at once "and in Christ
Jesus" God's glory is revealed. Our Church views react upon our views of
Christ and our sense of His love. Bigotry and exclusiveness towards His
brethren chill the heart towards Himself. Our sectarianism stints and narrows
our apprehensions of the Divine grace.

I. St Paul prays that we may "*know* [not *comprehend*] the love of Christ"; for
it "passes knowledge." Amongst the Greek words denoting mental activity,
that here employed signifies knowledge in the acquisition rather than
possession—*getting to know*. Hence it is rightly, and often used of things
Divine that "we know in part," our knowledge of which falls short of the
reality while it is growing up to it. Thus understood, the contradiction of the
apostle's wish disappears. We know the unknowable, just as we "clearly see
the invisible things of God" (Rom. i. 20). The idea is conveyed of an object
that invites our observation and pursuit, but which at every step outreaches
apprehension, each discovery revealing depths within it unperceived before.
Such was the knowledge of Christ to the soul of St Paul. To the Philippians
the aged apostle writes: "I do not reckon myself to have apprehended Him. I
am in pursuit! I forget the past; I press on eagerly to the goal. I have but one
object in view and sacrifice everything for it,—that I may *win Christ*!"

In all the mystery of Christ, there is nothing more wonderful and past finding
out than His love. For nigh thirty years Paul has been living in daily
fellowship with the love of Christ, his heart full of it and all the powers of his
mind bent upon its comprehension: he cannot understand it yet! At this

moment it amazes him more than ever.

Great as the Christian community is, and large as the place and part assigned to it by this epistle, that is still finite and a creation of time. The apostle's doctrine of the Church is not beyond the comprehension of a mind sufficiently loving and enlightened. But though we had followed him so far and had well and truly apprehended the mystery he has revealed to us, the love of Christ is still beyond us. Our principles of judgement and standards of comparison fail us when applied to this subject. Human love has in many instances displayed heroic qualities; it can rise to a divine height of purity and tenderness; but its noblest sacrifices will not bear to be put by the side of the cross of Christ. No picture of that love but shows poor and dull compared with the reality; no eloquence lavished upon it but lowers the theme. Our logical framework of doctrine fails to enclose and hold it; the love of Christ defies analysis and escapes from all our definitions. Those who know the world best, who have ranged through history and philosophy and the life of living men and have measured most generously the possibilities of human nature, are filled with a wondering reverence when they come to know the love of Christ. "Never man spake like this man," said one; but verily never man loved like Jesus Christ. He expects to be loved more than father or mother; for His love surpasses theirs. We cannot describe His love, nor delineate its features as Paul saw them when he wrote these lines. Go to the Gospels, and behold it as it lived and wrought for men. Stand and watch at the cross. Then if the eyes of your heart are open, you will see the great sight—the love that passeth knowledge.

When, turning from Christ Himself in His own person and presence, before whom praise is speechless, we contemplate the manifestations of His love to mankind; when we consider that its fountain lies in the bosom of the Eternal; when we trace its footsteps prepared from the world's foundation, and perceive it choosing a people for its own and making its promises and raising up its heralds and forerunners; when at last it can hide and refrain itself no longer, but comes forth incarnate with lowly heart to take our infirmities and carry our diseases—yea, to put away our sin by the sacrifice of itself; when we behold that same Love which the hands of men had slain, setting up its cross for the sign of its covenant of peace with mankind, and enthroned in the majesty of heaven waiting even as a bridegroom joyously for the time when its ransomed shall be brought home, redeemed from iniquity and gathered unto itself from all the kindreds of the earth; and when we see how this mystery of love, in its sufferings and glories and its deep-laid plans for all the creatures, engages the ardent study and sympathy of the heavenly principalities,—in view of these things, who can but feel himself unworthy to know the love of Christ or to speak one word on its behalf? Are we not ready to say like Peter, "Depart from me, for I am a sinful man, O Lord"?

This is a revelation that searches every man's soul who looks into it. What is there so confounding to our reason and our human self-complacency as the discovery: "He loved me; He gave Himself up for me"—that He should do it, and should *need* to do it! It was this that went to Saul's heart, that gave the mortal blow to the Jewish pride in him, strong as it was with the growth of centuries. The bearer of this grace and the ambassador of Christ's love to the Gentiles, he feels himself to be "less than the least of all the saints." We carry in our hands to show to men a heavenly light, which throws our own unloveliness into dark relief.

II. The *love of Christ* connects together, in the apostle's thoughts, *the greatness of the Church* and *the fulness of God*. The two former conceptions —Christ's love and the Church's greatness—go together in our minds; knowing them, we are led onwards to the realization of the last.

The "fulness [*pleroma*] of God," and the "filling" (or "completing") of believers in Christ are ideas characteristic of this group of epistles. The first of these expressions we have discussed already in its connexion with Christ, in chapter i. 23; we shall meet with it again as "the fulness of Christ" in chapter iv. 13. The phrase before us is, in substance, identical with that of the latter text. Christ contains the Divine plenitude; He embodies it in His person, and conveys it to the world by His redemption. St Paul desires for the Asian Christians that they may receive it; it is the ultimate mark of his prayer. He wishes them to gain the total sum of all that God communicates to men. He would have them "filled"—their nature made complete both in its individual and social relations, their powers of mind and heart brought into full exercise, their spiritual capacities developed and replenished—"filled unto all the plenitude of God."

This is no humanistic or humanitarian ideal. The mark of Christian completeness is on a different and higher plane than any that is set up by culture. The ideal Christian is a greater man than the ideal citizen or artist or philosopher: he may include within himself any or all of these characters, but he transcends them. He may conform to none of these types, and yet be a perfect man in Christ Jesus. Our race cannot rest in any perfection that stops short of "the fulness of God." When we have received all that God has to give in Christ, when the community of men is once more a family of God and the Father's will is done on earth as in heaven, then and not before will our life be complete. That is the goal of humanity; and the civilization that does not lead to it is a wandering from the way. "You are complete in Christ," says the apostle. The progress of the ages since confirms the saying.

The apostle prays that his readers may know the love of Christ. This is a part of the Divine plenitude; nor is there anything in it deeper. But there is more to know. When he asks for "*all* the fulness," he thinks of other elements of revelation in which we are to participate. God's *wisdom*, His *truth*, His *righteousness*, along with His *love* in its manifold forms,—all the qualities that, in one word, go to make up His *holiness*, are communicable and belong to the image stamped by the Holy Spirit on the nature of God's children. "Ye shall be holy, for I am holy" is God's standing command to His sons. So Jesus bids His disciples, "Be perfect, as your Father in heaven is perfect." St Paul's prayer "is but another way of expressing the continuous aspiration and effort after holiness which is enjoined in our Lord's precept" (Lightfoot).

While the holiness of God gathers up into one stream of white radiance the revelation of His character, "the fulness of God" spreads it abroad in its many-coloured richness and variety. The term accords with the affluence of thought that marks this supplication. The might of the Spirit that strengthens weak human hearts, the greatness of the Christ who is the guest of our faith, His wide-spreading kingdom and the vast interests it embraces and His own love surpassing all,—these objects of the soul's desire issue from the fulness of God; and they lead us in pursuing them, like streams pouring into the ocean, back to the eternal Godhead. The mediatorial kingdom has its end; Christ, when He has "put down all rule and authority," will at last "yield it up to His God and Father"; and "the Son Himself will be subjected to Him that put all things under Him, that God may be all in all" (1 Cor. xv. 24–28). This is the crown of the Redeemer's mission, the end which His love to the Father seeks. But when that end is reached, and the soul with immediate vision beholds the Father's glory, the Plenitude will be still new and unexhausted; the soul will then begin its deepest lessons in the knowledge of God which is life eternal.

St Paul is conscious of the extreme boldness of the prayer he has just uttered. But he protests that, instead of going beyond God's purposes, it falls short of them. This assurance rises, in verses 20 and 21, into a rapture of praise. It is a cry of exultation, a true song of triumph, that breaks from the apostle's lips:—

> "Now unto Him that is able to do above all things,—
> Yea, far exceedingly beyond what we ask or think,—
>   According to the power that worketh in us:
> To Him be glory in the Church and in Christ Jesus,
> Unto all generations of the age of the ages.—Amen!"
>   (vv. 20, 21).

Praise soars higher than prayer. When St Paul has reached in supplication the summit of his desires, he sees the plenitude of God's gifts still by a whole heaven outreaching him. But it is only from these mountain-tops hardly won in the exercise of prayer, in their still air and tranquil light, that the boundless realms of promise are visible. God's giving surpasses immeasurably our thought and asking; but there must be the asking and the thinking for it to surpass. He puts always more into our hand and better things than we expected—when the expectant hand is reached out to Him.

Man's desires will never overtake God's bounty. Hearing the prayer just offered, unbelief will say: "You have asked too much. It is preposterous to expect that raw Gentile converts, scarcely raised above their heathen debasement, should enter into these exalted notions of yours about Christ and the Church and should be filled with the fulness of God! Prayer must be rational and within the bounds of possibility, offered 'with the understanding' as well as 'with the spirit,' or it becomes mere extravagance."—The apostle gives a twofold answer to this kind of scepticism. He appeals to the Divine omnipotence. "With men," you say, "this is impossible." Humanly speaking, St Paul's Gentile disciples were incapable of any high spiritual culture; they were unpromising material, with "not many wise or many noble" amongst them, some of them before their conversion stained with infamous vices. Who is to make saints and godlike men out of such human refuse as this! But "with God," as Jesus said, "all things are possible." *Fæx urbis, lux orbis*: "the scum of the city is made the light of the world!" The force at work upon the minds of these degraded pagans—slaves, thieves, prostitutes, as some of them had been—is the love of Christ; it is the power of the Holy Ghost, the might of the strength which raises the dead to life eternal.

Let us therefore praise Him "who is able to do beyond all things"—beyond the best that His best servants have wished and striven for. Had men ever asked or thought of such a gift to the world as Jesus Christ? Had the prophets foreseen one tenth part of His greatness? In their boldest dreams did the disciples anticipate the wonders of the day of Pentecost and of the later miracles of grace accomplished by their preaching? How far exceedingly had these things already surpassed the utmost that the Church asked or thought.

St Paul's reliance is not upon the "ability" alone, upon the abstract omnipotence of God. The force upon which he counts is lodged in the Church, and is in visible and constant operation. "According to the power *that worketh in us*" he expects these vast results to be achieved. This power is the same as that he invoked in verse 16,—the might of the Spirit of God in the inward man. It is the spring of courage and joy, the source of religious intelligence (i. 17, 18) and personal holiness, the very power that raised the dead body of Jesus to life, as it will raise hereafter all the holy dead to share His immortality (Rom. viii. 11). St Paul was conscious at this time in a remarkable degree of the supernatural energy working within his own mind. It is of this that he speaks to the Colossians, in language very similar to that of our text, when he says: "I toil hard, striving according to His energy that works in me in power." As he labours for the Church in writing that epistle, he is sensible of another Power acting within his spirit and distinguished from it by his consciousness, which tasks his faculties to the utmost to follow its dictates and express its meaning.

The presence of this mysterious power of the Spirit St Paul constantly felt when engaged in prayer,—"The Spirit helpeth our infirmities"; He "makes intercession for us with groanings that cannot be uttered" (Rom. viii. 26, 27). On this point the experience of earnest Christian believers in all ages confirms that of St Paul. The sublime prayer to which he has just given utterance, is not his own. There is more in it than the mere Paul, a weak man, would have dared to ask or think. He who inspires the prayer will fulfil it. The Searcher of hearts knows better than the man who conceived it, infinitely better than we who are trying for our own help to interpret it, all that this intercession means. God will hear the pleading of His Spirit. The Power that prompts our prayers, and the Power that grants their answer are the same. The former is limited in its action by human infirmity; the latter knows no limit. Its only measure is the fulness of God. To Him who works in us all good desires, and works far beyond us to bring our good desires to good effect, be the glory of all for ever!

In such measure, then, shall glory be to God "in the Church and in Christ Jesus." We see how the Church takes up the foreground of Paul's horizon. This epistle has taught us that God desires far more than our individual salvation, however complete that might be. Christ came not to save men only, but mankind. It is "in the Church" that God's consummate glory will be seen. No man in his fragmentary self-hood, no number of men in their separate capacity can conceivably attain "unto the fulness of God." It will need all humanity for that,—to reflect the full-orbed splendour of Divine revelation. Isolated and divided from each other, we render to God a dimmed and partial glory. "With one accord, with one mouth" we are called to "glorify the God and Father of our Lord Jesus Christ." Wherefore the apostle bids us "receive one another, as Christ also received us, to the glory of God" (Rom. xv. 6, 7).

The Church, being the creation of God's love in Christ and the receptacle of His communicative fulness, is the vessel formed for His praise. Her worship is a daily tribute to the Divine majesty and bounty. The life of her people in the world, her witness for Christ and warfare against sin, her ceaseless ministries to human sorrow and need proclaim the Divine goodness, righteousness and truth. From the heavenly places where she dwells with Christ, she reflects the light of God's glory and makes it shine into the depths of evil at her feet. It was the Church's voice that St John heard in heaven as "the voice of a great multitude, and as the voice of many waters, and as the voice of mighty thunders, saying, Hallelujah: for the Lord our God, the Almighty reigneth!" Each soul new-born into the fellowship of faith adds another note to make up the multitudinous harmony of the Church's praise to God.

Nor does the Church by herself alone render this praise and honour unto God. The display of God's manifold wisdom in His dealings with mankind is drawing admiration, as St Paul believed, from the celestial spheres (ver. 10). The story of earth's redemption is the theme of endless songs in heaven. All creation joins in concert with the redeemed from the earth, and swells the chorus of their triumph. "I heard," says John in another place, "a voice of many angels round about the throne, and the living creatures, and the elders, saying with a great voice, Worthy is the Lamb that hath been slain! And every created thing which is in the heaven, and on the earth, and under the earth, and on the sea, and all things that are in them, heard I saying:

Unto Him that sitteth upon the throne, and unto the Lamb,
Be blessing and honour and glory and dominion—
For ever and ever."

But the Church is the centre of this tribute of the universe to God and to His Christ.

The Church and Christ Jesus are wedded in this doxology, even as they were in the foregoing supplication (vv. 18, 19). In the Bride and the Bridegroom, in the Redeemed and the Redeemer, in the many brethren and in the Firstborn is this perfect glory to be paid to God. "In the midst of the congregation" Christ the Son of man sings evermore the Father's praise (Heb. ii. 12). No glory is paid to God by men which is not due to Him; nor does He render to the Father any tribute in which His people are without a share. "The glory which thou hast given me I have given them," said Jesus to the Father praying for His Church, "that they may be one, even as we are one" (John xvii. 22). Our union with each other in Christ is perfected by our union with Him in realizing the Father's glory, in receiving and manifesting the fulness of God.

The duration of the glory to be paid to God by Christ and His Church is expressed by a cumulative phrase in keeping with the tenor of the passage to which it belongs: "unto all generations of the age of the ages." It reminds us of "the ages to come" through which the apostle in chapter ii. 7 foresaw that God's mercy to his own age would be celebrated. It carries our thoughts along the vista of the future, till time melts into eternity. When the apostle desires that God's praise may resound in the Church "unto *all generations*," he no longer supposes that the mystery of God may be finished speedily as men count years. The history of mankind stretches before his gaze into its dim futurity. The successive "generations" gather themselves into that one consummate "age" of the kingdom of God, the grand cycle in which all "the ages" are contained. With its completion time itself is no more. Its swelling current, laden with the tribute of all the worlds and all their histories, reaches the eternal ocean.

The end comes: God is all in all. At this furthest horizon of thought, Christ and His own are seen together rendering to God unceasing glory.

THE EXHORTATION.

CHAPTER iv. 1—vi. 20.

ON CHURCH LIFE.

CHAPTER iv. 1–16.

"It is good we return unto the ancient bond of unity in the Church of God, which was *one faith, one baptism*, and not *one hierarchy, one discipline*; and that we observe the league of Christians, as it was penned by our Saviour Christ, which is in substance of doctrine this: *He that is not with us is against us*; and in things indifferent and but of circumstance this: *He that is not against us is with us.*"—LORD BACON: *Certain Considerations touching the better Pacification and Edification of the Church of England*, addressed to King James I.

———————————————

CHAPTER XVI.

THE FUNDAMENTAL UNITIES.

"I therefore, the prisoner in the Lord, beseech you to walk worthily of the calling wherewith
ye were called, with all lowliness and meekness, with longsuffering, forbearing one another
in love; giving diligence to keep the unity of the Spirit in the bond of peace.
"There is one body, and one Spirit,
Even as also ye were called in one hope of your calling;
One Lord, one faith, one baptism,
One God and Father of all,
Who is over all, and through all, and in all."

EPH. iv. 1–6.

This Encyclical of St Paul to the Churches of Asia is the most formal and
deliberate of his writings since the great epistle to the Romans. In entering
upon its hortatory and practical part we are reminded of the transition from
doctrine to exhortation in that epistle. Here as in Romans xi., xii. the apostle's
theological teaching, brought with measured steps to its conclusion, has been
followed by an act of worship expressing the profound and holy joy which
fills his spirit as he views the purposes of God thus displayed in the gospel
and the Church. In this exalted mood, as one sitting in heavenly places with
Christ Jesus, St Paul surveys the condition of his readers and addresses
himself to their duties and necessities. His homily, like his argument, is
inwoven with the golden thread of devotion; and the smooth flow of the
epistle breaks ever and again into the music of thanksgiving.

The apostle resumes the words of self-description dropped in chapter iii. 1.
He appeals to his readers with pathetic dignity: "I the prisoner in the Lord";
and the expression gathers new solemnity from that which he has told us in
the last chapter of the mystery and grandeur of his office. He is *"the
prisoner"*—the one whose bonds were known through all the Churches and
manifest even in the imperial palace (Phil. i. 12–14). It was "in the Lord" that
he wore this heavy chain, brought upon him in Christ's service and borne
joyfully for His people's sake. He is now a martyr apostle. If his confinement
detained him from his Gentile flock, at least it should add sacred force to the
message he was able to convey. The tone of the apostle's letters at this time
shows that he was sensible of the increased consideration which the
afflictions of the last few years had given to him in the eyes of the Church. He
is thankful for this influence, and makes good use of it.

His first and main appeal to the Asian brethren, as we should expect from the
previous tenor of the letter, is an exhortation to *unity*. It is an obvious
conclusion from the doctrine of the Church that he has taught them. The

"oneness of the Spirit" which they must "earnestly endeavour to preserve," is the unity which their possession of the Holy Spirit of itself implies. "Having access in one Spirit to the Father," the antipathetic Jewish and Gentile factors of the Church are reconciled; "in the Spirit" they "are builded together for a habitation of God" (ii. 18–22). This unity when St Paul wrote was an actual and visible fact, despite the violent efforts of the Judaizers to destroy it. The "right hands of fellowship" exchanged between himself and James, Peter, and John at the conference of Jerusalem were a witness thereto (Gal. ii. 7–10). But it was a union that needed for its maintenance the efforts of right-thinking men and sons of peace everywhere. St Paul bids all who read his letter help to keep Christ's peace in the Churches.

The conditions for such pursuing and preserving of peace in the fold of Christ are briefly indicated in verses 1 and 2. There must be—

(1) *A due sense of the dignity of our Christian calling*: "Walk worthily," he says, "of the calling where with you were called." This exhortation, of course, includes much besides in its scope; it is the preface to all the exhortations of the three following chapters, the basis, in fact, of every worthy appeal to Christian men; but it bears in the first instance, and pointedly, upon Church unity. Levity of temper, low and poor conceptions of religion militate against the catholic spirit; they create an atmosphere rife with causes of contention. "Whereas there is among you jealousy and strife, are ye not carnal and walk as men?"

(2) Next to low-mindedness amongst the foes of unity comes *ambition*: "Walk with all lowliness of mind and meekness," he continues. Between the low-minded and the lowly-minded there is a total difference. The man *of lowly mind* habitually feels his dependence as a creature and his unworthiness as a sinner before God. This spirit nourishes in him a wholesome self-distrust, and watchfulness over his temper and motives.—The *meek* man thinks as little of his personal claims, as the humble man of his personal merits. He is willing to give place to others where higher interests will not suffer, content to take the lowest room and to be in men's eyes of no account. How many seeds of strife and roots of bitterness would be destroyed, if this mind were in us all. Self-importance, the love of office and power and the craving for applause must be put away, if we are to recover and keep the unity of the Spirit in the bond of peace.

(3) When St Paul adds "with longsuffering, forbearing one another in love," he is opposing a cause of division quite different from the last,—to wit, *impatience and resentfulness*. A high Christian ideal and a strict self-judgement will render us more sensitive to wrong-doing in the world around us. Unless tempered with abundant charity, they may lead to harsh and one-

sided censure. Gentle natures, reluctant to condemn, are sometimes slow and difficult in forgiveness. Humbleness and meekness are choice graces of the Spirit. But they are self-regarding virtues at the best, and may be found in a cold nature that has little of the patience which bears with men's infirmities, of the sympathetic insight that discovers the good often lying close to their faults. "Above all things"—above kindness, meekness, longsuffering, forgivingness—"put on love, which is the bond of perfectness" (Col. iii. 14). Love is the last word of St Paul's definition of the Christian temper in verse 2; it is the sum and essence of all that makes for Christian unity. In it lies a charm which can overcome both the lighter provocations and the grave offences of human intercourse,—offences that must needs arise in the purest society composed of infirm and sinful men. "Bind thyself to thy brother. Those who are bound together in love, bear all burdens lightly. Bind thyself to him, and him to thee. Both are in thy power; for whomsoever I will, I may easily make my friend" (Chrysostom).

Verses 1–3 exhibit the temper in which the unity of the Church is to be maintained. Verses 4–6 set forth the basis upon which it rests. This passage is a brief summary of Christian doctrine. It defines the "foundation of the apostles and prophets" asserted in chapter ii. 20,—the groundwork of "every building" in God's holy temple, the foundation upon which Paul's Gentile readers, along with the Jewish saints, were growing into one holy temple in the Lord. Seven elements of unity St Paul enumerates: one *body, Spirit, hope*; one *Lord, faith* and *baptism*; one *God and Father of all*. They form a chain stretching from the Church on earth to the throne and being of the universal Father in heaven.

Closely considered, we find that the seven unities resolve themselves into three, centring in the names of the Divine Trinity—the Spirit, the Lord, and the Father. The Spirit and the Lord are each accompanied by two kindred uniting elements; while the one God and Father, placed alone, in Himself forms a threefold bond to His creatures—by His sovereign power, pervasive action, and immanent presence: "Who is over all, and through all, and in all" (comp. i. 23).

The rhythm of expression in these verses suggests that they belonged to some apostolic Christian song. Other passages in Paul's later epistles betray the same character;[98] and we know from chapter v. 19 and Colossians iii. 16 that the Pauline Church was already rich in psalmody. This epistle shows that St Paul was touched with the poetic as well as the prophetical afflatus. He expected his people to sing; and we see no reason why he should not, like Luther and the Wesleys afterwards, have taught them to do so by giving voice to the joy of the new-found faith in "hymns and spiritual songs." These lines, we could fancy, belonged to some chant sung in the Christian assemblies; they form a brief metrical creed, the confession of the Church then and in all ages.

I. *One body* there is, *and one Spirit.*

The former was a patent fact. Believers in Jesus Christ formed a single body, the same in all essentials of religion, sharply distinguished from their Jewish and their Pagan neighbours. Although the distinctions now existing amongst Christians are vastly greater and more numerous, and the boundaries between the Church and the world at many points are much less visible, yet there is a true unity that binds together those "who profess and call themselves Christians" throughout the world. As against the multitudes of heathen and idolaters; as against Jewish and Mohammedan rejecters of our Christ; as against atheists and agnostics and all deniers of the Lord, we are "one body," and should feel and act as one.

In missionary fields, confronting the overwhelming forces and horrible evils of Paganism, the servants of Christ intensely realize their unity; they see how trifling in comparison are the things that separate the Churches, and how precious and deep are the things that Christians hold in common. It may need the pressure of some threatening outward force, the sense of a great peril hanging over Christendom to silence our contentions and compel the soldiers of Christ to fall into line and present to the enemy a united front. If the unity of believers in Christ—their oneness of worship and creed, of moral ideal and discipline—is hard to discern through the variety of human forms and systems and the confusion of tongues that prevails, yet the unity is there to be discerned; and it grows clearer to us as we look for it. It is visible in the universal acceptance of Scripture and the primitive creeds, in the large measure of correspondence between the different Church standards of the Protestant communions, in our common Christian literature, in the numerous alliances and combinations, local and general, that exist for philanthropic and missionary objects, in the increasing and auspicious comity of the Churches. The nearer we get to the essentials of truth and to the experience of living Christian men, the more we realize the existence of one body in the scattered limbs and innumerable sects of Christendom.

There is "one body and one Spirit": one body because, and so far as there is one Spirit. What is it constitutes the unity of our physical frame? Outward attachment, mechanical juxtaposition go for nothing. What I grasp in my hand or put between my lips is no part of *me*, any more than if it were in another planet. The clothes I wear take the body's shape; they partake of its warmth and movement; they give its outward presentment. They are not of the body for all this. But the fingers that clasp, the lips that touch, the limbs that move and glow beneath the raiment,—these are the body itself; and everything belongs to it, however slight in substance, or uncomely or unserviceable, nay, however diseased and burdensome, that is vitally connected with it. The life that thrills through nerve and artery, *the spirit* that animates with one will and being the whole framework and governs its ten thousand delicate springs and interlacing cords,—it is this that makes *one body* of an otherwise inert and decaying heap of matter. Let the spirit depart, it is a body no more, but a corpse. So with the body of Christ, and its members in particular. Am I a living, integral part of the Church, quickened by its Spirit? or do I belong only to the raiment and the furniture that are about it? "If any man have not the Spirit of Christ, he is none of His."

He who has the Spirit of Christ, will find a place within His body. The Spirit of Jesus Christ is a communicative, sociable spirit. The child of God seeks out his brethren; like is drawn to like, bone to bone and sinew to its sinew in the building up of the risen body. By an instinct of its life, the new-born soul forms bonds of attachment for itself to the Christian souls nearest to it, to those amongst whom it is placed in God's dispensation of grace. The ministry, the community through which it received spiritual life and that travailed for its birth claim it by a parental right that may not be disowned, nor at any time renounced without loss and peril.

Where the Spirit of Christ dwells as a vitalizing, formative principle, it finds or makes for itself a body. Let no man say: I have the spirit of religion; I can dispense with forms. I need no fellowship with men; I prefer to walk with God.—God will not walk with men who do not care to walk with His people. He "loved the world"; and we must love it, or we displease Him. "This commandment have we from Him, that he who loves God love his brother also."

The oneness of communion amongst the people of Christ is governed by a unity of aim: "Even as also you were called in *one hope* of your calling." Our fellowship has an object to realize, our calling a prize to win. All Christian organization is directed to a practical end. The old Pagan world fell to pieces because it was "without hope"; its golden age was in the past. No society can endure that lives upon its memories, or that contents itself with cherishing its privileges. Nothing holds men together like work and hope. This gives energy, purpose, progress to the fellowship of Christian believers. In this imperfect and unsatisfying world, with the majority of our race still in bondage to evil, it is idle for us to combine for any purpose that does not bear on human improvement and salvation. The Church of Christ is a society for the abolition of sin and death. That this will be accomplished, that God's will shall be done on earth as in heaven, is *the hope of our calling*. To this hope we "were called" by the first summons of the gospel. "Repent," it cried, "for the kingdom of heaven is at hand!"

For ourselves, in our personal quality, Christianity holds out a splendid crown of life. It promises our complete restoration to the image of God, the redemption of the body with the spirit from death, and our entrance upon an eternal fellowship with Christ in heaven. This hope, shared by us in common and affecting all the interests and relationships of daily life, is the ground of our communion. The Christian hope supplies to men, more truly and constantly than Nature in her most exalted forms,

"The anchor of their purest thoughts, the nurse,
The guide, the guardian of their heart, and soul
Of all their moral being."

Happy are the wife and husband, happy the master and servants, happy the circle of friends who live and work together as "joint-heirs of the grace of life." Well says Calvin here: "If this thought were fixed in our minds, this law laid upon us, that the sons of God may no more quarrel than the kingdom of heaven can be divided, how much more careful we should be in cultivating brotherly goodwill! What a dread we should have of dissensions, if we considered, as we ought to do, that those who separate from their brethren, exile themselves from the kingdom of God."

But the hope of our calling is a hope for mankind,—nay, for the entire universe. We labour for the regeneration of humanity. "We look for a new heavens and earth, wherein dwelleth righteousness;" for the actual gathering into one in Christ of all things in all worlds, as they are already gathered in God's eternal plan. Now if it were merely a personal salvation that we had to seek, Christian communion might appear to be an optional thing, and the Church no more than a society for mutual spiritual benefit. But seen in this larger light, Church membership is of the essence of our calling. As children of the household of faith, we are heirs to its duties with its possessions. We cannot escape the obligations of our spiritual any more than of our natural birth. One Spirit dwelling in each, one sublime ideal inspiring us and guiding all our efforts, how shall we not be one body in the fellowship of Christ? This hope of our calling it is our calling to breathe into the dead world. Its virtue alone can dispel the gloom and discord of the age. From the fountain of God's love in Christ springing up in the heart of the Church, there shall pour forth

"One common wave of thought and joy,
Lifting mankind again!"

II. The first group of unities leads us to the second. If one Spirit dwells within us, it is *one Lord* who reigns over us. We have one hope to work for; it is because we have *one faith* to live by. A common fellowship implies a common creed.

Thus Christ Jesus the Lord takes His place fourth in this list of unities, between hope and faith, between the Spirit and the Father. He is the centre of centres, the Lamb in the midst of the throne, the Christ in the midst of the ages. United with Christ, we are at unity with God and with our fellow-men. We find in Him the fulcrum of the forces that are raising the world, the corner-stone of the temple of humanity.

But let us mark that it is the one *Lord* in whom we find our unity. To think of Him as Saviour only is to treat Him as a means to an end. It is to make ourselves the centre, not Christ. This is the secret of much of the isolation and sectarianism of modern Churches. Individualism is the negation of Church life. Men value Christ for what they can get from Him for themselves. They do not follow Him and yield themselves up to Him, for the sake of what He is. "Come unto me, all ye that are burdened, and I will give you rest": they listen willingly so far. But when He goes on to say "Take my yoke upon you," their ears are deaf. There is a subtle self-seeking and self-pleasing even in the way of salvation.

From this springs the disloyalty, the want of affection for the Church, the indifference to all Christian interests beyond the personal and local, which is worse than strife; for it is death to the body of Christ. The name of the "one Lord" silences party clamours and rebukes the voices that cry, "I am of Apollos, I of Cephas." It recalls loiterers and stragglers to the ranks. It bids each of us, in his own station of life and his own place in the Church, serve the common cause without sloth and without ambition.

Christ's Lordship over us for life and death is signified by our *baptism* in His name. We have received, most of us in infancy through our parents' reverent care, the token of allegiance to the Lord Christ. The baptismal water that He bade all nations receive from His apostles, has been sprinkled upon you. Shall this be in vain? Or do you now, by the faith of your heart in Christ Jesus the Lord, endorse the faith of your parents and the Church exercised on your behalf? If so, your faith saves you. Your obedience is at once accepted by the Lord to whom it is tendered; and the sign of God's redemption of the race which greeted you at your entrance into life, assumes for you all its significance and worth. It is the seal upon your brow, now stamped upon your heart, of your eternal covenant with Christ.

But it is the seal of a *corporate* life in Him. Christian baptism is no private transaction; it attests no mere secret vow passing between the soul and its Saviour. "For in one Spirit we were all baptized *into one body*, whether Jews or Greeks, whether bond or free; and were all made to drink of one Spirit" (1 Cor. xii. 13). Our baptism is the sign of a common faith and hope, and binds us at once to Christ and to His Church.

One baptism there has been through all the ages since the ascending Lord said to His disciples: "Go, make disciples of all the nations, baptizing them into the name of the Father, and of the Son, and of the Holy Spirit." The ordinance has been administered in different ways and under varying regulations; but with few exceptions, it has been observed from the beginning by every Christian community in fulfilment of the word of Christ, and in acknowledgement of His dominion. Those who insist on the sole validity of this or that mode or channel of administration, recognize at least the intention of Churches baptizing otherwise than themselves to honour the one Lord in thus confessing His name; and so far admit that there is in truth "one baptism." Wherever Christ's sacraments are observed with a true faith, they serve as visible tokens of His rule.

In this rule lies the ultimate ground of union for men, and for all creatures. Our fellowship in the faith of Christ is deep as the nature of God; its blessedness rich as His love; its bonds strong and eternal as His power.

III. The last and greatest of the unities still remains. Add to our fellowship in the one Spirit and confession of the one Lord, our adoption by the *one God and Father of all.*

To the Gentile converts of the Asian cities this was a new and marvellous thought. "Great is Artemis of the Ephesians," they had been used to shout; or haply, "Great is Aphrodité of the Pergamenes," or "Bacchus of the Philadelphians." Great they knew was "Jupiter Best and Greatest" of conquering Rome; and great the *numen* of the Cæsar, to which everywhere in this rich and servile province shrines were rising. Each city and tribe, each grove or fountain or sheltering hill had its local *genius* or *daimon*, requiring worship and sacrificial honours. Every office and occupation, every function in life—navigation, midwifery, even thieving—was under the patronage of its special deity. These petty godships by their number and rivalries distracted the pious heathen with continual fear lest one or other of them might not have received due observance.

With what a grand simplicity the Christian conception of "the one God and Father" rose above this vulgar pantheon, this swarm of motley deities—some gay and wanton, some dark and cruel, some of supposed beneficence, all infected with human passion and baseness—which filled the imagination of the Græco-Asiatic pagans. What rest there was for the mind, what peace and freedom for the spirit in turning from such deities to the God and Father of our Lord Jesus Christ!

Here is no jealous Monarch regarding men as tribute-payers, and needing to be served by human hands. He is the Father of men, pitying us as His children and giving us all things richly to enjoy. Our God is no local divinity, to be honoured here but not there, tied to His temple and images and priestly mediators; but the "one God and Father of all, who is above all, and through all, and in all." This was the very God whom the logic of Greek thought and the practical instincts of Roman law and empire blindly sought. Through ages He had revealed Himself to the people of Israel, who were now dispersed amongst the nations to bear His light. At last He declared His full name and purpose to the world in Jesus Christ. So the gods many and lords many have had their day. By His manifestation the idols are utterly abolished. The proclamation of one God and Father signifies the gathering of men into one family of God. The one religion supplies the basis for one life in all the world.

God is *over all*, gathering all worlds and beings under the shadow of His beneficent dominion. He is *through all*, and *in all*: an Omnipresence of love, righteousness and wisdom, actuating the powers of nature and of grace, inhabiting the Church and the heart of men. You need not go far to seek Him; if you believe in Him, you are yourself His temple.

FOOTNOTES:

[98] See ch. v. 14; 1 Tim. i. 17, ii. 5, 6, vi. 15, 16; 2 Tim. ii. 11–13.

CHAPTER XVII.

THE MEASURE OF THE GIFT OF CHRIST.

"But unto each one of us was the grace given according to the measure of the gift of Christ. Wherefore He saith: 'When He ascended on high, He led captivity captive, and gave gifts unto men.' Now this, 'He ascended,' what is it but that He also descended into the lower parts of the earth? He that descended is the same also that ascended far above all the heavens, that He might fill all things. And He gave some *to be* apostles; and some, prophets; and some evangelists; and some, pastors and teachers; for the perfecting of the saints for work of ministration, for the building up of the body of Christ."—EPH. iv. 7–12.

In verse 7 the apostle passes from the unities of the Church to its diversities, from the common foundation of the Christian life to the variety presented in its superstructure. "To each single one of us was the grace given." The great gift of God in Christ is manifold in its distribution. Its manifestations are as various and fresh as the idiosyncrasies of human personality. There is no capacity of our nature, no element of human society which the gospel of Christ cannot sanctify and turn to good account.

All this the apostle keeps in view and allows for in his doctrine of the Church. He does not merge man in humanity, nor sacrifice the individual to the community. He claims for each believer direct fellowship with Christ and access to God. The earnestness with which in his earlier epistles St Paul insisted on the responsibilities of conscience and on the personal experience of salvation, leads him now to press the claims of the Church with equal vigour. He understands well that the person has no existence apart from the community, that our moral nature is essentially social and the religious life essentially fraternal. Its vital element is "the *communion* of the Holy Spirit." Hence, to gather the real drift of this passage we must combine the first words of verse 7 with the last of verse 12: "To each single one of us was the grace given—in order to build up the body of Christ." God's grace is not bestowed upon us to diffuse and lose itself in our separate individualities; but that it may minister to one life and work towards one end and build up one great body in us all. The diversity subserves a higher unity. Through ten thousand channels, in ten thousand varied forms of personal influence and action, the stream of the grace of God flows on to the accomplishment of the eternal purpose.

Like a wise master in his household and sovereign in his kingdom, the Lord of the Church distributes His manifold gifts. His bestowments and appointments are made with an eye to the furtherance of the state and house that He has in charge. As God dispenses His wisdom, so Christ His gifts "according to plan" (iii. 11). The purpose of the ages, God's great plan for mankind, determines "the measure of the gift of Christ." Now, it is to illustrate this *measure*, to set forth the style and scale of Christ's bestowments within His Church, that the apostle brings in evidence the words of Psalm lxviii. 18. He interprets this ancient verse as he cites it, and weaves it into the texture of his argument. In the original it reads thus:

"Thou hast ascended on high, Thou hast led Thy captivity captive,
Thou hast received gifts among men,—
Yea, among the rebellious also, that the LORD God might dwell with them." (R.V.)

Let us go back for a moment to the occasion of the old Hebrew song. Psalm lxviii, is, as Ewald says, "the greatest, most splendid and artistic of the temple-songs of Restored Jerusalem." It celebrates Jehovah's entry into Zion. This culminating verse records, as the crowning event of Israel's history, the capture of Zion from the rebel Jebusites and the Lord's ascension in the person of His chosen to take His seat upon this holy hill. The previous verses, in which fragments of earlier songs are embedded, describe the course of the Divine Leader of Israel through former ages. In the beat and rhythm of the Hebrew lines one hears the footfall of the Conqueror's march, as He "arises and His enemies are scattered" and "kings of armies flee apace," while nature trembles at His step and bends her wild powers to serve His congregation. The sojourn in the wilderness, the scenes of Sinai, the occupancy of Canaan, the wars of the Judges were so many stages in the progress of Jehovah, which had Zion always for its goal. To Zion, the new and more glorious sanctuary, Sinai must now give place. Bashan and all mountains towering in their pride in vain "look askance at the hill which God has desired for His abode," where "Jehovah will dwell for ever." So the day of the Lord's desire has come! From the Kidron valley David leads Jehovah's triumph up the steep slopes of Mount Zion. A train of captives defiles before the Lord's anointed, who sits down on the throne that God gives him and receives in His name the submission of the heathen. The vanquished chiefs cast their spoil at his feet; it is laid up in treasure to build the future temple; while, upon this happy day of peace, "the rebellious also" share in Jehovah's grace and become His subjects.

In this conquest David "gave to men" rather than "received"—gave even to his stubborn enemies (witness his subsequent transaction with Araunah the Jebusite for the site of the temple); for that which he took from them served to build amongst them God's habitation: "that," as the Psalmist sings, "the Lord God might dwell with them." St Paul's adaptation of the verse is both bold and true. If he departs from the letter, he unfolds the spirit of the prophetic words. That David's *giving* signified a higher *receiving*, Jewish interpreters themselves seem to have felt, for this paraphrase was current also amongst them.

The author of this Hebrew song has in no way exaggerated the importance of David's victory. The summits of the elect nation's history shine with a supernatural and prophetic light. The spirit of the Christ in the unknown singer "testified beforehand of the glory that should follow" His warfare and sufferings. From this victorious height, so hardly won, the Psalmist's verse flashes the light of promise across the space of a thousand years; and St. Paul has caught the light, and sends it on to us shining with a new and more spiritual brightness. David's "going up on high" was, to the apostle's mind, a picture of the ascent of Christ, his Son and Lord. David rose from deep humiliation to a high dominion; his exaltation brought blessing and enrichment to his people; and the spoil that he won with it went to build God's house amongst rebellious men. All this was true in parable of the dispensation of grace to mankind through Jesus Christ; and His ascension disclosed the deeper import of the words of the ancient Scripture. "Wherefore God saith" (and St Paul takes the liberty of putting in his own words *what* He saith)—"wherefore He saith: He ascended on high; He led captivity captive; He gave gifts to men."

———————

The three short clauses of the citation supply, in effect, a threefold measure of the gifts of Christ to His Church. They are gifts *of the ascended Saviour*. They are gifts bestowed *from the fruit of His victory*. And they are gifts *to men*. Measure them, first, by the height to which He has risen—from what a depth! Measure them, again, by the spoils He has already won. Measure them, once more, by the wants of mankind, by the need He has undertaken to supply.— As He is, so He gives; as He has, so He gives; as He has given, so He will give till we are filled unto all the fulness of God.

I. Think first, then, of Him. Think of what, and *where* He is! Consider "what is the height" of His exaltation; and then say, if you can, "what is the breadth" of His munificence.

We know well how He gave as a poor and suffering man upon earth—gave, with what affluence, pity and delight, bread to the hungry thousands, wine to the wedding-feast, health to the sick, sight to the blind, pardon to the sinful, sometimes life to the dead! Has His elevation altered Him? Too often it is so with vain and weak men like ourselves. Their wealth increases, but their hearts contract. The more they have to give, the less they love to give. They go up on high as men count it, and climb to places of power and eminence; and they forget the friends of youth and the ranks from which they sprang— low-minded men. Not so with our exalted Friend. "It is not one that went down, and another that went up," says Theodoret. "He that descended, *it is He* also that ascended up far above all the heavens!" (ver. 10). Jesus of Nazareth is on the throne of God,—"the same yesterday and to-day!" But now the resources of the universe are at His disposal. Out of that treasure He can choose the best gifts for you and me.

Mere authority, even Omnipotence, could not suffice to save and bless moral beings like ourselves; nor even the best will joined to Omnipotence. Christ gained by His humiliation, in some sense, a new fulness added to the fulness of the Godhead. This gain of His sufferings is implied in what the apostle writes in Colossians i. 19 concerning the risen and exalted Redeemer: "It was well-pleasing that *all* the fulness should make its dwelling in Him." His plenitude is that of the Ascended One *who had descended*. "If He ascended, what does it mean but that He also descended into the under regions of the earth?" (ver. 9). If He went up, why then He had been down!—down to the Virgin's womb and the manger cradle, wrapping His Godhead within the frame and the brain of a little child; down to the home and the bench of the village carpenter; down to the contradiction of sinners and the level of their scorn; down to the death of the cross,—to the nether abyss, to that dim populous underworld into which we look shuddering over the grave's edge! And from that lower gulf He mounted up again to the solid earth and the light of day and the world of breathing men; and up, and up again, through the rent clouds and the ranks of shouting angels, and under the lifted heads of the everlasting doors, until He took His seat at the right hand of the Majesty in the heavens.

Think of the regions He has traversed, the range of being through which the Lord Jesus passed in descending and ascending, "that He might fill all things." Heaven, earth, hades—hades, earth, heaven again are His; not in mere sovereignty of power, but in experience and communion of life. Each He has annexed to His dominion by inhabitation and the right of self-devoting love, as from sphere to sphere He "travelled in the greatness of His power, mighty to save." He is Lord of angels; but still more of men,—Lord of the living, and of the dead. To them that sleep in the dust He has proclaimed His accomplished sacrifice and the right of universal judgement given Him by the Father.

Nor did Abraham alone and Moses and Elijah have the joy of "seeing His day," but all the holy men of old, who had embraced its promise and "died in faith," who looked forward through their imperfect sacrifices "which could never quite take away sins" to the better thing which God provided for us, and for their perfection along with us.[99] On the two side-posts of the gate of death our great High Priest sprinkled His atoning blood. He turned the abode of corruption into a sweet and quiet sleeping chamber for His saints. Then at His touch those cruel doors swung back upon their hinges, and He issued forth the Prince of life, with the keys of death and hades hanging from His girdle. From the depths of the grave to the heaven of heavens His Mastership extends. With the perfume of His presence and the rich incense of His sacrifice Jesus Christ has "filled all things." The universe is made for us one realm of redeeming grace, the kingdom of the Son of God's love.

"So there crowns Him the topmost, ineffablest, uttermost crown;
And His love fills infinitude wholly, nor leaves up nor down
One spot for the creature to stand in!"[100]

So "Christ is all things, and in all." And we are nothing; but we have everything in Him.

How, pray, will He give who has thus given Himself,—who has thus endured and achieved on our behalf? Let our hearts consider; let our faith and our need be bold to ask. One promise from His lips is enough: "If ye shall ask anything in my name, I will do it."

II. A second estimate of the gifts to be looked for from Christ, we derive from *His conquests already won*. David as he entered Zion's gates "led captivity captive,"—led, that is in Hebrew phrase, a great, a notable captivity. Out of the gifts thus received he enriched his people. The resources that victory placed at his disposal, furnished the store from which to build God's house. In like fashion Christ builds His Church, and blesses the human race. With the spoils of His battle He adorns His bride. The prey taken from the mighty becomes the strength and beauty of His sanctuary. The prisoners of His love He makes the servants of mankind.

This "captivity" implies a warfare, even as the ascent of Christ a previous descending. The Son of God came not into His earthly kingdom as kings are said to have come sometimes disguised amongst their subjects, that they might learn better of their state and hear their true mind; nor as the Greeks fabled of their gods, who wandered unknown on earth seeking adventure and wearied haply of the cloying felicities of heaven, suffering contempt and doing to men hard service. He came, the Good Shepherd, to seek lost sheep. He came, the Mighty One of God, to destroy the works of the devil, to drive out "the strong one armed" who held the fortress of man's soul. He had a war to wage with the usurping prince of the world. In the temptations of the wilderness, in the strife with disease and demoniac powers, in the debate with Scribes and Pharisees, in the anguish of Gethsemane and Calvary that conflict was fought out; and by death He abolished him who holds the power of death, by His blood He "bought us for God." But with the spoils of victory, He bears the scars of battle,—tokens glorious for Him, humbling indeed to us, which will tell for ever how they pierced His hands and feet!

For Him pain and conflict are gone by. It remains to gather in the spoil of His victory of love, the harvest sown in His tears and His blood. And what are the trophies of the Captain of our salvation? what the fruit of His dread passion? For one, there was the dying thief, whom with His nailed hands the Lord Jesus snatched from a felon's doom and bore from Calvary to Paradise. There was Mary the Magdalene, out of whom He had cast seven demons, the first to greet Him risen. There were the three thousand whom on one day, in the might of His Spirit, the ascended Lord and Christ took captive in rebel Jerusalem, "lifted from the earth" that He might draw all men unto Him. And there was the writer of this letter, once His blasphemer and persecutor. By a look, by a word, Jesus arrested Saul at the height of his murderous enmity, and changed him from a Pharisee into an apostle to the Gentiles, from the destroyer into the wise master-builder of His Church.

St Paul's own case suggested, surely, the application he makes of this ancient text of the Psalter and lighted up its Messianic import. In the glory of His triumph Jesus Christ had appeared to make him captive, and put him at once to service. From that hour Paul was led along enthralled, the willing bond-slave of the Lord Jesus and celebrant of His victory. "Thanks be unto God," he cries, "who ever triumphs over us in the Christ, and makes manifest through us the savour of His knowledge in every place."[101]

Such, and of such sort are the prisoners of the war of Jesus; such the gifts that through sinners pardoned and subdued He bestows upon mankind,—"patterns to those who should hereafter believe." Time would fail to follow the train of the captives of the love of Christ, which stretches unbroken and ever multiplying through the centuries to this day. We, too, in our turn have laid our rebel selves at His feet; and all that we surrender to Him, by right of conquest He gives over to the service of mankind.

> "His love the conquest more than wins;
>   To all I shall proclaim:
> Jesus the King, the Conqueror reigns;
>   Bow down to Jesu's name!"

He gives out of the spoil of His war with evil,—gives what He receives. Yet He gives not *as* He receives. Everything laid in His hands is changed by their touch. Publicans and Pharisees become apostles. Magdalenes are made queens and mothers in His Israel. From the dregs of our streets He raises up a host of sons to Abraham. From the ranks of scepticism and anti-Christian hate the Lord Christ wins new champions and captains for His cause. He coins earth's basest metal into heaven's fine gold. He takes weak things of the earth and foolish, to strike the mightiest blows of battle.

What may we not expect from Him who has led captive such a captivity! What surprises of blessing and miracles of grace there are awaiting us, that shall fill our mouth with laughter and our tongue with singing—gifts and succours coming to the Church from unlooked-for quarters and reinforcements from the ranks of the enemy. And what discomfitures and captivities are preparing for the haters of the Lord,—if, at least, the future is to be as the past; and if we may judge from the apostle's word, and from his example, of the measure of the gift of Christ.

III. A third line of measurement is supplied in the last word of verse 8, and is drawn out in verses 11 and 12. "He gave gifts *to men*—He gave some apostles, some prophets, some evangelists, some pastors and teachers, with a view to the full equipment of the saints for work of ministration, for building up of the body of Christ." Yes, and some martyrs, some missionaries, some Church rulers and Christian statesmen, some poets, some deep thinkers and theologians, some leaders of philanthropy and helpers of the poor; all given for the same end—to minister to the life of His Church, to furnish it with the means for carrying on its mission, and to enable every saint to contribute his part to the commonwealth of Christ according to the measure of Christ's gift to each.

Comparison with verse 16 that follows and with verse 7 that precedes, seems to us to make it clear that we should read, without a comma, the second and third clauses of verse 12 as continuations of the first. The "work of ministering" and the "building up of the body of Christ" are not assigned to special orders of ministry as their exclusive calling. Such honour have all His saints. It is the office of the clergy to see that the laity do their duty, of "the ministry" to make each saint a minister of Christ, to guide, instruct and animate the entire membership of Christ's body in the work He has laid upon it. Upon this plan the Christian fellowship was organized and officered in the apostolic times. Church government is a means to an end. Its primitive form

149

was that best suited to the age; and even then varied under different circumstances. It was not precisely the same at Jerusalem and at Corinth; at Corinth in 58, and at Ephesus in 66 A.D. That is the best Church system, under any given conditions, which serves best to conserve and develope the spiritual energy of the body of Christ.

The distribution of Church office indicated in verse 11 corresponds closely to what we find in the Pastoral epistles. The apostle does not profess to enumerate all grades of ministry. The "deacons" are wanting; although we know from Philippians i. 1 that this order already existed in Pauline Churches. *Pastors* (shepherds)—a title only employed here by the apostle—is a fitting synonym for the "bishops" (*i.e.*, overseers) of whom he speaks in Acts xx. 28, Philippians i. 1, and largely in the epistles to Timothy and Titus, whose functions were spiritual and disciplinary as well as administrative. Addressing the Ephesian elders at Miletus four years before, St Paul bade them "shepherd the Church of God."

In 1 Peter v. 1, 2 the same charge is laid by the Jewish apostle upon his "fellow-elders," that they should "shepherd the flock of God, making themselves examples" to it; Christ Himself he has previously called "Shepherd and Bishop of souls" (1 Pet. ii. 25). The expression is derived from the words of Jesus recorded in John x., concerning the true and false shepherd of God's flock, and Himself the Good Shepherd,—words familiar and dear to His disciples.

The office of *teaching*, as in 1 Timothy v. 17, is conjoined with that of shepherding. From that passage we infer that the freedom of teaching so conspicuous in the Corinthian Church (1 Cor. xiv. 26, etc.) was still recognized. Teaching and ruling are not made identical, nor inseparable functions, any more than in Romans xii. 7, 8; but they were frequently associated, and hence are coupled together here.—Of apostolic *evangelists* we have examples in Timothy and the second Philip;[102] men outside the rank of the apostles, but who, like them, preached the gospel from place to place. The name apostles (equivalent to our *missionaries*) served, in its wider sense, to include ministers of this class along with those directly commissioned by the Lord Jesus.[103]

The *prophets*,[104] like the apostles and evangelists, belonged to the Church at large, rather than to one locality. But their gift of inspiration did not carry with it the claim to rule in the Church. This was the function of the apostles generally, and of the pastor-bishops, or elders, locally appointed.

The first three orders (apostles, prophets, evangelists) linked Church to Church and served the entire body; the last two (pastors and teachers) had charge of local and congregational affairs. The apostles (the Twelve and

Paul), with the prophets, were the founders of the Church. Their distinctive functions ceased when the foundation was laid and the deposit of revealed truth was complete. The evangelistic and pastoral callings remain; and out of them have sprung all the variety of Christian ministries since exercised. Evangelists, with apostles or missionaries, bring new souls to Christ and carry His message into new lands. Pastors and teachers follow in their train, tending the ingathered sheep, and labouring to make each flock that they shepherd and every single man perfect in Christ Jesus.

Marvellous were Christ's "gifts for men" bestowed in the apostolic ministry. What a gift to the Christian community, for example, was Paul himself! In his natural endowments, so rich and finely blended, in his training and early experience, in the supernatural mode of his conversion, everything wrought together to give to men in the apostle Paul a man supremely fitted to be Christ's ambassador to the Pagan world, and for all ages the "teacher of the Gentiles in faith and truth." "A *chosen vessel* unto me," said the Lord Jesus, "to bear my name."

Such a gift to the world was St Augustine: a man of the most powerful intellect and will, master of the thought and life of his time. Long an alien from the household of faith, he was saved at last as by miracle, and utterly subdued to the will of Christ. In the awful crisis of the fifth century, when the Roman empire was breaking up and the very foundations of life seemed to be dissolved, it was the work of this heroic man to reassert the sovereignty of grace and to re-establish faith in the Divine order of the world.

Such another gift to men was Martin Luther, the captive of justifying grace, won from the monastery and the bondage of Rome to set Germany and Europe free. What a soul of fire, what a voice of power was his! to whose lips our Lord Christ set the great trumpet of the Reformation; and he blew a blast that waked the sleeping peoples of the North, and made the walls of Babylon rock again to their foundation. Such a gift to Scotland was John Knox, who from his own soul breathed the spirit of religion into the life of a nation, and gave it a body and organic form in which to dwell and work for centuries.

Such a gift to England was John Wesley. Can we conceive a richer boon conferred by the Head of the Church upon the English race than the raising up of this great evangelist and pastor and teacher, at such a time as that of his appearance? Standing at the distance of a hundred years, we are able to measure in some degree the magnitude of this bestowment. In none of the leaders and commanders whom Christ has given to His people was there more signally manifest that combination of faculties, that concurrence of providences and adjustment to circumstances, and that transforming and attempering influence of grace in all—the "effectual working in the measure of each single part" of the man and his history, which marks those special gifts that Christ is wont to bestow upon His people in seasons of special emergency and need.

We are passing into a new age, such as none of these great men dreamed of, an age as exigent and perilous as any that have gone before it. The ascendency of physical science, the political enfranchisement of the masses, the universal spread of education, the emancipation of critical thought, the gigantic growth of the press, the enormous increase and aggregation of wealth, the multiplication of large cities, the world-wide facilities of intercourse,—these and other causes more subtle are rapidly transforming human society. Old barriers have disappeared; while new difficulties are being created, of a magnitude to overtask the faith of the strongest. The Church is confronted with problems larger far in their dimensions than those our fathers knew. Demands are being made on her resources such as she has never had to meet before. Shall we be equal to the needs of the coming times? —Nay, that is not the question; but will *He*?

There is nothing new or surprising to the Lord Jesus in the progress of our times and the developments of modern thought, nothing for which He is not perfectly prepared. He has taken their measure long ere this, and holds them within His grasp. The government is upon His shoulders—"the weight of all this unintelligible world"—and He can bear it well. He has gifts in store for the twentieth century, when it arrives, as adequate as those He bestowed upon the first or fifth, upon the sixteenth or the eighteenth of our era. There are Augustines and Wesleys yet to come. Hidden in the Almighty's quiver are shafts as polished and as keen as any He has used, which He will launch forth in the war of the ages at the appointed hour. The need, the peril, the greatness of the time will be the measure of the gift of Christ.

There is a danger, however, in waiting for great leaders and in looking for signal displays of Christ's power amongst men. His "kingdom comes not with observation," so that men should say, Lo here! or Lo there! It steals upon us unforeseen; it is amongst us before we know. "We looked," says Rutherford, "that He should take the higher way along the mountains; and lo, He came by the lower way of the valleys!" While men listen to the earthquake and the wind rending the mountains, a still, small voice speaks the message of God to prepared hearts. Rarely can we measure at the first the worth of Christ's best gifts. When the fruit appears, after long patience, the world will haply discover when and how the seed was sown. But not always then.

> "The sower, passing onward, was not known;
> And all men reaped the harvest as their own."

Those who are most ready to appraise their fellows are constantly at fault.

Our last may prove Christ's first; our first His last! "Each of us shall give account of himself to God": each must answer for his own stewardship, and the grace that was given to each. "Let us not therefore judge one another any more." But let every man see to it that his part in the building of God's temple is well and faithfully done. Soon the fire will try every man's work, of what sort it is.

FOOTNOTES:

[99] Comp. Hebrews x. 1, 2, 10–14 with xi. 13–16, 39, 40, xii. 23, 24; also vi. 12.

[100] The words of David in Browning's *Saul*, turned from the future tense into the present.

[101] 2 Cor. ii. 14; comp. Eph. ii. 6, 7.

[102] 2 Tim. iv. 5; Acts viii. 26–40, xxi. 8.

[103] In Acts xiv. 4, 14, *Barnabas and Paul* are "apostles"; 1 Thess. ii. 6, *Paul and Silas and Timothy*. Comp. Rom. xvi. 7; 2 Cor. viii. 23, xi. 13; Phil. ii. 25; Rev. ii. 2.

[104] Comp. ch. ii. 20, iii. 5 for the association of *prophets* with *apostles*.

CHAPTER XVIII.

THE GROWTH OF THE CHURCH.

"Till we all attain unto the unity of the faith and of the full knowledge of the Son of God, unto a full-grown man, unto the measure of the stature of the fulness of Christ: that we may be no more children, tossed to and fro and carried about with every wind of doctrine in the sport of men, in craftiness, unto the scheme of error; but dealing truly, in love may grow up in all things into Him, which is the head, *even* Christ; from whom all the body fitly framed and knit together, through that which every juncture supplieth, according to the working in *due* measure of each several part, maketh the increase of the body unto the building up of itself in love."—EPH. iv. 13–16.

We must spend a few moments in unravelling this knotty paragraph and determining the relation of its involved clauses to each other, before we can expound it. This passage is enough to prove St Paul's hand in the letter. No writer of equal power was ever so little of a literary craftsman. His epistles read, as M. Renan says, like "a rapid conversation stenographed." Sometimes, as in several places in Colossians ii., his ideas are shot out in disjointed clauses, hardly more continuous than shorthand notes; often, as in this epistle, they pour in a full stream, sentence hurrying after sentence and phrase heaped upon phrase with an exuberance that bewilders us. In his spoken address the interpretation of tone and gesture, doubtless, supplied the syntactical adjustments so often wanting in Paul's written composition.

The gifts pertaining to special office in the Church were bestowed to promote its corporate efficiency and to further its general growth (vv. 11, 12). Now, the purpose of these endowments sets a *limit* to their use. "Christ gave apostles, prophets," and the rest—"*till we all arrive* at our perfect manhood and reach the stature of His fulness." Such is the connexion of verse 13 with the foregoing context. The aim of the Christian ministry is to make itself superfluous, to raise men beyond its need. Knowledge and prophesyings, apostolates and pastorates, the missions of the evangelist and the schools of the teacher will one day cease; their work will be done, their end gained, when all believers are brought "to the unity of faith, to the full knowledge of the Son of God." The work of Christ's servants can have no grander aim, no further goal lying beyond this. Verse 14, therefore, does not disclose an ulterior purpose arising out of that affirmed in the previous sentence; it restates the same purpose. To make men of us (ver. 13) and to prevent our being children (ver. 14) is the identical object for which apostles, prophets, pastors, teachers are called to office. The goal marked out for all believers in the knowledge and the moral likeness of Christ (ver. 13), is set up that it may direct the Church's course through dangers shunned and enemies vanquished (ver. 14) to the attainment of her corporate perfection (vv. 15, 16). The whole thought of this section turns upon the idea of "the perfecting of the saints" in verse 12. Verse 16 looks backward to this; verse 7 looked forward to it.

So much for the general construction of the period. As to its particular words and phrases, we must observe:—

(1) The "perfect [full-grown] man" of verse 13 is the *individual*, not the generic man, not "the one [collective] new man" of chapter ii. 15. The Greek words for *man* in these two places differ.[105] The apostle proposes to the Christian ministry the end that he was himself pursuing, viz., to "present *every man* perfect in Christ."[106]

(2) "*Sleight* of men" (A.V. and R.V.) does not seem to us to express the precise meaning of the word so translated in verse 14. *Kubeia* (from *kubos*, a cube, or die) occurs only here in the New Testament; in classical Greek it appears in its literal sense of *dice-play, gambling*. The interpreters have drawn from this the idea of *trickery, cheating*—the common accompaniment of gambling. But the kindred verb (*to play dice, to gamble*) has another well-established use in Greek, namely, *to hazard*: this supplies for St Paul's noun the signification of *sport* or *hazarding*, preferred by Beza among the older expositors and by von Soden amongst the newest. *In the sport of men*, says von Soden: "conduct wanting in every kind of earnestness and clear purpose. These men *play* with religion, and with the welfare of Christian souls." This metaphor accords admirably with that of the restless waves and uncertain winds[107] just preceding it; while it leads fittingly to the further qualification "in craftiness," which is almost an idle synonym after "sleight."

(3) Another rare word is found in this verse, not very precisely rendered as "wiles"—a translation suiting it better in chapter vi. 11. Here the noun is singular in number: *methodeia*. It signifies *methodizing, reducing to a plan*; and then, in a bad sense, *scheming, plotting*. "Error" is thus personified: it "schemes," just as in 2 Thessalonians ii. 7 it "works." Amid the restless speculations and the unscrupulous perversions of the gospel now disturbing the infant faith of the Asian Churches, the apostle saw the outline of a great system of error shaping itself. There was a method in this madness. *Unto the scheme of error*—into the meshes of its net—those were being driven who yielded to the prevailing tendencies of speculative thought. With all its cross currents and capricious movements, it was bearing steadily in one direction. Reckless pilots steered ignorant souls this way and that over the wind-swept seas of religious doubt; but they brought them at last to the same rocks and quicksands.

(4) As the contrast between manhood and childhood links verses 13 and 14, so it is by the contrast of error and craftiness with *truth* that we pass from

verse 14 to verse 15. "*Speaking* truth" insufficiently renders the opening word of the latter verse. The "*dealing* truly" of the Revised margin is preferable. In Galatians iv. 16 the apostle employs the same verb, signifying not truth of speech alone, but of deed and life (comp. Eph. v. 9). The expression resembles that of 1 John iii. 19: "We are *of the truth*, and shall assure our hearts before Him," where truth and love are found in the like union.

(5) The last difficulty of this kind we have to deal with, lies in the connexion of the clauses of verse 16. "Through every joint of supply" is an incongruous adjunct to the previous clause, "fitly framed and knit together," although the rendering "joint" gives this connexion a superficial aptness. The apostle's word means *juncture* rather than *joint*.[108] The *points of contact* between the members of Christ's body form the channels of supply through which the entire frame receives nourishment. The clause "through every juncture of the supply"—an expression somewhat obscure at the best—points forwards, not backwards. It describes the means by which the Church of Christ, compacted in its general framework by those larger ligatures which its ministry furnishes (vv. 11, 12), builds up its inward life,—through a communion wherein "each single part" of the body shares, and every tie that binds one Christian soul to another serves to nourish the common life of grace. We may paraphrase the sentence thus: "Drawing its life from Christ, the entire body knit together in a well-compacted frame, makes use of every link that unites its members and of each particular member in his place to contribute to its sustenance, thus building itself up in love evermore."

These difficult verses unfold to us three main conceptions: *The goal of the Church's life* (ver. 13), *the malady which arrests its development* (ver. 14), and *the means and conditions of its growth* (vv. 15, 16).

I. The mark at which the Church has to arrive is set forth, in harmony with the tenor of the epistle, in a twofold way,—in its *collective* and its *individual* aspects. We must all "unitedly attain the oneness of the faith and the knowledge of the Son of God"; and we must attain, each of us, "a perfect manhood, the measure of the stature of the fulness of Christ."

The "one faith" of the Church's foundation (ver. 5) is, at the same time, its end and goal. The final unity will be the unfolding of the primal unity; the implicit will become explicit; the germ will be reproduced in the developed organism. "The faith" is still, in St Paul, the *fides qua credimus*, not *quam credimus*; it is the living faith of all hearts in the same Christ and gospel.[109] When "we all" believe heartily and understandingly in "the word of truth, the gospel of our salvation," the goal will be in sight. All our defects are, at the bottom, deficiencies of faith. We fail to apprehend and appropriate the fulness

156

of God in Christ. Faith is the essence of the heart's life: it forms the common consciousness of the body of Christ.

While faith is the central organ of the Church's life, *the Son of God* is its central object. The dangers assailing the Church and the divisions threatening its unity, touched His Person; and whatever touches the Head, vitally affects the health of the body and the well-being of every member in it. Many had believed in Jesus as the Christ and received blessing from Him, whose knowledge of Him as the Son of God was defective. This ignorance exposed their faith to perversion by the plausible errors circulating in the Churches of Asia Minor.[110] The haze of speculation dimmed His glory and distorted His image. Dazzled by the "philosophy and empty deceit" of specious talkers, these half-instructed believers formed erroneous or uncertain views of Christ. And a divided Christ makes a divided Church. We may hold divergent opinions upon many points of doctrine—in regard to Church order and the Sacraments, in regard to the nature of the future judgement, in regard to the mode and limits of inspiration, in regard to the dialect and expression of our spiritual life—and yet retain, notwithstanding, a large measure of cordial unity and find ourselves able to co-operate with each other for many Christian purposes. But when our difference concerns the Person of Christ, it is felt at once to be fundamental. There is a gulf between those who worship and those who do not worship the Son of God.

"Whosoever shall confess that Jesus is the Son of God, God abideth in him and he in God" (1 John iv. 15). This is the touchstone of catholic truth that the apostles have laid down; and by this we must hold fast. The kingship of the Lord Jesus is the rallying-point of Christendom. In His name we set up our banners. There are a thousand differences we can afford to sink and quarrels we may well forget, if our hearts are one towards Him. Let me meet a man of any sect or country, who loves and worships my Lord Christ with all his mind and strength, he is my brother; and who shall forbid us "with one mind and one mouth to glorify the God and Father of our Lord Jesus Christ"? It is nothing but our ignorance of Him, and of each other, that prevents us doing this already. Let us set ourselves again to the study of Christ. Let us strive "all of us" to "attain to the full knowledge of the Son of God"; it is the way to reunion. As we approach the central revelation, and the glory of Christ who is the image of God shines in its original brightness upon our hearts, prejudices will melt away; the opinions and interests and sentiments that divide us will be lost in the transcendent and absorbing vision of the one Lord Jesus Christ.

> "Names and sects and parties fall:
> Thou, O Christ, art all in all!"

The second and third *unto* of verse 13 are parallel with the first, and with each other. A truer faith and better knowledge of Christ uniting believers to each other, at the same time develope in each of them a riper character. Jesus Christ was the "perfect man." In Him our nature attained, without the least flaw or failure, its true end,—which is to glorify God. In His fulness the plenitude of God is embodied; it is made human, and attainable to faith. In Jesus Christ humanity rose to its ideal stature; and we see what is the proper level of our nature, the dignity and worth to which we have to rise. We are "predestinated to be conformed to the image of God's Son." All the many brethren of Jesus measure themselves against the stature of the Firstborn; and they will have to say to the end with St Paul: "Not as though I had attained, either were already perfect. I follow after; I press towards the mark." A true heart that has seen perfection, will never rest short of it.

"Till we arrive—till we *all* arrive" at this, the work of the Christian ministry is incomplete. Teachers must still school us, pastors shepherd us, evangelists mission us. There is work enough and to spare for them all—and will be, to all appearance, for many a generation to come. The goal of the regenerate life is never absolutely won; it is hid with Christ in God. But there is to be a constant approximation to it, both in the individual believer and in the body of Christ's people. And a time is coming when that goal will be practically attained, so far as earthly conditions allow. The Church after long strife will be reunited, after long trial will be perfected; and Christ will "present her to Himself" a bride worthy of her Lord, "without spot or wrinkle or any such thing." Then this world will have had its use, and will give place to the new heavens and earth.

II. The goal that the apostle marked out, did not appear to him to be in immediate prospect. The childishness of so many Christian believers stood in the way of its attainment. In this condition they were exposed to the seductions of error, and ready to be driven this way and that by the evil influences active in the world of thought around them. So long as the Church contains a number of unstable souls, so long she will remain subject to strife and corruption. When he says in verse 14, "that we may be *no longer children* tossed to and fro," etc., this implies that many Christian believers at that time were of this childish sort, and were being so distracted and misled. The apostle writes on purpose to instruct these "babes" and to raise them to a more manly style of Christian thought and life.[111]

It is a grievous thing to a minister of Christ to see those who for the time ought to be teachers, fit for the Church's strong meat and the harder tasks of her service, remaining still infantile in their condition, needing to be nursed and humoured, narrow in their views of truth, petty and personal in their aims, wanting in all generous feeling and exalted thought. Some men, like St Paul himself, advance from the beginning to a settled faith, to a large intelligence and a full and manly consecration to God. Others remain "babes in Christ" to the end. Their souls live, but never thrive. They suffer from every change in the moral atmosphere, from every new wind of doctrine. These invalids are objects full of interest to the moral pathologist; they are marked not unfrequently by fine and delicate qualities. But they are a constant anxiety to the Church. Till they grow into something more robust they must remain to crowd the Church's nursery, instead of taking part in her battle like brave and strenuous men.

The appearance of false doctrine in the Asian Churches made their undeveloped condition a matter for peculiar apprehension to the apostle. The Colossian heresy, for example, with which he is dealing at this present moment, would have no attraction for ripe and settled Christians. But such a "scheme of error" was exactly suited to catch men with a certain tincture of philosophy and in general sympathy with current thought, who had embraced Christianity under some vague sense of its satisfaction for their spiritual needs, but without an intelligent grasp of its principles or a thorough experience of its power.

St Paul speaks of "every wind of *the* doctrine," having in his mind a more or less definite form of erroneous teaching, a certain "plan of error." Reading this verse in the light of the companion letter to Colossæ and the letters addressed to Timothy when at Ephesus a few years later, we can understand its significance. We can watch the storm that was rising in the Græco-Asiatic Churches. The characteristics of early Gnosticism are well defined in the miniature picture of verse 14. We note, in the first place, its protean and capricious form, half Judaistic, half philosophical—ascetic in one direction, libertine in another: "tossed by the waves, and carried about with every wind." In the next place, its intellectual spirit,—that of a loose and reckless speculation: "in the hazarding of men,"—not in the abiding truth of God. Morally, it was vitiated by "craftiness." And in its issue and result, this new teaching was leading "to the scheme of error" which the apostle four years ago had sorrowfully predicted, in bidding farewell to the Ephesian elders at Miletus (Acts xx.). This scheme was no other than the gigantic Gnostic system, which devastated the Eastern Churches and inflicted deep and lasting wounds upon them.

The struggle with legalism was now over and past, at least in its critical phase. The apostle of the Gentiles had won the battle with Judaism and saved the Church in its first great conflict. But another strife is impending (comp. vi. 10); a most pernicious error has made its appearance within the Church itself. St Paul was not to see more than the commencement of the new movement, which took two generations to gather its full force; but he had a true prophetic insight, and he saw that the strength of the Church in the coming day of trial lay in the depth and reality of her knowledge of the Son of God.

At every crisis in human thought there emerges some prevailing method of truth, or of error, the resultant of current tendencies, which unites the suffrages of a large body of thinkers and claims to embody the spirit of the age. Such a method of error our own age has produced as the outcome of the anti-Christian speculation of modern times, in the doctrines current under the names of Positivism, Secularism, or Agnosticism. While the Gnosticism of the early ages asserted the infinite distance of God from the world and the intrinsic evil of matter, modern Agnosticism removes God still further from us, beyond the reach of thought, and leaves us with material nature as the one positive and accessible reality, as the basis of life and law. Faith and knowledge of the Son of God it banishes as dreams of our childhood. The supernatural, it tells us, is an illusion; and we must resign ourselves to be once more without God in the world and without hope beyond death.

This materialistic philosophy gathers to a head the unbelief of the century. It is the living antagonist of Divine revelation. It supplies the appointed trial of faith for educated men of our generation, and the test of the intellectual vigour and manhood of the Church.

III. In the midst of the changing perils and long delays of her history, the Church is called evermore to press towards the mark of her calling. The conditions on which her progress depends are summed up in verses 15 and 16.

To the craft of false teachers St Paul would have his Churches oppose the weapons only of *truth and love*. "Holding the truth in love," they will "grow up in all things into Christ." Sincere believers, heartily devoted to Christ, will not fall into fatal error. A healthy life instinctively repels disease. They "have an anointing from the Holy One" which is their protection (1 John ii. 20–29). In all that belongs to godliness and a noble manhood, such natures will expand; temptation and the assaults of error stimulate rather than arrest their growth. And with the growth and ripening in her fellowship of such men of God, the whole Church grows.

Next to the moral condition lies the spiritual condition of advancement,—viz., the full recognition of *the supremacy and sufficiency of Christ*. Christ assumes here two opposite relations to the members of His body. He is the Head *into* (or *unto*) which we grow in all things; but at the same time, *from* whom all the body derives its increase (ver. 16). He is the perfect ideal for us each; He is the common source of life and progress for us all. In our individual efforts after holiness and knowledge, in our personal aspirations and struggles, Jesus Christ is our model, our constant aim: we "grow into Him" (ver. 15). But as we learn to live for others, as we merge our own aims in the life of the Church and of humanity we feel, even more deeply than our personal needs had made us do, our dependence upon Him. We see that the forces which are at work to raise mankind, to stay the strifes and heal the wounds of humanity, emanate from the living Christ (ver. 16). He is the head of the Church and the heart of the world.

The third, practical condition of Church growth is brought out by the closing words of the paragraph. It is *organization*: "all the body fitly framed [comp. ii. 21] and knit together." Each local *ecclesia*, or assembly of saints, will have its stated officers, its regulated and seemly order in worship and in work. And within this fit frame, there must be the warm union of hearts, the frank exchange of thought and feeling, the brotherly counsel in all things touching the kingdom of God, by which Christian men in each place of their assembling are "knit together." From these local and congregational centres, the Christian fellowship spreads out its arms to embrace all that love our Lord Jesus Christ.

A building or a machine is *fitted* together by the adjustment of its parts. A body needs, besides this mechanical construction, a pervasive life, a sympathetic force *knitting* it together: "knit together in love," the apostle says in Colossians ii. 2; and so it is "in love" that this "body builds up itself." The tense of the participles in the first part of verse 16 is present (continuous); we see a body in process of incorporation, whose several organs, imperfectly developed and imperfectly co-operant, are increasingly drawn to each other and bound more firmly in one as each becomes more complete in itself. The perfect Christian and the perfect Church are taking shape at once. Each of them requires the other for its due realization.

The rest of the sentence, following the comma that we place at "knit together," has its parallel in Colossians ii. 19: "All the body, through its junctures and bands being supplied and knit together, increaseth with the increase of God." According to St Paul's physiology, the "bands" knit the body together, but the "junctures" are its means of supply. Each point of contact is a means of nourishment to the frame. In touch with each other, Christians communicate the life flowing from the common Head. The apostle would make *Christian intercourse a universal means of grace.* No two Christian men should meet anywhere, upon any business, without themselves and the whole Church being the better for it.

"Wherever two or three are met together in my name," said Jesus, "there am I in the midst." In the multitude of these obscure and humble meetings of brethren who love each other for Christ's sake, is the grace supplied, the love diffused abroad, by which the Church lives and thrives. The vitality of the

Church of Christ does not depend so much upon the large and visible features of its construction—upon Synods and Conferences, upon Bishops and Presbyteries and the like, influential and venerable as these authorities may be; but upon the spiritual intercourse that goes on amongst the body of its people. "Each several part" of Christ's great body, "according to the measure" of its capacity, is required to receive and to transmit the common grace.

However defective in other points of organization, the society in which this takes place fulfils the office of an ecclesiastical body. It will grow into the fulness of Christ; it "builds up itself in love." The primary condition of Church health and progress is that there shall be an unobstructed flow of the life of grace from point to point through the tissues and substance of the entire frame.

FOOTNOTES:

[105] Εἰς ἕνα καινὸν ἄνθρωπον (*homo*), ch. ii. 15; similarly in iv. 22, 24; Rom. vi. 6; 1 Cor. xv. 45, 47, etc. Here εἰς ἄνδρα τέλειον (*vir*); comp. 1 Cor. xiii. 11; James iii. 2. To call the Church ἀνήρ would be highly incongruous, in view of ch. v. 23, etc.; comp. 2 Cor. xi. 2.

[106] Col. i. 22, 28, 29; 2 Tim. ii. 10.

[107] For this association of metaphor, comp. Shakespeare: *Julius Cæsar*, Act V., Scene 1:—

"Blow, wind; swell, billow; and swim, bark!
The storm is up; and all is on the hazard!"

[108] Vulgate: *per omnem juncturam ministrationis*. St Paul's word here is διὰ πάσης ἀφῆς, *through every touching*. See Lightfoot's valuable note on the medical and philosophical use of the word by Greek authors, in his Commentary on Colossians (ii. 19).

[109] Comp. ch. i. 13: "in whom you also [Gentiles, along with us Jews] found hope"; also Rom. iii. 29, 30; Tit. i. 4, "my true child according to *a common faith*."

[110] See the connexion of thought in Col. ii. 8–10, 18, 19.

[111] Compare 1 Cor. ii. 6, iii. 1–3, xiv. 20, xvi. 13; Gal. iv. 19; Heb. v. 11–14.

ON CHRISTIAN MORALS.

Chapter iv. 17—v. 21.

Ἐν καινότητι ζωῆς περιπατήσωμεν.—Rom. vi. 4.

CHAPTER XIX.

THE WALK OF THE GENTILES.

"This I say, therefore, and testify in the Lord, that ye no longer walk as the Gentiles also walk, in the vanity of their mind, being darkened in their understanding, alienated from the life of God because of the ignorance that is in them, because of the hardening of their heart; who being past feeling gave themselves up to lasciviousness, to work all uncleanness with greediness."—EPH. iv. 17–19.

Christ has called into existence and formed around Him already a new world. Those who are members of His body, are brought into another order of being from that to which they had formerly belonged. They have therefore to walk in quite another way—"no longer as the Gentiles." St Paul does not say "as the other Gentiles" (A.V.); for his readers, though Gentiles by birth (ii. 11), are now of the household of faith and the city of God. They hold the franchise of the "commonwealth of Israel." As at a later time the apostle John in his Gospel, though a born Jew, yet from the standpoint of the new Israel writes of "the Jews" as a distant and alien people, so St Paul distinguishes his readers from "the Gentiles" who were their natural kindred.

When he "testifies," with a pointed emphasis, "that *you* no longer walk as do indeed the Gentiles," and when in verse 20 he exclaims, "But *you* did not thus learn the Christ," it appears that there were those bearing Christ's name and professing to have learnt of Him who did thus walk. This, indeed, he expressly asserts in writing to the Philippians (ch. iii. 18, 19): "Many walk, of whom I told you oftentimes, and now tell you even weeping,—the enemies of the cross of Christ; whose god is their belly, and their glory in their shame, who mind earthly things." We cannot but associate this warning with the apprehension expressed in verse 14 above. The reckless and unscrupulous teachers against whose seductions the apostle guards the infant Churches of Asia Minor, tampered with the morals as well as with the faith of their disciples, and were drawing them back insidiously to their former habits of life.[112]

The connexion between the foregoing part of this chapter and that on which we now enter, lies in the relation of the new life of the Christian believer to the new community which he has entered. The old world of Gentile society had formed the "old man" as he then existed, the product of centuries of debasing idolatry. But in Christ that world is abolished, and a "new man" is born. The world in which the Asian Christians once lived as "Gentiles in the flesh," is dead to them.[113] They are partakers of the regenerate humanity constituted in Jesus Christ. From this idea the apostle deduces the ethical doctrine of the following paragraphs. His ideal "new man" is no mere ego, devoted to his personal perfection; he is part and parcel of the redeemed society of men; his virtues are those of a member of the Christian order and commonwealth.

The representation given of Gentile life in the three verses before us is highly condensed and pungent. It is from the same hand as the lurid picture of Romans i. 18–32. While this delineation is comparatively brief and cursory, it carries the analysis in some respects deeper than does that memorable passage. We may distinguish the main features of the description, as they bring into view in turn the *mental*, *spiritual*, and *moral* characteristics of the existing Paganism. Man's intellect was confounded; religion was dead; profligacy was flagrant and shameless.

I. "The Gentiles walk," the apostle says, "in *vanity of their mind*"—with reason frustrate and impotent; "being *darkened in their understanding*"—with no clear or settled principles, no sound theory of life. Similarly, he wrote in Romans i. 21: "They were frustrated in their reasonings, and their senseless heart was darkened." But here he seems to trace the futility further back, beneath the "reasonings" to the "reason" (*nous*) itself. The Gentile mind was deranged at its foundation. Reason seemed to have suffered a paralysis. Man has forfeited his claim to be a rational creature, when he worships objects so degraded as the heathen gods, when he practises vices so detestable and ruinous.

The men of intellect, who held themselves aloof from popular beliefs, for the most part confessed that their philosophies were speculative and futile, that certainty in the greatest and most serious matters was unattainable. Pilate's question, "What is truth?"—no jesting question surely—passed from lip to lip and from one school of thought to another, without an answer. Five centuries before this time the human intellect had a marvellous awakening. The art and philosophy of Greece sprang into their glorious life, like Athené born from the head of Zeus, full-grown and in shining armour. With such leaders as Pericles and Phidias, as Sophocles and Plato, it seemed as though nothing was impossible to the mind of man. At last the genius of our race had blossomed; rich and golden fruit would surely follow, to be gathered from the tree of life. But the blossoms fell, and the fruit proved as rottenness. Grecian art had sunk into a meretricious skill; poetry was little more than a trick of words; philosophy, a wrangling of the schools. Rome towered in the majesty of her arms and laws above the faded glory of Greece. She promised a more practical and sober ideal, a rule of world-wide justice and peace and material plenty. But this dream vanished, like the other. The age of the Cæsars was an age of disillusion. Scepticism and cynicism, disbelief in goodness, despair of the future possessed men's minds. Stoics and Epicureans, old and new Academics, Peripatetics and Pythagoreans disputed the palm of wisdom in mere strife of words. Few of them possessed any earnest faith in their own systems. The one craving of Athens and the learned was "to hear some new thing," for of the old things all thinking men were weary. Only rhetoric and scepticism flourished. Reason had built up her noblest constructions as if in sport, to pull them down again. "On the whole, this last period of Greek philosophy, extending into the Christian era, bore the marks of intellectual exhaustion and impoverishment, and of despair in the solution of its high problem" (Döllinger). The world itself admitted the apostle's reproach that "by wisdom it knew not God." It knew nothing, therefore, to sure purpose, nothing that availed to satisfy or save it.

Our own age, it may be said, possesses a philosophic method unknown to the ancient world. The old metaphysical systems failed; but we have relaid the foundations of life and thought upon the solid ground of nature. Modern culture rests upon a basis of positive and demonstrated knowledge, whose value is independent of religious belief. Scientific discovery has put us in command of material forces that secure the race against any such relapse as that which took place in the overthrow of the Græco-Roman civilization. *Pessimism* answers these pretensions made for physical science by her idolaters. Pessimism is the nemesis of irreligious thought. It creeps like a slow palsy over the highest and ablest minds that reject the Christian hope. What avails it to yoke steam to our chariot, if black care still sits behind the rider? to wing our thoughts with the lightning, if those thoughts are no happier or worthier than before?

"Civilization contains within itself the elements of a fresh servitude. Man conquers the powers of nature, and becomes in turn their slave" (F. W. Robertson). Poverty grows gaunt and desperate by the side of lavish wealth. A new barbarism is bred in what science grimly calls the *proletariate*, a barbarism more vicious and dangerous than the old, that is generated by the inhuman conditions of life under the existing regime of industrial science.

Education gives man quickness of wit and new capacity for evil or good; culture makes him more sensitive; refinement more delicate in his virtues or his vices. But there is no tendency in these forces as we see them now in operation, any more than in the classical discipline, to make nobler or better men. Secular knowledge supplies nothing to bind society together, no force to tame the selfish passions, to guard the moral interests of mankind. Science has given an immense impetus to the forces acting on civilized men; it cannot change or elevate their character. It puts new and potent instruments into our hands; but whether those instruments shall be tools to build the city of God or weapons for its destruction, is determined by the spirit of the wielders. In the midst of his splendid machinery, master of the planet's wealth and lord of nature's forces, the civilized man at the end of this boastful century stands with a dull and empty heart—without God. Poor creature, he wants to know whether "life is worth living"! He has gained the world, but lost his soul.

In vanity of mind and darkness of reasoning men stumble onwards to the end of life, to the end of time. The world's wisdom and the lessons of its history give no hope of any real advance from darkness to light until, as Plato said, "We are able more safely and securely to make our journey, borne on some firmer vehicle, on some Divine word."[114] Such a vehicle those who believe in Christ have found in His teaching. The moral progress of the Christian ages is due to its guidance. And that moral progress has created the conditions and given the stimulus to which our material and scientific progress is due. Spiritual life gives permanence and value to all man's acquisitions. Both of this world and of that to come "godliness holds the promise." We are only beginning to learn how much was meant when Jesus Christ announced Himself as "the light of the world." He brought into the world a light which was to shine through all the realms of human life.

II. The delusion of mind in which the nations walked, resulted in a settled state of *estrangement from God*. They were "alienated from the life of God."

"Alienated from the commonwealth of Israel," St Paul said in chapter ii. 12, [115] using, as he does here, the Greek perfect participle, which denotes an abiding fact. These two alienations generally coincide. Outside the religious community, we are outside the religious life. This expression gathers to a point what was said in verses 11, 12 of chapter ii., and further back in verses 1–3; it discloses the spring of the soul's malady and decay in its separation from the living God. When shall we learn that in God only is our life? We may exist without God, as a tree cast out in the desert, or a body wasting in the grave; but that is not *life*.

Everywhere the apostle moved amongst men who seemed to him dead—joyless, empty-hearted, weary of an idle learning or lost in sullen ignorance, caring only to eat and drink till they should die like the beasts. Their so-called gods were phantasms of the Divine, in which the wiser of them scarcely even pretended to believe. The ancient natural pieties—not wholly untouched by the Spirit of God, despite their idolatry—that peopled with fair fancies the Grecian shores and skies, and taught the sturdy Roman his manfulness and hallowed his love of home and city, were all but extinguished. Death was at the heart of Pagan religion; corruption in its breath. Few indeed were those who believed in the existence of a wise and righteous Power behind the veil of sense. The Roman augurs laughed at their own auspices; the priests made a traffic of their temple ceremonies. Sorcery of all kinds was rife, as rife as scepticism. The most fashionable rites of the day were the gloomy and revolting mysteries imported from Egypt and Syria. A hundred years before, the Roman poet Lucretius expressed, with his burning indignation, the disposition of earnest and high-minded men towards the creeds of the later classic times:—

"Humana ante oculos fœde cum vita jaceret,
In terris oppressa gravi sub religione,
Quæ caput e cœli regionibus ostendebat
Horribili super aspectu mortalibus instans,
Primum Graius homo mortalis tollere contra
Est oculos ausus primusque obsistere contra."[116]
                    De Rerum Natura: Bk. I., 62–67.

How alienated from the life of God were those who conceived such sentiments, and those whose creed excited this repugnance. And when amongst ourselves, as it occurs in some unhappy instances, a similar bitterness is cherished, it is matter of double sorrow,—of grief at once for the alienation prompting thoughts so dark and unjust towards our God and Father, and for the misshapen guise in which our holy religion has been presented to make this aversion possible.

The phrase "alienated from the life of God" denotes an objective position rather than a subjective disposition, the state and place of the man who is far from God and and his true life. God exiles sinners from His presence. By a necessary law, their sin acts as a sentence of deprivation. Under its ban they go forth, like Cain, from the presence of the Lord. They can no longer partake of the light of life which streams forth evermore from God and fills the souls that abide in His love.

And this banishment was due to the cause already described,—to the radical perversion of the Gentile mind, which is re-affirmed in the double prepositional clause of verse 18: "because of the ignorance that is in them, because of the hardening of their heart." The repeated preposition (*because of*) attaches the two parallel clauses to the same predicate. Together they serve to explain this sad estrangement from the Divine life; the second *because* supplements the first. It is the ingrained "ignorance" of men that excludes them from the life of God; and this ignorance is no misfortune or unavoidable fate, it is due to a positive "hardening of the heart."

Ignorance is not the mother of devotion, but of indevotion. If men knew God, they would certainly love and serve Him. St Paul agreed with Socrates and Plato in holding that virtue is knowledge. The debasement of the heathen world, he declares again and again, was due to the fact that it "knew not God."[117] The Corinthian Church was corrupted and its Christian life imperilled by the presence in it of some who "had not the knowledge of God" (1 Cor. xv. 33, 34). At Athens, the centre of heathen wisdom, he spoke of the Pagan ages as "the times of ignorance" (Acts xvii. 30); and found in this want of knowledge a measure of excuse. But the ignorance he censures is not of the understanding alone; nor is it curable by philosophy and science. It has an intrinsic ground,—"existing *in* them."

Since the world's creation, the apostle says, God's unseen presence has been clearly visible (Rom. i. 20). Yet multitudes of men have always held false and corrupting views of the Divine nature. At this present time, in the full light of Christianity, men of high intellect and wide knowledge of nature are found proclaiming in the most positive terms that God, if He exists, is unknowable. This ignorance it is not for us to censure; every man must give account of himself to God. There may be in individual cases, amongst the enlightened deniers of God in our own days, causes of misunderstanding beyond the will, obstructing and darkening circumstances, on the ground of which in His merciful and wise judgement God may "overlook" that ignorance, even as He did the ignorance of earlier ages. But it is manifest that while this veil remains, those on whose heart it lies cannot partake in the life of God. Living in unbelief, they walk in darkness to the end, knowing not whither they go.

The Gentile ignorance of God was attended, as St Paul saw it, with an *induration of heart*, of which it was at once the cause and the effect. There is a wilful stupidity, a studied misconstruction of God's will, which has played a large part in the history of unbelief. The Israelitish people presented at this time a terrible example of such guilty callousness (Rom. xi. 7–10, 25). They professed a mighty zeal for God; but it was a passion for the deity of their partial and corrupt imagination, which turned to hatred of the true God and Father of men when He appeared in the person of His Son. Behind their pride of knowledge lay the ignorance of a hard and impenitent heart.

In the case of the heathen, hardness of heart and religious ignorance plainly went together. The knowledge of God was not altogether wanting amongst them; He "left Himself not without witness," as the apostle told them (Acts xiv. 17). Where there is, amid whatever darkness, a mind seeking after truth and right, some ray of light is given, some gleam of a better hope by which the soul may draw nigh to God,—coming whence or how perhaps none can tell. The gospel of Christ finds in every new land souls waiting for God's salvation. Such a preparation for the Lord, in hearts touched and softened by the preventings of grace, its first messengers discovered everywhere,—a remnant in Israel and a great multitude amongst the heathen.

But the Jewish nation as a whole, and the mass of the pagans, remained at present obstinately disbelieving. They had no perception of the life of God, and felt no need of it; and when offered, they thrust it from them. Theirs was another god, "the god of this world," who "blinds the minds of the unbelieving" (2 Cor. iv. 3, 4). And their "ungodliness and unrighteousness" were not to be pitied more than blamed. They might have known better; they were "holding down the truth in unrighteousness," putting out the light that was in them and contradicting their better instincts. The wickedness of that generation was the outcome of a hardening of heart and blinding of conscience that had been going on for generations past.

III. By two conspicuous features the decaying Paganism of the Christian era was distinguished,—its unbelief and its *licentiousness*. In his letter to the Romans St Paul declares that the second of these deplorable characteristics was the consequence of the former, and a punishment for it inflicted by God. Here he points to it as a manifestation of the hardening of heart which caused their ignorance of God: "Having lost all feeling, they gave themselves up to lasciviousness, so as to commit every kind of uncleanness in greediness."

Upon that brilliant classic civilization there lies a shocking stain of impurity. St Paul stamps upon it the burning word *Aselgeia (lasciviousness)*, like a brand on the harlot's brow. The habits of daily life, the literature and art of the Greek world, the atmosphere of society in the great cities was laden with corruption. Sexual vice was no longer counted vice. It was provided for by public law; it was incorporated into the worship of the gods. It was cultivated in every luxurious and monstrous excess. It was eating out the manhood of the Greek and Latin races. From the imperial Cæsar down to the horde of slaves, it seemed as though every class of society had abandoned itself to the horrid practices of lust.

The "greediness" with which debauchery was then pursued, is at the bottom self-idolatry, self-deification; it is the absorption of the God-given passion and will of man's nature in the gratification of his appetites. Here lies the reservoir and spring of sin, the burning deep within the soul of him who knows no God but his own will, no law above his own desire. He plunges into sensual indulgence, or he grasps covetously at wealth or office; he wrecks the purity, or tramples on the rights of others; he robs the weak, he corrupts the innocent, he deceives and mocks the simple—to feed the gluttonous idol of self that sits upon God's seat within him. The military hero wading to a throne through seas of blood, the politician who wins power and office by the sleights of a supple tongue, the dealer on the exchange who supplants every competitor by his shrewd foresight and unscrupulous daring, and absorbs the fruit of the labour of thousands of his fellow-men, the sensualist devising some new and more voluptuous refinement of vice,—these are all the miserable slaves of their own lust, driven on by the insatiate craving of the false god that they carry within their breast.

For the light-hearted Greeks, lovers of beauty and of laughter, self was deified as Aphrodité, goddess of fleshly desire, who was turned by their worship into *Aselgeia*,—she of whom of old it was said, "Her house is the way to Sheol." Not such as the chaste wife and house-keeping mother of Hebrew praise, but

Laïs with her venal charms was the subject of Greek song and art. Pure ideals of womanhood the classic nations had once known—or never would those nations have become great and famous—a Greek Alcestis and Antigoné, Roman Cornelias and Lucretias, noble maids and matrons. But these, in the dissolution of manners, had given place to other models. The wives and daughters of the Greek citizens were shut up to contempt and ignorance, while the priestesses of vice—*hetæræ* they were called, or *companions* of men—queened it in their voluptuous beauty, until their bloom faded and poison or madness ended their fatal days.

Amongst the Jews whom our Lord addressed, the choice lay between "God and Mammon"; in Corinth and Ephesus, it was "Christ or Belial." These ancient gods of the world—"mud-gods," as Thomas Carlyle called them—are set up in the high places of our populous cities. To the slavery of business and the pride of wealth men sacrifice health and leisure, improvement of mind, religion, charity, love of country, family affection. How many of the evils of English society come from this root of all evil!

Hard by the temple of Mammon stands that of Belial. Their votaries mingle in the crowded amusements of the day and rub shoulders with each other. Aselgeia flaunts herself, wise observers tell us, with increasing boldness in the European capitals. Theatre and picture-gallery and novel pander to the desire of the eye and the lust of the flesh. The daily newspapers retail cases of divorce and hideous criminal trials with greater exactness than the debates of Parliament; and the appetite for this garbage grows by what it feeds upon. It is plain to see whereunto the decay of public decency and the revival of the animalism of pagan art and manners will grow, if it be not checked by a deepened Christian faith and feeling.

Past feeling says the apostle of the brazen impudicity of his time. The loss of the religious sense blunted all moral sensibility. The Greeks, by an early instinct of their language, had one word for *modesty* and *reverence*, for self-respect and awe before the Divine. There is nothing more terrible than the loss of shame. When immodesty is no longer felt as an affront, when there fails to rise in the blood and burn upon the cheek the hot resentment of a wholesome nature against things that are foul, when we grow tolerant and familiar with their presence, we are far down the slopes of hell. It needs only the kindling of passion, or the removal of the checks of circumstance, to complete the descent. The pain that the sight of evil gives is a divine shield against it. Wearing this shield, the sinless Christ fought our battle, and bore the anguish of our sin.

FOOTNOTES:

[112] "The persons here denounced," says Lightfoot on Phil. iii. 18, "are not

the Judaizing teachers, but the antinomian reactionists.... The stress of Paul's grief lies in the fact that they degraded the true doctrine of liberty, so as to minister to their profligate and worldly living." Comp. 1 Peter iv. 3, 4; 2 Peter ii. 18–22.

[113] Comp. Col. ii. 20–iii. 4; Gal. vi. 14, 15.

[114] *Phæao*: § xxxv.

[115] See p. 129.

[116] "When human life to view lay foully prostrate upon earth, crushed down under the weight of religion, who showed her head from the quarters of heaven with hideous aspect lowering upon mortals, a man of Greece ventured first to lift up his mortal eyes to her face and first to withstand her to her face" (Munro).

[117] 1 Thess. iv. 5; 2 Thess. i. 8; Gal. iv. 8, 9.

CHAPTER XX.

THE TWO HUMAN TYPES.

"But ye did not so learn the Christ; if so be that ye heard Him, and were taught in Him, even as truth is in Jesus: that ye put away, as concerning your former manner of life, the old man, which waxeth corrupt after the lusts of deceit; and that ye be renewed in the spirit of your mind, and put on the new man, which after God hath been created in righteousness and holiness of the truth."—EPH. iv. 20–24.

But as for you!—The apostle points us from heathendom to Christendom. From the men of blinded understanding and impure life he turns to the cleansed and instructed. "Not thus did *you* learn the Christ"—not to remain in the darkness and filth of your Gentile state.

The phrase is highly condensed. The apostle, in this letter so exuberant in expression, yet on occasion is as concise as in Galatians. One is tempted, as Beza suggested[118] and Hofmann insists, to put a stop at this point and to read: "But with you it is not so:[119] you learned the Christ!" In spite of its abruptness, this construction would be necessary, if it were only "the Gentiles" of verse 17 with whose "walk" St Paul means to contrast that of his readers. But, as we have seen, he has before his eye a third class of men, unprincipled Christian teachers (ver. 14), men who had in some sense learnt of Christ and yet walked in Gentile ways and were leading others back to them.[120] Verse 20, after all, forms a coherent clause. It points an antithesis of solemn import. There are genuine, and there are supposed conversions; there are true and false ways of learning Christ.

Strictly speaking, it is not *Christ*, but *the Christ* whom St Paul presumes his readers to have duly learnt.[121] The words imply a comprehending faith, that knows who and what Christ is and what believing in Him means, that has mastered His great lessons. To such a faith, which views Christ in the scope and breadth of His redemption, this epistle throughout appeals; for its impartation and increase St Paul prayed the wonderful prayer of the third chapter. When he writes not simply, "You have believed in Christ," but "You have *learned the Christ*," he puts their faith upon a high level; it is the faith of approved disciples in Christ's school. For such men the "philosophy and vain deceit" of Colossæ and the plausibilities of the new "scheme of error" will have no charm. They have found the treasures of wisdom and knowledge that are hidden in Christ.

The apostle's confidence in the Christian knowledge of his readers is, however, qualified in verse 21 in a somewhat remarkable way: "If verily it is

He whom you heard, and in Him that you were taught, as truth is in Jesus." We noted at the outset the bearing of this sentence on the destination of the letter. It would never occur to St Paul to question whether the *Ephesian* Christians were taught Christ's true doctrine. If there were any believers in the world who, beyond a doubt, had heard the truth as in Jesus in its certainty and fulness, it was those amongst whom the apostle had "taught publicly and from house to house," "not shunning to declare all the counsel of God" and "for three years night and day unceasingly with tears admonishing each single one" (Acts xx. 18–35). To suppose these words written in irony, or in a modest affectation, is to credit St Paul with something like an ineptitude. Doubt was really possible as to whether all his readers had heard of Christ aright, and understood the obligations of their faith. Supposing, as we have done, that the epistle was designed for the Christians of the province of Asia generally, this qualification is natural and intelligible.

There are several considerations which help to account for it. When St Paul first arrived at Ephesus, eight years before this time, he "found certain disciples" there who had been "baptized into John's baptism," but had not "received the Holy Spirit" nor even heard of such a thing (Acts xix. 1–7). Apollos formerly belonged to this company, having preached and "taught carefully the things about Jesus," while he "knew only the baptism of John" (Acts xviii. 25). One very much desires to know more about this Church of the Baptist's disciples in Asia Minor. Its existence so far away from Palestine testifies to the power of John's ministry and the deep impression that his witness to the Messiahship of Jesus made on his disciples. The ready reception of Paul's fuller gospel by this little circle indicates that their knowledge of Jesus Christ erred only by defect; they had received it from Judæa by a source dating earlier than the day of Pentecost. The partial knowledge of Jesus current for so long at Ephesus, may have extended to other parts of the province, where St Paul had not been able to correct it as he had done in the metropolis.

Judaistic Christians, such as those who at Rome "preached Christ of envy and strife," were also disseminating an imperfect Christian doctrine. They limited the rights of uncircumcised believers; they misrepresented the Gentile apostle and undermined his influence. A third and still more lamentable cause of uncertainty in regard to the Christian belief of Asian Churches, was introduced by the rise of Gnosticizing error in this quarter. Some who read the epistle had, it might be, received their first knowledge of Christ through channels tainted with error similar to that which was propagated at Colossæ. With the seed of the kingdom the enemy was mingling vicious tares. The apostle has reason to fear that there were those within the wide circle to which his letter is addressed, who had in one form or other heard a different gospel and a Christ other than the true Christ of apostolic teaching.

Where does he find the test and touchstone of the true Christian doctrine?—In the historical Jesus: "as there is truth *in Jesus*." Not often, nor without distinct meaning, does St Paul use the birth-name of the Saviour by itself. Where he does, it is most significant. He has in mind the facts of the gospel history; he speaks of "the Jesus"[122] of Nazareth and Calvary. The Christ whom St Paul feared that some of his readers might have heard of was not the veritable *Jesus* Christ, but a shadowy and notional Christ, lost amongst the crowd of angels, such as was now being taught to the Colossians. This Christ was neither the image of God, nor the true Son of man. He supplied no sufficient redemption from sin, no ideal of character, no sure guidance and authority to direct the daily walk. Those who followed such a Christ would fall back unchecked into Gentile vice. Instead of the light of life shining in the character and words of Jesus, they must resort to "the doctrines and commandments of men" (Col. ii. 8–23).

Amongst the Gnostics of the second century there was held a distinction between the human (fleshly and imperfect) *Jesus* and the Divine *Christ*, who were regarded as distinct beings, united to each other from the time of the baptism of Jesus to His death. The critics who assert the late and non-Pauline authorship of the epistle, assert that this peculiar doctrine is aimed at in the words before us, and that the identification of Christ with Jesus has a polemical reference to this advanced Gnostic error. The verses that follow show that the writer has a different and entirely practical aim. The apostle points us to our true ideal, to "the Christ" of all revelation manifest in "the Jesus" of the gospel. Here we see "the new man created after God," whose nature we must embody in ourselves. The counteractive of a false spiritualism is found in the incarnate life of the Son of God. The dualism which separated God from the world and man's spirit from his flesh, had its refutation in "the Jesus" of Paul's preaching, whom we see in the Four Gospels. Those who persisted in the attempt to graft the dualistic theosophy upon the Christian faith, were in the end compelled to divide and destroy the Christ Himself. They broke up into *Jesus and Christ* the unity of His incarnatePerson.

It is an entire mistake to suppose that the apostle Paul was indifferent to the historical tradition of Jesus; that the Christ he taught was a product of his personal inspiration, of his inward experience and theological reflection. This preaching of an abstract Christ, distinct from the actual Jesus, is the very thing that he condemns. Although his explicit references in the epistles to the teaching of Jesus and the events of His earthly life are not numerous, they are such as to prove that the Churches St Paul taught were well instructed in that history. From the beginning the apostle made himself well acquainted with the facts concerning Jesus, and had become possessor of all that the earlier witnesses could relate. His conception of the Lord Jesus Christ is living and realistic in the highest degree. Its germ was in the visible appearance of the glorified Jesus to himself on the Damascus road; but that expanding germ struck down its roots into the rich soil of the Church's recollections of the incarnate Redeemer as He lived and taught and laboured, as He died and rose again amongst men. Paul's Christ was the Jesus of Peter and of John and of our own Evangelists; there was no other. He warns the Church against all unhistorical, subjective Christs, the product of human speculation.

The Asian Christians who held a true faith, had received Jesus as the Christ. So accepting Him, they accepted a fixed standard and ideal of life for themselves. With Jesus Christ evidently set forth before their eyes, let them look back upon their past life; let them contrast what they had been with what they are to be. Let them consider what things they must "put off" and what "put on," so that they may "be found in Him."

Strangely did the image of Jesus confront the pagan world; keenly its light smote on that gross darkness. There stood the Word made flesh—purity immaculate, love in its very self—shaped forth in no dream of fancy or philosophy, but in the veritable man Christ Jesus, born of Mary, crucified under Pontius Pilate,—truth expressed

"In loveliness of perfect deeds,
More strong than all poetic thought."

And this life of Jesus, living in those who loved Him (2 Cor. iv. 11), ended not when He passed from earth; it passed from land to land, speaking many tongues, raising up new witnesses at every step as it moved along. It was not a new system, a new creed, but *new men* that it gave the world in Christ's disciples, men redeemed from all iniquity, noble and pure as sons of God. It was the sight of Jesus, and of men like Jesus, that shamed the old world, so corrupt and false and hardened in its sin. In vain she summoned the gates of death to silence the witnesses of Jesus. At last

"She veiled her eagles, snapped her sword,
And laid her sceptre down;
Her stately purple she abhorred,
And her imperial crown.
She broke her flutes, she stopped her sports,
Her artists could not please;
She tore her books, she shut her courts,
She fled her palaces;
Lust of the eye and pride of life—
She left it all behind,
And hurried, torn with inward strife,
The wilderness to find" (*Obermann once more*).

The Galilean conquered! The new man was destined to convict and destroy the old. "God sending His Son in the likeness of sinful flesh, and for sin, condemned sin in the flesh" (Rom. viii. 3). When Jesus lived, died, and rose again, an inconceivable revolution in human affairs had been effected. The cross was planted on the territory of the god of this world; its victory was inevitable. The "grain of wheat" fell into the ground to die: there might be still a long, cruel winter; many a storm and blight would delay its growth; but the harvest was secure. Jesus Christ was the type and the head of a new moral order, destined to control the universe.

To see the new and the old man side by side was enough to assure one that the future lay with Jesus. Corruption and decrepitude marked every feature of Gentile life. It was gangrened with vice,—"wasting away in its deceitful lusts."

St Paul had before his eyes, as he wrote, a conspicuous type of the decaying Pagan order. He had appealed as a citizen of the empire to *Cæsar* as his judge. He was in durance as *Nero's* prisoner, and was acquainted with the life of the palace (Phil. i. 13). Never, perhaps, has any line of rulers dominated mankind so absolutely or held in their single hand so completely the resources of the world as did the Cæsars of St Paul's time. Their name has ever since served to mark the summit of autocratic power. It was, surely, the vision of Tiberius sitting at Rome that Jesus saw in the wilderness, when "the devil showed Him all the kingdoms of the world and their glory; and said, All this hath been delivered to me, and to whomsoever I will I give it." The Emperor was the topstone of the splendid edifice of Pagan civilization, that had been rearing for so many ages. And Nero was the final product and paragon of the Cæsarean house!

At this epoch, writes M. Renan,[123] "*Nero and Jesus*, Christ and Antichrist, stand opposed, confronting each other, if I may dare to say so, like heaven and hell.... In face of Jesus there presents itself a monster, who is the ideal of evil as Jesus of goodness.... Nero's was an evil nature, hypocritical, vain, frivolous, prodigiously given to declamation and display; a blending of false intellect, profound wickedness, cruel and artful egotism carried to an incredible degree of refinement and subtlety.... He is a monster who has no second in history, and whose equal we can only find in the pathological annals of the scaffold.... The school of crime in which he had grown up, the execrable influence of his mother, the stroke of parricide forced upon him, as one might say, by this abominable woman, by which he had entered on the stage of public life, made the world take to his eyes the form of a horrible comedy, with himself for the chief actor in it. At the moment we have now reached [when St Paul entered Rome], Nero had detached himself completely from the philosophers who had been his tutors. He had killed nearly all his relations. He had made the most shameful follies the common fashion. A large part of Roman society, following his example, had descended to the lowest level of debasement. The cruelty of the ancient world had reached its consummation…. The world had touched the bottom of the abyss of evil; it could only reascend."

Such was the man who occupied at this time the summit of human power and glory,—the man who lighted the torch of Christian martyrdom and at whose sentence St Paul's head was destined to fall, the Wild Beast of John's awful vision. Nero of Rome, the son of Agrippina, embodied the triumph of Satan as the god of this world. Jesus of Nazareth, the Son of Mary, reigned only in a few loving and pure hearts. Future history, as the scroll of the Apocalypse unfolded it, was to be the battle-field of these confronting powers, the war of Christ with Antichrist.

Could it be doubtful, to any one who had measured the rival forces, on which side victory must fall? St Paul pronounces the fate of the whole kingdom of evil in this world, when he declares that "the old man" is "perishing, according to the lusts of deceit." It is an application of the maxim he gave us in Galatians vi. 8: "He that soweth to his own flesh, shall of the flesh reap corruption." In its mad sensuality and prodigal lusts, the vile Roman world he saw around him was speeding to its ruin. That ruin was delayed; there were moral forces left in the fabric of the Roman State, which in the following generations re-asserted themselves and held back for a time the tide of disaster; but in the end Rome fell, as the ancient world-empires of the East had fallen, through her own corruption, and by "the wrath" which is "revealed from heaven against all ungodliness and unrighteousness of men." For the solitary man, for the household, for the body politic and the family of nations the rule is the same. "Sin, when it is finished, bringeth forth death."

The passions which carry men and nations to their ruin are "lusts *of deceit*." The tempter is the liar. Sin is an enormous fraud. "You shall not die," said the serpent in the garden; "Your eyes will be opened, and you will be as God!" So forbidden desire was born, and "the woman *being deceived* fell into transgression."

"So glistered the dire Snake, and into fraud
Led Eve, our credulous mother, to the tree
Of prohibition, root of all our woe."

By its baits of sensuous pleasure, and still more by its show of freedom and power to stir our pride, sin cheats us of our manhood; it sows life with misery, and makes us self-despising slaves. It knows how to use God's law as an incitement to transgression, turning the very prohibition into a challenge to our bold desires. "Sin taking occasion by the commandment deceived me, and by it slew me." Over the pit of destruction play the same dancing lights that have lured countless generations,—the glitter of gold; the purple robe and jewelled coronet; the wine moving in the cup; fair, soft faces lit with laughter. The straying foot and hot desires give chase, till the inevitable moment comes when the treacherous soil yields, and the pursuer plunges beyond escape into sin's reeking gulfs. Then the illusion is over. The gay faces grow foul; the glittering prize proves dust; the sweet fruit turns to ashes; the cup of pleasure burns with the fire of hell. And the sinner knows at last that his greed has cheated him, that he is as foolish as he is wicked.

Let us remember that there is but one way of escape from the all-encompassing deceit of sin. It is in "learning Christ." Not in learning *about* Christ, but in learning *Him*. It is a common artifice of the great deceit to "wash the outside of cup and platter." The old man is improved and civilized; he is baptized in infancy and called a Christian. He puts off many of his old ways, he dresses himself in a decorous garb and style; and so deceives himself into thinking that he is new, while his heart is unchanged. He may turn ascetic, and deny this or that *to* himself; and yet never deny *himself*. He observes religious forms and makes charitable benefactions, as though he would compound with God for his unforsaken sin. But all this is only a plausible and hateful manifestation of the lusts of deceit. To learn the Christ, is to learn the way of the cross. "Take my yoke upon you, and learn of me," He bids us; "for I am meek and lowly in heart." Till we have done this, we are not even at the beginning of our lesson.

From the perishing old man the apostle turns, in verses 23, 24, to the new. These two clauses differ in their form of expression more than the English rendering indicates.[124] When he writes, "that ye be renewed in the spirit of your mind," it is a *continual rejuvenation* that he describes; the verb is present in tense, and the newness implied is that of recency and youth, newness in point of age. But the "new man" to be "put on" (ver. 24) is of a *new kind and order*; and in this instance the verb is of the aorist tense signifying an event, not a continuous act. The new man is put on when the Christian way of life is adopted, when we enter personally into the new humanity founded in Christ. We "put on the Lord Jesus Christ" (Rom. xiii. 14), who covers and absorbs the old self, even as those who await in the flesh His second advent will "put on the house from heaven," when "the mortal" in them will be "swallowed up of life" (2 Cor. v. 2–4). Thus two distinct conceptions of the life of faith are placed before our minds. It consists, on the one hand, of a quickening, constantly renewed, in the springs of our individual thought and will; and it is at the same time the assumption of another nature, the investiture of the soul with the Divine character and form of its being.

Borne on the stream of his evil passions, we saw "the old man" in his "former manner of life," hastening to the gulf of ruin. For the man renewed in Christ the stream of life flows steadily in the opposite direction, and with a swelling tide moves upward to God. His knowledge and love are always growing in depth, in refinement, in energy and joy. Thus it was with the apostle in his advancing age. The fresh impulses of the Holy Spirit, the unfolding to his spirit of the mystery of God, the fellowship of Christian brethren and the interests of the work of the Church renewed Paul's youth like the eagle's. If in years and toil he is old, his soul is full of ardour, his intellect keen and eager; the "outward man decays, but the inward man is renewed day by day."

This new nature had a new birth. The soul reanimating itself perpetually from the fresh springs that are in God, had in God the beginning of its renovated life. We have not to create or fashion for ourselves the perfect life, but to *adopt* it,—to realize the Christian ideal (ver. 24). We are called to put on the new type of manhood as completely as we renounce the old (ver. 22). The new man is there before our eyes, manifest in the person of Jesus Christ, in whom we live henceforth. When we "learn the Christ," when we have become His true disciples, we "put on" His nature and "walk in Him." The inward reception of His Spirit is attended by the outward assumption of His character as our calling amongst men.

Now, the character of Jesus is human nature as God first formed it. It existed in His thoughts from eternity. If it be asked whether St Paul refers, in verse 24, to the creation of Adam in God's likeness, or to the image of God appearing in Jesus Christ, or to the Christian nature formed in the regenerate, we should say that, to the apostle's mind, the first and last of these creations are merged in the second. The Son of God's love is His primeval image. The race of Adam was created in Christ (Col. i. 15, 16). The first model of that image, in the natural father of mankind, was marred by sin and has become "the old man" corrupt and perishing. The new pattern replacing this broken type is the original ideal, displayed "in the likeness of sinful flesh"—wearing no longer the charm of childish innocence, but the glory of sin vanquished and sacrifice endured—in the Son of God made perfect through suffering. Through all there has been only one image of God, one ideal humanity. The

Adam of Paradise was, within his limits, what the Image of God had been in perfectness from eternity. And Jesus in His human personality represented, under the changed circumstances brought about by sin, what Adam might have grown to be as a complete and disciplined man.

The qualities which the apostle insists upon in the new man are two: "*righteousness* and *holiness* [or *piety*] of the truth." This is the Old Testament conception of a perfect life, whose realization the devout Zacharias anticipates when he sings how God has "shown mercy to our fathers, in remembrance of His holy covenant, ... that we being delivered from the hand of our enemies, might serve Him without fear, in holiness and righteousness before Him all the days of our life." Enchanting vision, still to be fulfilled! "Righteousness" is the sum of all that should be in a man's relations towards God's law; "holiness" is a right disposition and bearing towards God Himself. This is not St Paul's ordinary word for holiness (*sanctification, sanctity*), which he puts so often at the head of his letters, addressing his readers as "saints" in Christ Jesus. That other term designates Christian believers as devoted persons, claimed by God for His own;[125] it signifies holiness as a calling. The word of our text denotes specifically the holiness of temper and behaviour—"that becometh saints." The two words differ very much as *devotedness* from *devoutness*.[126]

A religious temper, a reverent mind marks the true child of grace. His soul is full of the loving fear of God. In the new humanity, in the type of man that will prevail in the latter days when the truth as in Jesus has been learnt by mankind, justice and piety will hold a balanced sway. The man of the coming times will not be atheistic or agnostic: he will be devout. He will not be narrow and self-seeking; he will not be pharisaic and pretentious, practising the world's ethics with the Christian's creed: he will be upright and generous, manly and godlike.

FOOTNOTES:

[118] Quid si post οὕτως distinctionem ascribas? *Vos autem non ita* (subaudi *facere convenit*), *qui didicistis*, etc.

[119] Comp. Numb. xii. 7; Ps. i. 4; Luke xxii. 26, for this Hebraistic turn of expression.

[120] Comp. Phil. iii. 2, 18; Titus i. 16.

[121] See pp. 47, 83, 169, 189.

[122] Ἐστὶν ἀλήθεια ἐν τῷ Ἰησοῦ. The article with the proper name is most significant. It points to the definite image of Jesus, in His actual person, that was made familiar by the preaching of Paul and the other apostles.

[123] *L'Antéchrist*, pp. i. ii. 1, 2. This is a powerful and impressive work, of whose value those who know only the *Vie de Jésus* can have little conception. Renan's faults are many and deplorable; but he is a writer of genius and of candour. His rationalism teems with precious inconsistencies. One hears in him

always the Church bells ringing under the sea, the witness of a faith buried in the heart and never silenced, to which he confesses touchingly in the Preface to his *Souvenirs*.

[124] ἀνανεοῦσθαι δὲ τῷ πνεύματι τοῦ νοὸς ὑμῶν, καὶ ἐνδυσασθαι τὸν καίνον ἄνθρωπον, τὸν κατὰ Θεὸν κτισθέντα.

[125] Comp. pp. 29, 30.

[126] It is important to distinguish the Greek adjectives ἅγιος and ὅσιος, with their derivatives. See Cremer's *N. T. Lexicon* on these words, and Trench's *N. T. Synonyms*, § lxxxviii. Of the latter word, 1 Thess. ii. 10; 1 Tim. i. 9, ii. 8; 2 Tim. iii. 3; Tit. i. 8 are the only examples in St Paul.

CHAPTER XXI.

DISCARDED VICES.

"Wherefore, having put away falsehood, 'speak ye truth each one with his neighbour': for we are members one of another.

"'Be ye angry, and sin not': let not the sun go down upon your provocation: neither give place to the devil.

"Let him that stole steal no more; but rather let him labour, working with his hands the thing that is good, that he may have whereof to give to him that hath need.

"Let no worthless speech proceed out of your mouth, but such as is good for edifying as the need may be, that it may give grace to them that hear. And grieve not the Holy Spirit of God, in whom ye were sealed unto the day of redemption.

"Let all bitterness, and wrath, and anger, and clamour, and railing be put away from you, with all malice: and be ye kind one to another, tenderhearted, forgiving each other, even as God also in Christ forgave you. Be ye therefore imitators of God, as beloved children; and walk in love, even as the Christ also loved you, and gave Himself up for us, an offering and a sacrifice to God for an odour of a sweet smell.

"But fornication, and all uncleanness, or covetousness, let it not even be named among you, as becometh saints; nor filthiness, nor foolish talking, nor jesting, which are not befitting: but rather giving of thanks. For this ye know of a surety, that no fornicator, nor unclean person, nor covetous man, which is an idolater, hath any inheritance in the kingdom of Christ and God. Let no man deceive you with empty words: for because of these things cometh the wrath of God upon the sons of disobedience."—EPH. iv. 25—v. 6.

The transformation described in the last paragraph (vv. 17–24) has now to be carried into detail. The vices of the old heathen self must be each of them replaced by the corresponding graces of the new man in Christ Jesus.

The peculiarity of the instructions given by the apostle for this purpose does not lie in the virtues enjoined, but in the light in which they are set and the motives by which they are inculcated. The common conscience condemns lying and theft, malice and uncleanness; they were denounced with eloquence by heathen moralists. But the ethics of the New Testament differed in many respects from the best moral philosophy: in its direct appeal to the conscience, in its vigour and decision, in the clearness with which it traced our maladies to the heart's alienation from God; but most of all, in the remedy which it applied, the new principle of faith in Christ. The surgeon's knife lays bare the root of the disease; and the physician's hand pours in the healing balm.

Let us observe at the outset that St Paul deals with the actual and pressing temptations of his readers. He recalls what they had been, and forbids them to be such again. The associations and habits of former life, the hereditary force of evil, the atmosphere of Gentile society, and added to all this, as we discover from chapter v. 6, the persuasions of the sophistical teachers now beginning to infest the Church, tended to draw the Asian Christians back to Gentile ways and to break down the moral distinctions that separated them from the pagan world.

Amongst the discarded vices of the forsaken Gentile life, the following are here distinguished: *lying, theft, anger, idle speech, malice, impurity, greed.* These may be reduced to sins of temper, of word, and of act. Let us discuss them in the order in which they are brought before us.

1. "The falsehood"[127] of verse 25 is the antithesis of "the truth" from which righteousness and holiness spring (ver. 24). In accepting the one, Paul's Gentile readers "had put off" the other. When these heathen converts became Christians, they renounced the great lie of idolatry, the system of error and deceit on which their lives were built. They have passed from the realm of illusion to that of truth. "Now," the apostle says, "let your daily speech accord with this fact: you have bidden farewell to falsehood; *speak* truth each with his neighbour." The true religion breeds truthful men; a sound faith makes an honest tongue. Hence there is no vice more hateful than jesuitry, nothing more shocking than the conduct of those who defend what they call "the truth" by disingenuous arts, by tricks of rhetoric and the shifts of an unscrupulous partizanship. "Will you speak unrighteously for God, and talk deceitfully for Him?" *As Christ's truth is in me* cries the apostle, when he would give the strongest possible assurance of the fact he wishes to assert.[128] The social conventions and make-believes, the countless simulations and dissimulations by which the game of life is carried on belong to the old man with his lusts of deceit, to the universal lie that runs through all ungodliness and unrighteousness, which is in the last analysis the denial of God.

St Paul applies here the words of Zechariah viii. 16, in which the prophet promises to restored Israel better days on the condition that they should "speak truth each with his neighbour, and judge truth and the judgement of peace in their gates. And let none of you," he continues, "imagine evil in his heart against his neighbour; and love no false oath. For all these things do I hate, saith the Lord." Such is the law of the New Covenant life. No doubt, St Paul is thinking of the intercourse of Christians with each other when he quotes this command and adds the reason, "For we are *members one of another*." But the word *neighbour*, as Jesus showed, has in the Christian vocabulary no limited import; it includes the Samaritan, the heathen man and publican. When the apostle bids his converts "Follow what is good towards one another, and towards all" (1 Thess. v. 15), he certainly presumes the neighbourly obligation of truthfulness to be no less comprehensive.

Believers in Christ represent a communion which in principle embraces all men. The human race is one family in Christ. For any man to lie to his fellow is, virtually, to lie to himself. It is as if the eye should conspire to cheat the hand, or the one hand play false to the other. Truth is the right which each man claims instinctively from his neighbour; it is the tacit compact that binds together all intelligences. Without neighbourly and brotherly love perfect truthfulness is scarcely possible. "Self-respect will never destroy self-seeking, which will always find in self-interest a side accessible to the temptations of falsehood" (Harless).

2. Like the first precept, the second is borrowed from the Old Testament and shaped to the uses of the New. "*Be ye angry, and sin not*": so the words of Psalm iv. 4 stand in the Greek version and in the margin of our Revised Bible, where we commonly read, "Stand in awe, and sin not. Commune with your own heart upon your bed, and be still." The apostle's further injunction, that anger should be stayed before nightfall, accords with the Psalmist's words; the calming effect of the night's quiet the apostle anticipates in the approach of evening. As the day's heat cools and its strain is relaxed, the fires of anger should die down. With the Jews, it will be remembered, the new day began at evening. Plutarch, the excellent heathen moralist contemporary with St Paul, gives this as an ancient rule of the Pythagoreans: "If at any time they happened to be provoked by anger to abusive language, before the sun set they would take each other's hands and embracing make up their quarrel." If Paul had heard of this admirable prescription, he would be delighted to recognize and quote it as one of those many facts of Gentile life which "show the work of the law written in their hearts" (Rom. ii. 15). The passion which outlives the day, on which the angry man sleeps and that wakes with him in the morning, takes root in his breast; it becomes a settled rancour, prompting ill thoughts and deeds.

There is no surer way of tempting the devil to tempt us than to brood over our wrongs. Every cherished grudge is a "place given" to the tempter, a new entrenchment for the Evil One in his war against the soul, from which he may shoot his "fire-tipped darts" (vi. 16). Let us dismiss with each day the day's vexations, commending as evening falls our cares and griefs to the Divine compassion and seeking, as for ourselves, so for those who may have done us wrong forgiveness and a better mind. We shall rise with the coming light armed with new patience and charity, to bring into the world's turmoil a calm and generous wisdom that will earn for us the blessing of the peacemakers, who shall be called sons of God.

Still the apostle says: "*Be angry*, and sin not." He does not condemn anger in itself, nor wholly forbid it a place within the breast of the saint. Wrath is a glorious attribute of God,—perilous, indeed, for the best of men; but he who cannot be angry has no strength for good. The apostle knew this holy passion, the flame of Jehovah that burns unceasingly against the false and foul and cruel. But he knew its dangers—how easily an ardent soul kindled to exasperation forgets the bounds of wisdom and love; how strong and jealous a curb the temper needs, lest just indignation turn to sin, and Satan gain over us a double advantage, first by the wicked provocation and then by the uncontrolled resentment it excites.

3. From anger we pass to *theft*.

The eighth commandment is put here in a form indicating that some of the apostle's readers had been habitual sinners against it. Literally his words read: "Let him *that steals* play the thief no more." The Greek present participle does not, however, necessarily imply a pursuit now going on, but an habitual or characteristic pursuit, that by which the agent was known and designated: "Let the thief no longer steal!" From the lowest dregs of the Greek cities— from its profligate and criminal classes—the gospel had drawn its converts (comp. 1 Cor. vi. 9–11). In the Ephesian Church there were converted thieves; and Christianity had to make of them honest workmen.

The words of verse 28, addressed to a company of thieves, vividly show the transforming effect of the gospel of Christ: "Let him toil, working with his hands what is good, that he may have wherewith to give to him that is in need." The apostle brings the loftiest motives to bear instantly upon the basest natures, and is sure of a response. He makes no appeal to self-interest, he says nothing of the fear of punishment, nothing even of the pride of honest labour. Pity for their fellows, the spirit of self-sacrifice and generosity is to set those pilfering and violent hands to unaccustomed toil. The appeal was as wise as it was bold. Utilitarianism will never raise the morally degraded. Preach to them thrift and self-improvement, show them the pleasures of an ordered home and the advantages of respectability, they will still feel that their own way of life pleases and suits them best. But let the divine spark of charity be kindled in their breast—let the man have love and pity and not self to work for, and he is a new creature. His indolence is conquered; his meanness changed to the noble sense of a common manhood. Love never faileth.

4. We have passed from speech to temper, and from temper to act; in the warning of verses 29, 30 we come back to speech again.

We doubt whether *corrupt talk* is here intended. That comes in for condemnation in verses 2 and 3 of the next chapter. The Greek adjective is the same that is used of the "*worthless* fruit" of the "*worthless* [*good-for-nothing*] tree" in Matthew xii. 33; and again of the "*bad* fish" of Matthew xiii. 48, which the fisherman throws away not because they are corrupt or offensive, but because they are useless for food. So it is against *inane*, inept and useless talk that St Paul sets his face. Jesus said that "for *every idle word* men must give account to God" (Matt. xii. 36).

Jesus Christ laid great stress upon the exercise of the gift of speech. "By thy words," He said to His disciples, "thou shalt be justified, and by thy words condemned." The possession of a human tongue is an immense responsibility. Infinite good or mischief lies in its power. (With the tongue we should include the pen, as being the tongue's deputy.) Who shall say how great is the sum of injury, the waste of time, the irritation, the enfeeblement of mind and dissipation of spirit, the destruction of Christian fellowship that is due to thoughtless speech and writing? The apostle does not simply forbid injurious words, he puts an embargo on all that is not positively useful. It is not enough to say: "My chatter does nobody harm; if there is no good in it, there is no evil." He replies: "If you cannot speak to profit, be silent till you can."

Not that St Paul requires all Christian speech to be grave and serious. Many a true word is spoken in jest; and "grace" may be "given to the hearers" by words clothed in the grace of a genial fancy and playful wit, as well as in the direct enforcement of solemn themes. It is the mere talk, whether frivolous or pompous—spoken from the pulpit or the easy chair—the incontinence of tongue, the flux of senseless, graceless, unprofitable utterance that St Paul desires to arrest: "let it not proceed out of your mouth." Such speech must not "escape the fence of the teeth." It is an oppression to every serious listener; it is an injury to the utterer himself. Above all, it "grieves the Holy Spirit."

The witness of the Holy Spirit is the seal of God's possession in us;[129] it is the assurance to ourselves that we are His sons in Christ and heirs of life eternal. From the day it is affixed to the heart, this seal need never be broken nor the witness withheld, "until the day of redemption." Dwelling within the Church as the guard of its communion, and loving us with the love of God, the Spirit of grace is hurt and grieved by foolish words coming from lips that He has sanctified. As Israel in its ancient rebellions "vexed His Holy Spirit" (Isai. lxiii. 10), so do those who burden Christian fellowship and who enervate their own inward life by speech without worth and purpose. As His fire is quenched by distrust (1 Thess. v. 19), so His love is vexed by folly. His witness grows faint and silent; the soul loses its joyous assurance, its sense of the peace of God. When our inward life thus declines, the cause lies not unfrequently in our own heedless speech. Or we have listened willingly and without reproof to "words that may do hurt," words of foolish jesting or idle gossip, of mischief and backbiting. The Spirit of truth retires affronted from His desecrated temple, not to return until the iniquity of the lips is purged and the wilful tongue bends to the yoke of Christ. Let us grieve before the Holy Spirit, that He be not grieved with us for such offences. Let us pray evermore: "Set a watch, O Jehovah, before my mouth; keep the door of my lips."

5. In his previous reproofs the apostle has glanced in various ways at love as the remedy of our moral disorders and defects. Falsehood, anger, theft, misuse of the tongue involve disregard of the welfare of others; if they do not spring from positive ill-will, they foster and aggravate it. It is now time to deal directly with this evil that assumes so many forms, the most various of our sins and companion to every other: "Let all bitterness, and wrath, and anger, and clamour, and railing be put away from you, with all malice."

The last of these terms is the most typical. *Malice* is badness of disposition, the aptness to envy and hatred, which apart from any special occasion is always ready to break out in bitterness and wrath. *Bitterness* is malice sharpened to a point and directed against the exasperating object. *Wrath* and *anger* are synonymous, the former being the passionate outburst of resentment in rage, the latter the settled indignation of the aggrieved soul: this passion was put under restraint already in verses 26, 27. *Clamour* and *railing* give audible expression to these and their kindred tempers. Clamour is the loud self-assertion of the angry man, who will make every one hear his grievance; while the railer carries the war of the tongue into his enemy's camp, and vents his displeasure in abuse and insult.

These sins of speech were rife in heathen society; and there were some amongst Paul's readers, doubtless, who found it hard to forgo their indulgence. Especially difficult was this when Christians suffered all manner of evil from their heathen neighbours and former friends; it cost a severe struggle to be silent and "keep the mouth as with a bridle" under fierce and malicious taunts. Never to return evil for evil and railing for railing, but contrariwise blessing,—this was one of the lessons most difficult to flesh and blood.

Kindness in act, *tenderheartedness* of feeling are to take the place of malice with its brood of bitter passions. Where injury used to be met with reviling and insult retorted in worse insult, the men of the new life will be found "forgiving one another, even as God in Christ forgave" them. Here we touch the spring of Christian virtue, the master motive in the apostle's theory of life. The cross of Jesus Christ is the centre of Pauline ethics, as of Pauline theology. The sacrifice of Calvary, while it is the ground of our salvation, supplies the standard and incentive of moral attainment. It makes life *an imitation of God*.

The commencement of the new chapter at this point makes an unfortunate division; for its first two verses are in close consecution with the last verse of chapter iv. By kindness and pitifulness of heart, by readiness to forgive, God's "beloved children" will "show themselves imitators" of their Father. The apostle echoes the saying of his Master, in which the law of His kingdom was laid down: "Love your enemies, and do good, and lend never despairing; and your reward shall be great, and you shall be called children of the Highest: for He is kind to the thankless and evil. Be ye therefore pitiful, as your Father is pitiful" (Luke vi. 35, 36). Before the cross of Jesus was set up, men could not know how much God loved the world and how far He was ready to go in the way of forgiveness. Yet Christ Himself saw the same love displayed in the Father's daily providence. He bids us imitate Him who makes His sun shine and His rain fall on the just and unjust, on the evil and the good. To the insight of Jesus, nature's impartial bounties in which unbelief sees only moral indifference, spoke of God's compassion; they proceed from the same love that gave His Son to taste death for every man.

In chapter iv. 32–v. 2 the Father's love and the Son's self-sacrifice are spoken of in terms precisely parallel. They are altogether one in quality. Christ does not by His sacrifice persuade an angry Father to love His children; it is the Divine compassion in Christ that dictates and carries into effect the sacrifice. At the same time it was "an *offering* and a *sacrifice* to God." God is love; but love is not everything in God. Justice is also Divine, and absolute in its own realm. Law can no more forgo its rights than love forget its compassions. Love must fulfil all righteousness; it must suffer law to mark out its path of obedience, or it remains an effusive, ineffectual sentiment, helpless to bless and save. Christ's feet followed the stern and strait path of self-devotion; "He humbled Himself and became obedient," He was "born under law." And the law of God imposing death as the penalty for sin, which shaped Christ's sacrifice, made it acceptable to God. Thus it was "an odour of a sweet smell."

Hence the love which follows Christ's example, is love wedded with duty. It finds in an ordered devotion to the good of men the means to fulfil the all-holy Will and to present in turn its "offering to God." Such love will be above the mere pleasing of men, above sentimentalism and indulgence; it will aim higher than secular ideals and temporal contentment. It regards men in their kinship to God and obligation to His law, and seeks to make them worthy of their calling. All human duties, for those who love God, are subordinate to this; all commands are summed up in one: "Thou shalt love thy neighbour as thyself." The apostle pronounced the first and last word of his teaching when he said: *Walk in love, as the Christ also loved us.*

6. Above all others, one sin stamped the Gentile world of that time with infamy,—its *uncleanness*.

St Paul has stigmatized this already in the burning words of verse 19. There we saw this vice in its intrinsic loathsomeness; here it is set in the light of Christ's love on the one hand (ver. 2), and of the final judgement on the other (vv. 5, 6). Thus it is banished from the Christian fellowship in every form—

even in the lightest, where it glances from the lips in words of jest: "Fornication and all uncleanness, let it not even be named among you." Along with "filthiness, foolish talk and jesting" are to be heard no more. Passing from verse 2 to verse 3 by the contrastive *But*, one feels how repugnant are these things to the love of Christ. The perfume of the sacrifice of Calvary, so pleasing in heaven, sweetens our life on earth; its grace drives wanton and selfish passions from the heart, and destroys the pestilence of evil in the social atmosphere. Lust cannot breathe in the sight of the cross.

The "good-for-nothing speech" of chapter iv. 29 comes up once more for condemnation in the *foolish speech* and *jesting* of this passage. The former is the idle talk of a stupid, the latter of a clever man. Both, under the conditions of heathen society, were tainted with foulness. Loose speech easily becomes low speech. Wit, unchastened by reverence, finds a tempting field for its exercise in the delicate relations of life, and displays its skill in veiled indecencies and jests that desecrate the purer feelings, while they avoid open grossness.

St Paul's word for "jesting" is one of the singular terms of this epistle. By etymology it denotes a *well-turned* style of expression, the versatile speech of one who can touch lightly on many themes and aptly blend the grave and gay. This social gift was prized amongst the polished Greeks. But it was a faculty so commonly abused, that the word describing it fell into bad odour: it came to signify banter and persiflage; and then, still worse, the kind of talk here indicated,—the wit whose zest lies in its flavour of impurity. "The very profligate old man in the *Miles Gloriosus* of Plautus (iii. I. 42–52), who prides himself, and not without reason, upon his wit, his elegance and refinement [*cavillator lepidus, facetus*], is exactly the εὐτράπελος. And keeping in mind that εὐτραπελία, being only once expressly and by name forbidden in Scripture, is forbidden to Ephesians, it is not a little notable to find him urging that all this was to be expected from him, being as he was an Ephesian by birth:—

Post *Ephesi sum natus*; non enim in Apulia, non Animulæ."[130]

In place of senseless prating and wanton jests—things unbefitting to a rational creature, much more to a saint—the Asian Greeks are to find in *thanksgiving* employment for their ready tongue. St Paul's rule is not one of mere prohibition. The versatile tongue that disported itself in unhallowed and frivolous utterance, may be turned into a precious instrument for God's service. Let the fire of Divine love touch the jester's lips, and that mouth will show forth His praise which once poured out dishonour to its Maker and shame to His image in man.

7. At the end of the Ephesian catalogue of vices, as at the beginning (iv. 19), uncleanness is joined with *covetousness*, or *greed*.

This, too, is "not even to be named amongst you, as becometh saints." *Money! property!* these are the words dearest and most familiar in the mouths of a large class of men of the world, the only themes on which they speak with lively interest. But Christian lips are cleansed from the service both of Belial and of Mammon. When his business follows the trader from the shop to the fireside and the social circle, and even into the Church, when it becomes the staple subject of his conversation, it is clear that he has fallen into the low vice of covetousness. He is becoming, instead of a man, a money-making machine, an "idolater" of

"Mammon, the least erected spirit that fell
From heaven."

The apostle classes the covetous man with the fornicator and the unclean, amongst those who by their worship of the shameful idols of the god of this world exclude themselves from their "inheritance in the kingdom of Christ and of God."

A serious warning this for all who handle the world's wealth. They have a perilous war to wage, and an enemy who lurks for them at every step in their path. Will they prove themselves masters of their business, or its slaves? Will they escape the golden leprosy,—the passion for accumulation, the lust of property? None are found more dead to the claims of humanity and kindred, none further from the kingdom of Christ and God, none more "closely wrapped" within their "sensual fleece" than rich men who have prospered by the idolatry of gain. Dives has chosen and won his kingdom. He "receives in his lifetime his good things"; afterwards he must look for "torments."

FOOTNOTES:

[127] Διὸ ἀποθέμενοι τὸ ψεῦδος. Despite the commentators, we must hold to it that *the lie, the falsehood* is objective and concrete; not *lying*, or *falsehood* as a subjective act, habit, or quality,—which would have been rather ψευδολογία (comp. μωρολογία, v. 4; and 1 Tim. iv. 2, ψευδολόγων), or τὸ ψευδές. So in Rom. i. 25, τὸ ψεῦδος is "the [one great] lie" which runs through all idolatry; and in 2 Thess. ii. 11 it denotes "the lie" which Antichrist imposes on those ready to believe it,—viz., that he himself is God. Accordingly, we take the participle ἀποθέμενοι to signify not what the readers are to do, but what they *had done* in renouncing heathenism. The apostle requires consistency: "Since you are now of the truth, be truth-speaking men."

[128] 2 Cor. i. 18, 19, xi. 10.

[129] See ch. i. 13, 14, and 18 (last clause).

[130] Trench: *N. T. Synonyms*, § xxxiv.

CHAPTER XXII.

DOCTRINE AND ETHICS.

"We are members one of another....

"Let the thief labour ... that he may have whereof to give to him that hath need....

"Grieve not the Holy Spirit of God, in whom ye were sealed unto the day of redemption....

"Forgive each other, even as God also in Christ forgave you. Be ye imitators of God, as beloved children, and walk in love, even as the Christ also loved you, and gave Himself up for us, an offering and a sacrifice to God....

"No fornicator, nor unclean person, nor covetous man, which is an idolater, hath any inheritance in the kingdom of Christ and God."—Eph. iv. 25–v. 6.

The homily that we have briefly reviewed in the last Chapter demands further consideration. It affords a striking and instructive example of St Paul's method as a teacher of morals, and makes an important contribution to evangelical ethics. The common vices are here prohibited on specifically Christian grounds. The new nature formed in Christ casts them off as alien and dead things; they are the sloughed skin of the old life, the discarded dress of the old man who was slain by the cross of Christ and lies buried in His grave.

The apostle does not condemn these sins as being contrary to God's law: that is taken for granted. But the legal condemnation was ineffectual (Rom. viii. 3). The wrath revealed from heaven against man's unrighteousness had left that unrighteousness unchastened and defiant. The revelation of law, approved and echoed by conscience, taught man his guilt; it could do no more. All this St Paul assumes; he builds on the ground of law and its acknowledged findings.

Nor does the apostle make use of the principles of philosophical ethics, which in their general form were familiar to him as to all educated men of the day. He says nothing of the rule of nature and right reason, of the intrinsic fitness, the harmony and beauty of virtue; nothing of expediency as the guide of life, of the inward contentment that comes from well-doing, of the wise calculation by which happiness is determined and the lower is subordinated to the higher good. St Paul nowhere discountenances motives and sanctions of this sort; he contravenes none of the lines of argument by which reason is brought to the aid of duty, and conscience vindicates itself against passion and false self-interest. Indeed, there are maxims in his teaching which remind us of each of the two great schools of ethics, and that make room in the Christian theory of life both for the philosophy of experience and that of intuition. The true theory recognizes, indeed, the experimental and evolutional as well as the fixed and intrinsic in morality, and supplies their synthesis.

But it is not the apostle's business to adjust his position to that of Stoics and Epicureans, or to unfold a new philosophy; but to teach the way of the new life. His Gentile disciples had been untruthful, passionate in temper, covetous, licentious: the gospel which he preached had turned them from these sins to God; from the same gospel he draws the motives and convictions which are to shape their future life and to give to the new spirit within them its fit expression. St Paul has no quarrel with ethical science, much less with the inspired law of his fathers; but both had proved ineffectual to keep men from iniquity, or to redeem them fallen into it. Above them both, above all theories and all external rules he sets the law of the Spirit of life in Christ.

The originality of Christian ethics, we repeat, does not lie in its detailed precepts. There is not one, it may be, even of the noblest maxims of Jesus that had not been uttered by some previous moralist. With the New Testament in our hands, it may be possible to collect from non-Christian sources—from Greek philosophers, from the Jewish Talmud, from Egyptian sages and Hindoo poets, from Buddha and Confucius—a moral anthology which thus sifted out of the refuse of antiquity, like particles of iron drawn by the magnet, may bear comparison with the ethics of Christianity. If Christ is indeed the Son of man, we should expect Him to gather into one all that is highest in the thoughts and aspirations of mankind. Addressing the Athenians on Mars' Hill, the apostle could appeal to "certain of your own poets" in support of his doctrine of the Fatherhood of God. The noblest minds in all ages witness to Jesus Christ and prove themselves to be, in some sort, of His kindred.

> "They are but broken lights of Thee;
> And Thou, O Lord, art more than they!"

It is Christ in us, it is the personal fellowship of the soul with Him and with the living God through Him, that forms the vital and constitutive factor of Christianity. Here is the secret of its moral efficacy. The Christ is the centre root and of the race; He is the image of God in which we were made. The life-blood of mankind flowed in Him as in its heart, and poured forth from Him as from its fountain in sacrifice for the common sin. Jesus gathered into Himself and restored the virtue of humanity broken into a thousand fragments; but He did much more than this. While He re-created in His personal character our lost manhood, by His death and resurrection He has gained for that ideal a transcendent power that seizes upon men and regenerates and transforms them. "With unveiled face beholding in the mirror the glory of the Lord, we are changed into the same image, [receiving the glory that we see] as from the Lord of the Spirit" (2 Cor. iii. 18).

There is, therefore, an evangelical ethics, a Christian science of life. "The law of the Spirit of life in Christ Jesus" has a system and method of its own. It has a rational solution and explanation to render for our moral problems. But its solution is given, as St Paul and as his Master loved to give it, in practice, not in theory. It teaches the art of living to multitudes to whom the names of ethics and moral science are unknown. Those who understand the method of Christ best are commonly too busy in its practice to theorize about it. They are physicians tending the sick and the dying, not professors in some school of medicine. Yet professors have their use, as well as practitioners. The task of developing a Christian science of life, of exhibiting the truth of revelation in its theoretical bearings and its relations to the thought of the age, forms a part of the practical duties of the Church and touches deeply the welfare of souls. For other times this work has been nobly accomplished by Christian thinkers. Shall we not pray the Lord of the harvest that He will thrust forth into this field fit labourers; that He will raise up men mighty through God to overthrow every high thing that exalts itself against His knowledge, and wise to build up to the level of the times the great fabric of Christian ethics and discipline?

There emerge in this exhortation four distinct principles, which lay at the basis of St Paul's views of life and conduct.

I. In the first place, the fundamental truth of *the Fatherhood of God*, "Be imitators of God," he writes, "as beloved children." And in chapter iv. 24: "Put on the new man, which *was created after God*."

Man's life has its law, for it has its source, in the nature of the Eternal. Behind our race-instincts and the laws imposed on us in the long struggle for existence, behind those imperatives of practical reason involved in the structure of our intelligence, is the presence and the active will of Almighty God our heavenly Father. His image we see in the Son of man.

Here is the fountainhead of truth, from which the two great streams of philosophical thought upon morals have diverged. If man is the child of a Being absolutely good, then moral goodness belongs to the essence of his nature; it is discoverable in the instincts of his reason and will. Were not our nature warped by sin, such reasoning must have commanded immediate assent and led to consistent and self-evident results. Again, if man is the *child* of God, the finite of the Infinite, his moral character must, presumably, have been in the beginning germinal rather than complete, needing—even apart from sin and its malformations—development and education, the discipline of a fatherly providence, inculcating the lessons and forming the habits which belong to his ripe manhood and full-grown stature. Intuitional morals bear witness to the God of creation; experimental morals to the God of providence and history. The Divine Fatherhood is the keystone of the arch in which they meet.

The command to "be imitators of God" makes *personality* the sovereign element in life. If consciousness is a finite and passing phenomenon, if God be but a name for the sum of the impersonal laws that regulate the universe, for the "stream of tendency" in the worlds, *Father* and *love* are meaningless terms applied to the Supreme and religion dissolves into an impalpable mist. Is the universe governed by personal will, or by impersonal force? Is reason, or is gravitation the index to the nature of the Absolute? This is the vital question of modern thought. The latter is the answer given by a large, if not a preponderant body of philosophical opinion in our own day,—as it was given, virtually, by the natural philosophers of Greece in the dawn of science. Man's triumphs over nature and the splendour of his discoveries in the physical realm bewilder his reason. The scientists, like other conquerors, have been intoxicated with victory. The universe, it seemed, was about to yield to them its last secrets; they were prepared to analyze the human soul and resolve the conception of God into its material elements. Religion and conscience, however, prove to be intractable subjects in the physical laboratory; they are coming out of the crucible unchanged and refined. We are able by this time to take a more sober measure of the possibilities of the scientific method, and to see what inductive logic and natural selection can do for us, and what they cannot do. We can walk in the light of the new revelation, without being dazzled by it. Things are less altered than we thought. The old boundaries reappear. The spirit resumes its place, and rules a wider realm than before. Reason refuses to be the victim of its own success, and to immolate itself for the deification of material law. "Forasmuch as we are God's offspring," we ought not to think, and we will not think that the Godhead is like to blind forces and reasonless properties of matter. Love, thought, will in us raise our being above the realm of the impersonal; and these faculties point us upward to Him from whom they came, the Father of the spirits of all flesh.

The great tide of joy, the victorious energy which the sense of God's love brings into the life of a Christian, is evidence of its reality. The believer is a child walking in the light of his Father's smile—dependent, ignorant, but the object of an Almighty love. A thousand tokens speak to him of the Divine care; his tasks and trials are sweetened by the confidence that they are appointed for wise ends beyond his present knowledge. To another in that same house there is no heavenly Father, no unseen hand that guides, no gleam of a brighter and purer day lighting up its dull chambers. There are human companions, weak, erring and wearying like oneself. There is work to do, with the night coming swiftly; and the brave heart girds itself to duty, finding in the service of man its motive and employment—but, alas, with how poor success and how faint a hope!

It is not the loss of strength for human service, nor the dying out of joy which unbelief entails, that is its chief calamity; but the unbelief itself. The sun in the soul's heaven is put out. The personal relationship to the Supreme which gave dignity and worth to our individual being, which imparted sacredness and enduring power to all other ties, is destroyed. The heart is orphaned; the temple of the spirit desolate. The mainspring of life is broken.

> "Make haste to answer me, O Jehovah; my spirit faileth!
> Hide not Thy face from me,
> Lest I be like unto them that go down into the pit!"

II. *The solidarity of mankind in Christ* furnishes the apostle with a powerful lever for raising the ethical standard of his readers. The thought that "we are members one of another" forbids deceit. That he may "have whereof to give to the needy" is the purpose that provokes the thief to industry. The desire to "give grace" to the hearers and to "build them up" in truth and goodness imparts seriousness and elevation to social intercourse. The irritations and injuries we inflict on each other, with or without purpose, furnish occasion for us to "be kind one to another, good-hearted, *forgiving yourselves*"—for this is the expression the apostle uses in chapter iv. 32, and in Colossians iii. 13. Self is so merged in the community, that in dealing censure or forgiveness to an offending brother the Christian man feels as though he were dealing with himself—as though it were the hand that forgave the foot for tripping, or the ear that pardoned some blunder of the eye.

Showing-grace is what the apostle literally says here, speaking both of human and Divine forgiveness.[131] In this lies the charm and power of true forgiveness. The forgiver after the order of grace does not pardon like a judge moved by magnanimity or pity for transgressors, but in love to his own kind and desire for their amendment. He identifies himself with the wrong-doer, weighs his temptation and all that drew him into error. Such forgiveness, while it never ignores the wrong, admits every qualifying circumstance and just extenuation. This is the kind of pardon that touches the sinner's heart; for it goes to the heart of the sin, isolating it from all other feelings and conditions that are not sin; it takes the wrong upon itself in understanding and perception; it puts its finger upon the aching, festering spot where the criminality lies and applies to that its healing balm.

"Even as God in Christ forgave you." And how did God forgive? Not by a grand imperial decree, as of some monarch too exalted to resent the injuries of men or to inquire into their futile proceedings. Had such forgiveness been possible to Divine justice, it could have wrought in us no real salvation. Our forgiveness is that of God in Christ. The Forgiver has sat down by the prisoner's side, has felt his misery and the force of his temptations, and in everything but the actual sin has made Himself one with the sinner, even to bearing the extreme penalty of his guilt. In the act of making sacrifice, Jesus prayed for those that slew Him: "Father, forgive them; they know not what they do!" This intercession breathed the spirit of the new forgiveness. There is a real remission of sins, a release granted justly and upon due satisfaction; but it is the act of justice charged with love, of a justice as tender and considerate as it is strong, and which eagerly takes account of all that bespeaks in the offender a possibility of better things. It is a forgiveness that does justice to the humanity as well as the criminality in the sinner.

To proclaim by word and deed this forgiveness of God to the sinful world is the vocation of the Church. And where she does thus declare it, by whatever means or ministry, Christ's promise to her is verified: "Whose-soever sins ye remit, they are remitted to them." We may so reconcile men to ourselves, as to bring them back to God. Has some one done you a wrong? there is your opportunity of saving a soul from death and hiding a multitude of sins. Thus Christ used the great wrong we all did Him. It is your privilege to show the wrong-doer that you and he are made one by the blood of Christ.

"Walk in love," St Paul says, "as the Christ also loved us and gave up Himself for us a sacrifice." When the apostle writes *the Christ*, he points us along the whole line of the revelation of the cross.[132] We think of the Christhood of Jesus, of the Christliness of such love as this. Christ's was a representative and exemplary love, with its forerunners and its followers all walking in one path. "The Christ loved *and gave*"; for love that does not give, that prompts to

197

no effort and puts itself to no sacrifice, is but a luxury of the heart,—useless and even selfish. And He "gave up *Himself*"—the only gift that could suffice. The rich who bestow many gifts in furtherance of humanitarian and religious work and still do not bestow themselves, their sympathetic thought, their presence and personal aid, are withholding the best thing, the one thing required to make their bounties efficacious. In what we give and forgive, it is the accent of sympathy, the giving of the heart with it that adds grace to the act. "Though I dole out all my goods, though I give my body to be burned, and have not love, it profiteth me nothing." We do a thousand things to serve and benefit our fellow-men, and yet evade the real sacrifice,—which is simply to love them.

In studying this epistle, we have felt increasingly that the Church is the centre of humanity. The love born and nourished in the household of faith goes out into the world with a universal mission. The solidarity of moral interests that is realized there, embraces all the kindreds of the earth. The incarnation of Christ knits all flesh into one redeemed family. The continents and races of mankind are members one of another, with Jesus Christ for head. We are brothers and sisters of humanity: He our elder brother, and God our common Father in heaven,—His Father and ours.

Auguste Comte writes in his *System of Positive Polity*: "The promises of supernatural religion appealed exclusively to man's selfish instincts…. The sympathetic instincts found no place in the theological synthesis."[133] It would be impossible to affirm anything more completely at variance with the truth, anything more absolutely opposed to the doctrine of Christ and the theological synthesis of the apostles. And yet it was upon this ground that the great French thinker renounced Christianity, proposing his new religion of humanity as a substitute for a selfish and effete supernaturalism! Why did he not go to the New Testament itself to find out what Christianity means? "To combine permanently concert with independence," Comte excellently says, "is the capital problem of society, a problem which religion alone can solve, by love primarily, then by faith on a basis of love."[134] Precisely so; and this is the solution offered by Jesus Christ. His self-sacrificing love is the basis on which our faith rests; and that faith works by love in all those who truly possess it. This is the evangelical theory. The morale of the Church, it is true, has fallen shamefully below its doctrine; but this doctrine is, after all, the one fruitful and progressive moral force in the world; and it is certain to be carried into effect.

In the darkest hour of Israel's oppression and of international hate, one of her great prophets thus described the triumph of supernatural religion: "In that day shall Israel be the third with Egypt and Assyria, a blessing in the midst of the earth; for that the LORD of hosts hath blessed them, saying, Blessed be Egypt my people, and Assyria the work of my hands, and Israel my inheritance" (Isai. xix. 24, 25). This is our programme still.

III. Another of St Paul's ruling ideas lying at the basis of Christian ethics, is his conception of *man's future destiny*. The apostle warns his readers that they "grieve not the Holy Spirit, in whom they were sealed till the day of redemption." He tells them that "the impure and the covetous have no inheritance in the kingdom of Christ and God."

There is thus disclosed a world beyond the world, a life growing out of life, an eternal and invisible kingdom of whose possession the Spirit that lives in Christian men is the earnest and firstfruits. This kingdom is the joint inheritance of the sons of God, brethren with Christ and in Christ, who are conformed to His image and found worthy to "stand before the Son of man." Those are excluded from the inheritance, who by their moral nature are alien to it: "Without are dogs, sorcerers, whoremongers, idolaters, and every one that loveth and maketh a lie." This revelation has had a most powerful influence on the progress of ethics. It has given a momentous importance to individual conduct, a new grandeur to the moral issues of the present life. "Man's life," viewed in the light of the Christian gospel, "has duties that are alone great, that go up to Heaven, and down to Hell." The tangled skein is at last to be unravelled, the mysterious problem of mortal life will have its solution at the judgement-seat of Jesus Christ.

It is true that the wicked flourish and spread themselves like green trees in the sunshine; and the covetous boast of their hearts' desire. To see this was the trial of ancient faith; and the good man had to charge himself constantly that he should not fret because of evil-doers. It required an heroic faith to believe in God's kingdom and righteousness, when the visible course of things made all against them, and there was no clear light beyond. God's saints had to learn first that God is Himself the sufficient good, and must be trusted to do right. But this was the faith of defence rather than of victory,—of endurance, not enthusiasm. In the knowledge of Christ's victory over death and entrance on our behalf into the heavenly world, "in hope of life eternal which God who cannot lie hath promised," men have fought against their own sins, have struggled for the right and spent themselves to save their fellows with a vigour and success never witnessed before, and in numbers far exceeding those that all other creeds and systems have enlisted in the holy cause of humanity.

Human reason had guessed and hope had dreamed of the soul's immortality. Christianity gives this hope certainty, and adds to it the assurance of the resurrection of the body. Man's entire nature is thus redeemed. Chastity takes its due place amongst the virtues, and becomes the mark of a Christian as distinguished from a pagan life. "The body is not for fornication, but for the Lord, and the Lord for the body. God who raised up the Lord Jesus, will raise us also through His power. Your bodies are limbs of Christ, ... a temple of the Holy Spirit which you have from God.... Glorify God in your body." So St Paul exhorts the Christians of Corinth (1 Ep. vi.), living in the centre and shrine of heathen vice. This doctrine of the sanctity of the body has been the salvation of the family. It has saved civilization from perishing through sexual corruption, and is still our chief defence against this fearful evil.

Our bodily dress, we now learn, is one with the spirit that it infolds. We shall lay it aside only to resume it,—transfigured, but with a form and impress continuous with its present being. This identical self, the same both in its outward and inward personality, will appear before the tribunal of Christ, that it may "receive the things done in the body." This announcement gives reasonableness and distinctness to the expectation of future judgement. The judgement assumes, with its solemn grandeur, a matter-of-fact reality, an immediate bearing on the daily conduct of life, which lends a powerful reinforcement to the conscience, while it supplies a fitting and glorious conclusion to our course as moral beings.

IV. Finally, *the atonement of the cross* stamps its own character and spirit on the entire ethics of Christianity. The Fatherhood of God, the unity and solidarity of mankind, the issues of eternal life or death awaiting us in the unseen world—all the great factors and fundamentals of revealed religion gather about the cross of Christ; they lend to it their august significance, and gain from it new import and impressiveness.

The fact that Christ "gave Himself up for us an offering and sacrifice to God"—gave Himself, as it is put elsewhere, "for our sins"—throws an awful light upon the nature of human transgression. The blood spilt in the strife with our sin and shed to wash out its stain, reveals its foulness and malignity. All that inspired men had taught, that good men had believed and felt and penitent men confessed in regard to the evil of human sin, is more than verified by the sacrifice which the Holy One of God has undergone in order to put it away. It was felt that "the blood of bulls and goats could never take away sins," that the sacrifices man could offer for himself, or the creatures on his behalf, were ineffectual; the guilt was too real to be expiated in this fashion, the wound too deep to be healed by those poor appliances. But who had suspected that such a remedy as this was needed, and forthcoming? How deep the resentment of eternal Justice against the transgressions of men, if the blood of God's own Son alone could make propitiation! How rank the offence against the Divine holiness, if to purge its abomination the vessel containing the most sweet fragrance of His sinless nature must be broken! What tears of contrition, what cleansing fires of hate against our own sins, what scorn of their baseness, what stern resolves against them are awakened by the sight of the cross of our Lord Jesus Christ!

This negative side of the ethical bearing of Christ's sacrifice is implied in the words of the apostle in the second verse, and in the contrast indicated between its sweet savour and those unclean things whose very names it should banish from our midst (ver. 3). On its positive effects—the love and self-devotion it inspires, the conformity of our lives to its example—we have dwelt already. Let us add, however, that the sacrifice of Christ demands from us, above all, *devotion to Christ Himself.* Our first duty as Christians is to love Christ, to serve and follow Christ. "He died for all," says the apostle, "that the living should live no longer to themselves, but to Him that died for them and rose again." When Mary of Bethany poured on the Saviour's head her box of precious ointment, the Master accepted the tribute and approved the act; and the poor have been gainers by it a thousand times the pence which Judas deemed wasted on the head he was watching to betray. There is no conflict between the claims of Christ and those of philanthropy, between the needs of His worship and the needs of the destitute and suffering in our streets. Every new subject won to the kingdom of Christ is another helper won for His poor. Every act of love rendered to Him deepens the channel of sympathy by which relief and blessing come to sorrowful humanity.

Let the gospel of Christ's kingdom be preached in word and deed to all nations, let the love of Christ be brought to bear upon the great masses of mankind, and the time of the world's salvation will be come. Its sin will be hated, forsaken, forgiven. Its social evils will be banished; its weapons of war turned to ploughshares and pruning hooks. Its scattered races and nations will be reunited in the obedience of faith, and formed into one Christian confederacy and commonwealth of the peoples, a peaceful kingdom of the Son of God's love.

FOOTNOTES:

[131] Χαριζόμενοι ἑαυτοῖς, καθὼς καὶ ὁ Θεὸς ἐν Χριστῷ ἐχαρίσατο ὑμῖν. So in Col. ii. 13, iii. 13; Rom. viii. 32; 2 Cor. ii. 7, 10; Luke vii. 42, 43.

[132] Comp. pp. 47, 83, 169, 189.

[133] Vol. iv., pp. 22, 41 (Eng. Trans.).

[134] Comte, vol. iv., p. 30.

CHAPTER XXIII.

THE CHILDREN OF THE LIGHT.

"Be not ye therefore partakers with them; for ye were once darkness, but are now light in the Lord; walk as children of light (for the fruit of the light is in all goodness and righteousness and truth), proving what is well-pleasing unto the Lord; and have no fellowship with the unfruitful works of darkness, but rather even reprove them. For the things which are done by them in secret it is a shame even to speak of; but all things when they are reproved are made manifest by the light: for everything that is made manifest is light. Wherefore He saith:—
  'Awake, thou that sleepest, and arise from the dead;
  And the Christ shall shine upon thee.'"

EPH. V. 7–14.

The contrast between the Christian and heathen way of life is now, finally, to be set forth under St Paul's familiar figure of *the light and the darkness*. He bids his Gentile readers not to be "joint-partakers with them"—with the sons of disobedience upon whom God's wrath is coming (ver. 6)—for he has hailed them already, in chapter iii. 6, as "joint-partakers of the promise in Christ Jesus through the gospel." "Once" indeed they shared in the lot of the disobedient; but for them the darkness has past, and the true light now shineth.

In wrath or promise, in hope of life eternal or in the fearful looking for of judgement they, and we, must partake. This future participation depends upon present character. "Do not," the apostle entreats, "cast in your lot again with the unclean and covetous. Their ways you have renounced, and their doom you have exchanged for the heritage of the saints. Let no vain words deceive you into supposing that you may keep your new inheritance, and yet return to your old sins. Show yourselves worthy of your calling. Walk as children of the light, and you will possess the eternal kingdom." Each man carries with him into the next state of being the entail of his past life. That heritage depends on his own choice; yet not upon his individual will working by itself, but on the grace and will of God working with him, as that grace is accepted or rejected. He has light: he must walk in it; and he will reach the realm of light. Thus the apostle, in verses 7 and 8, concludes his warning against relapse into heathen sin.

Verses 9 and 10 delineate *the character of the children of the light*: verses 11–14 set forth *their influence upon the surrounding darkness*. Into these two divisions the exposition of this paragraph naturally falls.

I. "The fruit *of the light*" (not *of the Spirit*) is the true text of verse 9, as it stands in the older Greek copies, Versions, and Fathers. Calvin showed his judgement and independence in preferring this reading to that of the received Greek text. Similarly Bengel,[135] and most of the later critics. The sentence is parenthetical, and contains a singular and instructive figure. It is one of those sparks from the anvil, in which great writers not unfrequently give us their finest utterances,—sentences that get a peculiar point from the eagerness with which they are struck off in the heat and clash of thought, as the mind reaches forward to some thought lying beyond. The clause is an epitome, in five words, of Christian virtue, whose qualities, origin and method are all defined. It sums up exquisitely the moral teaching of the epistle. Galatians v. 22, 23 (*the fruit of the Spirit*) and Philippians iv. 8 (*Whatsoever things are true*, etc.) are parallel to this passage, as Pauline definitions, equally perfect, of the virtues of a Christian man. This has the advantage of the others in brevity and epigrammatic point.

"You are light in the Lord," the apostle said; "walk as children of the light." But his readers might ask: "What does this mean? It is poetry: let us have it translated into plain prose. How shall we walk as children of the light? Show us the path."—"I will tell you," the apostle answers: "the fruit of the light is in all goodness and righteousness and truth. Walk in these ways; let your life bear this fruit; and you will be true children of the light of God. So living, you will find out what it is that pleases God, and how joyful a thing it is to please Him (ver. 10). Your life will then be free from all complicity with the works of darkness. It will shine with a brightness clear and penetrating, that will put to shame the works of darkness and transform the darkness itself. It will speak with a voice that all must hear, bidding them awake from the sleep of sin to see in Christ their light of life." Such is the setting in which this delightful definition stands.

But it is more than a definition. While this sentence declares what Christian virtue is, it signifies also whence it comes, how it is generated and maintained. It asserts the connexion that exists between Christian character and Christian faith. The fruit cannot be grown without the tree, any more than the tree can grow soundly without yielding its proper fruit. *Right is the fruit of light.*

The principle that religion is the basis of moral virtue, is one that many moralists disputed in St Paul's time; and it has fallen into some discredit in our own. In philosophical theory, and to a large extent in popular maxim and belief, it is assumed that faith and morals, character and creed, are not only distinct but independent things and that there is no necessary connexion between the two. Christians are themselves to blame for this fallacy, through the discrepancy not seldom visible between their creed and life. Our narrowness of view and the harshness of our ethical judgements have helped to foster this grave error.

Great Christian teachers have spoken of the virtues of the heathen as "splendid sins." But Christ and His apostles never said so. He said: "Other sheep I have, which are not of this fold." And they said: "In every nation he that feareth God and worketh righteousness, is accepted of Him." The Christian creed has no jealousy in regard to human excellence. "Whatsoever things are true and honourable and just and pure," wherever and in whomsoever they are found, our faith honours and delights in them, and accepts them to the utmost of their worth. But then it claims them all for its own,—as the fruit of the one "true light which lighteth every man." Wherever this fruit appears, we know that that light has been, though its ways are past finding out. Through secret crevices, by subtle refractions and multiplied reflections, the true light reaches many a life lying far outside its visible course.

All goodness has one source; for, said Jesus, "there is none good but one, that is God." The channels may be tortuous, obstructed and obscure: the stream is always one. There is nothing more touching, and nothing more encouraging to our faith in God's universal love and His will that all men should be saved, than to see, as we do sometimes under conditions most adverse and in spots the most unlikely, features of moral beauty and Christlike goodness appearing like springs in the desert or flowers blooming in Alpine snows,—signs of the universal light,

> "Which yet in the absolutest drench of dark
> Ne'er wants its witness, some stray beauty-beam
> To the despair of hell!"

The action of God's grace in Christ is by no means limited to the sphere of its recognized working. All the more earnestly on this account do we vindicate this grace against those who deny its necessity or the permanence of its moral influence. The fruit, in the main, they approve. But they would cut down the plant from which it came; they seek to quench the light under which it grew. They are like men who should take you to some lofty tree that has flourished for ages rooted in the rock, and who should say: "See how wide its branches and how stout its stem, how firmly it stands upon its native soil! Let us cut it loose from those dark and ugly roots—that mysterious theology, those superstitions of the past. The human mind has outgrown them. Virtue can support itself on its own proper basis. It is time to assert the dignity of man, and to proclaim the independence of morality." If these men have their way, and if European society renounces the authority of God, how quickly will that tree of the Lord's planting, the vast growth of Christian virtue and beneficence, wither to its topmost bough; and the next storm will bring it to the ground, with all its stately strength and summer beauty. Unbelief in God lays the axe at the root of human society. Our life—the life of individuals, of families and nations—is rooted in the unseen and hid with Christ in God. Thence it draws its vitality and virtue, through those spiritual fibres by which we are linked to God and lay hold on eternal life. Since Christ Jesus our forerunner entered the heavenly places, the anchor of human hopes has been cast within the veil; if that anchor drags, there is no other that will hold. The rocks are plain to see on which our richly freighted ship of life will founder. Without the religion of Jesus Christ, our civilization is not worth a hundred years' purchase.

Moral effects do not follow upon their causes as rapidly as physical effects: they follow as certainly. We live largely upon the accumulated ethical capital of our forefathers. When that is spent, we are left to our intrinsic poverty of soul, to our faithlessness and feebleness. The scepticism of one generation bears fruit in the immorality of the next, or the next after that; the unbelief and cynicism of the teacher in the vice of his disciple. Such fruit of blasting and mildew the decay of faith has never failed to bear.

The corresponding truth will be at once acknowledged. There is no real religion without virtue. If the godly man is not a good man, if he is not a sincere and pure-hearted man, "that man's religion is vain": no matter what his professions or his emotions, no matter what his services to the Church. He is one of those to whom Jesus Christ will say: "I know you not; depart from me, all ye that work iniquity." There is a flaw in him somewhere, a rift within the lute that spoils all its music. "A good tree cannot bring forth corrupt fruit."

In Christ's garden there forms in clustered beauty and perfectness the ripe growth of virtue, which in the sunshine of His love and under the freshening breath of His Spirit sends forth its spices and "yieldeth its fruit every month." In it there abide *goodness, righteousness, truth*—these three; and who shall say which of them is greatest?

I. *Goodness* stands first, as the most visible and obvious form of Christian excellence,—that which every one looks for in a religious man, and which every one admires when it is to be seen. Righteousness, regarded by itself, is not so readily appreciated. There is something austere and forbidding in it. "For a righteous man scarcely would one die"—you respect, even revere him; but you do not love him: "but for the good man peradventure, one would even dare to die."

Christian goodness is the sanctification of the heart and its affections, renewed and governed by the love of God in Christ. It is, notwithstanding, but seldom inculcated in the New Testament;[136] because it is referred to its spring and principle in *love*. Goodness is love embodied. Now love, as the

Christian knows it, is of God. "We love," says the apostle John, "because He first loved us…. He loved us, and sent His Son to be the propitiation for our sins." This is the faith that makes good men,—the best the world has ever known, the best that it holds now. Vanity, selfishness, evil temper and desire are shamed and burnt out of the soul by the holy fire of the love of God in Jesus Christ our Lord. In the warm, tender light of the cross the heart is softened and cleansed, and expanded to the widest charity. It becomes the home of all generous instincts and pure affections. So "the fruit of the light is in all goodness."

2. And *righteousness*.

This second and central definition applies a searching test to all spurious forms of goodness, superficial or sentimental,—to the goodness of mere good manners, or good nature. The principle of righteousness, fully understood, includes everything in moral worth, and is often used to denote in one word the entire fruit of God's grace in man. For righteousness is the sanctification of the conscience. It is loyalty to God's holy and perfect law. It is no mere outward keeping of formal rules, such as the legal righteousness of Judaism, no submission to necessity or calculation of advantages: it is a love of the law in a man's inmost spirit; it is the quality of a heart one with that law, reconciled to it as it is reconciled to God Himself in Jesus Christ.

At the bottom, therefore, righteousness and goodness are one. Each is the counterface and complement of the other. Righteousness is to goodness as the strong backbone of principle, the firm hand and the vigorous grasp of duty, the steadfast foot that plants itself on the eternal ground of the right and true and stands against a world's assault. Goodness without righteousness is a weak and fitful sentiment: righteousness without goodness is a dead formality. He cannot love God or his neighbour truly, who does not love God's law; and he knows nothing aright of that law, who does not know that it is the law of love.

This also, this above all is "the fruit of the light." Two watchwords we have from the lips of Jesus, two mottoes of His own life and mission,—the one given at the end, the other at the beginning of His course: "Greater *love* hath none than this, that one lay down his life for his friends"; and, "Thus it becometh us to fulfil all *righteousness*." By a double flame was He consumed a sacrifice upon the cross,—by the passion of His zeal for God's righteousness, and by the passion of His pity for mankind. In that twofold light we see light, and become "light in the Lord." Therefore the fruit of the light, the moral product of a true faith in the gospel, is in all *goodness and righteousness*.

There is a danger of merging the latter in the former of these attributes.

Evangelical piety is credited with an excess of the sentimental and emotional disposition, cultivated at the expense of the more sterling elements of character. High principle, scrupulous honour, stern fidelity to duty are no less essential to the image of Christ in the soul than are warm feeling and zealous devotion to His service. *Jesus Christ the righteous*, as His apostles loved to call Him, is the pattern of a manly faith, up to which we must grow in all things. *"He* is the propitiation for our sins." Never was there an act of such unswerving integrity and absolute loyalty to the law of right as the sacrifice of Calvary. God forbid that we should magnify love at the expense of law, or make good feeling a substitute for duty.

3. *Truth* comes last in this enumeration, for it signifies the inward reality and depth of the other two.

Truth does not mean veracity alone, the mere truth of the lips. Heathen honesty goes as far as this. Men of the world expect as much from each other, and brand the liar with their contempt. Truth of words requires a reality behind itself. The acted falsehood is excluded, the hinted and intended lie no less than that expressly uttered. Beyond all this, it is the truth of the man that God requires—speech, action, thought, all consistent, harmonious and transparent, with the light of God's truth shining through them. Truth is the harmony of the inward and the outward, the correspondence of what the man is in himself with that which he appears and wishes to appear to be.

Now, it is only children of the light, only men thoroughly good and upright who can, in this strict sense, be men of truth. So long as any malice or iniquity is left in our nature, we have something to conceal. We cannot afford to be sincere. We are compelled to pay, by very shame, the degrading tribute which vice renders to virtue, the homage of hypocrisy. But find a man whose intellect, whose heart and will, tried at whatever point, ring sound and true, in whom there is no affectation, no make-believe, no pretence or exaggeration, no discrepancy, no discord in the music of his life and thought, "an Israelite indeed, in whom is no guile"—there is a saint for you, and a man of God; there is one whom you may "grapple to your soul with hoops of steel."

Truth is the hall-mark of entire sanctification; it is the highest and rarest attainment of the Christian life. It is equally the charm of an innocent, unspoilt childhood, and of a ripe and purified old age. The apostle John, "the disciple whom Jesus loved," is the most perfect embodiment, after his Master, of this consummating grace. In him righteousness and love were blended in the translucence of an utter simplicity and truth.

We must beware of giving a subjective and merely personal aspect to this divine quality. While truth is the unity of the outward and inward, of heart and act and word in the man, it is at the same time the agreement of the man with the reality of things as they exist in God. The former kind of truth rests upon the latter; the subjective upon the objective order. The truth of God makes us true. We magnify our own sincerity, until it becomes vitiated and pretentious. In our eagerness to realize and express our own convictions, we give too little pains to form them upon a sound basis; we make a great virtue of *speaking out* what is in our hearts, but take small heed of what *comes in* to the heart, and speak out of a loose self-confidence and idolatry of our own opinions. So the Pharisees were true, who called Christ an impostor. So every careless slanderer, and scandalmonger credulous of evil, who believes the lies he propagates. "Imagination has pictured to itself a domain in which every one who enters should be compelled to speak only what he thought, and pleased itself by calling such domain the Palace of Truth. A palace of veracity, if you will; but no temple of the truth. A place where each one would be at liberty to utter his own crude unrealities, to bring forth his delusions, mistakes, half-formed, hasty judgements; where the depraved ear would reckon discord harmony, and the depraved eye mistake colour; the depraved moral taste take Herod or Tiberius for a king, and shout beneath the Redeemer's cross, 'Himself He cannot save!' A temple of the truth? Nay, only a palace echoing with veracious falsehoods, a Babel of confused sounds, in which egotism would rival egotism, and truth would be each man's own lie."[137] In the pride of our veracity, we miss the verity of things; we are true only to our blind self, false to the light of God. "Every one that is of the truth heareth my voice:" so said He who was Truth incarnate, making His word a law for all true men.

"In *all* goodness and righteousness and truth," says the apostle. Let us seek them all. We are apt to become specialists in virtue, as in other departments of life. Men will endeavour even to compensate by extreme efforts in one direction for deficiencies in some other direction, which they scarcely desire to make good. So they grow out of shape, into oddities and moral malformations. There is a want of balance and of finish about a multitude of Christian lives, even of those who have long and steadily pursued the way of faith. We have sweetness without strength, and strength without gentleness, and truth spoken without love, and words of passionate zeal without accuracy and heedfulness.

All this is infinitely sad, and infinitely damaging to the cause of our religion.

"It is the little rift within the lute
That by-and-by will make the music mute,
    And ever widening slowly silence all;
The little rift within the lover's lute,
Or little pitted speck in garnered fruit,
    That rotting inward slowly moulders all."

Let us judge ourselves, that we be not judged by the Lord. Let us count no wrong a trifle. Let us never imagine that our defects in one kind will be atoned for by excellencies in another. Our friends may say this, in charity, for us; it is a fatal thing when a man begins to say so to himself. "May the God of peace sanctify you fully. May your whole spirit, soul, and body in blameless integrity be preserved to the coming of the Lord Jesus Christ" (1 Thess. v. 23).

II. The *effect* upon surrounding darkness of the light of God in Christian lives is described in verses 11–14, in words which it remains for us briefly to examine.

Verse 12 distinguishes "the things secretly done" by the Gentiles, "of which it is a shame even to speak," from the open and manifest forms of evil in which they invite their Christian neighbours to join (ver. 11). Instead of doing this and "having fellowship with the unfruitful works of darkness," they must "rather reprove them." Silent absence, or abstinence is not enough. Where sin is open to rebuke, it should at all hazards be rebuked. On the other hand, St Paul does not warrant Christians in prying into the hidden sins of the world around them and playing the moral detective. Publicity is not a remedy for all evils, but a great aggravation of some, and the surest means of disseminating them. "It is a shame"—a disgrace to our common nature, and a grievous peril to the young and innocent—to fill the public prints with the nauseous details of crime and to taint the air with its putridities.

"But all things," the apostle says—whether it be those open works of darkness, profitless of good, which expose themselves to direct conviction, or the depths of Satan that hide their infamy from the light of day—"all things being reproved by the light, are made manifest" (ver. 13). The fruit of the light convicts the unfruitful works of darkness. The daily life of a Christian man amongst men of the world is a perpetual reproof, that tells against secret sins of which no word is spoken, of which the reprover never guesses, as well as against open and unblushing vices.

"This is the condemnation," said Jesus, "that light is come into the world." And this condemnation every one who walks in Christ's steps, and breathes His Spirit amid the corruptions of the world, is carrying on, more frequently in silence than by spoken argument. Our unconscious and spontaneous influence is the most real and effective part of it. Life is the light of men—

words only as the index of the life from which they spring. Just so far as our lives touch the conscience of others and reveal the difference between darkness and light, so far do we hold forth the word of life and carry on the Holy Spirit's work in convincing the world of sin. "Let your light so shine."

This manifestation leads to a transformation: "For everything that is made manifest *is light*" (ver. 13). "You are light in the Lord," St Paul says to his converted Gentile readers,—you who were "once darkness," once wandering in the lusts and pleasures of the heathen around you, without hope and without God. The light of the gospel disclosed, and then dispelled the darkness of that former time; and so it may be with your still heathen kindred, through the light you bring to them. So it will be with the night of sin that is spread over the world. The light which shines upon sin-laden and sorrowful hearts, shines on them to change them into its own nature. *The manifested is light*: in other words, if men can be made to see the true nature of their sin, they will forsake it. If the light can but penetrate their conscience, it will save them. "Wherefore He saith:—

> Awake, O sleeper; and arise from out of the dead!
> And the Christ shall dawn upon thee!"

The speaker of this verse can be no other than God, or the Spirit of God in Scripture. The sentence is no mere quotation. It re-utters, in the style of Mary's or Zechariah's song, the promise of the Old Covenant from the lips of the New. It gathers up the import of the prophecies concerning the salvation of Christ, as they sounded in the apostle's ears and as he conveyed them to the world. Isaiah lx. 1–3 supplies the basis of our passage, where the prophet awakens Zion from the sleep of the Exile and bids her shine once more in the glory of her God and show forth His light to the nations: "Arise," he cries, "shine, for thy light is come!" There are echoes in the verse, besides, of Isaiah li. 17, xxvi. 19; perhaps even of Jonah i. 6: "What meanest thou, O sleeper? arise, and call upon thy God!" We seem to have here, as in chapter iv. 4–6, a snatch of the earliest Christian hymns. The lines are a free paraphrase from the Old Testament, formed by weaving together Messianic passages— belonging to such a hymn as might be sung at baptisms in the Pauline Churches. Certainly those Churches did not wait until the second century to compose their hymns and spiritual songs (comp. ver. 19). Our Lord's sublime announcement (John v. 25), already verified, that "the hour had come when the dead should hear the voice of the Son of God, and they that heard should live," gave the key to the prophetic sayings which promised through Israel the light of life to all nations.

With this song on her lips the Church went forth, clad in the armour of light, strong in the joy of salvation; and darkness and the works of darkness fled before her.

FOOTNOTES:

[135] Mr. Wesley adopted this and other emendations from Bengel, "that great light of the Christian world," in the translation accompanying his *Explanatory Notes upon the New Testament*. He there supplied the Methodist preachers with many of the most valuable improvements made in the Revised Version, a hundred years before the time.

[136] The word belongs to Paul's vocabulary; it is found besides in 2 Thess. i. 11; Rom. xv. 14; and Gal. v. 22. See the Commentary on this last epistle in the *Expositor's Bible*, pp. 384, 385.

[137] F. W. Robertson: *Sermons* (First Series), xix., on "The Kingdom of the Truth."

CHAPTER XXIV.

THE NEW WINE OF THE SPIRIT.

"Look therefore carefully how ye walk, not as unwise, but as wise; redeeming the time, because the days are evil. Wherefore be ye not foolish, but understand what the will of the Lord is.

"And be not drunken with wine, wherein is riot, but be filled with the Spirit; speaking one to another in psalms and hymns and spiritual songs, singing and making melody with your heart to the Lord; giving thanks always for all things in the name of our Lord Jesus Christ to God, even the Father; subjecting yourselves one to another in the fear of Christ."—EPH. v. 15–21.

Very solemnly did the moral homily to the Asian Christians begin in chapter iv. 17: "This therefore I say and testify in the Lord, that you must no longer walk as the Gentiles walk." So much has now been said and testified in the intervening paragraphs, by way both of dehortation and exhortation. Here the apostle pauses; and casting his eye over the whole pathway of life he has marked out in this discourse, he bids his readers: "Look then carefully how you walk. Show that you are not fools, but wise to observe your steps and to seize your opportunities in these evil times,—days so perilous that you need your best wisdom and knowledge of God's will to save you from fatal stumbling."

So far St Paul's renewed exhortation, in verses 15–17, inculcates care and wary discretion,—the skill that in the strategy of life finds its vantage in unequal ground, that makes opposing winds help forward the seafarer. In this sober wisdom it is likely the Asian Christians were deficient. In many ways, both directly and indirectly, the need of increased thoughtfulness on the readers' part has been indicated. But there is another side to the Christian nature: it has its moods of exhilaration, as well as of caution and reflection; ardent emotion, eager speech and exultant song are things proper to a high religious life. For these the apostle makes room in verses 18–20, while the three foregoing verses enjoin the circumspection and vigilance that become the good soldier of Christ Jesus.

A striking contrast thus arises between the *sobriety* and the *excitement* that mark the life of grace. We see with what strictness we must watch over ourselves, and guard the character and interests of the Church; and with what joyousness and holy freedom we may take our part in its communion. Temperament and constitution modify these injunctions in their personal application. The Holy Spirit does not enable us all to speak with equal fervour and freedom, nor to sing with the same tunefulness. His power operates in the limbs of Christ's body "according to the measure of each single part." But the self-same Spirit works in both these contrasted ways,—in the sanguine and the melancholic disposition, in the demonstrative and in the reserved, in the quick play of fancy and the brightness and impulsiveness of youth no less than in the sober gait and solid sense of riper age. Let us see how the two opposite aspects of Christian experience are set out in the apostle's words.

I. First of all, upon the one side, *heedfulness* is enjoined. The children of light must use the light to see their way. To "stumble at noonday" is a proof of folly or blindness. So misusing our light, we shall quickly lose it and return to the paths of darkness.

According to the preferable (Revised) order of the words, the qualifying adverb "carefully" belongs to the "look," not to the "walk." The circumspect *look* precedes the wise step. The spot is marked on which the foot is to be planted; the eye ranges right and left and takes in the bearings of the new position, forecasting its possibilities. "Look before you leap," our sage proverb says. According to the carefulness of the look, the success of the leap is likely to be.

There is no word in the epistle more apposite than this to

> "our day
> Of haste, half-work, and disarray."

We are too restless to think, too impatient to learn. Everything is sacrificed to speed. The telegraph and the daily newspaper symbolize the age. The public ear loves to be caught quickly and with new sensations: a premium is set on carelessness and hurry. Earnest men, eager for the triumph of a good cause, push forward with unsifted statements and unweighed denunciations, that discredit Christian advocacy and wound the cause of truth and charity. Time, thus wronged and driven beyond her pace, has her revenge; she deals hardly with these light judgements of the hour. They are as the chaff which the wind carrieth away. After all, it is still truth that lives; thorough work that lasts; accuracy that hits the mark. And the time-servers are "unwise," both intellectually and morally. They are most unwise who think to succeed in life's high calling without self-distrust, and without scrupulous care and pains in all work they do for the kingdom of God.

In the evil of his own times St Paul sees a special reason for heedfulness: "Walk not as unwise, but as wise, buying up the opportunity, *because the days are evil.*" In Colossians iv. 5 the parallel sentence shows that in giving this caution he is thinking of the relation of Christians to the world outside:"Walk in wisdom toward those without, buying up the opportunity." Evil days they were, when Paul lay in Nero's prison; when that wild beast was raging against everything that resisted his mad will or reproved his monstrous vices. With supreme power in the hands of such a creature of Satan, who could tell what fires of persecution were kindling for the people of Christ, or what terrible revelation of God's anger against the present evil world might be impending. At Ephesus the spirit of heathenism had shown itself peculiarly menacing. Here, too, in the rich and cultivated province of Asia where the currents of Eastern and Western thought met, heresy and its corruptions made their first decided appearance in the Churches of the Gentiles. Conflicts are approaching which will try to the uttermost the strength of the Christian faith and the temper of its weapons (vi. 10–16).

As wise men, reading thoughtfully the signs of the times, the Asian Christians will "redeem the [present] season." They will use to the utmost the light given them. They will employ every means to increase their knowledge of Christ, to confirm their faith and the habits of their spiritual life. They are like men expecting a siege, who strengthen their fortifications and furbish their weapons and practise their drill and lay up store of supplies, that they may "stand in the evil day." Such wisdom Ecclesiastes preaches to the young man: "Remember now thy Creator in the days of thy youth, or ever the evil days come."

Within a year after this epistle was penned, Rome was burnt and the crime of its burning washed out, at Nero's caprice, in Christian blood. In four years more St Paul and St Peter had died a martyr's death at Rome; and Nero had fallen by the assassin's hand. At once the Empire was convulsed with civil war; and the year 68–69 was known as that of the Four Emperors. Amid the storms threatening the ruin of the Roman State, the Jewish war against Rome was carried on, ending in the year 70 with the capture of Jerusalem and the destruction of the Jewish temple and nationality. These were the days of tribulation of which our Lord spoke, "such as had not been since the beginning of the world" (Matt. xxiv. 21, 22). The entire fabric of life was shaken; and in the midst of earthquake and tempest, blood and fire, Israel met its day of judgement and the former age passed away. In the year 63, when the apostle wrote, the sky was everywhere red and lowering with signs of coming storm. None knew where or how the tempest might break, or what would be its issue.

When men amid evil days and portents of danger must be told not to be "foolish" nor "drunken with wine," one is disposed to tax them with levity. It was difficult for these Asian Greeks to take life seriously, and to realize the gravity of their situation. St Paul appeals to them by their duty, still more than by their danger: "Be not foolish, but understand what *the will of the Lord* is." As he bade the Thessalonians consider that chastity was not matter of choice and of their own advantage only, it was "God's will" (1 Ep. iv. 3), so the Ephesians must understand that Christ is no mere adviser, nor the Christian life an optional system that men may adopt when and so far as it suits them. He is our Lord; and it is our business to understand, in order that we may execute, His designs. For this Christ's servants require a watchful eye and an alert intelligence. They must be no dullards nor simpletons, who would enter into the Divine Master's plans; no triflers, no creatures of sentiment and impulse, who are to be the agents of His will. He can and does employ every sincere heart that gives itself in love to Him. But His nobler tasks are for the wise taught by His Spirit, for those who can "understand," with penetrating sympathy and breadth of comprehension, "what the will of the Lord is." Hence the distinction of St Paul himself, and of John the beloved disciple, amongst His ministers and witnesses,—men great in mind as they were in heart, whose thoughts about Christ were as grand as their love to Him was fervent.

Nowhere does the apostle say so much of "the will of God" in regard to the dispensation of grace as he does in this epistle.[138] For he sees life and salvation here in their largest bearings and proportions. He prayed at the outset that the Gentile readers might realize the value that God puts upon them, and the mighty forces He has set at work for their salvation (i. 18–20); and again, that they might comprehend the vast dimensions of His plan for the building of the Church (iii. 18). Now that he has shown the relation of this eternal purpose to the character and everyday life of the converted Gentiles, "the will of God" becomes matter of immediate import; it is revealed in its bearing upon conduct, upon the affairs of business and society. It is not the purpose, the promises, the doctrine of the Lord alone, but "the *will* of the Lord" that they have to understand, as it touches their spirit and behaviour day by day. They must realize the practical demands of their religion,—how it is to make them truthful, gracious, pure and wise. They must translate creed into life and act. Such is the wisdom which their apostle strives to instil into the Asian Christians. Their first need was spiritual enlightenment; their second need was moral intelligence. Might they only have sense to understand and loyalty to obey the will of Christ.—And oh may we!

II. There were converted thieves in the Ephesian Church, who still needed to be warned against their old propensities (iv. 28); there were men who had been sorcerers and fortune-tellers (Acts xix. 18, 19). It appears that there were in this circle converted *drunkards* also, men to whom the apostle is obliged to say: "Be not drunk with wine, wherein is riot."

In view of the following context (vv. 19–21), and remembering how the Lord's table was defiled by excess at Corinth (1 Cor. xi. 17–34), it seems to us probable that the warning of verse 18 had special reference to the Christian assemblies. The institution of the common meal, the *Agapé* or Lovefeast accompanying the Lord's Supper, suited the manners of the early Christians, and was long continued. The cities of Asia Minor were full of trade-guilds and clubs for various social and religious purposes, in which the common supper, or club-feast, furnished usually by each member bringing his contribution to the table, was a familiar bond of fellowship. This afforded to the Church a natural and pleasant means of intercourse; but it must be purified from sensual indulgence. *Wine* was its chief danger.

The eastern coast of the Ægean is an ancient home of the vine. And the Greeks of the Asian towns, on those bright shores and under their genial sky, were a light-hearted, sociable race. They sought the wine-cup not for animal indulgence, but as a zest to good-fellowship and to give a freer flow to social joys. This was the influence that ruled their feasts, that loosened their tongues and inspired their gaiety. Hence their wit was prone to become ribaldry (ver. 4); and their songs were the opposite of the "spiritual songs" that gladden the feasts of the Church (ver. 19). The quick imagination and the social instincts of the Ionian Greeks, the aptness for speech and song native to the land of Homer and Sappho, were gifts not to be repressed but sanctified. The lyre is to be tuned to other strains; and poetry must draw its inspiration from a higher source. Dionysus and his reeling Fauns give place to the pure Spirit of Jesus and the Father. "The Aonian mount" must now pay tribute to "Sion hill"; and the fountain of Castalia yields its honours to

> "Siloa's brook that flowed
> Fast by the oracle of God."

Our nature craves excitement,—some stimulus that shall set the pulses dancing and thrill the jaded frame, and lift the spirit above the taskwork of life and the dreary and hard conditions which make up the daily lot of multitudes. It is this craving that gives to strong drink its cruel fascination. Alcohol is a mighty magician. The tired labouring man, the household drudge shut up in city courts refreshed by no pleasant sight or cheering voice, by its aid can leave fretted nerves and aching limbs and dull care behind, and taste, if it be only for a feverish moment, of the joy of bounding life. Can such cravings be hindered from seeking their relief? The removal of temptation will accomplish little, unless higher tastes are formed and springs of purer pleasure opened to the masses for whom our civilization makes life so drab and colourless. "One finds traces of the primitive greatness of our nature even in its most deplorable errors. Just as impurity proceeds at the bottom from an abuse of the craving for love, so drunkenness betrays a certain demand for ardour and enthusiasm, which in itself is natural and even noble.... Man loves to *feel* himself alive; he would fain live twice his life at once; and he would rather draw excitement from horrible things than have no excitement at all" (Monod).

For the drunkards of Ephesus the apostle finds a cure in the joys of the Holy Ghost. The mightiest and most moving spring of feeling is in the spirit of man kindred to God. There is a deep excitement and refreshment, a "joy that human thought transcends," in the love of God shed abroad in the heart and the communion of true saints, which makes sensuous delights cheap and poor. Toil and care are forgotten, sickness and trouble seem as nothing; we can glory in tribulation and laugh in the face of death, when the strong wine of God's consolations is poured into the soul.

"Be filled with the Spirit," says the apostle—or more strictly, "filled *in* the Spirit"; since the Holy Spirit of God is the element of the believer's life, surrounding while it penetrates his nature: it is the atmosphere that he breathes, the ocean in which he is immersed. As a flood fills up the river-banks, as the drunkard is filled with the wine that he drains without limit, so the apostle would have his readers yield themselves to the tide of the Spirit's coming and steep their nature in His influence. The Greek imperative, moreover, is present, and "describes this influence as ever going forth from the Spirit" (Beet). This is to be a continual replenishment. Paul has prayed that we may "be filled unto all the fulness of God" (iii. 19), and has bidden us grow "to the measure of the stature of the fulness of Christ" (iv. 13) in whom we "are made full" (Col. ii. 9): in the replenishment of the Spirit the fulness of God in Christ is sensibly imparted. God's fulness is the hidden and eternal spring of all that can fill our nature; Christ's fulness is its revelation and renewed communication to the race; the Holy Spirit's fulness is its abiding energy within the soul and within the Church. Thus possessed, the Church is truly the body of Christ (iv. 4), and the habitation of God (ii. 21, 22).

The words of verses 19, 20 show that St Paul is thinking of that presence of the Spirit in the Christian community, which is the spring of its affections and activities. The Spirit of Jesus, the Son of man, is a kindly and gracious Spirit, the guardian of brotherhood and friendship, the inspirer of pure social joys and genial converse. The joy in the Holy Ghost that in its warmth and freshness filled the hearts of the first Christians, soared upward on the wings of song. Their very talk was music: they "spoke to each other in psalms and hymns and spiritual songs, singing and making melody with their heart to the Lord." Love loves to sing. Its joys

> "from out our hearts arise,
> And speak and sparkle in our eyes,
> And vibrate on our tongue."

All exalted sentiment tends to rhythmical expression. There is a mystical alliance, which is amongst the most significant facts in our constitution, between emotion and art. The rudest natures, touched by high feeling, will shape themselves to some sort of beauty, to some grace and refinement of expression. Each new stirring of the pulse of man's common life has been marked by a re-birth of poetry and art. The songs of Mary and Zechariah were the parents and patterns of a multitude of holy canticles. In the Psalms of Scripture the New Testament Church found already an instrument of wide compass strung and tuned for her use. We can imagine the delight with which the Gentile Christians would take up the Psalter and draw out one and another of its pearls, and would in turn recite them at their meetings, and adapt them to their native measures and modes of song. After a while, they began to mix with the praise-songs of Israel newer strains—"hymns" to the glory of Christ and the Father, such as that with which this epistle opens, needing but little change in form to make it a true poem, and such as those which break in upon the dread visions of the Apocalypse; and added to these, "spiritual songs" of a more personal and incidental character, like Simeon's *Nunc dimittis* or Paul's swan-song in his last letter to Timothy. In verse 14 above we detected, as we thought, an early Church paraphrase of the Old Testament. In later epistles addressed to Ephesus, there are fragments of just such artless chants as the Asian Christians, exhorted and taught by their apostle, were wont to sing in their assemblies: see 1 Timothy iii. 16, and 2 Timothy ii. 11–13.

Upon this congenial soil, we trace the beginnings of Christian psalmody. The parallel text of Colossians (iii. 16) discloses in the songs of the Pauline Churches a didactic as well as a lyric character. The apostle bids his readers *"teach and admonish* one another by psalms, hymns, spiritual songs." The form of the sentence of chapter iv. 4–6 in this letter, and of 1 Timothy iii. 16, suggests that these passages were destined for use as a chanted rehearsal of Christian belief. Thus "the word of Christ dwelling richly" in the heart, poured itself freely from the lips, and added to its grave discourse the charms of gladdening and spirit-stirring song.

As in their heathen days they were used to "speak to each other," in festive or solemn hours, with hymns to Artemis of the Ephesians, or Dionysus giver of the vine, or to Persephoné sad queen of the dead—in songs merry and gay, too often loose and wanton; in songs of the dark underworld and the grim Furies and inexorable Fate, that told how life fleets fast and we must pluck its pleasures while we may;—so now the Christians of Ephesus and Colossæ, of Pergamum and of Smyrna would sing of the universal Father whose presence fills earth and sky, of the Son of His love, His image amongst men, who died in sacrifice for their sins and asked grace for His murderers, of the joys of forgiveness and the cleansed heart, of life eternal and the treasure laid up for the just in the heavenly places, of Christ's return in glory and the judgement of the nations and the world quickly to dissolve and perish, of a brotherhood dearer than earthly kindred, of the saints who sleep in Jesus and in peace await His coming, of the Good Shepherd who feeds His sheep and leads them to fountains of living water calling each by his name, of creation redeemed and glorified by His love, of pain and sorrow sanctified and the trials that make perfect in Christ's discipline, of the joy that fills the heart in suffering for Him, and the vision of His face awaiting us beyond the grave. So reciting and chanting—now in single voice, now in full chorus—singing the Psalms of David to their Greek music, or hymns composed by their leaders, or sometimes improvised in the rapture of the moment, the Churches of Ephesus and of the Asian cities lauded and glorified "the name of our Lord Jesus Christ" and the counsels of redeeming love. So their worship and fellowship were filled with gladness. Thus in their great Church meetings, and in smaller companies, many a joyous hour passed; and all hearts were cheered and strengthened in the Lord.

"Singing and *playing*," says the apostle. For music aided song; voice and instrument blended in His praise whose glory claims the tribute of all creatures. But it was "with the heart," even more than with voice or tuneful strings, that melody was made. For this inward music the Lord listens. Where other skill is wanting and neither voice nor hand can take its part in the concert of praise, He hears the silent gratitude, the humble joy that wells upward when the lips are still or the full heart cannot find expression.

But the Spirit who dwelt in the praises of the new Israel, was not confined to its public assemblings. The people of Christ should be "*always giving thanks, for all things, in the name of our Lord Jesus Christ.*" It is one of St Paul's commonest injunctions. "In *everything* give thanks," he wrote to the Thessalonians in his earliest extant letter (1 Ep. v. 18). "For all things," he says to the Ephesians,—"though fallen on evil days." Do we not "know that to them that love God all things work together for good"—evil days as well as good days? Nothing comes altogether amiss to the child of God. In the heaviest loss, the severest pain, the sharpest sting of injury—"in everything" the ingenuity of love and the sweetness of patience will find some token of mercy. If the evil is to our eyes all evil and we can see in it no reason for thanksgiving, then faith will give thanks for that which we "know not now, but shall know hereafter."

Always, the apostle says,—*for all things*! No room for a moment's discontent. In this perfecting of praise he had himself undergone a long schooling in his four years' imprisonment. Now, he tells us, he "has learnt the secret of contentment, in whatsoever state" (Phil. iv. 12). Let us try to learn it from him. These words, which we treat, almost unconsciously, as the exaggeration of homiletical appeal, state no more than the sober possibility, the experience attained by many a Christian in circumstances of the greatest suffering and deprivation. The love of God in Jesus Christ our Lord suffices for the life and joy of man's spirit.

The twenty-first verse, which seems to belong to a different line of thought, in reality completes the foregoing paragraph. In the Corinthian Church, as we remember, with its affluence of spiritual gifts, there were so many ready to prophesy, so many to sing and recite, that confusion arose and the Church meetings fell into disedifying uproar (1 Cor. xiv. 26–34). The apostle would not have such scenes occur again. Hence when he urges the Asian Christians to seek the full inspiration of the Spirit and to give free utterance in song to the impulses of their new life, he adds this word of caution: "being subject to one another in fear of Christ." He reminds them that "God is not the author of confusion." His Spirit is a spirit of seemliness and reverence. "In fear of Christ," the unseen witness and president of its assemblies, the Church will comport herself with the decorum that befits His bride. The spirits of the prophets will be subject to the prophets. The voices of the singers and the hands of them that play upon the strings of the harp or the keys of the organ, will keep tune with the worship of Christ's congregation. Each must consider that it is his part to serve and not rule in the service of God's house.

In our common work and worship, in all the offices of life this is the Christian law. No man within Christ's Church, however commanding his powers, may set himself above the duty of submitting his judgement and will to that of his fellows. In mutual subjection lies our freedom, with our strength and peace.

FOOTNOTES:

[138] See ch. i. 5–11, ii. 21, iii. 11, v. 10, vi. 6; comp. Col. i. 9, 27, iv. 12; Phil. ii. 13,—epistles of the same group.

ON FAMILY LIFE.

CHAPTER v. 22–vi. 9.

Θέλω δὲ ὑμᾶς εἰδέναι ὅτι παντὸς ἀνδρὸς ἡ κεφαλὴ ὁ Χριστός ἐστιν, κεφαλὴ δὲ γυναικὸς ὁ ἀνήρ, κεφαλὴ δὲ τοῦ Χριστοῦ ὁ Θεός.—1 Cor. xi. 3.

"And pure Religion breathing household laws."

W. WORDSWORTH.

220

CHAPTER XXV.

CHRISTIAN MARRIAGE.

"Wives, *be in subjection* to your own husbands, as unto the Lord. For the husband is the head of the wife, as the Christ also is the head of the Church, *being* Himself the saviour of the body. But as the Church is subject to the Christ, so let the wives also *be* to their husbands in everything.

"Husbands, love your wives, even as the Christ also loved the Church, and gave Himself up for her; that He might sanctify her, having cleansed her by the washing of water with the word, that He might present the Church to Himself a glorious *Church*, not having spot or wrinkle or any such thing; but that she should be holy and without blemish.

"Even so ought husbands also to love their wives as their own bodies. He that loveth his wife loveth himself: for no man ever hated his own flesh; but nourisheth and cherisheth it, even as the Christ also the Church; because we are members of His body. 'For this cause shall a man leave his father and mother, and shall cleave to his wife; and the twain shall become one flesh.' This mystery is great: but I speak in regard of Christ and of the Church. Nevertheless do ye also severally love each one his own wife even as himself; and *let* the wife *see* that she fear her husband."—Eph. v. 22–33.

In mutual subjection the Christian spirit has its sharpest trials and attains its finest temper. "Be subject one to another," was the last word of the apostle's instructions respecting the "walk" of the Asian Churches. By its order and subjection the gifts of all the members of Christ's body are made available for the upbuilding of God's temple. The inward fellowship of the Spirit becomes a constructive and organizing force, reconstituting human life and framing the world into the kingdom of Christ and God. "In fear of Christ" the loyal Christian man submits himself to the community; not from the dread of human displeasure, but knowing that he must give account to the Head of the Church and the Judge of the last day, if his self-will should weaken the Church's strength and interrupt her holy work. "For the Lord's sake" His freemen submit to every ordinance of men. This is such a fear as the servant has of a good master (vi. 5), or the true wife for a loving husband (ver. 33),— not that which "perfect love casts out," but which it deepens and sanctifies.

Of this subjection to Christ the relationship of marriage furnishes an example and a mirror. St Paul passes on to the new topic without any grammatical pause, verse 22 being simply an extension of the participial clause that forms verse 21: "Being in subjection to one another in fear of Christ—ye wives to your own husbands, as to the Lord." The relation of the two verses is not that of the particular to the general, so much as that of image and object, of type and antitype. Submission to Christ in the Church suggests by analogy that of the wife to her husband in the house. Both have their origin in Christ, in whom all things were created, the Lord of life in its natural as well as in its spiritual and regenerate sphere (Col. i. 15–17). The bond that links husband and wife, lying at the basis of collective human existence, has in turn its ground in the relation of Christ to humanity.

The race springs not from a unit, but from a united pair. The history of mankind began in wedlock. The family is the first institution of society, and the mother of all the rest. It is the life-basis, the primitive cell of the aggregate of cities and bodies politic. In the health and purity of household life lies the moral wealth, the vigour and durability of all civil institutions. The mighty upgrowth of nations and the great achievements of history germinated in the nursery of home and at the mother's breast. Christian marriage is not an expedient—the last of many that have been tried—for the satisfaction of desire and the continuance of the human species. The Institutor of human life laid down its principle in the first frame of things. Its establishment was a great prophetic mystery (ver. 32). Its law stands registered in the eternal statutes. And the Almighty Father watches over its observance with an awful jealousy. Is it not written: "Fornicators and adulterers God will judge"; and again, "The Lord is an avenger concerning all these things"?

St Paul rightly gives to this subject a conspicuous place in this epistle of Christ and the Church. The corner-stone of the new social order which the gospel was to establish in the world lies here. The entire influence of the Church upon society depends upon right views on the relationship of man and woman and on the ethics of marriage.

In wedlock there are blended most completely the two principles of association amongst moral beings,—viz., authority and love, submission and self-surrender.

I. On the one side, *submission to authority.*

"Wives, be in subjection, as to the Lord,"—as is fitting in the Lord (Col. iii. 18). Again, in 1 Timothy ii. 11, 12, the apostle writes: "I suffer not a woman to teach, nor to have dominion," or (as the word may rather signify) "to act independently of the man." Were these directions temporary and occasional? Were they due, as one hears it suggested, to the uneducated and undeveloped condition of women in the apostle's time? Or do they not affirm a law that is deeply seated in nature and in the feminine constitution? The words of 1 Corinthians xi. 2–15 show that, in the apostle's view of life, this subordination is fundamental. "The head of woman is the man," as "the head of every man is the Christ" and "the head of Christ is God." "The woman," he says, "is of the man," and "was created because of the man." Whether these sentences square with our modern conceptions or not, there they stand, and their import is unmistakable.[139] They teach that in the Divine order of things it is the man's part to lead and rule, and the woman's part to be ruled. But the Christian woman will not feel that there is any loss or hardship in this. For in the Christian order, ambition is sin. To obey is better than to rule. She remembers who has said: "I am amongst you as he that serveth." The children of the world strive for place and power; but "it shall not be so amongst you."

Such subordination implies no inferiority, rather the opposite. A free and sympathetic obedience—which is the true submission—can only subsist between equals. The apostle writes: "Children, obey; ... Servants, obey" (vi. 1, 5); but "Wives, submit yourselves to your own husbands, as to the Lord." The same word denotes submission within the Church, and within the house. It is here that Christianity, in contrast with Paganism, and notably with Mohammedanism, raises the weaker sex to honour. In soul and destiny it declares the woman to be man, endowed with all rights and powers inherent in humanity. "In Christ Jesus there is no male and female," any more than there is "Jew and Greek" or "bond and free." The same sentence which broke down the barriers of Jewish caste, and in course of time abolished slavery, condemned the odious assumptions of masculine pride. It is one of the glories of our faith that it has enfranchised our sisters, and raises them in spiritual calling to the full level of their brothers and husbands. Both sexes are children of God by the same birthright; both receive the same Holy Spirit, according to the prediction quoted by St Peter on the day of Pentecost: "Your sons and your daughters shall prophesy.... Yea, on my servants and on my handmaidens in those days will I pour out of my Spirit, saith the Lord" (Acts ii. 17, 18). This one point of headship, of public authority and guidance, is reserved. It is the point on which Christ forbids emulation amongst His people.

Christian courtesy treats the woman as "the glory of the man"; it surrounds her from girlhood to old age with protection and deference. This homage, duly rendered, is a full equivalent for the honour of visible command. When, as it happens not seldom in the partnership of life, the superior wisdom dwells with the weaker vessel, the golden gift of persuasion is not wanting, by which the official ruler is guided, to his own advantage, and his adviser accomplishes more than she could do by any overt leadership. The chivalry of the Middle Ages, from which the refinement of European society takes its rise, was a product of Christianity grafted on the Teutonic nature. Notwithstanding the folly and excess that was mixed with it, there was a beautiful reverence in the old knightly service and championship of women. It humanized the ferocity of barbarous times. It tamed the brute strength of warlike races and taught them honour and gentleness. Its prevalence marked a permanent advance in civilization.

Shall we say that this law of St Paul is that laid down specifically for *Christian* women? is it not rather a law of nature—the intrinsic propriety of sex, whose dictates are reinforced by the Christian revelation? The apostle takes us back to the creation of mankind for the basis of his principles in dealing with this subject (ver. 31). The new commandments are the old which were in the world from the beginning, though concealed and overgrown with corruption. Notwithstanding the debasement of marriage under the non-Christian systems, the instincts of natural religion taught the wife her place in the house and gave rise to many a graceful and appropriate custom expressive of the honour due from one sex to the other. So the apostle regarded the man's bared and cropped head and the woman's flowing tresses as symbols of their relative place in the Divine order (1 Cor. xi. 13–15). These and such distinctions—between the dignities of strength and of beauty—no artificial sentiment and no capricious revolt can set aside, while the world stands. St Paul appeals to the common sense of mankind, to that which "nature itself teaches," in censuring the forwardness of some Corinthian women who appeared to think that the liberty of the gospel released them from the limitations of their nature.

Some earnest promoters of women's rights have fallen into the error that Christianity, to which they owe all that is best in their present status, is the obstacle in the way of their further progress. It is an obstacle to claims that are against nature and against the law of God,—claims only tolerable so long as they are exceptional. But the barriers imposed by Christianity, against which these people fret, are their main protection. "The moment Christianity disappears, the law of strength revives; and under that law women can have no hope except that their slavery may be mild and pleasant." To escape from the "bondage of Christian law" means to go back to the bondage of paganism.

"As unto the Lord" gives the pattern and the principle of the Christian wife's submission. Not that, as Meyer seems to put it, the husband in virtue of marriage "represents Christ to the wife." Her relation to the Lord is as full, direct, and personal as his. Indeed, the clause inserted at the end of verse 23 seems expressly designed to guard against this exaggeration. The qualification that Christ is "Himself Saviour of the body," thrown in between the two sentences comparing the marital headship to that which Christ holds towards the Church, has the effect of limiting the former.[140] The subjection of the Christian wife to her husband reserves for Christ the first place in the heart and the undiminished rights of Saviourship. St Paul indicates a real, and not unfrequent danger. The husband may eclipse Christ in the wife's soul, and be counted as her all in all. Her absorption in him may be too complete. Hence the brief guarding clause: "He Himself [and no other] Saviour of the body [to which all believers alike belong]." As the Saviour of the Church,

Christ holds an unrivalled and unqualified lordship over every member of the same.

"Nevertheless, as the Church is subject to the Christ, so also wives [should be] to their husbands in everything" (ver. 24). Again, in verse 33: "Let the wife see that she fear her husband"—with the reverent and confiding fear which love makes sweet. As the Christian wife obeys the Lord Christ in the spiritual sphere, in the sphere of marriage she is subject to her husband. The ties that bind her to Christ, bind her more closely to the duties of home. These duties illustrate for her the submissive love that Christ's people, and herself as one of them, owe to their Divine Head. Her service in the Church, in turn, will send her home with a quickened sense of the sacredness of her domestic calling. It will lighten the yoke of obedience; it will check the discontent that masculine exactions provoke; and will teach her to win by patience and gentleness the power within the house that is her queenly crown.

II. The apostle alludes to submission as the wife's duty; for she might, possibly, be tempted to think this superseded by the liberty of the children of God. Love he need not enjoin upon her; but he writes: "Husbands, *love your wives*, even as the Christ also loved the Church and gave up Himself for her" (comp. Col. iii. 18, 19).

The danger of selfishness lies on the masculine side. The man's nature is more exacting; and the self-forgetfulness and solicitous affection of the woman may blind him to his own want of the truest love. Full of business and with a hundred cares and attractions lying outside the domestic circle, he too readily forms habits of self-absorption and learns to make his wife and home a convenience, from which he takes as his right the comfort they have to give, imparting little of devotion and confidence in return. This lack of love denies the higher rights of marriage; it makes the wife's submission a joyless constraint. Along with this selfishness and the uneasy conscience attending it, there supervenes sometimes an irritability of temper that chafes over domestic troubles and makes a grievance of the most trifling mishap or inadvertence, ignoring the wife's patient affection and anxiety to please. Too often in this way husbands grow insensibly into family tyrants, forgetting the days of youth and the kindness of their espousals. "There are many," says Bengel (on this point unusually caustic), "who out of doors are civil and kind to all; when at home, toward their wives and children, whom they have no need to fear, they freely practise secret bitterness."

"Love your wives, *even as the Christ loved the Church*." What a glory this confers upon the husband's part in marriage! His devotion pictures, as no other love can, the devotion of Christ to His redeemed people. His love must therefore be a spiritual passion, the love of soul to soul, that partakes of God and of eternity. Of the three Greek words for love,—*eros*, familiar in Greek poetry and mythology, denoting the flame of sexual passion, is not named in the New Testament; *philia*, the love of friendship, is tolerably frequent, in its verb at least; but *agapé* absorbs the former and transcends both. This exquisite word denotes love in its spiritual purity and depth, the love of God and of Christ, and of souls to each other in God. This is the specific Christian affection. It is the attribute of God who "loved the world and gave His Son the Only-begotten," of "the Christ" who "loved the Church and gave up Himself for her." Self-devotion, not self-satisfaction, is its note. Its strength and authority it uses as material for sacrifice and instruments of service, not as prerogatives of pride or titles to enjoyment. Let this mind be in you, O husband, toward your wife, which was also in Christ Jesus, who was meek and lowly in heart, counting it His honour to serve and His reward to save and bless.

From verse 26 we gather that Christ is the husband's model, not only in the rule of self-devotion, but in the end toward which that devotion is directed: "that He might sanctify the Church,—that He might present her to Himself a glorious Church without spot or wrinkle,—*that she might be holy and without blemish*." The perfection of the wife's character will be to the religious husband one of the dearest objects in life. He will desire for her that which is highest and best, as for himself. He is put in charge of a soul more precious to him than any other, over which he has an influence incomparably great. This care he cannot delegate to any priest or father-confessor. The peril of such delegation and the grievous mischiefs that arise when there is no spiritual confidence between husband and wife, when through unbelief or superstition the head of the house hands over his priesthood to another man, are painfully shown by the experience of Roman Catholic countries. The irreligion of laymen, the carelessness and unworthiness of fathers and husbands are responsible for the baneful influences of the confessional. The apostle bade the Corinthian wives, who were eager for religious knowledge, to "ask their husbands at home" (1 Cor. xiv. 35). Christian husbands should take more account of their office than they do; they should not be strangers to the spiritual trials and experiences of the heart so near to them. It might lead them to walk more worthily and to seek higher religious attainments, if they considered that the shepherding of at least one soul devolves upon themselves, that they are unworthy of the name of husband without such care for the welfare of the soul linked to their own as Christ bears toward His bride the Church. Those who have no father or husband to look to, or who look in vain to this quarter for spiritual help, St Paul refers, beside the light and comfort of Scripture and the public ministry and fellowship of the Church, to the "aged women" who are the natural guides and exemplars of the younger in their own sex (Titus ii. 3–5).

The selfishness of the stronger sex, supported by the force of habit and social usage, was hard to subdue in the Greek Christian Churches. Through some eight verses St Paul labours this one point. In verse 28 he adduces another reason, added to the example of Christ, for the love enjoined. "So ought men indeed to love their wives as their own bodies. He that loveth his wife loveth himself." The "So" gathers its force from the previous example. In loving us Christ does not love something foreign and, as it were, outside of Himself. "We are members of His body" (ver. 30). It is the love of the Head to the members, of the Son of man to the sons of men, whose race-life is founded in Him. Jesus Christ laid it down as the highest law, under that of love to God: "Thou shalt love thy neighbour *as thyself*." His love to us followed this rule. His life was wrapped up in ours. By such community of life self-love is transfigured, and exalted into the purest self-forgetting.

Thus it is with true marriage. The wedding of a human pair makes each the other's property. They are "one flesh" (ver. 31); and so long as the flesh endures there remains this consciousness of union, whose violation is deadly sin. As the Church is not her own, nor Christ His own since He became man with men, so the husband and wife are no longer independent and self-complete personalities, but incorporated into a new existence common to both. Their love must correspond to this fact. If the man loves himself, if he values his own limbs and tends and guards from injury his bodily frame (ver. 29), he must do the same equally by his wife; for her life and limbs are as a part of his own. This the apostle lays down as an obvious duty. Nature teaches the obligation, by every manly instinct.

The saying the apostle quotes in verse 31 dates from the origin of the human family; it is taken from the lips of the first husband and father of the race, while as yet unstained by sin (Gen. ii. 23, 24). Christ infers from it the singleness and indelibility of the marriage covenant. But this doctrine, natural as it is, was not inferred by natural religion. The cultivated Greek took a wife for the production of children. Her rights put no restriction upon his appetite. Love was not in the marriage contract. If she received the maintenance due to her rank and the mistress-ship of the house, and was the mother of his lawful children, she had all that a free-born woman could demand. The slave-woman had no rights. Her body was at her owner's disposal. Nothing in Christianity appeared more novel and more severe, in comparison with the dissolute morals of the time, than the Christian view of marriage. Even Christ's Jewish disciples seemed to think the state of wedlock intolerable under the condition He imposed. This want of reverence and constancy between the sexes was a main cause of the degeneracy of the age. All virtues disappear with this one.

Roman manliness and uprightness, Greek courtesy and courage, filial piety, civic worth, loyalty in friendship—the qualities that once in a high degree adorned the classic nations, were now rare amongst men. In the most exalted ranks infamous vices flourished; and purity of life was a cause for odium and suspicion.

Amidst this seething mass of corruption the Spirit of life in Christ Jesus created new hearts and new homes. It kindled a pure fire on the desecrated hearth. It taught man and woman a chaste love; and their alliances were formed "in sanctification and honour, not in the passion of lust as it is with the Gentiles who know not God" (1 Thess. iv. 3–6). Every Christian house, thus based on an honourable and religious union, became the centre of a leaven that wrought upon the corrupt society around. It held forth an example of wedded loyalty and domestic joy beautiful and strange in that loveless Pagan world. Children grew up trained in pure and gentle manners. From that hour the hope of a better day began. The influence of the new ideal, filtrating everywhere into the surrounding heathenism and assimilating even before it converted the hostile world, raised society, though gradually and with many relapses, from the extreme debasement of the age of the Cæsars. Never subsequently have the morals of civilized mankind sunk to a level quite so low. The Christian conception of love and marriage opened a new era for mankind.

FOOTNOTES:

[139] See Dr. Maclaren's admirable words on this subject in *Colossians and Philemon* (Expositor's Bible), pp. 336–40; and Dr. Dale's *Lectures on Ephesians*, Lect. xix., "Wives and Husbands."

[140] In verse 24 St Paul resumes with ἀλλά, the *but* of opposition and not mere contrast, indicating a case where the claims of husband and Saviour may, conceivably, be in competition.

CHAPTER XXVI.

CHRIST AND HIS BRIDE.

"The Christ is the head of the Church, *being* Himself the Saviour of the body.... The Church is subject to the Christ in everything....

"The Christ loved the Church, and gave Himself up for her; that He might sanctify her, having cleansed her by the washing of water with the word, that He might present the Church to Himself a glorious *Church*, not having spot or wrinkle or any such thing; but that she should be holy and without blemish....

"The Christ [nourisheth and cherisheth] the Church; because we are members of His body. 'For this cause shall a man leave his father and mother, and shall cleave to his wife; and the twain shall become one flesh.' This mystery is great: but I speak in regard of Christ and of the Church."—EPH. v. 23–32.

We have extracted from the apostle's homily upon marriage the sentences referring to Christ and His Church, in order to gather up their collective import. The main topic of the epistle here again asserts itself; and under the figure of marriage St Paul brings to its conclusion his doctrine on the subject of the Church. This passage answers, theologically, a purpose similar to that of the allegory of Hagar and Sarah in the epistle to the Galatians: it lights up for the imagination the teaching and argument of the former part of the epistle; it shows how the doctrine of Christ and the Church has its counterpart in nature, as the struggle between the legal and evangelical spirit had its counterpart in the patriarchal history. The three detached paragraphs present us three considerations, of which we shall treat the second first in order of exposition: Christ's *love to the Church*; His *authority over the Church*; and *the mystery of the Church's origin in Him.*

I. "Husbands, love your wives, even as the Christ also loved the Church, and gave up Himself for her." This is parallel to the declaration of Galatians ii. 20: "He loved me; He gave up Himself for me." The sacrifice of the cross has at once its personal and its collective purpose. Both are to be kept in mind.

On the one hand, we must value infinitely and joyfully assert our individual part in the redeeming love of the Son of God; but we must equally admit the sovereign rights of the Church in the Redeemer's passion. Our souls bow down before the glory of the love with which He has from eternity sought her for His own. There is in some Christians an absorption in the work of grace within their own hearts, an individualistic salvation-seeking that, like all selfishness, defeats its end; for it narrows and impoverishes the inner life thus sedulously cherished. The Church does not exist simply for the benefit of individual souls; it is an eternal institution, with an affiance to Christ, a calling and destiny of its own; within that universal sphere our personal destiny holds its particular place.

It is "the Christ" who stands, throughout this context (vv. 23–29), over against "the Church" as her Lover and Husband; whereas in the context of Galatians ii. 20 we read "Christ"—the bare personal name—repeated again and again without the distinguishing article. *Christ* is the Person whom the soul knows and loves, with whom it holds communion in the Spirit. *The Christ* is the same regarded in the wide scope of His nature and office,—the Christ of humanity and of the ages. "The Christ" of this epistle expands the Saviour's title to its boundless significance, and gives breadth and length to that which in "Christ" is gathered up into a single point.[141]

This Christ "gave Himself up for the Church,"—yielded Himself to the death which the sins of His people merited and brought upon Him. Under the same verb, the apostle says in Romans iv. 25: He "*was delivered* because of our trespasses, and raised up because of our justification"—the sacrifice being there regarded on its passive side. Here, as in Galatians ii. 20, the act is made His own,—a voluntary surrender. "No man taketh my life from me," He said (John x. 18). In His case alone amongst the sons of men, death was neither natural nor inevitable. His surrender of life was an absolute sacrifice. He "laid down His life for His friends," as no other friend of man could do—the One who died for all. The love measured by this sacrifice is proportionately great.

The sayings of verses 25–27 set the glory of the vicarious death in a vivid light. Of such worth was the person of the Christ, of such significance and moral value His sacrificial death, that it weighed against the trespass, not of a man—Paul or any other—but of a world of men. He "purchased through His own blood," said Paul to the Ephesian elders, "the Church of God" (Acts xx. 28)—the whole flock that feeds in the pastures of the Great Shepherd, that has passed or will pass through the gates of His fold. Great was the honour and glory with which he was crowned, when led as victim to the altar of the world's atonement (Heb. ii. 9). Who will not say, as the meek Son of man treads so willingly His mournful path to Calvary, "Worthy is the Lamb!" Is not the heavenly Bridegroom worthy of the bride, that He consents to win by the sacrifice of Himself!

He is worthy; and *she must be made worthy*. "He gave up Himself, that He might sanctify her,—that He might Himself present to Himself a glorious Church, not having spot or wrinkle or anything of the kind,—that she may be holy and without blemish." The sanctification of the Church is the grand purpose of redeeming grace. This was the design of God for His sons in Christ before the world's foundation, "that we should be holy and unblemished before Him" (i. 4). This, therefore, was the end of Christ's mission upon earth; this was the intention of His sacrificial death. "For their sakes," said Jesus concerning His disciples, "I sanctify myself, that they also may be sanctified in truth" (John xvii. 19). His purchase of the Church is no selfish act. To God His Father Christ devotes every spirit of man that is yielded to Him. As the Priest of mankind it was His office thus to consecrate humanity, which is already in purpose and in essence "sanctified through the offering of the body of Jesus Christ once for all" (Heb. x. 10).

Only in this passage, where the apostle is thinking of the preparation of the Church for its perfect union with its Head, does he name Christ as our *Sanctifier*; in 1 Corinthians i. 2 he comes near this expression, addressing his readers as men "sanctified in Christ Jesus." In the epistle to the Hebrews this character is largely ascribed to Him, being the function of His priesthood. One in nature with the sanctified, Jesus our great Priest "sanctifies us through His own blood," so that with cleansed consciences we may draw near to the living God.[142] As Christ the Priest stands towards His people, so Christ the Husband towards His Church. He devotes her with Himself to God. He cleanses her that she may dwell with Him for ever, a spotless bride, dead unto sin and living unto God through Him.

"That He might sanctify her, *having cleansed her* in the laver of water by the word." The Church's purification is antecedent in thought to her sanctification through the sacrifice of Christ; and it is a means thereto. "Ye were washed, ye were sanctified," writes the apostle in 1 Corinthians vi. 11, putting the two things in the same order. It is the order of doctrine which he has laid down in the epistle to the Romans, where sanctification is built on the foundation laid in justification through the blood of Christ. Through the virtue of the sacrificial death the Church in all her members was washed from the defilements of sin, that she might enter upon God's service. Of the same initial purification of the heart St John writes in his first epistle (i. 7–9): "The blood of Jesus, God's Son, cleanses us from all sin…. He is faithful and just, that He should forgive us our sins and cleanse us from all unrighteousness." This is "the redemption through Christ's blood," for which St Paul in his first words of praise called upon us to bless God (i. 7). It is the special distinction of the New Covenant, which renders possible its other gifts of grace, that "the worshippers once cleansed" need have "no further consciousness of sins" (Heb. x. 2, 14–18). In the theological use here made of the idea of *cleansing*, St Paul comes into line with St John and the epistle to the Hebrews. The purification is nothing else than that which he has elsewhere styled *justification*. He employs the terms synonymously in the later epistle to Titus (ii. 14; iii. 7).

"Having cleansed" is a phrase congruous with the figure of *the laver*, or *bath* (comp. again Tit. iii. 5–7),—an image suggested, as one would think, by the bride-bath of the wedding-day in the ancient marriage customs. To this St Paul sees a counterpart in baptism, "the laver of water in the word." The cleansing and withal refreshing virtues of water made it an obvious symbol of regeneration. The emblem is twofold; it pictures at once the removal of guilt, and the imparting of new strength. One goes into the bath exhausted, and covered with dust; one comes out clean and fresh. Hence the baptism of the new believer in Christ had, in St Paul's view, a double aspect.[143] It looked backward to the old life of sin abandoned, and forward to the new life of holiness commenced. Thus it corresponded to the burial of Jesus (Rom. vi. 4), the point of juncture between death and resurrection. Baptism served as the visible and formal expression of the soul's passage through the gate of forgiveness into the sanctified life.

Along with this older teaching, a further and kindred significance is now given to the baptismal rite. It denotes the soul's affiance to its Lord. As the maiden's bath on the morning of her marriage betokened the purity in which she united herself to her betrothed, so the baptismal laver summons the Church to present herself "a chaste virgin unto Christ" (2 Cor. xi. 2). It signifies and seals her forgiveness, and pledges her in all her members to await the Bridegroom in garments unspotted from the world, with the pure and faithful love which will not be ashamed before Him at His coming. For this end Christ set up the baptismal laver. Upon our construction of the text, the words "that He might sanctify her" express a purpose complete in itself— viz., that of the Church's consecration to God. Then follow the means to this sanctification: "having cleansed her in the water-bath through the word,"— which washing, at the same time, has its purpose on the part of the Lord who appointed it—viz., "that He might present her to Himself" a glorious and spotless Church.

At the end of verse 27 the sentence doubles back upon itself, in Paul's characteristic fashion. The twofold aim of Christ's sacrifice of love on the Church's behalf—viz., her consecration to God, and her spotless purity fitting her for perfect union with her Lord—is restated in the final clause, by way of contrast with the "spots and wrinkles and such-like things" that are washed out: "but that she may be holy and without blemish."

We passed by, for the moment, the concluding phrase of verse 26, with which the apostle qualifies his reference to the baptismal cleansing; we are by no means forgetting it. "Having cleansed her," he writes, "by the laver of water *in [the] word*." This adjunct is deeply significant. It impresses on baptism a spiritual character, and excludes every theurgic conception of the rite, every doctrine that gives to it in the least degree a mechanical efficacy. "Without the word the sacrament could only influence man by magic, outward or inward" (Dorner). The "word" of which the apostle speaks,[144] is that of chapter vi. 17, "God's word—the Spirit's sword"; of Romans x. 8, "the word of faith which we proclaim"; of Luke i. 37, "the word from God which shall not be powerless"; of John xvii. 8, etc., "the words" that the Father had given to the Son, and the Son in turn to men. It is the Divine utterance, spoken and believed. In this accompaniment lies the power of the laver. The baptismal affusion is the outward seal of an inward transaction, that takes place in the spirit of believing utterers and hearers of the gospel word. This saving word receives in baptism its concrete expression; it becomes the *verbum visibile*.

The "word" in question is defined in Romans x. 8, 9: "If thou shalt confess with thy mouth the Lord Jesus, and believe in thy heart that God raised Him from the dead, thou shalt be saved!" Let the hearer respond, "I do so confess and believe," on the strength of this confession he is baptized, and in the conjoint act of faith and baptism—in the *obedience* of faith signified by his baptism—he is saved from his past sins and made an heir of life eternal. The rite is the simplest and most universal in application one can conceive. In heathen countries baptism recovers its primitive significance, as the decisive act of rupture with idolatry and acceptance of Christ as Lord, which in our usage is often overlaid and forgotten.

This interpretation gives a key to the obscure text of St Peter upon the same subject (1 Ep. iii. 21): "Baptism saves you—not the putting away of the filth of the flesh, but the questioning with regard to God of a good conscience, through the resurrection of Jesus Christ." The vital constituent of the rite is not the application of water to the body, but the challenge which the word makes therein to the conscience respecting the things of God,—the inquiry thus conveyed, to which a sincere believer in the resurrection of Christ makes joyful and ready answer. It is, in fine, *the appeal to faith* contained in baptism that gives to the latter its saving worth.

The "word" that makes Christian ordinances valid, is not the past utterance of God alone, which may remain a dead letter, preserved in the oracles of Scripture or the official forms of the Church, but that word alive and active, re-spoken and transmitted from soul to soul by the breath of the Holy Spirit. Without this animating word of faith, baptism is but the pouring or sprinkling of so much water on the body; the Lord's Supper is only the consumption of so much bread and wine.

All the nations will at last, in obedience to Christ's command, be baptized into the thrice-holy Name; and the work of baptism will be complete. Then the Church will issue from her bath, cleansed more effectually than the old world that emerged with Noah from the deluge. Every "spot and wrinkle" will pass from her face: the worldly passions that stained her features, the fears and anxieties that knit her brow or furrowed her cheek, will vanish away. In her radiant beauty, in her chaste and spotless love, Christ will lead forth His Church before His Father and the holy angels, "as a bride adorned for her husband." From eternity He set His love upon her; on the cross He won her back from her infidelity at the price of His blood. Through the ages He has been wooing her to Himself, and schooling her in wise and manifold ways that she might be fit for her heavenly calling. Now the end of this long task of redemption has arrived. The message goes forth to Christ's friends in all the worlds: "Come, gather yourselves to the great supper of God! The marriage of the Lamb is come, and His wife hath made herself ready! He hath given her fine linen bright and pure, that she may array herself. Let us rejoice and exult, and give to Him the glory!" Through what cleansing fires, through what baptisms even of blood she has still to pass ere the consummation is reached, He only knows who loved her and gave Himself for her. He will spare to His Church nothing, either of bounty or of trial, that her perfection needs.

II. Concerning Christ's lordly *authority* over His Church we have had occasion to speak already in other places. A word or two may be added here.

We acknowledge the Church to be "subject to Christ in everything." We proclaim ourselves, like the apostle, "slaves of Christ Jesus." But this subjection is too often a form rather than a fact. In protesting our independence of Popish and priestly lords of God's heritage, we are sometimes in danger of ignoring our dependence upon Him, and of dethroning, in effect, the one Lord Jesus Christ. Christian communities act and speak too much in the style of political republics. They assume the attitude of self-directing and self-responsible bodies.

The Church is no democracy, any more than it is an aristocracy or a sacerdotal absolutism: it is a *Christocracy*. The people are not rulers in the house of God; they are the ruled, laity and ministers alike. "One is your Master, even the Christ; and all ye are brethren." We acknowledge this in theory; but our language and spirit would oftentimes be other than they are, if we were penetrated by the sense of the continual presence and majesty of the Lord Christ in our assemblies. Royalties and nobilities, and the holders of popular power—all whose "names are named in this world," along with the principalities in heavenly places, when they come into the precincts of the Church must lay aside their robes and forget their titles, and speak humbly as in the Master's presence. What is it to the glorious Church of Jesus Christ that Lord So-and-so wears a coronet and owns half a county? or that Midas can fill her coffers, if he is pleased and humoured? or that this or that orator guides at his will the fierce democracy? He is no more than a man who will die, and appear before the judgement-seat of Christ. The Church's protection from human tyranny, from schemes of ambition, from the intrusion of political methods and designs, lies in her sense of the splendour and reality of Christ's dominion, and of her own eternal life in Him.

III. We come now to the profound mystery disclosed, or half-disclosed at the end of this section, that of *the origination of the Church from Christ*, which accounts for His love to the Church and His authority over her. He nourishes and cherishes the Church, we are told in verses 29, 30, "because we are members of His body."

Now, this membership is, in its origin, as old as creation. God "chose us in Christ before the world's foundation" (i. 4). We were created in the Son of God's love, antecedently to our redemption by Him. Such is the teaching of this and the companion epistle (Col. i. 14–18). Christ recovers through the cross that which pertains inherently to Him, which belonged to Him by nature and is as a part of Himself. From this standpoint the connexion of verses 30 and 31 becomes intelligible.[145] It is not, strictly speaking, "on account of this"; but "in correspondence with this"[146] says the apostle, suiting the original phrase to his purpose. The derivation of Eve from the body of Adam, as that is affirmed in the mysterious words of Genesis, is analogous to the derivation of the Church from Christ. The latter relationship existed in its ideal, and as conceived in the purpose of God, prior to the appearance of the human race. In St Paul's theory, the origin of woman in man which forms the basis of marriage in Scripture, looked further back to the origin of humanity in Christ Himself.

The train of thought that the apostle resumes here he followed in 1 Corinthians xi. 3–12: "I would have you know that the head of every man is the Christ, and the head of the woman is the man, and the head of Christ is God.... Man is the image and glory of God: but the woman is the glory of the man. For the man is not of the woman; but the woman of the man." So it is with Christ and His bride the Church.

"The LORD God caused a deep sleep to fall upon the man, and he slept; and He took one of his ribs, and closed up the flesh instead thereof: and the rib which the LORD God had taken from the man, made He a woman, and brought her to the man. And the man said,

> This is now bone of my bones, and flesh of my flesh:
> She shall be called Woman [*Isshah*], because she was taken out of Man [*Ish*].
> Therefore shall a man leave his father and his mother, and shall cleave unto his wife:
> And they shall be one flesh" (Gen. ii. 21–24).

Thus the first father of our race prophesied, and sang his wedding song. In some mystical, but real sense, marriage is a *reunion*, the reincorporation of what had been sundered. Seeking his other self, the complement of his nature, the man breaks the ties of birth and founds a new home. So the inspired author of the passage in Genesis explains the origin of marriage, and the instinct which draws the bridegroom to his bride.

But our apostle sees within this declaration a deeper truth, kept secret from the foundation of the world. When he speaks of "this great *mystery*," he means thereby not marriage itself, but *the saying of Adam about it*. This text was a standing problem to the Jewish interpreters. "But for my part," says the apostle, "I refer it to Christ and to the Church." St Paul, who has so often before drawn the parallel between Adam and Christ, by the light of this analogy perceives a new and rich meaning in the old dark sentence. It helps him to see how believers in Christ, forming collectively His body, are not only grafted into Him (as he puts it in the epistle to the Romans), but were derived from Him and formed in the very mould of His nature.

What is affirmed in Colossians i. 16, 17 concerning the universe in general, is true in its perfect degree of redeemed humanity: "*In Him* were created all things," as well as "through Him and for Him." Eve was created in Adam; and Adam in Christ. We are "partakers of a Divine nature," by our spiritual origin in Him who is the image of God and the root of humanity. The union of the first human pair and every true marriage since, being in effect, as Adam puts it, a restoration and redintegration, symbolizes the fellowship of Christ with mankind. This intention was in the mind of God at the institution of human life; it took expression in the prophetic words of the Book of Genesis, whose deeper sense St Paul is now able for the first time to unfold.

In our union through grace and faith with Christ crucified, we realize again the original design of our being. Christ has purchased by His blood no new or foreign bride, but her who was His from eternity,—the child who had wandered from the Father's house, the betrothed who had left her Lord and Spouse. In regard to this "mystery of our coherence in Christ," Richard Hooker says, in words that suggest many aspects of this doctrine: "The Church is in Christ, as Eve was in Adam. Yea, by grace we are every one of us in Christ and in His Church, as by nature we are in our first parents. God made Eve of the rib of Adam. And His Church He frameth out of the very flesh, the very wounded and bleeding side of the Son of man. His body crucified and His blood shed for the life of the world are the true elements of that heavenly being which maketh us such as Himself is of whom we come. For which cause the words of Adam may be fitly the words of Christ concerning His Church, 'flesh of my flesh and bone of my bones—a true native extract out of mine own body,' So that in Him, even according to His manhood, we according to our heavenly being are as branches in that root out of which they grow."[147]

FOOTNOTES:

[141] Compare pp. 47, 83, 169, 189.

[142] Heb. ii. 9–12, ix. 14, 15, x. 5–22, xiii. 12.

[143] See Rom. vi. 1–11; Col. ii. 11, 12; 1 Cor. x. 2, xii. 13.

[144] Ἐν ῥήματι. Λόγος is word as expressive of *thought*. Ῥῆμα, the utterance of a living voice,—a *sentence, pronouncement, message*; it is the Greek term employed in all the passages here cited.

[145] The words "of His flesh and of His bones," following "members of His body" in the A.V., appear to be an ancient gloss adopted by the Greek copyists, which was suggested by Gen. ii. 23. They are unsuitable to the idea of a spiritual union, and interrupt rather than help the apostle's exposition.

[146] St Paul changes the Ἕνεκεν τούτου of the original to Ἀντὶ τούτου, which conveys the idea that marriage has its counterpart in the fact that we are members of Christ.

[147] *Ecclesiastical Polity*; v. 56 7.

CHAPTER XXVII.

THE CHRISTIAN HOUSEHOLD.

"Children, obey your parents in the Lord: for this is right. 'Honour thy father and mother,' which is a first commandment, *given* in promise,—'that it may be well with thee, and thou mayest live long on the earth.' And, ye fathers, provoke not your children to wrath: but nurture them in the chastening and admonition of the Lord.

"Servants, be obedient to them that according to the flesh are your lords, with fear and trembling, in singleness of your heart, as unto the Christ; not in the way of eye-service, as men-pleasers; but as servants of Christ, doing the will of God from the soul; with good will doing service, as unto the Lord, and not unto men: knowing that whatsoever good thing each one doeth, the same shall he receive again from the Lord, whether *he be* bond or free. And, ye lords, do the same things unto them, and forbear threatening: knowing that both their Lord and yours is in heaven, and there is no respect of persons with Him."—EPH. vi. 1–9.

The Christian family is the cradle and the fortress of the Christian faith. Here its virtues shine most brightly; and by this channel its influence spreads through society and the course of generations. Marriage has been placed under the guardianship of God; it is made single, chaste and enduring, according to the law of creation and the pattern of Christ's union with His Church. With parents thus united, family honour is secure; and a basis is laid for reverence and discipline within the house.

I. Thus the apostle turns, in the opening words of chapter vi., from the husband and wife to the *children* of the household. He addresses them as present in the assembly where his letter is read. St Paul accounted the children "holy," if but one parent belonged to the Church (1 Cor. vii. 14). They were baptized, as we presume, with their fathers or mothers, and admitted, under due precautions,[148] to the fellowship of the Church so far as their age allowed. We cannot limit this exhortation to children of adult age. The "discipline and admonition of the Lord" prescribed in verse 4, belong to children of tender years and under parental control.

Obedience is the law of childhood. It is, in great part, the child's religion, to be practised "in the Lord." The reverence and love, full of a sweet mystery, which the Christian child feels towards its Saviour and heavenly King, add new sacredness to the claims of father and mother. Jesus Christ, the Head over all things, is the orderer of the life of boys and girls. His love and His might guard the little one in the tendance of its parents. The wonderful love of parents to their offspring, and the awful authority with which they are invested, come from the source of human life in God.

The Latin *pietas* impressed a religious character upon filial duty. This word signified at once dutifulness towards the gods, and towards parents and kindred. In the strength of its family ties and its deep filial reverence lay the secret of the moral vigour and the unmatched discipline of the Roman commonwealth. The history of ancient Rome affords a splendid illustration of the fifth commandment.

For this is right, says the apostle, appealing to the instincts of natural religion. The child's conscience begins here. Filial obedience is the primary form of duty. The loyalties of after life take their colour from the lessons learnt at home, in the time of dawning reason and incipient will. Hard indeed is the evil to remove, where in the plastic years of childhood obedience has been associated with base fear, with distrust or deceit, where it has grown sullen or obsequious in habit. From this root of bitterness there spring rank growths of hatred toward authority, jealousies, treacheries, and stubbornness. Obedience rendered "in the Lord" will be frank and willing, careful and constant, such as that which Jesus rendered to the Father.

St Paul reminds the children of the law of the Ten Words, taught to them in their earliest lessons from Scripture. He calls the command in question "*a first* [or *chief*] commandment"—just as the great rule, "Thou shalt love the Lord thy God," is *the* first commandment; for this is no secondary rule or minor precept, but one on which the continuance of the Church and the welfare of society depend. It is a law fundamental as birth itself, written not on the statute-book alone but on the tables of the heart.

Moreover, it is a "command *in promise*"—that takes the form of promise, and holds out to obedience a bright future. The two predicates—"first" and "in promise"—as we take it, are distinct. To merge them into one blunts their meaning. This commandment is primary in its importance, and promissory in its import. The promise is quoted from Exodus xx. 12, as it stands in the Septuagint, where the Greek Christian children would read it. But the last clause is abbreviated; St Paul writes "upon *the earth*" in place of "the good land which the Lord thy God giveth thee." This blessing is the heritage of dutiful children in every land. Those who have watched the history of godly families of their acquaintance, will have seen the promise verified. The obedience of childhood and youth rendered to a wise Christian rule, forms in the young nature the habits of self-control and self-respect, of diligence and promptitude and faithfulness and kindliness of heart, which are the best guarantees for happiness and success in life. Through parental nurture "godliness" secures its "promise of the life that now is."

Children are exhorted to submission: fathers to *gentleness*. "Do not," the apostle says, "anger your children"; in the corresponding place in Colossians, "Do not irritate your children, lest they be disheartened" (ch. iii. 21). In these parallel texts two distinct verbs are rendered by the one English word "provoke." The Colossian passage warns against the chafing effect of parental exactions and fretfulness, that tend to break the child's spirit and spoil its temper. Our text warns the father against angering his child by unfair or oppressive treatment. From this verb comes the noun "wrath" (or "provocation") used in chapter iv. 26, denoting that stirring of anger which gives peculiar occasion to the devil.

Not that the father is forbidden to cross his child's wishes, or to do anything or refuse anything that may excite its anger. Nothing is worse for a child than to find that parents fear its displeasure, and that it will gain its ends by passion. But the father must not be exasperating, must not needlessly thwart the child's inclinations and excite in order to subdue its anger, as some will do even of set purpose, thinking that in this way obedience is learnt. This policy may secure submission; but it is gained at the cost of a rankling sense of injustice.

Household rule should be equally firm and kind, neither provoking nor avoiding the displeasure of its subjects, inflicting no severity for severity's sake, but shrinking from none that fidelity demands. With much parental fondness, there is sometimes in family government a want of seriousness and steady principle, an absence in father or mother of the sense that they are dealing with moral and responsible beings in their little ones, and not with toys, which is reflected in the caprice and self-indulgence of the children's maturer life. Such parents will give account hereafter of their stewardship with an inconsolable grief.

It is almost superfluous to insist on the apostle's exhortation to treat children kindly. For them these are days of Paradise, compared with times not far distant. Never were the wants and the fancies of these small mortals catered for as they are now. In some households the danger lies at the opposite extreme from that of over-strictness. The children are idolized. Not their comfort and welfare only, but their humours and caprices become the law of the house. They are "nourished" indeed, but not "in the discipline and admonition of the Lord." It is a great unkindness to treat our children so that they shall be strangers to hardship and restriction, so that they shall not know what real obedience means, and have no reverence for age, no habits of deference and self-denial. It is the way to breed monsters of selfishness, pampered creatures who will be useless and miserable in adult life.

"Discipline and admonition" are distinguished as positive and negative terms. The first is the "training up of the child in the way that he should go"; the second checks and holds him back from the ways in which he should not go. The former word (*paideia*)—denoting primarily *treating-as-a-boy*—signifies very often "chastisement";[149] but it has a wider sense, embracing instruction besides.[150] It includes the whole course of training by which the boy is reared into a man.—*Admonition* is a still more familiar word with St Paul.[151] It may be reproof bearing upon errors in the past; or it may be warning, that points out dangers lying in the future. Both these services parents owe to their children. Admonition implies faults in the nature of the child, and wisdom in the father to see and correct them.

"Foolishness," says the Hebrew proverb, "is bound up in the heart of a child." In the Old Testament discipline there was something over-stern. The "hardness of heart" censured by the Lord Jesus, which allowed of two mothers in the house, put barriers between the father and his offspring that rendered "the rod of correction" more needful than it is under the rule of Christ. But correction, in gentler or severer sort, there must be, so long as children spring from sinful parents. The child's conscience responds to the kindly and searching word of reproof, to the admonition of love. This faithful dealing with his children wins for the father in the end a deep gratitude, and makes his memory a guard in days of temptation and an object of tender reverence.

The child's "obedience *in the Lord*" is its response to "the discipline and admonition *of the Lord*" exercised by its parents. The discipline which wise Christian fathers give their children, is the Lord's discipline applied through them. "Correction and instruction should proceed from the Lord and be directed by the Spirit of the Lord, in such a way that it is not so much the father who corrects his children and teaches them, as the Lord through him" (Monod). Thus the Father of whom every family on earth is named, within each Christian house works all in all. Thus the chief Shepherd, through His under-shepherds, guides and feeds the lambs of His flock. By the gate of His fold fathers and mothers themselves have entered; and the little ones follow with them. In the pastures of His word they nourish them, and rule them with His rod and staff. To their offspring they become an image of the Good Shepherd and the Father in heaven. Their office teaches them more of God's fatherly ways with themselves. From their children's humbleness and confidence, from their simple wisdom, their hopes and fears and ignorances, the elders learn deep and affecting lessons concerning their own relations to the heavenly Father.

St Paul's instruction to fathers applies to all who have the charge of children: to schoolmasters of every degree, whose work, secular as it may be called, touches the springs of moral life and character; to teachers in the Sunday school, successors to the work that Christ assigned to Peter, of shepherding His lambs. These instructors supply the Lord's nurture to multitudes of children, in whose homes Christian faith and example are wanting. The ideas which children form of Christ and His religion, are gathered from what they see and hear in the school. Many a child receives its bias for life from the influence of the teacher before whom it sits on Sunday. The love and meekness of wisdom, or the coldness or carelessness of the one who thus stands between Christ and the infant soul, will make or mar its spiritual future.

II. From the children of the house the apostle proceeds to address the *servants* —slaves as they were, until the gospel unbound their chains. The juxtaposition of children and slaves is full of significance; it is a tacit prophecy of emancipation. It brings the slave within the household, and gives a new dignity to domestic service.[152]

The Greek philosophers regarded slavery as a fundamental institution, indispensable to the existence of civilized society. That the few might enjoy freedom and culture, the many were doomed to bondage. Aristotle defines the slave as an "animated tool," and the tool as an "inanimate slave." Two or three facts will suffice to show how utterly slaves were deprived of human rights in the brilliant times of the classic humanism. In Athens it was the legal rule to admit the evidence of a slave only upon torture, as that of a freeman was received upon oath. Amongst the Romans, if a master had been murdered in his house, the whole of his domestic servants, amounting sometimes to hundreds, were put to death without inquiry. It was a common mark of hospitality to assign to a guest a female slave for the night, like any other convenience. Let it be remembered that the slave population outnumbered the free citizens of the Roman and Greek cities by many times; that they were frequently of the same race, and might be even superior in education to their masters. Indeed, it was a lucrative trade to rear young slaves and train them in literary and other accomplishments, and then to let them out in these capacities for hire. Let any one consider the condition of society which all this involved, and he will have some conception of the degradation in which the masses of mankind were plunged, and of the crushing tyranny that the world laboured under in the boasted days of republican liberty and Hellenic art.

No wonder that the new religion was welcome to the slaves of the Pagan cities, and that they flocked into the Church. Welcome to them was the voice that said: "Come unto me, all ye that are burdened and heavy laden"; welcome the proclamation that made them Christ's freedmen, "brethren beloved" where they had been "animated tools" (Philem. 16). In the light of such teaching, slavery was doomed. Its re-adoption by Christian nations, and the imposition of its yoke on the negro race, is amongst the great crimes of history,—a crime for which the white man has had to pay rivers of his blood.

The social fabric, as it then existed, was so entirely based upon slavery, that for Christ and the apostles to have proclaimed its abolition would have meant universal anarchy. In writing to Philemon about his converted slave Onesimus, the apostle does not say, "Release him," though the word seems to be trembling on his lips. In 1 Corinthians vii. 20–24 he even advises the slave who has the chance of manumission to remain where he is, content to be "the Lord's freedman." To the Christian slave what mattered it who ruled over his perishing body! his spirit was free, death would be his discharge and enfranchisement. No decree is issued to abolish bond-service between man and man; but it was destroyed in its essence by the spirit of Christian brotherhood. It melted away in the spread of the gospel, as snow and winter melt before the face of spring.

"Ye slaves, obey your lords according to the flesh." The apostle does not disguise the slave's subservience; nor does he speak in the language of pity or of condescension. He appeals as a man to men and equals, on the ground of a common faith and service to Christ. He awakens in these degraded tools of society the sense of spiritual manhood, of conscience and loyalty, of love and faith and hope. As in Colossians iii. 22–iv. 1, the apostle designates the earthly master not by his common title (*despotēs*), but by the very word (*kyrios*) that is the title of the *Lord* Christ, giving the slave in this way to understand that he has, in common with his master (ver. 9), a higher Lord in the spirit. "Ye are slaves to the Lord Christ!" (Col. iii. 24). St Paul is accustomed to call himself "a slave of Christ Jesus."[153] Nay, it is even said, in Philippians ii. 7, that Christ Jesus "took the form of a slave!"

How much there was, then, to console the Christian bondman for his lot. In self-abnegation, in the willing forfeiture of personal rights, in his menial and unrequited tasks, in submission to insult and injustice, he found a holy joy. His was a path in which he might closely follow the steps of the great Servant of mankind. His position enabled him to "adorn the Saviour's doctrine" above other men (Tit. ii. 9, 10). Affectionate, gentle, bearing injury with joyful courage, the Christian slave held up to that hardened and jaded Pagan age the example which it most required. God chose the base things of the world to bring to nought the mighty.

The relations of servant and master will endure, in one shape or other, while the world stands. And the apostle's injunctions bear upon servants of every order. We are all, in our various capacities, servants of the community. The moral worth of our service and its blessing to ourselves depend on the conditions that are here laid down.

1. There must be *a genuine care for our work.*

"Obey," he says, "with fear and trembling, in singleness of your heart, as unto the Christ." The fear enjoined is no dread of human displeasure, of the master's whip or tongue. It is the same "fear and trembling" with which we are bidden to "work out our own salvation" (Phil. ii. 12). The inward work of the soul's salvation and the outward work of the busy hands labouring in the mine or at the loom, or in the lowliest domestic duties,—all alike are to be performed under a solemn responsibility to God and in the presence of Christ, the Lord of nature and of men, who understands every sort of work, and will render to each of His servants a just and exact reward. No man, whether he be minister of state or stable-groom, will dare to do heedless work, who lives and acts in that august Presence,—

"As ever in the great Task-master's eye."

2. The sense of Christ's Lordship ensures *honesty in work.*

So the apostle continues: "Not with *eye-service*, as *men-pleasers*." Both these are rare compound words,—the former indeed occurring only here and in the companion letter, being coined, probably, by the writer for this use. It is the common fault and temptation of servants in all degrees to observe the master's eye, and to work busily or slackly as they are watched or not. Such workmen act as they do, because they look to men and not to God. Their work is without conscience and self-respect. The visible master says "Well done!" But there is another Master looking on, who says "Ill done!" to all pretentious doings and works of eye-service,—who sees not as man sees, but judges with the act the motive and intent.

> "Not on the vulgar mass
> Called 'work' must sentence pass,
> Things done, which took the eye and had the price."

In His book of accounts there is a stern reckoning in store for deceitful dealers and the makers-up of unsound goods, in whatever handicraft or headcraft they are engaged.

Let us all adopt St Paul's maxim; it will be an immense economy. What armies of overlookers and inspectors we shall be able to dismiss, when every servant works as well behind his master's back as to his face, when every manufacturer and shopkeeper puts himself in the purchaser's place and deals as he would have others deal with him. It was for the Christian slaves of the Greek trading cities to rebuke the Greek spirit of fraud and trickery, by which the common dealings of life in all directions were vitiated.

3. To the carefulness and honesty of the slave's daily labour he must even add *heartiness*: "as slaves of Christ doing the will of God from the soul, with good will doing service, as to the Lord and not to men."

They must do *the will of God* in the service of men, as Jesus Christ Himself did it,—and with His meekness and fortitude and unwearied love. Their work will thus be rendered from inner principle, with thought and affection and resolution spent upon it. That alone is the work of a man, whether he preaches or ploughs, which comes from the soul behind the hands and the tongue, into which the workman puts as much of his soul, of himself, as the work is capable of holding.

4. Add to all this, the servant's *anticipation of the final reward*. In each case, "whatsoever one may do that is good, this he will receive from the Lord, whether he be a bondman or a freeman." The complementary truth is given in the Colossian letter: "He who does wrong, will receive back the wrong that he did."

The doctrine of equal retribution at the judgement-seat of Christ matches that of equal salvation at the cross of Christ. How trifling and evanescent the differences of earthly rank appear, in view of these sublime realities. There is a "Lord in heaven," alike for servant and for master, "with whom is no respect of persons" (ver. 9). This grand conviction beats down all caste-pride. It teaches justice to the mighty and the proud; it exalts the humble, and assures the down-trodden of redress. No bribery or privilege, no sophistry or legal cunning will avail, no concealment or distortion of the facts will be possible in that Court of final appeal. The servant and the master, the monarch and his meanest subject will stand before the bar of Jesus Christ upon the same footing. And the poor slave, wonderful to think, who was faithful in the "few things" of his drudging earthly lot, will receive the "many things" of a son of

God and a joint-heir with Christ!

"*And, ye lords*, do the same things towards them"—be as good to your slaves as they are required to be towards you. A bold application this of Christ's great rule: "What you would that men should do to you, do even so to them." In many instances this rule suggested *liberation*, where the slave was prepared for freedom. In any case, the master is to put himself in his dependant's place, and to act by him as he would desire himself to be treated if their positions were reversed.

Slaves were held to be scarcely human. Deceit and sensuality were regarded as their chief characteristics. They must be ruled, the moralists said, by the fear of punishment. This was the only way to keep them in their place. The Christian master adopts a different policy. He "desists from threatening"; he treats his servants with even-handed justice, with fit courtesy and consideration. The recollection is ever present to his mind, that he must give account of his charge over each one of them to his Lord and theirs. So he will make, as far as in him lies, his own domain an image of the kingdom of Christ.

FOOTNOTES:

[148] We cannot absolutely *prove* infant baptism from the New Testament texts adduced on its behalf; but they afford a strong presumption in its favour, which is confirmed on the one hand by the analogy of circumcision, and on the other by the immemorial usage of the early Church. Titus i. 6 shows that stress was laid on the faith of children, and that discrimination was used in their recognition as Church members.

[149] 1 Cor. xi. 32; Heb. xii. 5, 11, etc.

[150] Acts vii. 22, xxii. 3; Rom. ii. 20; 2 Tim. ii. 25, iii.14.

[151] 1 Cor. x. 11; Col. i. 28, iii. 16; 1 Thess. v. 14, etc.

[152] The word *family* (Latin *familia*) denoted originally the servants of the establishment, the domestic slaves. Its modern usage is an index to the elevating influence of Christianity upon social relations.

[153] Rom. i. 1; 2 Cor. iv. 5; Gal. i. 10, etc.

ON THE APPROACHING CONFLICT.

CHAPTER vi. 10–20.

Ἰδοὺ ὁ Σατανᾶς ἐξῃτήσατο ὑμᾶς, τοῦ σινιάσαι ὡς τὸν σῖτον.

CHAPTER XXVIII.

THE FOES OF THE CHURCH.

"From henceforth be strong in the Lord, and in the might of His strength. Put on the whole armour of God, that ye may be able to stand against the wiles of the devil. For our wrestling is not against flesh and blood, but against the principalities, against the powers, against the world-rulers of this darkness, against the spiritual *hosts* of wickedness, in the heavenly *places*."—Eph. vi. 10–12.

We follow the Revised reading of the opening word of this paragraph, and the preferable rendering given by the Revisers in their margin. The adverb is the same that is found in Galatians vi. 17 ("*Henceforth* let no man trouble me"); not that used in Philippians iii. 1 and elsewhere ("*Finally*, my brethren," etc.). The copyists have conformed our text, seemingly, to the latter passage. We are recalled to the circumstances and occasion of the epistle. High as St Paul soars in meditation, he does not forget the situation of his readers. The words of chapter iv. 14 showed us how well aware he is of the dangers looming before the Asian Churches.

The epistle to the Colossians is altogether a letter of conflict (see ch. ii. 1 ff.). In writing that letter St Paul was wrestling with spiritual powers, mighty for evil, which had commenced their attack upon this outlying post of the Ephesian province. He sees in the sky the cloud portending a desolating storm. The clash of hostile arms is heard approaching. This is no time for sloth or fear, for a faith half-hearted or half-equipped. "You have need of your best manhood and of all the weapons of the spiritual armoury, to hold your ground in the conflict that is coming upon you. *Henceforth be strong in the Lord, and in the might of His strength.*"

It is the apostle's call to arms!—"Be strengthened in the Lord," he says (to render the imperative literally: so in 2 Timothy ii. I). *Make His strength your own.* The strength he bids them assume is *power*, *ability*, strength adequate to its end.[154] "The might of His strength" repeats the combination of terms we found in chapter i. 19. That sovereign power of the Almighty which raised Jesus our Lord from the dead, belongs to the Lord Christ Himself. From its resources He will clothe and arm His people. "In the Lord," says Israel evermore, "is righteousness and strength. The rock of my salvation and my refuge is in God." The Church's strength lies in the almightiness of her risen Lord, the Captain of her warfare.

"The *panoply* of God" (ver. II) reminds us of the saying of Jesus in reference to His casting out of demons, recorded in Luke xi. 21, 22—the only other instance in the New Testament of this somewhat rare Greek word. The Lord Jesus describes Himself in conflict with Satan, who as "the strong one armed keeps his possessions in peace,"—until there "come upon him the stronger than he," who "conquers him and takes away his panoply wherein he trusted, and divides his spoils." In this text the situation is reversed; and the "full armour" belongs to Christ's servants, who are equipped to meet the counter-attack of Satan and the powers of evil. There is a Divine and a Satanic panoply—arms tempered in heaven and in hell, to be wielded by the sons of light and of darkness respectively (comp. Rom. xiii. 12). The weapons of warfare on the two sides are even as the two leaders that furnish them—"the strong one armed" and the "Stronger than he." Mightier are faith and love than unbelief and hate; "greater is He that is in you than he that is in the world."

Let us review the forces marshalled against us,—their *nature*, their *mode of assault*, and *the arena of the contest*.

1. The Asian Christians had to "stand against *the wiles* [*schemes*, or *methods*[155]] *of the devil*."

Unquestionably, the New Testament assumes the personality of Satan. This belief runs counter to modern thought, governed as it is by the tendency to depersonalize existence. The conception of evil spirits given us in the Bible is treated as an obsolete superstition; and the name of the Evil One with multitudes serves only to point a profane or careless jest. To Jesus Christ, it is very certain, Satan was no figure of speech; but a thinking and active being, of whose presence and influence He saw tokens everywhere in this evil world (comp. ii. 2). If the Lord Jesus "speaks what He knows, and testifies what He has seen" concerning the mysteries of the other world, there can be no question of the existence of a personal devil. If in any matter He was bound, as a teacher of spiritual truth, to disavow Jewish superstition, surely Christ was so bound in this matter. Yet instead of repudiating the current belief in Satan and the demons, He earnestly accepts it; and it entered into His own deepest experiences. In the visible forms of sin Jesus saw the shadow of His great antagonist. "From the Evil One" He taught His disciples to pray that they might be delivered. The victims of disease and madness whom He healed, were so many captives rescued from the malignant power of Satan. And when Jesus went to meet His death, He viewed it as the supreme conflict with the usurper and oppressor who claimed to be "the prince of this world."[156]

Satan is the consummate form of depraved and untruthful intellect. We read of his "thoughts," his "schemes," his subtlety and deceit and impostures;[157] of his slanders against God and man,[158] from which, indeed, the name devil (*diabolus*) is given him. Falsehood and hatred are his chief qualities. Hence Jesus called him "the manslayer" and "the father of falsehood" (John viii. 44). He was the first sinner, and the fountain of sin (1 John iii. 8). All who do unrighteousness or hate their brethren are, so far, his offspring (1 John iii. 10). With a realm so wide, Satan might well be called not only "the prince," but the very "god of this world" (2 Cor. iv. 4). Plausibly he said to Jesus, in showing Him the kingdoms of the world, at the time when Tiberius Cæsar occupied the imperial throne: "All this authority and glory are delivered unto me. To whomsoever I will, I give it." His power is exercised with an intelligence perhaps as great as any can be that is morally corrupt; but it is limited on all sides. In dealing with Jesus Christ he showed conspicuous ignorance.

Chief amongst the wiles of the devil at this time was the "scheme of error," the cunningly woven net of the Gnostical delusion, in which the apostle feared that the Asian Churches would be entangled. Satan's empire is ruled with a settled policy, and his warfare carried on with a system of strategy which takes advantage of every opening for attack.[159] The manifold combinations of error, the various arts of seduction and temptation, the ten thousand forms of the deceit of unrighteousness constitute "the wiles of the devil."

Such is the gigantic opponent with whom Christ and the Church have been in conflict through all ages. But Satan does not stand alone. In verse 12 there is called up before us an imposing array of spiritual powers. They are "the angels of the devil," whom Jesus set in contrast with the angels of God that surround and serve the Son of man (Matt. xxv. 41). These unhappy beings are, again, identified with the "demons," or "unclean spirits," having Satan for their "prince," whom our Lord expelled wherever He found them infesting the bodies of men.[160] They are represented in the New Testament as fallen beings, expelled from a "principality" and "habitation of their own" (Jude 6) which they once enjoyed, and reserved for the dreadful punishment which Christ calls "the eternal fire prepared for the devil and his angels." They are here entitled *principalities* and *powers* (or *dominions*), after the same style as the angels of God, to whose ranks, as we are almost compelled to suppose, these apostates once belonged.

In contrast with the "angels of light" (2 Cor. xi. 14) and "ministering spirits" of the kingdom of God (Heb. i. 14), the angels of Satan have constituted themselves *the world-rulers of this darkness*. We find the compound expression *cosmo-krator* (world-ruler) in later rabbinical usage, borrowed from the Greek and applied to "the angel of death," before whom all mortal things must bow. Possibly, St Paul brought the term with him from the school of Gamaliel. Satan being the god of this world and swaying "the dominion of darkness,"[161] according to the same vocabulary his angels are "the rulers of the world's darkness"; and the provinces of the empire of evil fall under their direction.

The darkness surrounding the apostle in Rome and the Churches in Asia —"this darkness," he says—was dense and foul. With Nero and his satellites the masters of empire, the world seemed to be ruled by demons rather than by men. The frightful wish of one of the Psalmists was fulfilled for the heathen world: "Set a wicked man over him, and let Satan stand at his right hand."

The last of St Paul's synonyms for the satanic forces, "the spiritual [powers] of wickedness," may have served to warn the Church against reading a political sense into the passage and regarding the civil constitution of society and the visible world-rulers as objects for their hatred. Pilate was a specimen, by no means amongst the worst, of the men in power. Jesus regarded him with pity. His real antagonist lurked behind these human instruments. The above phrase, "spirituals of wickedness," is Hebraistic, like "judge" and "steward of unrighteousness,"[162] and is equivalent to "wicked spirits." The adjective "spiritual," which does duty for a substantive—"the spiritual [forces, or elements] of wickedness"[163]—brings out the collective character of these hostile powers.

St Paul's demonology[164] is identical with that of Jesus Christ. The two doctrines stand or fall together. The advent of Christ appears to have stirred to extraordinary activity the satanic powers. They asserted themselves in Palestine at this particular time in the most open and terrifying manner. In an age of scepticism and science like our own, it belongs to "the wiles of the devil" to work obscurely. This is dictated by obvious policy. Moreover, his power is greatly reduced. Satan is no longer the god of this world, since Christianity rose to its ascendant. The manifestations of demonism are, at least in Christian lands, vastly less conspicuous than in the first age of the Church. But those are more bold than wise who deny their existence, and who profess to explain all occult phenomena and phrenetic moral aberrations by physical causes. The popular idolatries of his own day, with their horrible rites and inhuman orgies, St Paul ascribed to devilry. He declared that those who sat at the feast of the idol and gave sanction to its worship, were partaking of "the cup and the table of demons" (1 Cor. x. 20, 21). Heathen idolatries at the present time are, in many instances, equally diabolical; and those who witness them cannot easily doubt the truth of the representations of Scripture upon this subject.

II. The conflict against these spiritual enemies is essentially a *spiritual* conflict. "Our struggle is not against blood and flesh."

They are not human antagonists whom the Church has to fear,—mortal men whom we can look in the face and meet with equal courage, in the contest where hot blood and straining muscle do their part. The fight needs mettle of another kind. The foes of our faith are untouched by carnal weapons. They come upon us without sound or footfall. They assail the will and conscience; they follow us into the regions of spiritual thought, of prayer and meditation. Hence the weapons of our warfare, like those which the apostle wielded (2 Cor. x. 2–5), "are not carnal," but spiritual and "mighty toward God."

It is true that the Asian Churches had visible enemies arrayed against them. There were the "wild beasts" with whom St Paul "fought at Ephesus," the heathen mob of the city, sworn foes of every despiser of their great goddess Artemis. There was Alexander the coppersmith, ready to do the apostle evil, and "the Jews from Asia," a party of whom all but murdered him in Jerusalem (Acts xxi. 27–36); there was Demetrius the silversmith, instigator of the tumult which drove him from Ephesus, and "the craftsmen of like occupation," whose trade was damaged by the progress of the new religion. These were formidable opponents, strong in everything that brings terror to flesh and blood. But after all, these were of small account in St Paul's view; and the Church need never dread material antagonism. The centre of the struggle lies elsewhere. The apostle looks beyond the ranks of his earthly foes to the power of Satan by which they are animated and directed,—"impotent pieces of the game he plays." From this hidden region he sees impending an attack more perilous than all the violence of persecution, a conflict urged with weapons of finer proof than the sharp steel of sword and axe, and with darts tipped with a fiercer fire than that which burns the flesh or devours the goods.

Even in outward struggles against worldly power, our wrestling is not simply against blood and flesh. Calvin makes a bold application of the passage when he says: "This sentence we should remember so often as we are tempted to revengefulness, under the smart of injuries from men. For when nature prompts us to fling ourselves upon them with all our might, this unreasonable passion will be checked and reined in suddenly, when we consider that these men who trouble us are nothing more than darts cast by the hand of Satan; and that while we stoop to pick up these, we shall expose ourselves to the full force of his blows." *Vasa sunt*, says Augustine of human troublers, *alius utitur; organa sunt, alius tangit.*

The crucial assaults of evil, in many instances, come in no outward and palpable guise. There are sinister influences that affect the spirit more directly, fires that search its inmost fibres, a darkness that sweeps down upon the very light that is in us threatening its extinction. "Doubts, the spectres of the mind," haunt it; clouds brood over the interior sky and fierce storms sweep down on the soul, that rise from beyond the seen horizon. "Jesus was led of the Spirit into the wilderness, to be tempted of the devil." Away from the tracks of men and the seductions of flesh and blood the choicest spirits have been tested and schooled. So they are tempered in the spiritual furnace to a fineness which turns the edge of the sharpest weapons the world may use against them.

Some men are constitutionally more exposed than others to these interior assaults. There are conditions of the brain and nerves, tendencies lying deep in the organism, that give points of vantage to the enemy of souls. These are the opportunities of the tempter; they do not constitute the temptation itself, which comes from a hidden and objective source. Similarly in the trials of the Church, in the great assaults made upon her vital truths, historical conditions and the external movements of the age furnish the material for the conflicts through which it has to pass; but the spring and moving agent, the master will that dominates these hostile forces is that of Satan.

The Church was engaged in a double conflict—of the flesh and of the spirit. On the one hand, it was assailed by the material seductions of heathenism and the terrors of ruthless persecution. On the other hand, it underwent a severe intellectual conflict with the systems of error that were rooted in the mind of the age. These forces opposed the Christian truth from without; but they became much more dangerous when they found their way within the Church, vitiating her teaching and practice, and growing like tares among the wheat. It is of heresy more than persecution that the apostle is thinking, when he writes these ominous words. Not blood and flesh, but the mind and spirit of the Asian believers will bear the brunt of the attack that the craft of the devil is preparing for the apostolic Church.

III. The last clause of verse 12, *in the heavenly places*, refuses to combine with the above description of the powers hostile to the Church. The heavenly places are the abode of God and the blessed angels. This is the region where the Father has blessed us in Christ (i. 3); where He seated the Christ at His own right hand (i. 20), and has in some sense seated us with Christ (ii. 6); and where the angelic princedoms dwell who follow with keen and studious sympathy the Church's fortunes (iii. 10). To locate the devil and his angels *there* seems to us highly incongruous; the juxtaposition is out of the question with St Paul. Chapter ii. 2 gives no real support to this view: supposing "the air" to be literally intended in that passage, it belongs to *earth* and not to heaven.[165] Nor do the parallels from other Scriptures adduced supply any but the most precarious basis for an interpretation against which the use of the exalted phrase in our epistle revolts.

No; Satan and his hosts do not dwell with Christ and the holy angels "in the heavenly places." But the Church dwells there already, by her faith; and it is in the heavenly places of her faith and hope that she is assailed by the powers of hell. This final prepositional clause should be separated by a comma from the words immediately foregoing; it forms a distinct predicate to the sentence contained in verse 12. It specifies the *locality* of the struggle; it marks out the battle-field. "Our wrestling is ... in the heavenly places."[166] So we construe the sentence, following the ancient Greek commentators.

The life of the Church "is hid with the Christ in God"; her treasure is laid up in heaven. She is assailed by a philosophy and vain deceit that perverts her highest doctrines, that clouds her vision of Christ and limits His glory, and threatens to drag her down from the high places where she sits with her ascended Lord.[167] Such was, in effect, the aim of the Colossian heresy, and of the great Gnostical movement to which this speculation was a prelude, that for a century and more entangled Christian faith in its metaphysical subtleties and false mysticism. The epistles to the Colossians and Ephesians strike the leading note of the controversies of the Church in this region during its first ages. Their character was thoroughly transcendental. "The heavenly things" were the subject-matter of the great conflicts of this epoch.

The questions of religious controversy characteristic of our own times, though not identical with those of Colossæ or Ephesus, concern matters equally high and vital. It is not this or that doctrine that is now at stake—the nature or extent of the atonement, the procession of the Holy Spirit from the Son with the Father, the verbal or plenary inspiration of Scripture; but the personal being of God, the historical truth of Christianity, the reality of the supernatural,—these and the like questions, which formed the accepted basis and the common assumptions of former theological discussions, are now brought into dispute. Religion has to justify its very existence. Christianity must answer for its life, as at the beginning. God is denied. Worship is openly renounced. Our treasures in heaven are proclaimed to be worthless and illusive. The entire spiritual and celestial order of things is relegated to the region of obsolete fable and fairy tales. The difficulties of modern religious thought lie at the foundation of things, and touch the core of the spiritual life. Unbelief appears, in some quarters, to be more serious and earnest than faith. While we quarrel over rubrics and ritual, thoughtful men are despairing of God and immortality. The Churches are engaged in trivial contentions with each other, while the enemy pushes his way through our broken ranks to seize the citadel.

"The apostle incites the readers," says Chrysostom, "by the thought of the prize at stake. When he has said that our enemies are powerful, he adds thereto that these are great possessions which they seek to wrest from us.

When he says *in the heavenly places*, this implies *for the heavenly things*. How it must rouse and sober us to know that the hazard is for great things, and great will be the prize of victory. Our foe strives to take *heaven* from us." Let the Church be stripped of all her temporalities, and driven naked as at first into the wilderness. She carries with her the crown jewels; and her treasure is unimpaired, so long as faith in Christ and the hope of heaven remain firm in her heart. But let these be lost; let heaven and the Father in heaven fade with our childhood's dreams; let Christ go back to His grave—then we are utterly undone. We have lost our all in all!

FOOTNOTES:

[154] Ἐνδυναμοῦσθε [from δύναμις] ἐν Κυρίῳ καὶ ἐν τῷ κράτει τῆς ἰσχύος αὐτοῦ. See the note on these synonyms, on p. 76. Comp., for this verb, Col. i. 11; 2 Tim. iv. 17; Phil. iv. 13: Πάντα ἰσχύω ἐν τῷ ἐνδυναμοῦντί με,—"I have strength for everything in Him that *enables* me."

[155] Comp. remark on μεθοδεία (iv. 14), p. 247.

[156] John xii. 31, xiv. 30, xvi. 11: comp. Luke iv. 5–7; Heb. ii. 14.

[157] 2 Cor. ii. 11, xi. 3; 2 Thess. ii. 9, 10; 2 Tim. ii. 26, etc.

[158] Rev. xii, 7–10; Gen. iii. 4, 5; Zech. iii. 1; Job i.

[159] Ch. iv. 27; 2 Cor. ii. 11; Luke xxii. 31.

[160] Luke x. 17–20, xi. 14–26.

[161] Col. i. 13: comp. Acts xxvi. 18, etc.

[162] Luke xvi. 8, xviii. 6.

[163] Τὰ πνευματικὰ τῆς πονηρίας.

[164] Mr. Moule aptly observes, in his excellent and most useful Commentary on Ephesians in the *Cambridge Bible for Schools and Colleges*: St Paul's "testimony to the real and objective existence" of evil spirits "gains in strength when it is remembered that the epistle was addressed (at least, among other designations) to Ephesus, and that Ephesus (see Acts xix.) was a peculiarly active scene of asserted magical and other dealings with the unseen darkness. Supposing that the right line to take in dealing with such beliefs and practices had been to say that the whole basis of them was a fiction of the human mind, not only would such a verse as this [vi. 12] not have been written, but, we may well assume, something would have been written strongly contradictory to the thought of it" (p. 176).

[165] See p. 103.

[166] The objection against the common rendering taken from the absence of the Greek article (τά) before the phrase ἐν τοῖς ἐπουρανίοις, required to link it to τὰ πνευματικὰ τῆς πονηρίας, is not decisive.

[167] Col. ii. 8–10, iii. 1–4; Phil. iii. 20, 21: comp. Eph. i. 3, ii. 6, 18, iv. 10, 15; Heb. vi. 19, 20, etc.

CHAPTER XXIX.

THE DIVINE PANOPLY.

"Wherefore take up the whole armour of God, that ye may be able to withstand in the evil day, and, having conquered all, to stand. Stand therefore, having girded your loins with truth, and having put on the breastplate of righteousness, and having shod your feet with the readiness of the gospel of peace; withal taking up the shield of faith, wherewith ye shall be able to quench all the fiery darts of the evil *one*. And take the helmet of salvation, and the sword of the Spirit, which is the word of God: with all prayer and supplication praying at all seasons in the Spirit, and watching thereunto in all perseverance and supplication for all the saints."—Eph. vi. 13–18.

Stand is the watchword for this battle, the apostle's order of the day: "that you may be able to *stand* against the stratagems of the devil, … that you may be able to *withstand* in the evil day, and mastering all your enemies[168] to *stand…. Stand* therefore, girding your loins about with truth." The apostle is fond of this martial style, and such appeals are frequent in the letters of this period.[169] The Gentile believers are raised to the heavenly places of fellowship with Christ, and invested with the lofty character of sons and heirs of God: let them hold their ground; let them maintain the honour of their calling and the wealth of their high estate, standing fast in the grace that is in Christ Jesus. *Pro aris et focis* the patriot draws his sword, and manfully repels the invader. Even so the good soldier of Christ Jesus contends for his heavenly city and the household of faith. He defends the dearest interests and hopes of human life.

This defence is needed, for an "evil day" is at hand! This emphatic reference points to something more definite than the general day of temptation that is co-extensive with our earthly life. St Paul foresaw a crisis of extreme danger impending over the young Church of Christ. The prophecies of Jesus taught His disciples, from the first, that His kingdom could only prevail by means of a severe conflict, and that some desperate struggle would precede the final Messianic triumph. This prospect looms before the minds of the New Testament writers, as "the day of Jehovah" dominated the imagination of the Hebrew prophets. Paul's apocalypse in 1 and 2 Thessalonians is full of reminiscences of Christ's visions of judgement. It culminates in the prediction of the evil day of Antichrist, which is to usher in the second, glorious coming of the Lord Jesus. The consummation, as the apostle was then inclined to think, might arrive within that generation (1 Thess. iv. 15, 17), although he declares its times and seasons wholly unknown. In his later epistles, and in this especially, it is clear that he anticipated a longer duration for the existing order of things; and "the evil day" for which the Asian Churches are to prepare can scarcely have denoted, to the apostle's mind, the final day of Antichrist, though it may well be an epoch of similar nature and a token and shadow of the last things.

In point of fact, a great secular crisis was now approaching. The six years (64–70 after Christ) extending from the fire of Rome to the fall of Jerusalem, were amongst the most fateful and calamitous recorded in history. This period was, in a very real sense, the day of judgement for Israel and the ancient world. It was a foretaste of the ultimate doom of the kingdom of evil amongst men; and through it Christ appears to have looked forward to the end of the world. Already "the days are evil" (v. 16); and "the evil day" is at hand—a time of terror and despair for all who have not a firm faith in the kingdom of God.

Two chief characteristics marked this crisis, as it affected the people of Christ: *persecution from without*, and *apostasy within the Church* (Matt. xxiv. 5, 8–12). To the latter feature St Paul refers elsewhere.[170] Of persecution he took less account, for this was indeed his ordinary lot, and had already visited his Churches; but it was afterwards to assume a more violent and appalling form.

When we turn to the epistle to the Seven Churches (Rev. ii., iii.) written in the next ensuing period, we find a fierce battle raging, resembling that for which this letter warns the Asian Churches to prepare. The storm which our apostle foresees, had then burst. The message addressed to each Church concludes with a promise to "him that overcometh." To the faithful it is said: "I know thy endurance." The angel of the Church of Pergamum dwells where is "the throne of Satan," and where "Antipas the faithful martyr was killed." There also, says the Lord Jesus, "are those who hold the teaching of Balaam, and the teaching of the Nicolaitans," with whom "I will make war with the sword of my mouth" (comp. Eph. vi. 17). Laodicea has shrunk from the trial, and grown rich by the world's friendship. Thyatira "suffers the woman Jezebel, who calls herself a prophetess, to teach and to seduce" the servants of Christ. Sardis has but "a few names that have not defiled their garments." Even Ephesus, though she had tried the false teachers and found them wanting (surely Paul's epistles to Timothy had helped her in this examination), has yet "left her first love." The day of trial has proved an evil day to these Churches. Satan has been allowed to sift them; and while some good wheat remains, much of the faith of the numerous and prosperous communities of the province of Asia has turned out to be faulty and vain. The presentiments that weighed on St Paul's mind when four years ago he took leave of the Ephesian elders at Miletus, and which reappear in this passage, were only too well justified by the course of events. Indeed, the history of the Church in this region has been altogether mournful and admonitory.

257

But it is time to look at the *armour* in which St Paul bids his readers equip themselves against the evil day. It consists of seven weapons, offensive or defensive—if we count prayer amongst them: the *girdle of truth*, the *breastplate of righteousness*, the *shoes of readiness to bear the message of peace*, the *shield of faith*, the *helmet of salvation*, the *sword of the word*, and the continual *cry of prayer*.

1. In girding himself for the field, the first thing the soldier does is to fasten round his waist the military *belt*. With this he binds in his under-garments, that there may be nothing loose or trailing about him, and braces up his limbs for action. Peace admits of relaxation. The girdle is unclasped; the muscles are unstrung. But everything about the warrior is tense and firm; his dress, his figure and movements speak of decision and concentrated energy. He stands before us an image of resolute conviction, of *a mind made up*. Such a picture the words "girt about with truth" convey to us.

The epistle is pervaded by the sense of the Church's need of intellectual conviction. Many of the Asian believers were children, half-enlightened and irresolute, ready to be "tossed to and fro and carried about with every wind of doctrine" (iv. 14). They had "heard the truth as it is in Jesus," but had an imperfect comprehension of its meaning.[171] They required to add to their faith knowledge,—the knowledge won by searching thought respecting the great truths of religion, by a thorough mental appropriation of the things revealed to us in Christ. Only by such a process can truth brace the mind and knit its powers together in "the full assurance of the understanding in the knowledge of the mystery of God, which is Christ" (Col. ii, 2, 3).

Such is the faith needed by the Church, now as then, the faith of an intelligent, firm and manly assurance. There is in such faith a security and a vigour of action that the faith of mere sentiment and emotional impression, with its nerveless grasp, its hectic and impulsive fervours, cannot impart. The luxury of agnosticism, the languors of doubt, the vague sympathies and hesitant eclecticism in which delicate and cultured minds are apt to indulge; the lofty critical attitude, as of some intellectual god sitting above the strife of creeds, which others find congenial—these are conditions of mind unfit for the soldier of Christ Jesus. He must have sure knowledge, definite and decided purposes—a soul girdled with truth.

2. Having girt his loins, the soldier next fastens on his *breastplate*, or cuirass.

This is the chief piece of his defensive armour; it protects the vital organs. In the picture drawn in 1 Thessalonians v. 8, the breastplate is made "of faith and love." In this more detailed representation, faith becomes the outlying defensive "shield," while righteousness serves for the innermost defence, the rampart of the heart. But, in truth, the Christian righteousness is compounded of faith and love.

This attribute must be understood in its full Pauline meaning. It is the state of one who is right with God and with God's law. It is the righteousness both of standing and of character, of imputation and of impartation, which begins with justification and continues in the new, obedient life of the believer. These are never separate, in the true doctrine of grace. "The righteousness that is of God by faith," is the soul's main defence against the shafts of Satan. It wards off deadly blows, both from this side and from that. Does the enemy bring up against me my old sins? I can say: "It is God that justifieth; who is he that condemneth?"—Am I tempted to presume on my forgiveness, and to fall into transgression once more? From this breastplate the arrow of temptation falls pointless, as it resounds: "He that doeth righteousness is righteous. He that is born of God doth not commit sin." The completeness of pardon for past offence and the integrity of character that belong to the justified life, are woven together into an impenetrable mail.

3. Now the soldier, having girt his loins and guarded his breast, must look well to his feet. There are lying ready for him *shoes* of wondrous make.

What is the quality most needed in the soldier's shoes? Some say, it is *firmness*; and they so translate the Greek word employed by the apostle, occurring only here in the New Testament, which in certain passages of the Septuagint seems to acquire this sense, under the influence of Hebrew idiom. [172] But firmness was embodied in the girdle. *Expedition* belongs to the shoes. The soldier is so shod that he may move with alertness over all sorts of ground.

Thus shod with speed and willingness were "the beautiful feet" of those that brought over desert and mountain "the good tidings of peace," the news of Israel's return to Zion (Isai. lii. 7–9). With such swift strength were the feet of our apostle shod, when "from Jerusalem round about unto Illyricum" he had "fulfilled the gospel of Christ," and is "ready," as he says, "to preach the glad tidings to you also that are in Rome" (Rom. i. 15). This readiness belonged to His own holy feet, who "came and preached peace to the far off and the near" (ii. 17),—when, for example, sitting a weary traveller by the well-side at Sychar, He found refreshment in revealing to the woman of Samaria the fountain of living water. Such readiness befits His servants, who have heard from Him the message of salvation and are sent to proclaim it everywhere.

The girdle and breastplate look to one's own safety. They must be supplemented by the evangelic zeal inseparable from the spirit of Christ. This is, moreover, a safeguard of Church life. Von Hofmann says admirably upon this point: "The objection [brought against the above interpretation] that the apostle is addressing the faithful at large, who are not all of them called to preach the gospel, is mistaken. Every believer should be prepared to witness for Christ so often as opportunity affords, and needs a *readiness* thereto. The knowledge of Christ's peace qualifies him to convey its message. He brings it with him into the strife of the world. And it is the consciousness that he possesses himself such peace and has it to communicate to others, which enables him to walk firmly and with sure step in the way of faith." When we are bidden to "*stand* in the evil day," that does not mean to stand idle or content to hold our ground. Attack is often the best mode of defence. We keep our faith by spreading it. We defend ourselves from our opponents by converting them to the gospel, which breathes everywhere reconciliation and fraternity. Our Foreign Missions are our grand modern apologetic; and God's peacemakers are His mightiest warriors.

4. With his body girt and fenced and his feet clad with the gospel shoes, the soldier reaches out his left hand to "take up withal the *shield*," while his right hand grasps first the helmet which he places on his head, and then the sword that is offered to him in the word of God.

The shield signified is not the small round buckler, or target, of the light-armed man; but the door-like shield,[173] measuring four feet by two-and-a-half and rounded to the shape of the body, that the Greek hoplite and the Roman legionary carried. Joined together, these large shields formed a wall, behind which a body of troops could hide themselves from the rain of the enemy's missiles. Such is the office of faith in the conflicts of life: it is the soldier's main defence, the common bulwark of the Church. Like the city's outer wall, faith bears the brunt and onset of all hostility. On this shield of faith the darts of Satan are caught, their point broken and their fire quenched. These military shields were made of wood, covered on the outside with thick leather, which not only deadened the shock of the missile, but protected the frame of the shield from the "fire-tipped darts" that were used in the artillery of the ancients. These flaming arrows, armed with some quickly burning and light combustible, if they failed to pierce the warrior's shield, fell in a moment extinguished at his feet.

St Paul can scarcely mean by his "fiery darts" incitements to passion in ourselves, inflammatory temptations that seek to rouse the inward fires of anger or lust. For these missiles are "fire-pointed darts *of the Evil One*." The fire belongs to the enemy who shoots the dart. It signifies the malignant hate with which Satan hurls slanders and threats against the people of God through his human instruments. A bold faith wards off and quenches this fire even at a distance, so that the soul never feels its heat. The heart's confidence is unmoved and the Church's songs of praise are undisturbed, while persecution rages and the enemies of Christ gnash their teeth against her. Such a shield to him was the faith of Stephen the proto-martyr.

"I heard the defaming of many; there was terror on every side.
But I trusted in Thee, O Jehovah: I said, Thou art my God!"

To "take up the shield of faith," is it not, like the Psalmist, to meet injuries and threats, the boasts of unbelief and of worldly power, the poisoned arrows of the deceitful and the bitter words of unjust reproach, with faith's quiet counter-assertion? "Who shall separate us from the love of Christ?" says the apostle in the midst of tribulation. "God is my witness, whom I serve in the gospel of His Son," he answers when his fidelity is questioned. No shaft of malice, no arrow of fear can pierce the soul that holds such a shield.

5. At this point (ver. 17), when the sentence beginning at verse 14 has drawn itself out to such length, and the relative clause of verse 16*b* makes a break and eddy in the current of thought, the writer pauses for a moment. He resumes the exhortation in a form slightly changed and with rising emphasis, passing from the participle to the finite verb: "And take *the helmet of salvation.*"

The word *take*, in the original, differs from the *taking up* of verses 13 and 16. It signifies the *accepting* of something offered by the hand of another. So the Thessalonians "*accepted* the word" brought them by St Paul (1 Thess. i. 6) and Titus "*accepted* the consolation" given him by the Corinthians (2 Cor. viii. 17)—in each case a welcome gift. God's hand is stretched out to bestow on His chosen warrior the helmet of salvation and the sword of His word, to complete his equipment for the perilous field. We accept these gifts with devout gratitude, knowing from what source they come and where the heavenly arms were fashioned.

The "helmet of salvation" is worn by the Lord Himself, as He is depicted by the prophet coming to the succour of His people (Isai. lix. 17). This helmet, on the head of Jehovah, is the crest and badge of their Divine champion. Given to the human warrior, it becomes the sign of his protection by God. The apostle does not call it "the *hope* of salvation," as he does in 1 Thessalonians v. 8, thinking of the believer's assurance of victory in the last struggle. Nor is it the sense and assurance of past salvation that here guards the Christian soldier. The presence of his Saviour and God in itself constitutes his highest safeguard.

"O Jehovah my Lord, the strength of my salvation,
Thou hast covered my head in the day of battle."

The warrior's head rising above his shield was frequently open to attack. The arrow might shoot over the shield's edge, and inflict a mortal blow. Our faith, at the best, has its deficiencies and its limits; but God's salvation reaches beyond our highest confidence in Him. His overshadowing presence is the crown of our salvation, His love its shining crest.

Thus the equipment of Christ's soldier is complete; and he is arrayed in the full armour of light. His loins girt with truth, his breast clad with righteousness, his feet shod with zeal, his head crowned with safety, while faith's all-encompassing shield is cast about him, he steps forth to do battle with the powers of darkness, "strong in the Lord, and in the might of His strength."

6. It only remains that "the *sword* of the Spirit" be put into his right hand, while his lips are open in continual prayer to the God of his strength.

The "cleansing word" of chapter v. 26, by whose virtue we passed through the gate of baptism into the flock of Christ, now becomes the guarding and smiting word, to be used in conflict with our spiritual foes. Of the Messiah it was said, in language quoted by the apostle against Antichrist (2 Thess. ii. 8): "He shall smite the earth with the rod of His mouth, and with the breath of His lips shall He slay the wicked" (Isai. xi. 4). Similarly, in Hosea the Lord tells how He has "hewed" the unfaithful "by His prophets, and slain them by the words of His mouth" (Hos. vi. 5). From such sayings of the Old Testament the idea of the sword of the Divine word is derived. We find it again in Hebrews iv. 12: "The word of God, living and active, sharper than any two-edged sword"; and in the "sword, two-edged, sharp," which John in the Revelation saw "coming out of the mouth of the Son of man": it belongs to Him whose name is "the word of God," and with it "He shall smite the nations."[174]

This sword of the inspired word Paul himself wielded with supernatural effect, as when he rebuked Elymas the sorcerer, or when he defended his gospel against the Judaizers of Galatia and Corinth. In his hand it was even as

> "The sword
> Of Michael, from the armoury of God,
> ... tempered so that neither keen
> Nor solid might resist that edge."

With what piercing reproofs, what keen thrusts of argument, what double-edged irony and dexterous sword-play did this mighty combatant smite the enemies of the cross of Christ! In times of conflict never may such leaders be wanting to the Church, men using weapons of warfare not carnal, but mighty to "cast down strongholds," to "bring down every high thing that exalts itself against the knowledge of God and make captive every thought to Christ's obedience."

In her struggle with the world's gigantic lusts and tyrannies, the Israel of God must be armed with this lofty and lightning-like power, with the flaming sword of the Spirit. No less in the secret, internal conflicts of the religious life, the sword of the word is the decisive weapon. The Son of man put it to proof in His combat in the wilderness. Satan himself sought to wrest this instrument to his purpose. With pious texts in his mouth he addressed our Lord, like an angel of light, fain to deceive Him by the very Scripture He had Himself inspired! until, with the last thrust of quotation, Jesus unmasked the tempter and drove him from the field, saying, "Get thee behind me, Satan!"

7. We have surveyed the Christian soldier with his harness on. From head to foot he is clothed in arms supernatural. No weapon of defence or offence is lacking, that the spiritual combat needs. Nothing seems to be wanting: yet everything is wanting, if this be all. Our text began: "Be strong in the Lord." It is *prayer* that links the believer with the strength of God.

What avails Michael's sword, if the hand that holds it is slack and listless? what the panoply of God, if behind it beats a craven heart? He is but a soldier in semblance who wears arms without the courage and the strength to use them. The life that is to animate that armed figure, to beat with high resolve beneath the corslet, to nerve the arm as it lifts the strong shield and plies the sharp sword, to set the swift feet moving on their gospel errands, to weld the Church together into one army of the living God, comes from the inspiration of God's Spirit received in answer to believing prayer. So the apostle adds: "With all prayer and supplication praying at every time in the Spirit."

There is here no needless repetition. "Prayer" is the universal word for reverent address to God; and "supplication" the entreaty for such help as "on every occasion"—at each turn of the battle, in each emergency of life—we find ourselves to need. And Christian prayer is always "in the Spirit,"—being offered in the grace and power of the Holy Spirit, who is the element of the believer's life in Christ, who helps our infirmities and, virtually, intercedes for us (Rom. viii. 26, 27). When the apostle continues, "*watching* [or *keeping awake*] thereunto," he reminds us, as perhaps he was thinking himself, of our Lord's warning to the disciples sleeping in Gethsemane: "Watch and pray, lest ye enter into temptation." The "perseverance" he requires in this wakeful attention to prayer, is the resolute persistence of the suppliant, who will neither be daunted by opposition nor wearied by delay.[175]

The word "supplication" is resumed at the end of verse 18, in order to enlist the prayers of the readers for the service of the Church at large: "with wakeful heed thereto, in all persistence and *supplication for all the saints*." Prayer for ourselves must broaden out into a catholic intercession for all the servants of our Master, for all the children of the household of faith. By the bands of prayer we are knit together,—a vast multitude of saints throughout the earth, unknown by face or name to our fellows, but one in the love of Christ and in our heavenly calling, and all engaged in the same perilous conflict.

"All the saints," St Paul said (i. 15), were interested in the faith of the Asian believers; they were called "with all the saints" to share in the comprehension of the immense designs of God's kingdom (iii. 18). The dangers and temptations of the Church are equally far-reaching; they have a common origin and character in all Christian communities. Let our prayers, at least, be catholic. At the throne of grace, let us forget our sectarian divisions. Having access in one Spirit to the Father, let us realize in His presence our communion with all His children.

FOOTNOTES:

[168] Comp. Rom. viii. 37, xvi. 20. *To bring down, overpower, conquer* is the military sense of **κατεργάζομαι**,—not found elsewhere in the New Testament, but, as it seems to us, unmistakable here. It occurs in Ezek. xxxiv. 4 (LXX), and 1 Esdr. iv. 4.

[169] Col. i. 23, ii. 5; Phil. i. 27–30, iv. 1: comp. 1 Thess. v. 8; Rom. xiii. 11–14; 1 Cor. xvi. 13; 2 Cor. x. 3–6.

[170] 2 Thess. ii. 3; Acts xx. 29, 30; 1 Tim. iv. 1; 2 Tim. iii. 1.

[171] Ch. 1. 17–23, iii. 16–19, iv. 13–15, 20–24.

[172] Ἑτοιμασία is adopted by the Greek translators as the equivalent of the Hebrew word for *foundation*, or *base*, in Ps. lxxxix. 14; Ezra ii. 68, iii. 3; Dan. xi. 7, 20, 21. See, however, the note of Meyer, who thinks that they misunderstood the Hebrew.

[173] Θυρεός: Latin *scutum*; only here in N.T.

[174] Rev. i. 16, ii. 12, xix. 13–15.

[175] Ἐν πάσῃ προσκαρτερήσει: *in every kind of persistence,*—a perseverance that tries all arts and holds its ground at every point. The verb προσκαρτερέω appears in the parallel passages: Col. iv. 2; Rom. xii. 12; also in Acts i. 14.

THE CONCLUSION.

CHAPTER vi. 19–24.

Πέπεισμαι γὰρ ὅτι οὔτε θάνατος οὔτε ζωὴ οὔτε ἄγγελοι οὔτε ἀρχαὶ οὔτε ἐνεστῶτα οὔτε μέλλοντα οὔτε δυνάμεις οὔτε ὕψωμα οὔτε βάθος οὔτε τις κτίσις ἑτέρα δυνήσεται ἡμᾶς χωρίσαι ἀπὸ τῆς ἀγάπης τοῦ Θεοῦ τῆς ἐν Χριστῷ Ἰησοῦ τῷ Κυρίῳ ἡμῶν—Rom. viii. 38, 39.

"Love for Christ is immortal."—R. W. DALE.

CHAPTER XXX.

REQUEST: COMMENDATION: BENEDICTION.

"And [pray] on my behalf, that the word may be given unto me in opening my mouth, to make known with boldness the mystery of the gospel, for which I am an ambassador in chains; that in it I may speak boldly, as I ought to speak.

"But that ye also may know my affairs, how I do, Tychicus, the beloved brother and faithful minister in the Lord, shall make known to you all things: whom I have sent unto you for this very purpose, that ye may know our state, and that he may comfort your hearts."—Eph. vi. 19–22.

The apostle has bidden his readers apply themselves with wakeful and incessant earnestness to prayer (ver. 18). For this is, after all, the chief arm of the spiritual combat. By this means the soul draws reinforcements of mercy and hope from the eternal sources (ver. 10). By this means the Asian Christians will be able not only to carry on their own conflict with vigour, but to help all the saints (ver. 18); and through their aid the whole Church of God will be sustained in its war with the prince of this world.

The apostle Paul himself stood in the forefront of this battle. He was suffering for the cause of common Christendom; he was a mark for the attack of the enemies of the gospel.[176] On him, more than on any other man, the safety and progress of the Church depended (Phil. i. 25). In this position he naturally says: "Watching unto prayer in all perseverance and supplication for all the saints—*and for me*." If his heart should fail him, or his mouth be closed, if the word of inspiration ceased to be given him and the great teacher of the Gentiles in faith and truth no longer spoke as he ought to speak, it would be a heavy blow and sore discouragement to the friends of Christ throughout the world. "My afflictions are your glory (iii. 13). My unworthy testimony to Christ is showing forth His praise to all men and angels.[177] Pray for me then, that I may speak and act in this hour of trial in a manner worthy of the dispensation given to me."

Strong and confident as the apostle Paul was, he felt himself to be nothing without prayer. It is his habit to expect the support of the intercessions of all who love him in Christ.[178] He knew that he was helped by this means, on numberless occasions and in wonderful ways. He asks his present readers to entreat that "the word[179] may be given me when I open my mouth, so that I may freely make known the mystery of the gospel, on which behalf I serve as ambassador in bonds, that in it I may speak freely, as I ought to speak." This sentence hangs upon the verb "may-be-given." Jesus said to His apostles: "It shall be *given* you in that hour what you shall speak, when brought before rulers and kings" (Matt x. 18–20). The apostle stands now before the Roman world. He has appealed to Cæsar, and awaits his trial. If he has not yet appeared at the Emperor's tribunal, he will shortly have to do so. Christ's ambassador is about to plead in chains before the highest of human courts. It is not his own life or freedom that he is concerned about; the ambassador has only to consider how he shall represent his Sovereign's interests. The importance which Paul attached to this occasion, is manifest from the words written to Timothy (2 Ep. iv. 17) referring to his later trial. St Paul has this special need in his thoughts, in addition to the help from above continually required in the discharge of his ministry, under the hampering conditions of his imprisonment (comp. Col. iv. 3, 4).

The Church must entreat on Paul's behalf that the word he utters may be God's, and not his own. It is in vain to "open the mouth," unless there is this higher prompting and through the gates of speech there issues a Divine message, unless the speaker is the mouthpiece of the Holy Spirit rather than of his individual thought and will. "The words that I speak unto you," Jesus said, "I speak not of myself." The bold apostle intends to open his mouth; but he must have the true "word given" him to say. We should pray for Christ's ambassadors, and especially for the more public and eloquent pleaders of the Christian cause, that it may be thus with them. Rash and vain words, that bear the stamp of the mere man who utters them and not of the Spirit of his Master, do a hurt to the cause of the gospel proportioned to the blessing that comes from such lips when they speak the word given to them.

Such inspiration would enable the apostle to "make known the mystery of the gospel *with freedom and confidence of speech*": the expression rendered "with boldness"[180] means all this. Before the emperor Nero, or the slave Onesimus, he will be able with the same aptness and dignity and self-command to declare his message and to vindicate his Master's name. "The mystery of the gospel" is no other secret than that which this epistle unfolds (iii. 3–9), the great fact that Jesus Christ is the Saviour and the Lord of the whole world. Jesus proclaimed Himself to Pilate, who represented at Jerusalem the imperial rule, as the King of all who are of the truth; and the apostle Paul has the like message to convey to the head of the Empire. It needed the greatest boldness and the greatest wisdom in the ambassador of the Messianic King to play his part at Rome; an unwise word might make his own life forfeit, and bring incalculable dangers on the Church.

St Paul's trial, we suppose, passed off successfully, as he at this time anticipated.[181] The Roman government was perfectly aware that the political charge against their prisoner was frivolous; and Nero, if he personally gave Paul a hearing on this earlier trial, in all probability viewed his spiritual pretensions on his Master's behalf with contemptuous tolerance. If he did so, the toleration was not due to any want of courage or clearness on the defendant's part. It is possible even that the courage and address of the advocate of the "new superstition" pleased the tyrant, who was not without his moments of good humour nor without the instincts of a man of taste. The apostle, we may well believe, made an impression on the supreme court at Rome similar to that made on his judges in Cæsarea.

St Paul's bonds in Christ have now become widely "manifest" in Rome (Phil. i. 13). He pleads in circumstances of disgrace. But God brings good for His servants out of evil. As he said at a later time, so he could say now: "They have bound me; but they cannot bind the word of God."[182] He was "not ashamed of the gospel" in the prospect of coming to Rome years before (Rom. i. 16); and he is not ashamed now, though he has come in chains as an evil-doer. Through the intercessions of Christ's people all these injuries of Satan are turning to his salvation and to the "furtherance of the gospel"; and Paul rejoices and triumphs in them, well assured that Christ will be magnified whether by his life or death, whether by his freedom or his chains (Phil. i. 12–26). The prayers which the imprisoned apostle asks from the Church were fulfilled. For we read in the last verses of the Acts of the Apostles, which put into a sentence the history of this period: "He received all that came to him, preaching the kingdom and teaching the things concerning the Lord Jesus Christ, *with all boldness*, none forbidding him."

The paragraph relating to Tychicus is almost identical with that of Colossians iv. 7, 8. It begins with a "But" connecting what follows with the statement the apostle has just made respecting his position at Rome. As much as to say: "I want your prayers, set as I am for the defence of the gospel and in circumstances of difficulty and peril. But Tychicus will tell you more about me than I can convey by letter. I am sending him, in fact, for this very purpose."

St Paul knew the great anxiety of the Christians of Asia on his account. Epaphras of Colossæ had "shown him the love in the Spirit" that was felt towards him even by those in this region who had never seen him in the flesh (Col. i. 8). The tender heart of the apostle is touched by this assurance. So he sends Tychicus to visit as many of the Asian Churches as he may be able to reach, bringing news that will cheer their hearts and relieve their discouragement (iii. 13).[183] The note sent at this time to Philemon indicates the hopeful tidings that Tychicus was able to convey to Paul's friends in the East: "I trust that through your prayers I shall be given to you" (Philem. 22). To the Philippians he writes, perhaps a little later, in the same strain: "I trust in the Lord that I myself shall come shortly" (Phil. ii. 24). He anticipates, with some confidence, his speedy acquital and release: it is not likely that this expectation, on the part of such a man as St Paul, was disappointed. The good news went round the Asian and Macedonian Churches: "Paul is likely soon to be free, and we shall see and hear him again!"

In the parallel epistle he writes, "that you may know" (Col. iv. 8); here it is, "that you *also* may know my affairs." The added word is significant. The writer is imagining his letter read in the various assemblies which it will reach. He has the other epistle in his mind, and remembering that he there introduced Tychicus in similar terms, he says to this wider circle of Asian disciples: "That you also, as well as the Churches of the Lycus valley, may know how things are with me, I send Tychicus to give you a full report." It is not necessary, however, to look beyond the last two verses for the reference of the *also* of verse 21: "I have asked your prayers on my behalf; and I wish you in turn to know how things go with me." Possibly, there were some matters connected with St Paul's trial at Rome that could not be fitly or safely communicated by letter. Hence he adds: "He shall make known unto you all things." When he writes "that ye may know my affairs, how I do," we gather that Tychicus was to communicate to those he visited everything about the beloved apostle that would be of interest to his Asian brethren.

The apostle commends Tychicus in language identical in the two letters, except that in Colossians "fellow-servant" is added to the honourable designations of "beloved brother and faithful minister," under which he is here introduced. We find him first associated with St Paul in Acts xx. 4, where "Tychicus and Trophimus" represent Asia in the number of those who accompanied the apostle on his voyage to Jerusalem, when he carried the contributions of his Gentile Churches to the relief of the Christian poor in Jerusalem. Trophimus, his companion, is called a "Greek" and an "Ephesian" (Acts xxi. 28, 29). Whether Tychicus belonged to the same city or not, we cannot tell. He was almost certainly a Greek. The Pastoral epistles show Tychicus still in the apostle's service in his last years. He appears to have joined St Paul's staff and remained with him from the time that he accompanied him to Jerusalem in the year 59. From 2 Timothy iv 9–12 we gather that Tychicus was sent to Ephesus to relieve Timothy, when St Paul desired the presence of the latter at Rome. It is evident that he was a man greatly valued by the apostle and endeared to him.

Tychicus was well known in the Asian Churches, and suitable therefore to be sent upon this errand. And the commendation given to him would be very welcome to the circle to which he belonged. The apostle has great tact in these personal matters, the tact which belongs to delicate feeling and a generous mind. He calls his messenger "the beloved brother" in his relation to the Church in general, and "faithful minister in the Lord" in his special relation to himself. So he describes Epaphroditus to the Philippians as "your apostle and minister of my need." In conveying these letters and messages, this worthy man was Paul's apostle and minister of his need in regard to the Asian Churches. He is a "*minister in the Lord*," inasmuch as this office lies within the range of his service to the Lord Christ.

We observe that in writing to the Colossians the apostle applies to Onesimus, the converted slave, the honourable epithets applied here to this long-tried friend: "the faithful and beloved brother" (Col. iv. 9). Every Christian believer should be in the eyes of his fellows a "beloved brother." And every true servant of Christ and His people is a "faithful minister in the Lord," be his rank high or low, and whether official hands have been laid upon his head or not. We are apt, by a trick of words, to limit to the order which we suitably call "the ministry" expressions that the New Testament applies to the common ministry of Christ's saints (comp. iv. 12). This devoted servant of Christ is employed just now as a newsman and letter-carrier. But what a high responsibility it was, to be the bearer to the Asian cities, and to the Church for all time, of the epistles of Paul the apostle to the Ephesians, Colossians and Philemon. Had Tychicus been careless or dishonest, had he lost these precious documents or tampered with them, how great the loss to mankind! We cannot read them without feeling our debt to this beloved brother and faithful servant of the Church. Those who travel upon Christ's business, who link distant communities to each other and convey from one to another the Holy Spirit's fellowship and grace, are "the messengers of the Churches and the glory of Christ" (2 Cor. viii. 23).

THE BENEDICTION.

"Peace be to the brethren, and love with faith,
  From God the Father and the Lord Jesus Christ.
Grace be with all them that love our Lord Jesus Christ
      In incorruption" (vv. 23, 24).

Grace and Peace were the first words of the epistle,—the apostle's salutation to all his Churches. In *Peace and Grace* he breathes out his final blessing. The benediction is fuller than in most of the epistles, and exhibits several peculiar features.

To the Thessalonians (2 Ep. iii. 16) St Paul wished: "Peace continually, in all ways, from the Lord of peace Himself"; and he commends the Romans twice to "the God of peace" (ch. xv. 33, xvi. 20): the Corinthians he bids to "live in peace," so that "the God of love and peace" may be with them (2 Cor. xiii. 11). There is nothing in the least degree strange or un-Pauline in the wishes here expressed, except the fact that they are put in the third person—"*Peace to the brethren*," etc.—instead of being addressed directly to the readers in the second person, as in all other of the apostle's extant closing benedictions. This peculiarity, as we observed in the first Chapter, is in accordance with the encyclical and impersonal stamp of the epistle.[184] It is Paul's most catholic benediction, his blessing upon "all the Israel of God" (comp. Gal. vi. 16).

"With faith," that "love" is desired whereby, according to the Pauline ethics of salvation, faith works (Gal. v. 6), the love which as a vitalizing organic force creates the new man, formed in all his doings and dispositions after the image of Jesus Christ. From chapter iv. 1–3 we have learnt how "peace" and "love" attend each other. Love is the source of the forbearance, the mutual consideration and self-sacrifice, without which there is no peace within the Church. Peace springs from love: love waits on faith. Amongst brethren in Christ, members of the same household of faith, peace and love have their home. These are the sons of peace: with good will and good hope, entering or quitting their abode, we say, "Peace be to this house!"

The peace that the apostle looks for amongst Christian brethren is the fruit of peace with God through Christ. Such "peace guarding the thoughts and heart" of each Christian man, nothing contrary thereto will arise amongst them. Calm and quiet hearts make a peaceful Church. There are no clashing interests, no selfish competitions, no strife as to who shall be greatest. Differences of opinion and taste are kept within the bounds of mutual submission. The awe of God's presence with His people, the remembrance of the dear price at which His Church was purchased, the sense of Christ's Lordship in the Spirit and of the sacredness of our brotherhood in Him, check all turbulence and rivalry and teach us to seek the things that make for peace.

"Peace *and love*," the apostle desires. Love includes peace, and more; for it labours not to prevent contention only, but to help and enrich in all ways the body of Christ. By such "toil of love" faith is made complete. We are bidden indeed, in certain matters, to "have faith to ourselves before God" (Rom. xiv. 22). This maxim holds where one has a special faith in regard to such things as eating flesh or drinking wine, in which any one of us may without offence differ from his brethren. But it is a poor faith that dwells upon questions of this nature, and makes its religion of them. The essentials of faith, as we saw them delineated in chapter iv. 1–6, are things that unite and not distinguish us.

As faith grows and deepens, it makes new channels in which love may flow. "We are bound to thank God always for you," writes St Paul to the Thessalonians (2 Ep. i. 3), "for that your faith groweth exceedingly, and the love of each one of you all toward one another multiplieth." This is the sound and true growth of faith. Where an intenser faith makes men disputatious and exclusive; where it fails to breed meekness and courtesy, we cannot but suspect its quality. Such faith may be sincere; but it is mixed with a lamentable ignorance, and a resistance to the Holy Spirit that is likely to end in grave offence. "Contending earnestly for the faith" does not mean contending angrily, with the weapons of satire and censoriousness. It is well to remember that we are not the judges of our brethren. There are many questions raised and discussed amongst us, which we may safely leave to the judgement of the last day. It is too easy to fill the air with matters of contention, and to excite a sore and suspicious temper destructive of peace, and in which nothing but fault-finding will flourish. If we must contend, we may surely debate quietly on secondary matters, while we are one in Christ. If we have not *love with faith*, our faith is worthless (1 Cor. xiii. 2).

Deep beneath the peace that dwells in the Church and the love that fills each believer's heart, is the eternal fountain of *grace*. "Grace be with all those who love our Lord Jesus Christ," says the apostle. Grace is theirs already; and they desire nothing so much as its increase. Their love to Christ is the fruit of the grace of God that is with them. This wish includes all good wishes; it surpasses both our deservings and desires. All that God prepared for us in His eternal counsels, and that Christ purchased by His redeeming love, all of good that our nature can receive now and for ever, is embraced in this one word: *Grace be with you.*

"With all them that love our Lord Jesus Christ," Paul says; for it is to lovers of Christ that God gives the continuance of His grace. If our love to Christ fails, grace leaves us. God cannot look with favour upon the man who has no love to His Son Jesus Christ. In giving his blessing to the Corinthians, St Paul was compelled to write with his own hand: "If any man love not the Lord, let him be anathema." The blessing involves the anathema. God's love is not a love of indifference, an indiscriminate, immoral affection. It is a love of choice and predilection—"If any man love me," said Jesus, "my Father will love him." Is not the condition reasonable,—and the inference inevitable? The Father cannot grant His grace to those who have seen and hated Him in His Son and image. By that hatred they refuse His grace, and cast it from them.

On the other hand, a sincere love to the Lord Jesus Christ opens the heart to all the rich and purifying influences of Divine grace. The sinful woman, stained with false and foul love, who washed the Saviour's feet with her tears, attained in that act to a height of purity undreamed of by the virtuous Pharisee. This new and holy flame burns out impure passion from the soul: it kindles lofty thoughts; it makes crooked natures straight, and timid and weak natures brave and strong. "To them that love God, we know, all things work together for good." To them that love Christ, all things contribute blessing; all conditions and events of life become means of grace. If we love Christ, we shall love His people,—the Church, the bride of Christ from whom He will never be parted in our thoughts. If we love Christ, we shall love the work He has laid upon us, and the word He has taught us, and the sacramental pledges He has given us in remembrance of Him and assurance of His coming. If we love Him, we shall "keep His commandments," and He will keep His promise to send us the "other Helper, to be with us for ever, even the Spirit of truth." The gift of the Holy Spirit is the all-sufficiency of grace.[185] Here is the innermost sanctuary of our religion, the fountain and beginning of the soul's eternal life,—in the love which joins it to the Lord in one spirit.

In incorruption is the last and sealing word of this letter, which we have been so long studying together. It "stands as the crown and climax of this glorious epistle" (Alford). Like so many other words of the epistle, at first sight its interpretation is not clear. The apostle has used the term in several other passages, as synonymous with *immortality*[186] and denoting the state of the blessed after the resurrection, when they will stand before God complete in body and in spirit, with all that is mortal in them swallowed up of life —"raised in incorruption." But there is nothing in this context to lead up to the idea of personal, bodily immortality. Those who construe the apostle's words in this sense, place a comma before the final clause and treat it as a qualification of the main predicate of the sentence: "Grace be with all them that love our Lord,—grace [culminating] in incorruption"—or in other words, "grace crowned with glory!" But it must be admitted that this is somewhat strained.

The rendering of our ordinary version, "in sincerity" (in the Revised rendering, "uncorruptness"), gives an ethical sense to the word that is scarcely borne out by usage. It is a different, though kindred expression that St Paul employs to express "uncorruptness" in Titus ii. 7.[187]

It appears to us that the term "incorruption," in its ordinary significance, applies fitly to the believer's love for the Lord, when the word is read in accordance with the symbolism of the epistle. This love is the life of the body of Christ. In it lies the Church's immortality. The gates of death prevail not against her, rooted and grounded as she is in love to the risen and immortal Christ. "May that love be maintained," the apostle says, "in its deathless power. Let it be an unspoilt and unwasting love."

Of earthly love we often say with sadness:—

> "Space is against thee: it can part!
> Time is against thee: it can chill!"

Not so with the love of Christ. Neither death nor life parts the soul from Him. Our love to the Lord Jesus Christ seats us with Him in the heavenly places,— above the realm of decay, above this wasting flesh and perishing world.

Lightning Source UK Ltd.
Milton Keynes UK
UKHW012010120123
415233UK00004B/347